HITMEN

Four Tales of Magick, Monsters, and Murder

Also By Greg Mitchell

THE COMING EVIL TRILOGY
The Strange Man
Enemies of the Cross
Dark Hour

Rift Jump
Rift Jump II: Sara's Song

Infernal City

"A destroyer will come against Babylon; her warriors will be captured, and their bows will be broken. For the Lord is a God of retribution; he will repay in full."
-Jeremiah 51:56

HITMEN

FOUR TALES OF MAGICK, MONSTERS, AND MURDER

GREG MITCHELL

GENRE
EXPERIENCE

Published by Genre Experience

Cover Art and Illustrations by Bob Freeman
www.occultdetective.com

Impacted font created by Phil Campbell

Visit Greg Mitchell at
www.thecomingevil.com

Dedicated to
Johnny, Jeff, Meghan, Drake, James, Dad, Zach,
and the rest of the cast and crew.

TABLE OF CONTENTS

FOREWORD

"You did *what?*"

That was the initial reaction when I told friends and family that I wrote the book you now hold in your hands.

A bit of backstory: The year was 1998. I was a couple years out of high school and trying to figure out what I wanted to do with my life. My childhood love of the horror genre was newly rekindled and I decided I wanted to write monster movies. I was getting my feet wet in independent Christian films and was starting to put together the story that would eventually become the novels in *The Coming Evil Trilogy*.

In a show of support of my new filmic aspirations, my parents bought me a video camera. I was thrilled and set out to draft my friends into my own amateur horror movies. I was still toying with the idea of merging horror and religion and set out to make an '80s style slasher flick with a twist. The original concept was simple: Jason Voorhees (of *Friday the 13th* fame) does great against half-naked camp counselors, but how would he fare against hardened hitmen with guns? I had a cheap plastic "blue skull" voice-changer mask that I bought on a lark at a *Kay Bee Toys* store some years prior and decided that would be the perfect frightening visage for my Jason-esque killer.

In the winter of '98, I shot the first "HITMEN" movie on that little camera. I paid a small fee to go over to my friend, and *Time Changer* director, Rich Christiano's house and cut it together onto a VHS tape. The movie was terrible—wonderfully so—but I was proud of that thing. I *made* a movie. My friends were supportive and didn't complain too much when I called them at all hours of the day and night and gave them a simple "What are you doing? Are you busy? Let's go film." They showed up on time, faithful to read over my rewrites and spout out my silly lines with zero practice or rehearsal. We finished the movie, had a popcorn night with our parents, and laughed at the fact that we'd made our very own movie. I'm sure everyone thought that it would end there.

But, hey. This is me we're talking about here.

Less than a year later, I had the idea for a sequel to my gruesome masterpiece. Once more, my friends (and now my little brother) simply got the call—"Let's go film another one". It didn't end with *that* movie either, as I was now determined to create an epic home movie saga! Over the ensuing years, my loyal cast and crew followed me like a crazy-eyed Captain Ahab as I soldiered on through late nights and lunch hours and early Saturday mornings in search of a Moby Dick-sized vision. There was no pay. There was no distribution. There was no audience! Just the simple satisfaction that we were making something with our own two hands.

In 2006, I finished editing "HITMEN IV: THE FINAL CHAPTER". By that time, I'd made the transition to digital editing and DVD authoring, complete with trailers, outtakes, commentaries, and deleted scenes. I made a couple new friends along the way, and had even gotten married—and, yes, they were all eventually drafted into my massive ongoing storyline of "HITMEN". In the films, I starred as guilt-ridden reformed hitman Eli, my brother Jeff portrayed precocious young ghost hunter Flynn, my wife Meghan became the seductive villainess Marcie, and my best friend Johnny pulled double-duty as lovable Vinnie Caponi: Urban Mythologist and our fearsome supernatural foe, the Blue Skull himself.

Man, it was a ride. Writing each new script at a feverish pace; throwing my camera, lights, and tripod in the back seat of my car on a whim to go pick up "one more shot"; sneaking out to the woods and having a hulking monster chase my wife screaming through the foliage; staying up at all hours of the night editing with Johnny, laughing and dreaming up even wilder scenarios for future installments—that *was* my twenties. They were some of the best times of my life.

I never intended to show anyone outside our circle of friends our amateur movies. They are for us: a snapshot of a more innocent time. But, like the supernatural Blue Skull who slashed his way through our films, the "HITMEN" saga refused to stay buried for long. Fast forward to 2012. I'm right in the middle of publishing my magnum opus, *The Coming Evil Trilogy*, and I have this quirky idea to adapt some old stories I wrote in high school into a novel. That book eventually became *Rift Jump*, first published in 2012 by Splashdown Darkwater. I had a lot of fun revisiting those old concepts and, as my mind is wont to do…I began to wonder: "What if I adapted those old 'HITMEN' movies?" They'd be greatly expanded on, of course, giving me the opportunity to do things we never had the budget to do in the original films. It could be bloodier, more action-packed—and way more ambitious, both in terms of character and story. A "Director's Cut", if you will. I was pretty excited, even as I laughed at myself for completely going off the deep end. That's when I went to my former crew and cast mates and told them my idea of turning the four main *Hitmen* installments (we made a lot of spin-offs, you see) into a single "braided novel".

And the response was near-unanimous: "You're going to do *what?*" We all had a good laugh and I didn't really think I'd follow it through, to be honest.

But, just for fun one night, I watched through those movies again, lost in bittersweet nostalgia and remembering all the funny and poignant behind-the-scenes stories. I began thinking about what I would do differently now if I had the budget and with my improved writing skills. I started writing the first part—herein called "The Saint"—and surprised myself by how natural it felt. Cautiously optimistic, I adapted the second movie and then let my wife read what I had so far. She actually *liked* it. Hey, maybe I was on to something.

I finished the book a couple months later and sought a publisher for over a year while working on other projects. No one was biting and, through it all, I kept thinking about putting the book out myself. It seemed only fitting. After all, all those movies we made, we made on our dime, with our own blood, sweat, and tears. I longed to experience that feeling of *making* something from scratch again. So, that's what I did. You'll note that this book is published by Genre Experience: the same company that "produced" all those *Hitmen* movies back in the day. And, reminiscent of those bygone days of youth and excitement, I called up my pal, author/artist Bob Freeman at a moment's notice and said, "Bob. I'm making a book. Can you do the cover?" Just like that, I'm fifteen years younger again, rushing off into the night to make monster movies with my best friends, making our own rules, entertaining ourselves.

I hope you'll come along for the ride.

-Greg Mitchell
January 20, 2014

PROLOGUE

Joey's twisted ankle swelled. He spat out a curse, gripping his leg while hopping on his other. Sweat drenched his disheveled bangs and they dangled in his face, obscuring his vision. The late afternoon sun leveled its glare on him, casting everything in dazzling diamond sparkles, but he could not slow or falter.

He slipped against the alley wall, knocking over a trash can, but righted himself on the grimy brick, hobbling along. His chest hurt from panting so hard, but he forced himself to keep moving, to get away. Tossing a glance behind him, he was momentarily relieved to see that the thing was no longer following.

Maybe I got a shot at this.

Turning back to the alley mouth, he saw the highway traffic blitzing by up ahead. No way would anyone stop for him—not in his torn jacket with embroidered patches depicting topless biker babes riding atop anarchy symbols, and a prominent upraised middle finger with angel wings across his shoulders. Fatigue threatened to undo him, but he *knew* he could survive this encounter, if he could just get a ride. Trembling too-thin fingers reached underneath his denim coat to brush the handles of the dual Ruger Super Redhawk .44 Magnums he had tucked in shoulder holsters. He was ready to draw them, to make someone stop for him, when the dark shape stepped into his path seemingly from nowhere, blocking the sun's warm rays, suffusing him in cold black.

"N-NO!" Joey screamed as a black-gloved hand—impossibly icy—palmed the left side of his face and slammed him against the brick wall. Joey grunted in surprise, spitting out a geyser of blood and a couple teeth. His whole body shaking with shock, he slipped to the wet pavement, sputtering. "Stop…" he pleaded.

One giant boot stepped over him as the shadow descended, reaching for him. The right side of his face was raw meat and he couldn't see out of that eye anymore, but Joey wasn't ready to die. Not today. Not by the hand of this *thing*. Weeping, he rolled onto his back and drew his revolvers. Roaring now, he fired at the looming shape, hurling expletives as fast as bullets.

The thing twitched under the lead assault and Joey laughed, triumphant. He scooped himself up and wobbled back towards the end of the alley, headed for the road again. *I'm gonna make it…I'm gonna make it…*

His vision was blurry with tears, sweat, and blood, but he could just make out the speeding shapes of traffic. "Pull over," he mumbled, not nearly loud enough for anyone to oblige. "Please, let me in…"

Weakly he emerged out of the alley, waving his pistols. "Hey," he said, dreamily, fearing he was slipping into unconsciousness. Upon seeing him, nearby drivers swerved out of his way, honking.

"Wait! Wait, you gotta stop…"

Horns blared, tires screeched, and motorists dodged him as he approached the highway shoulder. "Wait!" he wept after them. "Let me in!"

He watched in helpless dejection as, one by one, cars passed by, his only hope of salvation leaving him behind.

Then he heard the crunch.

Joey whirled around and saw the thing rising to a stand in the alley, no sign of injury. No sign of slowing down. "Aw, no…" he whimpered.

What horrified him the most was the thing's face. As the creature stood tall, drawing its strength, its face—that terrible skull face—began to radiate a soft phosphorescent blue glow. Against the backdrop of the shadowed alley, that head almost seemed to float, detached, and Joey could see nothing now but the grinning blue death's head staring back at him. Moving for him.

"No!" he held out his hands as though they would keep the monster at bay. The thing stalked for him, ready to leave the alley behind and join him any second. Joey stumbled back into traffic, still flapping his arms, begging, weeping. "Get back! Stay away from me! I didn't do nuthin!"

A thunderous horn roared in his ear and Joey glimpsed the eighteen-wheeler bearing down on him too late.

PART I
THE SAINT

CHAPTER ONE

At one o'clock in the afternoon, the phone rang.

James Lenderman lazily answered the call, expecting Theresa on the other end. She'd been on his case for weeks, demanding that he find a better job to provide for her and the baby on the way. She was staying with her parents and getting nothing but grief for being stupid enough to make a baby with James.

Prove them wrong, James, she would scold him, thinking emasculation was a good motivator. He continually shooed her away, trying not to hear her hurtful words. He could get the job done. He just needed a chance.

"Hello?" he greeted, gulping down a bite of ham sandwich.

A voice with a British accent answered. "James. Mr. Marcon has an important job opportunity for you. Are you interested?"

James' heart quickened.

Today would be his chance to prove himself.

After donning his navy overcoat, James left his house behind for the afternoon. Underneath his coat, he felt the weight of the Beretta M9 holstered to his chest. It felt good there. Reassuring. He'd trained with that gun. It had become an extension of him, by now.

I can do this.

The mission was simple. Some determined P.I. had been sticking his nose in places where it didn't belong and Adrian Marcon was finally pushed to take drastic measures. James had scribbled the address down quickly on the notepad sitting next to the phone when the Brit called. Now it rested in his jeans pocket, a death sentence. It was nothing personal. James had no ill feelings towards the P.I. He hadn't even met the guy.

This was just business, and once his business was done, he would be ten thousand dollars richer. He and Theresa could finally move in somewhere together, since Theresa hated his creaky house by the tracks, and they could raise their baby without Theresa's old man shouting and complaining.

The thought encouraged James as he slid into his car and started the engine.

This was his first solo hit. He had ridden with Eli before—had been there with him in that big fiasco a year ago that had gotten them into all this trouble with Marcon in the first place—but he'd yet to pull a job by himself. For too long, James had been relegated to the outside of Marcon's inner circle, just an arms dealer. But he knew he had more to offer than selling stolen guns. He could be trusted with the big jobs—and the big paychecks.

His hands grew sweaty as he gripped the steering wheel.

All at once, he was hit by the seriousness of what he was about to do. Driving to a house where an innocent man lived so that he could put a bullet through his forehead. It wasn't the first time he'd killed, but that had been during his tour in the sandbox. Those had been soldiers.

Never a civilian.

This P.I. had earned Marcon's wrath because he was a *good* man, trying to end the Boss' empire. And now James was going to kill him. Not because they were enemies, but for a paycheck.

I'm a mercenary, he told himself, unsure if the label was a condemnation or an encouragement.

So many thoughts filled his mind, a mixture of pride and shame. Fear and exhilaration. Hoping to drown out the raging storm within him, James turned the radio dial, switching through the stations. Static filled the airwaves until he finally found a clear reception.

Blue Öyster Cult's "Don't Fear the Reaper" was already in progress and immersed the car in its haunting melody. He took a deep, calming breath and leaned back in the seat, forcing himself to focus on the road ahead. It was such a drab, dreary day. The sun was hidden behind bland, steel grey clouds and the road was still damp from this morning's showers. It was depressing, and James reflected that today would be a crappy day to die.

Gravel churned underneath tires as James slowly crept down the secluded country road. The car bucked as he rounded the hill and crossed the washed-out gravel path. His prize lay before him, hidden behind a small grove of trees. The house was brick with cheap, moldy lawn furniture slumbering in a mess of tall grass. A couple broken down cars rested in eternal graves out back and James marveled at how run-down and empty the place looked.

Gumshoe business must not be much for revenue. He pulled into the lonesome drive. His hands were slick with perspiration, making it harder to slip on his black latex gloves. Pressed against his chest, his Beretta constantly reminded him why he was here.

To kill. To murder.

James had never been a religious man, but he prayed that, if there were a God, He would forgive him for what he was about to do.

I'm doing this for Theresa. I'm doing this for me.

Pocketing his keys, James opened the car door and glided towards the house like a phantom. He carried that image further, imagining how Eli would do this job. Eli was cold like the grave, and he would kill this man with no thought to tomorrow and no anticipation of the nightmares to come. It was how he had survived so long in Marcon's empire, and James knew he needed to be like that right now.

Stiffening as he approached the front screen door, he knocked on the aluminum frame, drawing his pistol. No reply came and he waited impatiently, tapping the gun against his leg. His throat felt dry and his tongue thick as he raised his gloved fist to knock again, to summon the P.I. to his death.

Then he noticed something on the window. A taped sign for Bakerman Realty, with a number attached.

A FOR SALE sign.

The house was empty.

The sound of rubber soles crunching on gravel met his ears and James slowly turned. A slender dark-haired man in a tailored black suit waited for him by the car.

"Eli?" James said, chuckling slightly at the sight of his best friend. "What are you doin—?"

Eli stood stock still, a hard-faced statue. James noticed, then, that Eli's hands were behind his back, and he knew. He had no idea what he had done wrong, what the final straw had been.

"Why?" he asked.

Eli withdrew his hands from behind his back, the steel of his SIG Sauer P229 glistening as the first rays of sunlight broke through the rainy clouds. Randomly, James thought, *It might turn out to be a pretty day after all.*

Then the shot was fired, and James thought no more.

His body blasted against the screen door, slid to the front porch, and remained still.

Eli Ross stood over the body of his friend for a moment, his weathered face unflinching. After a moment, he turned and walked away. For long minutes, he sat in his car, his gloved hands wringing the steering wheel.

He'd done it. He'd actually gone through with it.

Still stationary in the driveway, he glanced at James' body, bleeding out on the ground. *What did I do…?*

He'd have to remove the body. Get rid of the car too. He'd done it before, erasing the existence of Adrian Marcon's enemies. But he'd never had to do it to a friend. Reaching to the visor above the wheel, he brought out the Polaroid that used to give him comfort. He stared down at the small square sporting his own hard-cut face, too angular and thin for his twenty-five years. His deep-set dark blue eyes looked so happy in the picture, free of the intensity they bore now when he faced himself in the rearview mirror. Beside his former likeness, though, he saw hers. The girl, dark-eyed, with a smooth porcelain face and long dark hair, who smiled back at him. They were so happy when this picture was taken, so much in love.

Was it worth it? he asked himself, watching James' paling body, as if fearing his best friend would return from the dead, seeking his revenge. It wasn't supposed to be like this. Love was supposed to set him free, not bind him to more death.

Eli thought of Theresa. How much she'd worry when James didn't come home. How heartbroken she'd be, thinking he'd finally left her, taking the coward's way out of raising their baby. He couldn't let her think that, instead deciding to leave James' body, as inglorious as it was. Let it bleach under the sun, bloat with gases. It'd be disgusting when the police finally discovered him, but at least they *would* discover him and Theresa would know that James had been taken from her and hadn't left by choice.

It was the least Eli could do for his best friend.

The first of many tears began to build in his eyes.

Adrian would be furious about his leaving the body, no doubt. Perhaps so furious that he'd send a hitman after Eli next. But Eli gauged that if Adrian discovered the truth about that brown-eyed girl in the photo, laughing and loving with Eli, then his death would be shortly coming anyway.

He touched the photo girl's face one last time, thinking of the moments of passion they had shared, the way she had loved him, so wild and fierce. It'd been amazing, and he'd felt empowered, sneaking behind the Old Man's back. Yet now, Eli's secrets were finally coming into the light, and James had died because of them.

Slipping the picture back into the visor, he stared at James' body, a peaceful breeze lightly tousling its hair, then banged on the steering wheel, finally voicing his rage and regret in a singular throaty roar.

Something in the backseat stirred and Eli shot a panicked glance to the rearview mirror, shaken from his outburst. Much to his horror, he saw a dark shape staring back, its face a cerulean death mask—a glowing blue skull.

It was him. The *thing* from the video—

In a fright, Eli seized his gun and whirled to face his would-be assailant…only there was no one there. Eyes darting back to the rearview mirror, he saw only empty backseat.

So, he was next. It made sense, he guessed. He was one of the only ones left.

He exhaled, his heart heavy. That was it then. He *was* damned.

And now the Devil was coming to collect.

CHAPTER TWO

The Little White Church, one of the oldest buildings in Willowbrook, had begun life as one of many small country churches down here in the Bible Belt where farmers congregated to pray to the heavens for rain and good harvest. Over the decades, as the town spread, the church was assimilated into civilization. Buildings grew around it, pricey neighborhoods surrounded its meager white-washed wooden structure, but the church remained true to its simple folk spirit.

Perhaps that was why Eli felt comfortable approaching it. It had a home-like quality, a nostalgic pull, beckoning him to its bright red door, reminding him of a life before Adrian Marcon, even before the Army. Years ago, when he and Alex were boys staying with their father in Willowbrook during the summers. Things had been so much sweeter then.

But boys become men and men do questionable things.

Eli stepped closer to the church, facing the steeple as though it were the finger of God boring down on him in accusation. Closing his eyes, seeing nothing but James' body in the red space, he pushed through into the building.

Inside, the church was empty. Surrounded by the soothing hush of the darkened sanctuary, Eli trailed along the deserted pews, his shoes creaking on the wooden planks that had been there for over a hundred years. He wondered what people found in this building that kept it here so long. Did they find God? Did they find peace and redemption?

Eli stood before the cross that hung behind the pulpit. It had meant so little to him growing up, even though his father was a religious man. Eli found little use in those old beliefs; life didn't seem to be so bad that it merited the divine intervention of some cosmic being. He had a good life, for the most part, until Alex died. Now, Eli was stuck in a quagmire of his own bitterness, trapped and drowning in empty rage. Would he find solace here? Was solace possible for someone who had slaughtered other souls?

"Oh, hello, there," a voice startled Eli out of his grim reflection. "I didn't see anyone come in."

Eli turned and regarded the preacher: a short, plump man with graying black hair, unkempt and misshapen as though he'd just woken from a nap in his study, and tiny dark eyes looming behind thick orange-tinted glasses. He wore casual black loafers, slacks, and a turtleneck. The preacher adjusted his frames to get a better look at his guest. Suddenly, his pleasant public face dropped and his jowls trembled with contempt. "Oh, it's *you*."

The preacher's name was Pastor Matthew Loomis, a quirky fellow known around the community as a gloom-and-doom type. On the street corners, he'd wave his Bible and proclaim that "The End Is Nigh", urging everyone to repent before "The Great Beast" claimed them all. He was a joke, a branded lunatic with a tiny congregation of evangelical fanatics, locking themselves in their rickety wooden church Sunday after Sunday, passing condemnation on those unfortunate enough not to be on their church roster. Bold as a jungle cat, if not crazy as a loon, Pastor Loomis had also made it his one-man crusade to shout from the rooftops the dirty details of the corruption in town, laying a large amount of the blame on Boss Marcon and his goons.

Even amongst the religious in town—and there were many in this area—Loomis was a pariah, a wild-eyed doomsayer. Yet, there was something about him. Something strange and unkillable. Perhaps it was the pull of his passion, but even now Eli felt the power in his presence, as though Loomis had someone on his side—some supernatural force that protected him.

That was the reason why Eli needed to see him today.

"It's Eli, isn't it? You're one of Boss Marcon's men," Loomis drawled, puffing his broad chest. "You've come to threaten me again." Sighing, as though bored by the confrontation, he moved to a small table by the door to the study where the day's mail rested. Loomis picked up the stack and went about shuffling through the envelopes, barely paying Eli any attention. "Well, as I've told you before, I'm not afraid of you. I answer to a *much* higher authority than yours."

Eli kept his gaze steady as the suspicious pastor circled. "I know."

Loomis moved closer to one of the exits, and Eli spotted a phone mounted on the wall inside the hall. Before he had a chance to react, the preacher had the receiver in his hand, brandishing it like a weapon.

"So, give me one good reason why I shouldn't call the cops on you, you two-bit worthless punk."

Eli drew his SIG 229. "You don't think he already owns the police?"

The pastor's face fell, and the phone slumped in his hand. "Oh."

Eli held out his hands in surrender and slowly laid the gun on the pulpit before backing two steps away. Loomis' brow cinched in confusion. Eli said, "I need to get things right with God. And I need you to show me how to do it."

Relieved, the pastor grinned, a sparkle of hope in his eye. "You've come to the right place, my son."

As Eli sat in Loomis' study amidst shelves of dusty books, listening to the odd man ramble, he wondered if he'd made a mistake in coming here. The pastor was eccentric, to be sure, one moment calling him a "punk", the next kindly inviting him into the parlor to discuss his eternal salvation—all without missing a beat. But Eli waited patiently, his sins weighing on his soul. He'd already made up his mind that he'd have to leave Adrian and the family. That was decided for him the moment he pulled the trigger that robbed Theresa of her baby's father. Killing James was the final straw, the last bit of weight to sink a ship that had been bobbing uncertainly for months now. What started as a rage quest to avenge his brother's death had evolved into a self-destructive journey into more and more misery. Eli had felt a pressure in his gut for some time, and with each passing second, he felt more certain that leaving the empire was exactly what he must do. It would never be enough to redeem him for the atrocities he'd committed in the name of revenge, but it might at least provide him some measure of peace.

But leaving Adrian would be near impossible. Adrian hadn't made himself king of the hill in this town just to let loose ends fray in the breeze. He was a particular man, one who meticulously covered all the angles, and Eli would be an unacceptable variable. Eli needed something in his corner, something beyond luck.

"My dad believed in God," Eli said as Pastor Loomis deposited his opened bills on his cluttered desk. "He always told my brother and me that God delivered anyone who came to Him for help."

"So, it's deliverance you seek," Loomis said, touching a knuckle to his head, as if concentrating on something.

Eli eyed him strangely. "Adrian hates you, you know."

"As do many." The short man held his head up, proud. "My message is not a popular one."

"But Adrian's not made a move against you. That's...irregular. Either you're really lucky—"

"Luck has nothing to do with it, m'boy," the preacher said, taking a seat behind his desk.

"My point exactly. You've got something on your side that even Adrian is scared of. I want to know what it is."

The preacher considered Eli, perhaps suspicious. "You think I don't know what people think of me? You think I don't hear their whispers and their gossip?"

Eli shifted in the hard-backed wooden chair, silent.

"They think I'm crazy!" The man gesticulated, then smoldered. "Always spouting off about the end of the world, right? I'm just a quack." Loomis leaned across the desk, either madness or great wisdom glinting in his eyes. Maybe a bit of both. "But I've seen it. I've visited remote African villages, done battle with their witch doctors. I've combated the powers of the Haitian mambos in New Orleans, cast out demons out of the sick and drug-addicted. Seen haints in the Deep South. There are *things* in the darkness, young sir. Battles being fought every second in the heavenlies by the principalities and powers. And let me tell you, the darkness is *winning*."

Eli's mind flashed to the image of the skull-faced intruder in his rearview mirror.

"I know."

Loomis carried on, leaning back in his chair, pondering. "The Church has lost much of her power because she's forsaken her greatest strength—faith. She's forgotten about the spirit-world, so caught up in her meetings and potluck fellowships and gospel singings. She's lost sight of the war, but not me. I've been to the frontlines and back...and I've picked up a thing or two."

Eli soon lost focus on the possibility of God's protection, the image of the blue skull figure filling his memory, blocking out everything—Adrian, murdering James, and the untamed brown-eyed girl he'd done it all for.

Loomis perked up, grinning, his flesh tight around his lips. "You've seen it too, haven't you? I can tell."

"Yeah."

"Not surprising. I assume you've heard the stories. It's happening to *your* men, after all."

Eli's heart thudded. A number of Adrian's men had met unexpected deaths, slain without explanation. At first, Eli assumed it was just Rufus retaliating against the soldiers of his own that had been gunned down by Eli and others among Adrian's circle. But the *ruthlessness* behind these killings...It was a brutality Eli had never encountered.

Then there was the video. The man with the glowing blue skull.

Still, the preacher couldn't have known about any of that.

"How...?" Eli made to ask, but Loomis cut him off.

"I told you, m'boy. I've *seen* things. Mind you, I haven't seen it in the flesh, so to speak, but I've felt its presence. A wraith has descended on Willowbrook, no doubt drawn by the suffering that people like Boss Marcon and the other crime families have created."

"A demon?" Eli asked automatically, instantly feeling ridiculous. Perhaps it was just this mysterious prophet's words getting to him, but in that room—and after seeing that thing in the car for himself—he was willing to believe anything.

The preacher tapped at his dimpled chin in meditation. "I'm not sure. It could be an angel."

"An *angel*? No, I've seen this. It wasn't all halos and fluffy wings."

Loomis did not laugh, only shook his head seriously. "No, you misunderstand. In the Bible, angels were sent by God to bring good tidings to Man, yes. But, also, to bring swift and fiery retribution." The man paused and looked to the heavens, recalling, "'And it came to pass that night, that the angel of the Lord went out, and smote in the camp of the Assyrians an hundred fourscore and five thousand: and when they arose early in the morning, behold, they were all dead corpses.'"

Eli frowned, and Pastor Loomis clarified, "It's from the Bible. Second Kings nineteen thirty-five. It tells an account of one angel coming to earth and laying waste to an entire army. All by himself."

"So, you think it could be an angel killing us."

"Looks like you've got more to worry about than the wars of Boss Marcon and his rivals."

Eli scratched at the dark stubble on his jawline, blowing out an anxious sigh. "I'm not a good guy," he finally told the preacher, figuring this was as good a time as any to begin his confession. "But I want to change. I *need* to."

Loomis folded his hands, the excited shine in his eyes softening. "First John one nine says that 'If we confess our sins, He is faithful and just to forgive us our sins, and to cleanse us from all unrighteousness.'"

"That's it?"

Loomis eyed the young man, surprised. "What did you expect? Light a bunch of candles, dance around with feathers, and say a chant in Latin?"

"I don't know. I guess I just thought it'd be harder than that. Like I'd have to atone, or something."

The man smoothed his hair, as if just now realizing the mess it'd been. "God offers all free redemption, young man. The problem lies with us. Can we accept such a gift on faith? Or will our desire to work for our salvation—to pull ourselves up by our bootstraps—hinder us from all that the Good Lord would provide?"

Was it really so simple? To confess and believe? Was that enough to keep him out of hell, sparing him from a just punishment that he'd brought on himself?

"I'm trapped," Alex used to tell him. It amazed Eli how much his brother's

voice in his memory sounded like his own these days. That same lost sound, devoid of life and hope. But his father had believed in something, relying on that simple faith to carry him through everything, even until the moment a blood clot extinguished his flame.

Eli stood. Night was falling, and Adrian would be waiting for him to return with a report on James. Then he'd have to tell him that he was leaving the empire behind.

"I need to go," Eli said.

Loomis seemed distracted by faraway thoughts. He was an odd duck, indeed. He finally snapped back to attention, and stood as well. "Tread carefully, m'boy. God is not mocked. Whatever a man sows, he also reaps."

Eli frowned. "Then I've got a bad harvest coming my way."

CHAPTER THREE

Eli drove for another hour to clear his thoughts. Much of what the preacher said was outlandish, but some of it also rang of truth to Eli. The words from Scripture had warmed something in him, reminding him of the way he'd felt with his father. His dad protected him, soothed his broken heart, eased his concerns. The man would speak of God as though He were a trusted close friend, and, in those times, Eli listened. He wanted to believe. Now his dad was years gone, but hearing those verses brought back that security he'd missed more than anything. His father was dead, Alex was dead, and he was stuck down a deep, dark well.

Eli prayed in that hour as he toured the town, his mind drifting from Adrian, to that strange thing stalking Adrian's men, even to the brown-eyed girl and what he'd tell *her*. Would she still want him? Where would he go once he left Adrian's side—was there any place he could hide?

Or would only Death be waiting for him?

If that were the case, he had a call to make. One long overdue.

With one hand on the steering wheel, Eli shuffled in his jacket pocket until he found his cell phone. He dialed. Waited, his throat tightening with each ring.

Finally, she answered. "Hello?"

He grinned. How might things have been different if he'd only listened to her so long ago. "Hey, Kylie."

He heard her gasp. "Eli? Are you okay? Where are you? Is everything all right?"

Eli felt a pang of longing stab his stomach. "I'm okay."

It'd been a year since he'd talked to Alex's widow. A year since he'd seen Hannah and Niah, his nieces. He'd pushed their faces out of his mind until he forgot how much he missed them, but hearing Kylie's voice brought fresh heartache.

"Oh, Eli," she breathed, and he thought she was sobbing. "I was so worried…"

"I know. I'm sorry. It wasn't safe to call before. Listen, I wanted to tell you that…" He paused. "You told me once that we get ourselves into our own traps. And that we can get ourselves out of them. I'm ready to get out now."

She *was* weeping, and laughing too. He felt like doing the same.

"What will you do?" she asked.

He shook his head. "I'm quitting. Tonight. I don't expect it to go very well."

"Eli…"

"I just wanted you to know that, no matter what happens—no matter how it turns out—I'm free."

Kylie sniffled on the other end. "Come find us."

"I will," he said. "If I'm able. Bye, Kylie."

She remained silent for the longest time, and said so much in that silence. At length she said, "Good-bye, Eli."

Eli ended the call and released a breath. His chest heaved with cries longing to get out, but he felt cleansed. It was almost time, now. But he had one more good-bye to make.

Eli crossed the railroad tracks and pulled up to James' house, with only its orange-yellow porch light warding off the surrounding black night. He parked the car and placed his head on the steering wheel. He'd go meet Adrian and whatever fate waited for him, but first he needed to come back to James' house. He didn't know why, for sure, but he supposed it was his feeble way of apologizing.

Stepping out of the car, Eli stalked towards the rickety two-story on Buckingham Road. The place was up for sale. James had planned to finally ditch this dump and find a nice, respectable home for his new little family, to give the baby a safe place to grow up.

That baby… Eli didn't know if his prayers meant anything to God above, but even if all that unrighteousness were washed away like 1 John said, he knew that baby would haunt him to the day he died. *I took away that kid's dad.*

He felt nauseous.

Eli dug around in his pants pocket, fishing out the key James had given him. *He trusted me. We were friends. We looked out for each other.*

Feeling hot tears stinging his eyes, his gut wrenching, he reached to unlock the door, preparing himself to face a barrage of happy memories that he had tarnished with one selfish act.

Only…the door was ajar. A light was on inside. Eli heard murmuring.

On alert, he reached into the holster under his jacket and pulled out the SIG 229. Was Theresa here? Had she come looking for James? Did she not know that he was dead? Would he have to tell her?

It might not be Theresa, though. Adrian's soldiers had many enemies. He couldn't let his grief and guilt guide him into a trap. His survival instinct took over, and his military training made his next moves for him. Carefully, he gripped his gun, backed off the porch, and made his way around back. Keeping low and quiet, his mind attentive, Eli eased around the corner, his gun raised and ready to rock-n-roll. With a vigilant eye on every shadow, every tree, every bush, he slid under the windows as the voices grew louder. Here, he could tell that they were men, not Theresa.

Light cascaded through the screened-in back porch, painting the grass in white. Eli stayed in the shadows, peering with one eye around the edge of the screen frame to look inside the porch. There he saw two men playing cards, yucking it up. One wore a too-small tweed sportscoat and a too-big dusty black fedora. His chubby fingers squeezed his hand of cards and his eye twitched, the look of a guy hopped up on too much caffeine. His playing buddy was the shorter of the two, wearing a frumpy leather jacket and worn ball cap. He looked hopped up on something else as he reclined in James' wicker patio furniture, sedated, gazing at his cards as though they were speaking poetry to him.

Eli recognized them both. The one in the fedora, Stan. Ball Cap was Lee. They were Adrian's personal bodyguards. The Old Man was *here*.

Stan set down his cards, bowing his head in quiet contemplation, and lifted a poignant finger. "It was a political move set up by the feminists."

Lee lazily kicked back in the chair, sifting through his hand. "How d'ya figger?"

"Well, look," Stan began, explaining with his hands. "You got one guy. Two girls. It was a statement saying how the male population is being doubled by the female, that's it!" Wagging his limp finger, he finished, "They wanna take us over, man."

"They wanna outnumber us?"

"And knock us down too! Look. Take the poor guy. He was such a fool, he didn't even notice. Not even with that blonde, running loose, playing stupid. It was just another form of manipulation."

Lee waved off the comment, nodding in agreement. "Ah, those dames pull that stuff on us all the time."

Quieting, throwing furtive glances over his tweed-clad shoulder, Stan spoke in conspiratorial whispers, "The blonde, see, she lured him in with her good looks and no brains and then the other girl, with her cool wits and commanding nature, sneaks up...and *snap!*" Stan snapped his fingers, roaring now in indignation. "Springs up on that poor sap and he's trapped! The whole t'ing was a freakin' conspiracy, I say."

Stan gave a good shake of his head, as if that settled it, and Lee echoed, "Yup."

"But Mr. Roper!" Stan burst out into hysterics, his eyes darting every which way, as though the whole world were falling apart around him, and he alone were faced with the struggle to keep it together. "*He* was catching on! And what did those Commie feminists do? They shipped him off to his own spin-off series, mhm. They knew that show wasn't going to last, but did they care? No! They put him out to sea, just to shut him up."

Lee managed another dazed, mute jerk of his chin, as Stan exploded with revelation. "Oh! And then you know what they did! They brought in Don Knotts! You knew *he* wasn't going to bust the whole thing wide open, mhm!"

Eli could take no more. After the day he'd had, the idiotic ramblings of Stan were more than he could handle. He opened the back door and met their startled glances with a cold glare.

"What are you doing here?" Eli asked, coming inside.

Stan and Lee were bottom feeders—kiss-ups who followed Adrian around. They were good for little more than taking a bullet for the Old Man. They'd botched enough jobs, but Eli heard from the others that Stan and the Boss were distant relations, and Adrian always respected blood family. Rather than putting these clowns out on the streets where they could screw things up, Adrian seemed to prefer having them close by, out of trouble.

At once, Stan relaxed and coolly picked up his cards again. "Well, well. Eli. We've been waiting up for ya. Sorry about the lock on the front door. Hope we didn't scare ya."

"Is Adrian here?" Eli said.

Lee casually stood and went through the regular routine of patting Eli down, slipping the SIG out of its holster and laying it on the table. "Yup."

Eli watched the gun, knowing now he'd have no way to defend himself from the Old Man if things went south.

"Must feel pretty weird comin' back, huh?" Stan sneered, watching Eli with disdain. "Back to the guy's house you just double-crossed. Lotta ghosts here, huh? Pretty spooky."

Eli grimaced in the face of Stan's self-righteous smirk. Leaving the duo behind, Eli entered James' house, unable to quell the rampaging guilt within him.

As Eli ascended the few steps into the house proper, Stan shook the encounter from his thoughts and turned back to his cards. Forgetful, he glanced up at Lee. "Now, what were we talking about?"

Lee played his hand, nonchalant. "The feminist conspiracy behind *Three's Company.*"

"Oh." Stan brightened. "Right!"

Eli stepped into the darkened house, entering the kitchen. Only a small lamp in the next room cast any kind of glow in the gloom.

"Hello, Eli," a rumbling voice greeted him in the darkness.

Adrian Marcon was a small-town crook all grown up. He'd started out life on the streets as a "go-getter" for a chop shop back in the day. Eventually, he rose to prominence and inherited the chop shop. After that, he'd branched out to money laundering, offering his protection to local businesses, eventually dabbling in small time drug trafficking. He had a hand in everything in Willowbrook, both legal and illegal.

But he didn't get to the top by accident. He was a cunning businessman and a paranoid gangster. Few had ever spoken face-to-face with the Old Man. Most often, when Adrian needed to speak with his men, it was through his liaison, Darius Domingo. Domingo had only been with the empire a little longer than Eli, but Adrian trusted him explicitly and he served as the Boss' public face except for the rare occasions when the Old Man arranged one of these shadowy rendezvous.

"Have a seat," Adrian said somewhere in the dark, only his hand visible in the faint light of the distant lamp. The Boss was seated at the kitchen table, moonlight splashing across the fine finish. Eli took a seat, unsure of where to look.

"Sorry if we scared you," the Old Man said, his gravelly voice monotone, his intentions unreadable. He always sounded like a machine, hollow and straight to business. "We got worried when you didn't call. Stan thought maybe you'd left town."

Eli felt sweat soaking under his arms, but remained calm. "I'm not stupid."

"Yeah, but we all get scared sometimes. I take it the job went well?"

Eli clenched his jaw. He saw James in his mind, lying dead on the doorstep, exposed to the elements. Here, in his house, he realized he was surrounded by photos of James and Theresa, accusing him with their smiles. "Same as always."

"Good," the shadow spoke, then the illuminated hand slipped into the darkness. When it returned, it held a briefcase. Adrian set the case on the table. Slid it over.

Eli caught the case and unlocked it. Monetary gain was the last thing on his mind, though his promised pay was substantial, but he wanted something to do with his hands and someplace to focus his eyes. Anything other than staring into that void where the man who held his destiny watched. A cursory glance inside the briefcase told him his money was accounted for. Thirty thousand dollars. "So where was Joey? I thought he was supposed to pull this job."

The dark remained quiet. Eli closed the lid on the case, unnerved.

At last, Adrian spoke, "Joey ran into some…complications. Or, I should say that they ran into him. A Mack truck. Odd, wouldn't you say? Domingo and I think our friend with the skull mask has struck again."

Pastor Loomis' crazy words returned to Eli's mind: *"There are things in the darkness, young sir."*

He blew out a sigh.

"You seem different tonight, Eli. Something wrong?"

A pause. "No."

"Nobody likes a liar," Adrian drawled, and Eli feared that maybe the Old Man had found out. Not about his deep personal struggle for redemption, but about the girl who had started it all—the one who had tipped Eli into the downward spiral at the bottom of which he now found himself.

Marcie. The brown-eyed girl in the photo in his car. Adrian's daughter.

Eli blushed uncontrollably, terrified that the Old Man knew. "I hate this," he said, clenching his jaw, unable to look in Adrian's direction.

Adrian tapped on the table, a maddening steady rhythm. "Go on."

Eli cooled, thinking maybe the Old Man didn't know after all. "I'm tired of hurting people."

"You never seemed to mind before."

Eli's thoughts lingered on Alex. To their happy childhood playing with Matchbox cars. When they raced their bikes. Played football in the dirt.

"Don't grow a conscience on me now," Adrian said matter-of-factly. "You're my very own Angel of Death, remember?"

No. Eli had seen the Angel of Death. The thing had been leaving body parts of Adrian's thugs all over town for months now. Now Eli had even glimpsed its face, like some sort of omen of his own impending doom. Like the preacher said, he would have to reap what he'd sown, and his crop would be murder, terror, and bloodshed.

Eli spoke quietly. "But there's gotta be some kind of reckoning, don't you think?"

Adrian hesitated, twirling his fingers about. "You mean, like, God? Sounds like you've been talking to that crazy old preacher Loomis. You converting on me, kid?"

Eli shook his head, weary of dealing in death. Desperate to live again.

"We don't have room for philosophers in this business." Adrian said.

"I'm not talking philosophy. I'm talking fate. There has to be something more than this."

Adrian took a breath, and when he spoke again his tone was suddenly harsh. "You saying you want to quit? You want to join a monastery or the Peace Corps? After the things you've done, do you honestly think there's any going back for you?"

Eli looked away, terse, Adrian's words cutting into him like barbs.

"Your brother thought that once. He thought he could just leave. Be *normal*. But this was in his blood, just like it's in yours. You're a killer, boy. A cold-blooded murderer. And, face it, you like it." When Eli did not protest, Adrian tapped at the table again, thoughtfully. "You're not through."

"I can't do this anymore," Eli whispered, staring at nothing, afraid of the sound of his own voice.

Adrian shifted in his seat, his tapping ceased, his entire body rigid. Eli braced for anything—maybe the Old Man would pull a gun and shoot him right there, just as ruthlessly as *he'd* gunned down James. Fearing these were his final moments on Earth, Eli felt he should make the most of them. Do something that would make his dad proud of him again.

"I *did* talk to the preacher today," Eli said, growing bolder. "He said some things. Joey's not the first one to die under 'mysterious circumstances'. You want to think it's Rufus, and maybe it is. But something is out there. It's killing us, one by one, working its way up the ladder. It's only a matter of time before it comes for me."

Eli's memory violently slammed back to that blue skull staring at him in the rearview mirror, moving closer, ready to mete out its justice.

"I don't want to die. Not for this. That's why…that's why I have to leave. I'm getting out," he said, stronger this time, forcing his eyes to look to the shadows where his inevitable death awaited. "I need a fresh start."

The darkness only watched him. Even Adrian's hand remained limp and unmoving on the table. Eli fought the urge to fidget, confused by this reaction. He'd expected Adrian to laugh at him, berate him, yell, even *shoot* him. But he hadn't counted on him just sitting there.

Long seconds passed, and Eli felt sweat rolling down his face.

Unable to endure the silence any longer, Eli ventured, "Come on, Adrian. Say something."

But the Boss did not. Eli's throat ran dry. He felt the empty holster under his jacket and remembered that he was defenseless. James was a gun nut—had weapons stashed all over this house. But could Eli get to something fast enough should the Old Man try something? "Adrian?"

From the quiet black where Adrian sat, Eli heard a wet snapping sound, like elastic stretched to its limits and then popping apart.

Adrian's hand twitched, a small dot of blood landing on the polished table beside it.

Eli paled. "Adrian?"

There was a shuffle in the unseen and, suddenly, a basketball tumbled out of the darkness, rolling across the table, bouncing into Eli's lap. It only took Eli half a breath to understand that it wasn't a basketball.

It was Adrian's bloodied head.

Not severed, not cut with any kind of utensil, but rather *pulled*. Nerves and tendons dangled loose from the neck like tentacles, and Adrian's aged face was slack with horror, its eyes horribly cognizant, its mouth under a grey Old West-style handlebar mustache twitching open and closed, like a fish on dry land.

Eli jerked to his feet, dropping the head to the floor, brushing himself off in a mad panic as though he were covered in thousands of ants. He spat out curse after curse like they were burning his tongue, all the while smearing Adrian's blood on his jacket, his slacks—anything to be free of the gruesome sight—then looked back to the table where the Old Man's headless body slumped forward into the light, spilling gore all over the polish.

From the other side of Adrian's lifeless body, two firm hands wrapped in tight leather gloves slowly touched down on the table. A hulking shape loomed over them, then peered out of the darkness, its face caught in the moonlight.

No, Eli understood. Not a face, but a skull.

A glowing blue skull.

CHAPTER FOUR

Breathless, Eli stumbled backwards, his mouth agape.

From the shadows, the behemoth emerged. Dressed in a simple black London fog coat, with leather gloves, black jeans, and black boots, the shape was a living shadow. Floating in the dark space just above its shoulders was that blue skull that faintly shimmered like a solar-powered lawn light after dark. In that moment of fright, Eli could not tell if this thing had a skull for a face, or if he were only wearing some kind of mask. All he knew for certain was that this dark giant exuded animal lethality. The thing stalked for Eli, slow and deliberate, reaching with its blood-soaked hands, and Eli forgot his training, forgot the death he had dealt to so many. His experience as a soldier and as a hitman was stripped from him, reducing him to the small frightened boy he'd been before the war. The one who needed big brother Alex and his father to defend him.

Alex is dead. Dad is dead.

I'm going to die too.

"No!" he shouted, tears streaming down his cheeks. "Wait!"

But the thing moved, despite his pleas.

The back door exploded in, Stan's fat foot following close behind. Both Stan and Lee hurried into the kitchen, pistols drawn, suspecting perhaps that Eli had shot the Old Man. Nothing could prepare them for the sickening truth.

As one, their eyes moved to Adrian's head, wobbling slightly on the hardwood floor, then to the blue-faced monster reaching out for Eli.

"He killed Adrian!" Eli shrieked, his chest heaving.

Despite Stan and Lee's reputed incompetence, the duo put up a brave effort. Without hesitation, they raised their weapons and shot off a volley of deafening rounds. Eli instinctively covered his ears, flinching as bullets tore into the shape's coat. Dust plumed from the entry wounds, but no blood flowed. One bullet connected with the skull but merely evaporated in a flash of blue fire.

The monster paused, regarding its attackers with curiosity.

Stan and Lee froze too, their minds shutting down at the sight of the impossible.

Eli remembered what the preacher had said about a single angel butchering an entire army of trained soldiers. *Is that what this is? God's own hitman coming after us?*

Its broad shoulders raising up, bringing the creature to its full mighty stature,

40

the blue skull monstrosity turned its gaze—dark, empty, without eyeballs—towards Stan and Lee. Lee yelped, more animation than Eli had ever seen in the crony, and slipped past the monster, running away. Eli cowered without shame as the thing brushed past him, all its focus directed on poor Stan. With fluttering hands, Stan removed the empty clip from his gun and replaced it with a fresh one. He racked the slide, trembling as he did so, and lifted the barrel to face the monster. But his trigger finger seemed petrified. Instead of shooting, he just stood there, quaking, as a delirious grin spread across his clean-shaven face. In a feat of incredible speed, the monster thrust out its strong hands, wrapping them tightly around Stan's throat, then lifted him clear out of his loafers. Stan sputtered, white spittle at the corner of his mouth, dribbling down his cheeks. His grin grew grotesquely wide and he laughed, shrill and maniacal, twitching in the vise-like grip of his captor. The thing regarded him, cocking its head to the side—

Then twirled Stan around, pulled him in, and wrenched his neck.

Stan's spine broke with a dry *crack*, his socked feet still convulsing, his over-sized fedora sliding to the floor. Now the beast loosed the dead man and Stan's corpse collapsed, nerves still jittery.

Eli felt bile rising in his throat, and forced himself to reach for Stan's discarded gun. Numb fingertips made contact with the cold steel, but he didn't dare move any further. *Do something,* his instinct screamed at him, *or you're going to die!*

Once more, the creature looked to Eli, its skull face devoid of any sort of intelligence. But there *was* a sort of cunning there, all the same. Eli sensed it. It emanated from the thing in waves, eliciting in him a feeling he remembered from a childhood summer vacation when his dad drove him and Alex through the mountains. He had stared at those mountains, aged and permanent, knowing they had been on the Earth for millennia longer than he'd existed, and they'd stand for millennia once his insignificant life had passed. This thing before him now was immovable. Ancient. And surely, it would outlast him.

Just as before, the creature bypassed him, moving into the other room where Lee had fled. Eli's knees gave way and he wobbled, bracing himself on James' kitchen counter. Now was his time to run. For whatever reason, this thing had given him a second chance. Adrian was dead. Stan, too. Lee would be dead in a matter of moments, and no one would come looking for Eli.

Leave, he commanded his legs. *Find Marcie. Start over.*

But he could hear Lee shuffling around in the next room. And although it might have been the smart thing to do, he couldn't abandon the man to that monster. Inside, he felt a strange, warm assurance, a still soft voice telling him that he was making the *right* decision. Eli hadn't felt that certainty in a long time, and it empowered him.

Certain, his constitution solidifying along with his resolve, he cocked his gun and gave chase.

Eli slid into the living room, right behind the monster. Lee was by the staircase, making his last stand. He had to have known after seeing what the thing did to Adrian that his chances of survival were slim—he should have bolted out the front door. Perhaps Lee's loyalty to old friends kept him fighting, or perhaps he, like Eli, was hoping to do the right thing for once. Or maybe he was just too scared to think straight.

Lee raised his gun, freshly reloaded, and fired off a shot into the glowing skull. The bullet fizzled, worthless. For all his previous kicked-back attitude, Lee made a good showing. Once more, the creature moved so fast that Eli could have sworn it teleported. In the blink of an eye, the thing was standing on the bottom step, snatching one of James' decorative swords from its hanger on the wall. Eli roared in protest, raising his gun, but hesitated in firing, knowing already that bullets had no effect on the creature. In his moment's pause, the beast plunged the sword through Lee's stomach. Lee screamed as the thing pulled out the weapon, dragging with it a pile of steaming guts. Lee looked to the floor, seeing what had been on his inside, and blanched, his lip trembling.

"No!" Eli shouted, tears building.

The beast did not stop. It stabbed once more, this time leaving the sword protruding from Lee's stomach. Lee clutched at it, his blood-soaked hands slipping over the hilt, then fell back, groaning as he slowly died. "Eli..." he wheezed, pleading for salvation, "...do something..."

"Stop it!" Eli screamed, pointing the gun at the monster, feeling completely helpless.

The monster whipped its head about, the hollow void where its eyes should have been pinning Eli in place. "I-I know what you a-are," Eli stuttered. "You're Death."

The phantom marched towards Eli now, flickering in and out of the visible realm, appearing inches from Eli's face. It slapped the useless gun away, then encircled cold, strong fingers around his tender throat. Eli gasped and sputtered in the grip, hoping that he hadn't squandered his only chance of survival in choosing to return for Lee. *Please, God,* he begged. At once he felt that strange sense of peace inside, and a voice like his father's reminded him of a verse—a prayer—he'd taught Eli by his bedside in his youth. Shutting his eyes, feeling oxygen leaving him, Eli mumbled, "Yea, though I walk through the valley of the shadow of Death, I will fear no evil, for Thou art with me."

Fingers loosed, and Eli felt a whoosh of fresh air filling his lungs. He crumpled to the floor, then looked up to his would-be killer. The monster stared at its hand as though it'd never seen it before, then reared back, its whole body language communicating impotent wrath.

Run, Eli's father's voice urged him. This time, he did.

He raced through the dimly lit house, groping along the walls with quavering hands, until, in his haste, he tripped over Adrian's lolling head. Eli lost his footing and tumbled to the ground, his polished shoes squeaking on the bloody boards as he scrambled to pull himself away. Gasping now, desperate to live, he pushed with all his might, sliding across the floor, until the monster grabbed him by the collar of his suit and hefted him up.

Before he could react, Eli was flung across the room, rebounding off the wall, leaving behind a large crack. In a puff of plaster, he landed hard on the floor, coughing up blood. The beast was on him, ruthlessly yanking him to his dumb feet by his jacket, pressing its face to his.

Eli felt himself losing consciousness. The thing's uncaring blue skull filled his vision, dimming in and out. The thing seemed to be studying him, looking for something. Eli didn't know what. He no longer cared. *I tried, God*, he prayed. *I'm not a good man…I don't deserve to live…But I did my best. Do whatever you want, God. I'm okay with that. It's Your call.*

The blue-faced creature snorted, as though repelled by some offensive odor, and let Eli slip from its hands. Eli's face kissed the floor, and he felt the black closing in. He looked up, though, just before all turned to nothing, and saw the monster—the Bogeyman—leaving through the front door without incident, as though the beast had just realized it had some pressing matter to attend to. Miraculously, Eli had been spared.

Dragging himself to his feet, Eli staggered to the door, pushing it closed, then slid to sit on the floor, his breathing ragged. He staved off the cold oblivion of unconsciousness, resting his head on the door. He'd made it. Baptized in blood, he'd faced Death and yet lived. And, he realized, the man he'd feared so much, who he was afraid he'd be forced to serve forever, was gone. Adrian was dead—his empire might crumble in a matter of days. Suddenly, Eli's life spread out before him, his to spend again without the chains of his past dragging him down in misery. He was free.

He was redeemed.

PART II
THE SEEKER

CHAPTER ONE

Vinnie Caponi eyed the house. Cops surrounded the joint, taking pictures, handing off clear plastic bags of evidence, swapping stories. He pulled a root beer-flavored Dum Dum out of the pocket of his black trenchcoat, unwrapped it, and popped it in his mouth. It'd been storming on and off for the last few days—presently it was on, a sheet of rain pelting the crime scene, running like a waterfall off the edge of his black fedora's rim.

The house on Buckingham Road belonged to some local gun shop owner named James Lenderman. The man was ex-Army and did mostly honest work, but word was he sold a few modified items out his back door to the likes of Boss Marcon, although the cops could never stick anything to him. Lenderman was a lightweight as criminals went. His house was old and creaking—a bit imposing, really. A FOR SALE sign was stuck in the front yard. Vinnie couldn't imagine who would want to live here *now*, now that it was the scene of a triple homicide.

Pulling his coat collar tighter, Vinnie crossed the lawn from where he'd parked his busted-up white Ford Taurus, doing his best not to let his gigantic boots sink into the soggy earth. Already a few of the cops had taken notice of him and started whispering amongst themselves. Vinnie ignored their words and was careful not to meet eyes with the men. He knew what they thought about him—he thought the same of them.

An especially burly officer stood guard on the front porch. He looked young and Vinnie didn't immediately recognize him. *Must be a rook.* Vinnie figured he had about forty pounds on the guy—though the cop's build was muscle; Vinnie's not so much.

"Whoa, whoa." The cop bristled, holding out an authoritative hand upon Vinnie's approach. "Where do you think you're going?"

Vinnie took the sucker out of his mouth for a sec. "Easy, junior. Just here to investigate."

"This is a police investigation. You're gonna have to turn around, and you and your funny little tie—what is that, Scooby Doo? —head back to your hunk a'junk at the end of the driveway or I'm gonna have to get physical."

Before Vinnie could respond, a scratchy voice called from inside the house. "That's okay, Rudy. Let him through."

Officer Rudy squinted in disgust at Vinnie, who simply tipped his fedora respectfully and walked inside where he saw even more cops. Little numbered cards decorated the floor, points of interest for the investigation. The bodies had already been moved, but the blood...

The blood was everywhere.

At the center of the circus, he spotted the lanky, bent-over form of Lt. Frank Dutton of the Willowbrook P.D. Frank, a two-pack-a-day smoker, puffed on his latest coffin nail, his dark but graying beard growing in. He had the shakes about him, a bit wild-eyed, but he was steady with a pistol. Vinnie knew the man's skills with a gun firsthand—he had often lost competitions to him on the range.

"Thanks, Frank," Vinnie said, taking a stand next to his old friend.

Frank stood over a bloodied sword that rested on the ground. A couple green-at-the-gills officers were handling a small body bag filled with remains. "Gotta say that I'm surprised to see you here."

Vinnie shrugged. "Heard the ruckus on my scanner. Thought I'd come by and try to help."

He was partially honest with the lieutenant. He did want to help—but more than that, he wanted to be here, to find out if the talk was true. If so, he had to see it for himself. *I owe her that much.* "What do we got?"

Frank eyed him cautiously. "Off the record?"

"Of course."

"Three stiffs. Two bodyguards and the man himself. Boss Marcon."

Vinnie stuck his hands in his pockets, mulling that over. Was he happy that it had finally happened, or disappointed that he wasn't around to witness it? He couldn't tell. "Then it's true."

"Yep. Head torn off."

Vinnie blinked and cut a sharp look at Frank, who just nodded solemnly.

"One of the other stiffs had his head turned around backwards. The other was impaled with the fancy sword." Frank paused. "Multiple times."

Vinnie's memory flashed to the video tape. The one he'd seen thousands of times—the one that had started him down this path to begin with. In the video, one of Marcon's thugs went up against *something* that emerged out of the shadows. Something that took the goon's head completely off in a single move.

Something that had a skull for a face.

"Hmm," Vinnie paused, connecting dots.

"What are you thinking?"

Skullface. "Any leads?"

"Eli Ross. Some kid moving up the ranks. His prints are all over the house, but not on any of the murder weapons."

"You brought him in yet?"

"Still looking. He might've skipped town, which leads us to believe that we're on the right track. Maybe there was some bad blood and he did the deed himself or had an unknown accomplice. Who knows, maybe he's working with that Rufus guy who's making all the noise these days. Besides…there's another vic. Not here, though."

Curious, Vinnie faced Frank. "Who?"

"James Lenderman. The owner of the house."

"I figured he was one of the bodyguards."

"Nope. He was found some miles away this afternoon." Frank paused, his mood darkening as he studied Vinnie. "On the front step of *your* old house."

Vinnie did not expect that. "My place? Why's that?"

"Don't know." Frank looked over his shoulder and Vinnie followed his gaze. More than one cop was keeping tabs on Vinnie, all of them whispering to each other. "Looks suspicious, doesn't it?"

"You think I did this?"

"No, of course not. But you gotta look at the evidence, Vinnie. We got a shooting at your place—"

"I haven't lived there in months."

"True. But we all know how you felt about Marcon. He's why you left the force. Started the P.I. thing. Besides, this isn't the first of Marcon's gang to wind up butchered like this. There haven't been many eyewitnesses, but the ones we got said they saw someone big—in a black trenchcoat."

Frank's eyes flicked to Vinnie's own black trenchcoat. Feeling cornered, Vinnie defended, "It's a fashion statement."

The lieutenant laughed. "Like the cartoon ties? The fedora?"

"It's a classic. Never goes out of style."

Frank stepped in, reminding Vinnie of the friend he once had in him. "If I really thought you were capable of this, I'd've brought you in already. You say you're not involved, I'll take you at your word. But you don't have too many friends left on the force. You keep walking onto crime scenes like this, you're gonna give them the rope they need to hang you. Understand?"

Vinnie did, but the situation carried too much personal importance for him to back down now. He'd come here to make sure Adrian Marcon was dead, but something didn't sit right about the details. "I've seen this M.O. before, Frank. You're right—something's killing the Boss' men."

"Not some *thing*. Some*one*."

He frowned. "What's your point?"

"I heard about…" Frank grew quiet, and Vinnie shifted uncomfortably.

Vinnie looked away. "Yeah."

"I was sorry to hear that. I can only imagine what losing Lucy would do to me. I'm sure I'd start seeing things that weren't there."

Vinnie's jaw went taut, crunching on his sucker unexpectedly. Frank said, "I heard what you been doing these days. You're some kind of Ghostbuster or something, right? I know you think a ghost was responsible for…what happened, but don't lose touch with reality, partner."

Vinnie stiffened, having heard enough.

"Let us handle this, Vinnie. Please. For your own good."

Vinnie shoved his hands in his pockets, marching for the front door. "Thanks for not kicking me out, Frank. I'll see you around."

"Vinnie—" Frank called, his tone sympathetic, but Vinnie was in no mood to continue their heart-to-heart. The lieutenant didn't understand. No one did. There was some kind of monster killing gangsters in Willowbrook, but if they didn't want to listen to Vinnie Caponi about it, so be it. He had other cases to take. Let the P.D. handle this if they thought they could.

He just felt sorry for whatever poor schmuck moved into this house. Place like this, tainted with evil…

Moving in here would just be asking for trouble.

CHAPTER TWO

FIFTEEN MONTHS LATER

Snow drifted to the ground, covering the quiet countryside in a layer of sparkling white frosting. Brian Setzer and his orchestra proclaimed, *"It's Christmas-time, pretty baby"* from the radio, but Flynn Spanger felt little of the holiday spirit. Slumped in the passenger seat of his dad's car, Flynn sulked, watching strange surroundings speed past the window. He tried to convince himself that this was home, now, but the sentiment felt empty even in his own heart. Home was back in Wisconsin. Home was back with his mom.

"Right up there," his dad muttered, leaning his girth over the steering wheel to get a better peek through the windshield.

Flynn casually turned his attention front and center, to the towering country home on Buckingham Road, it too blanketed in untouched snow. The white fluff nearly buried the decrepit house, only its dark windows visible from the winding road.

"Looks cold," Flynn said, frowning.

His dad either ignored him or simply hadn't heard. Both possibilities were plausible. His dad had never been a very good listener. *Mom used to listen*, Flynn thought sourly.

The car dipped and rocked across the train tracks and pulled into the driveway, the snow making uncomfortable grinding noises beneath the tires. Dad stared at the house, and Flynn caught a reflection of his own thoughts in the man's eyes. A pang of sympathy stabbed Flynn's heart, but he did his best not to feel it. He was tired of feeling these days.

At last Dad pulled the keys from the ignition with a sigh, and the Spanger men stepped out of the car, Flynn pulling his bulky coat tighter around him. The coat was huge on his slight twelve-year old frame, and Flynn felt lost in it. He wished he could shrink inside the coat's warmth, disappearing forever from the fate that awaited him in this strange house.

Dad kept his back to him, his hands shoved deep into his pockets, as if bracing for the inevitable. "We'll be happy here, Flynn," the man said, his voice nearly lost in the wintry wind. "You'll see."

Flynn hung his head. He didn't want to cause his father any more grief, but he couldn't help speaking. "We were happy in Wisconsin."

Dad exhaled, his breath a frosty plume, and regarded his son, a mixture of understanding and guilt on his face. "We need to go where the money is. With all your mom's doctor bills…"

Flynn bit his lip, the pain close to the surface, and absently adjusted his glasses. He wondered if the hurt would ever go away or if the very thought of her would always push him to tears.

"Hey," his dad gently switched gears. "I'll let you have first pick of the bedrooms."

"Even the master?"

"Not the master." Dad cracked a grin.

Flynn pushed up his glasses and donned his best put-upon expression, but only as a means of clinging to normal father-son strife. He slipped under his dad's meaty arm and together they looked upon their new home.

Home, Flynn thought. *Not hardly.*

Steven Segal was on TV, doing his thing. Dad sat kicked back in the recliner, his large socked feet pointing up like rabbit ears from the raised footstool. He drifted in and out of sleep, no doubt exhausted from the drive and first wave of moving in, but Flynn remained wide awake, decked out in sweat pants and sweatshirt to ward off the chill that filled the creaky old house. He absently watched the action movie—edited for television, meaning all the good parts were cut out—looking past the screen. As he stared into space, Flynn's mind drifted, and he felt awash in an ocean of the surreal. This was his *home*. The thought seemed impossible to him. He'd start school in a new place, filled with strangers, forced to navigate the maze of a brand new campus he'd never even laid eyes on.

Flynn liked to keep to himself; he didn't have a lot of friends back home— his *real* home, in Wisconsin. But he'd learned to blend into the status quo. He knew who the worst bullies were and had developed proven methods of avoiding them. Back home, he had figured he could continue the rest of his life living just under the radar, neither admired or despised by anyone, just a piece of the scenery. He had a plan worked out, a nice normal routine that didn't compensate for terminal cancer that claimed one's mother. No, Flynn certainly had not prepared for that.

Dad snorted awake, bleary-eyed, first spotting Segal, then the clock on the wall. He jerked towards the couch where Flynn lay, as though he'd forgotten his son existed. Once he saw Flynn, he groggily wrestled with the remote and clicked off the TV. "All right, time for bed," he groaned.

"It's not even ten-thirty. Can't I stay up a *little* bit?"

Dad yawned. "No, you've got school in the morning."

Flynn sat up, draping his hands over his knees. He felt queasy inside. Thanks to Dad's new job that he had to start immediately, they had moved here with only two weeks of school left before Christmas break. Flynn supposed that was some sort of comfort. He'd have time away from his new peers pretty soon in case things were miserable—which he knew they would be—but that left two whole weeks of being "the new kid".

He slumped towards his room, dodging unpacked boxes, the fears of tomorrow and the strange looks he'd receive weighing across his shoulders.

Flynn walks to his mother's bedside. Even as he does so, he knows this is a dream. She lays there in the hospital, her long curly tresses spread out on the pillow. It's a lie, of course. In reality, the last time Flynn saw his mother she was bald, dark shadows under her eyes, tubes running into her nose and mouth. The chemo had done that to her.

But here, she is still vibrant. Beautiful.

"Flynn," she breathes through a smile.

She extends one trembling hand and Flynn takes it. "I'm here, Mom."

"Don't be afraid," she says, still smiling, and Flynn's stomach churns. "We all die."

"No."

"Oh, yes," she grins even wider, her mouth filling with rows of sharp, tiny teeth. Her eyes roll up in the back of her head, her skin turning white and papery, clinging to her skull. "Even you, child." Her voice becomes shrill and so loud that Flynn releases her grip and clamps his hands over his ears. "Your time will come soon."

Flynn's eyes shot open and he found himself alone in the darkness of a strange room. No. It was his room. His new bedroom. His new home.

He swung his legs over the side of the bed and sat up, shivering. The quiet of the night soothed him, but when he closed his eyes he still saw the ghost image of his mother—twisted and deformed, smiling at him.

Putting his face in his hands, he sobbed.

His tears broke free, his chest heaving as he expunged all the sorrow he'd been storing up since his mother died. Had he even cried at her funeral? Surely, he had. He couldn't remember, now. Couldn't remember anything about that day that they buried his mom.

Flynn heard his Dad snoring loudly, still in the recliner in the living room, and he tried to contain his emotion, hoping to avoid alerting his father.

Dad had cried a lot since Mom died. He did it privately, but Flynn heard him sometimes behind the bathroom door in the mornings. He thought to say something to his dad, to tell him he missed her, too, but... He never did. He just couldn't.

A train suddenly roared right outside his bedroom window, rattling the glass, filling the drafty house with a high-pitched roar. Flynn jumped to his feet, caught off guard by the unfamiliar sound, his heart thundering in fright. *Great*, he thought. *One more thing to get used to.*

His breathing slowed as the train rocketed by. Flynn relaxed and moved to the window, peeking through the blinds. He watched the train dash past a lone street lamp, casting his yard in staccato light. At last the train carried on and away, taking its noise with it. The clattering sound of the locomotive faded in the distance, and Flynn's eyes adjusted to the light that cut a blue swath through the fair snow and insidious shadows.

A shape stood out against the light. Moving?

Flynn squinted his eyes, then reached for his glasses. Slipping them onto his nose, he leaned forward against the windowpane, casting his search across the dark tree line beyond.

The shadow moved, pulling apart from the others, and Flynn recognized it as a man, staring into his bedroom window.

Flynn gasped, his father's snores in the other room constant reminders that his only protector was fast asleep while a stranger lurked just outside. Petrified, Flynn's gaze traveled up, from the man's thick black boots, to his black pants, a long black coat, black gloves, and finally—

A skull with just the faintest of blue luminescence, watching him.

"AHH!" Flynn hollered, stumbling away from the blinds, watching as, before his eyes, the shape of the man flickered, popped, then vanished from sight. "*Dad!*"

He heard the grinding gears of the retracting recliner moments before his dad burst through the room like a stampeding buffalo. "What?" he snapped, his eyes red and puffy from sleep.

"Out there!" Flynn pointed to the window.

Dad hurried to investigate, then let the blinds fall back into place after a moment. "I don't see anything. What was it?"

Flynn's body trembled, jittery with adrenaline. "I-I don't know. A man."

"Probably just a neighbor or something."

"No, he had this...this *skull* and he—he disappeared!"

Dad deflated and faced his son. "It was just a nightmare, Flynn. I...I get them too."

He reached out a sympathetic hand, but Flynn jerked away. "No! It wasn't a dream! I saw something out there!"

"Flynn..." Dad shook his head.

"Forget it." Flynn climbed back into bed, turning his back to his father.

He heard Dad shuffling for the door. "We're going to get through this, Flynn."

Flynn ignored him, clenching his jaw until his father left and quietly shut the door behind him. He slept fitfully that night.

CHAPTER THREE

The next morning, Flynn and his father ate breakfast in the silence of two separate rooms. They still didn't speak in the uneventful car ride to school, except for the quick, "Have a good day" that Dad mumbled as Flynn stumbled out of the vehicle. They were both lost in their own thoughts. Truth be told, Flynn no longer wanted to talk to his dad about last night's incident, preferring to ponder over it on his own.

The thing outside his window had disappeared, completely dematerialized. He was sure of it. *What could do that?*

Most of the morning at school went by in a blur of noise and motion. He kept his head down, getting lost twice in the unfamiliar halls. One of his classmates, a blonde girl who worked as an office aide—very pretty, which only worsened his anxiety—guided him to his destination.

In his classes, Flynn was subjugated to introducing himself to the other students, met only by the blank, uninterested faces of his classmates, while his teachers politely interrogated him on his reasons for moving. He stuck to the basics, simply stating that his father got a new job—careful to avoid the sadder truth. The last thing Flynn wanted was to be branded "the kid whose mom died" for the rest of his time in Willowbrook.

With the embarrassing probing complete, he was cast to the wolves. The other kids watched him closely, looking over his baggy clothes, his unruly mid-length locks, and his "nerdy" glasses. At least, Flynn imagined he was under their scrutiny. Perhaps they didn't care at all. He was too red-faced to look up to confirm or deny their interest in him.

At lunch, he took his tray and sat at a smaller table out of the way. He wasn't alone. At the other end sat a group of rambunctious older kids. They danced around and threw things at each other, squawking with obnoxious laughter.

He tried his best to ignore them, poking at his lukewarm meal, counting the seconds until school let out.

"Psst. Yo. Chief."

Flynn heard the voice behind him and turned in his chair. A pale, scruffy kid wearing a thick, woolly multi-colored hoodie and sporting long, curly hair and overgrown peach fuzz leaned across the aisle in Flynn's direction. The boy looked older than Flynn—maybe fifteen or sixteen.

"Hey," he said. "You new around here?"

Flynn said, "Yeah."

"What's yer name?"

"Flynn Spanger."

"Spanker?"

Flynn grimaced. "*Spanger.*"

"Yeah." He nodded, looked around the cafeteria real quick, and leaned in a little closer. "Hey, man, I'm carrying. You need a little pick-me-up to get you through the day?"

"Drugs?" Flynn balked.

"*Shhh,*" the guy hissed, then glanced over his shoulder. "Keep it down, Chief. *Sheesh.*"

Flynn squirmed in his seat. "Ah… No. No, thanks. I'm fine."

He'd never been offered drugs before.

Curly Head shrugged. "Suit yourself. Just sayin' you look like you could use a little help. I'm Jeremy, but people call me 'Chigger'."

Flynn blinked in surprise. "*Chigger?*"

"Not important. What's your name, again?"

"Flynn."

"Man. Flynn Spanger. I always thought 'Chigger' was bad. What are you sitting with the gleeks for? Swerve over here."

Flynn cast one last look at the group he now knew were the choir clique—they were watching Chigger in revulsion—then took his tray and swapped tables. Chigger scooted over a couple inches to make room and Flynn fit easily enough at the new table.

"Have you been in town long?" Chigger said.

"Uh, two days. We just moved in yesterday afternoon."

Chigger cursed. "You guys move fast."

"Yeah, my dad had to take a job as soon as it came up. It's kind of a long story."

"What about you?" The boy took a swig of his small carton of milk and set it down. "*You* looking for work?"

Flynn creased his brow. "What do you mean?"

"Little guy like you could make a lot of cash. They don't suspect you, you know?"

Flynn deduced what brand of "work" Chigger was hinting at and blushed. "Nah."

"There's good money in it. Believe me, it's the only way you're going to make any kind of real money in Willowbrook."

"What do you mean?"

"The Bosses own *everything*."

"Bosses?"

"The family heads. Adrian used to be the Big Dog, but he got axed a year ago. I never met him. But the guy who's taking over is Rufus. I mean, if you're happy just being normal like *those* clowns—" Chigger paused and cast a nod towards the choir group again, who were all making silly faces and sticking out their tongues at each other like they were still in pre-school, "—then go for it, but if you want to get ahead, you better let me hook you up with Rufus. He's always looking for new kids."

"That's okay," Flynn tittered. "I'm good."

Chigger eyed him suspiciously. "Yeah. You are, aren't you? Real goody goody, huh?"

Flynn broke eye contact and went back to poking at his food. He and Chigger didn't speak for the rest of lunch period.

So much for my new friend.

Vinnie Caponi unwrapped a Dum Dum sucker and popped it into his mouth.

He winced against the unpleasant artificial pineapple taste and surveyed the room. The furniture lay toppled over. The sheer white drapes were shredded. Books were off their shelves and scattered about the floor.

"It's bad," the anxious woman next to him said, her voice betraying the slightest quake. "Isn't it?"

Vinnie nodded without a word and stuck his hands in his trenchcoat's deep pockets. "Just like the other times? Windows and door still locked? No sign of forced entry?"

He turned to get her answer, and the woman nodded, her widened eyes beseeching him to save her.

Frowning, he slowly paced about the room, carefully stepping over the family's ransacked belongings.

"This is ridiculous," the husband cut in from his place at the edge of the living room. The dumpy young man with a mustache-less beard crossed his hairy arms and shook his head.

"Give him a chance!" the wife snapped back. Looking back to Vinnie, she said in a softer tone, "I've always been sensitive about these sorts of things, you know? I think it runs in my family. My second cousin had this dog and I *swear* she could read its mind. It was amazing!"

Vinnie paused in his investigation, unsure of how to respond. He declined to comment, heading for the equipment he'd set up in the house the night before. His old Sony HandyCam Vision rested on a dinged-up tripod.

"It's a ghost, isn't it?" she asked, her fear giving way to hope. Excitement.

Vinnie remembered a time when he was green like that. Desperate to find any proof that life beyond death existed. Desperate for comfort. But with all he'd seen, he couldn't find any reason to be excited anymore. There were things waiting for them on the Other Side…things that crossed over from time to time. He wasn't excited to meet those things. And the comfort he'd sought when he started looking…well, it just wasn't there.

"Is this really how you make a living?" The husband huffed a condescending laugh. "Chasing ghosts?"

Vinnie unclipped the camera from the tripod and flipped a switch, changing the setting to PLAYER. "Not a ghost. Hauntings are relatively harmless. Just an echo of a spirit, unable to cross over to the Other Side. What you have here is a physical manifestation of incredible psychic energy."

The husband chuckled, still shaking his head.

Vinnie continued, unfazed, "Judging by the amount of disturbance here, I'm almost certain you have a poltergeist."

"A poltergeist!" the wife exclaimed. "Like in that movie!"

· "Yeah, what if you're wrong?" Angry Husband barked.

If I'm wrong, Vinnie thought to say, *then your problems could be a whole lot worse.* Some poltergeist activity could also be attributed to demons, but Vinnie wasn't prepared to consider that possibility just yet. Real true-blue demons were rare— they usually kept to their hidey holes beyond the Veil.

"Only one way to know," Vinnie said, rewinding the tape he'd placed in the camcorder last night to record the spook in action.

"Let me see," the wife whispered, huddling close to Vinnie's brawny arm. "Can you see it?"

Vinnie frowned, playing back the footage. "Oh."

"Hey!" the woman shouted, angry. "That's me!"

"What?" her husband yelled, stomping across the room to look at the flipscreen as well.

Vinnie watched in sickening dread as the woman's recorded self tore up her own home.

"What *is* this?" the man demanded.

Vinnie felt his stomach plummet. Shutting his eyes and taking a deep breath, he turned to the woman. "So, tell me. You have a history of sleepwalking?"

She blushed. "Well…sort of."

"Unbelievable!" The husband jammed a fat finger in the wife's direction. "You're cleaning this up! That's it!" Next, he turned his finger on Vinnie. "And you! Get out of my house!"

Vinnie closed up the camera and turned it off, trying to maintain his composure.

"I shoulda listened to my gut!" the man said. "Ghosts! Ha! Get out, you phony!"

Vinnie gathered his tripod. "There's a little matter of the two hundred dollars you still owe me for the investigation."

"You can forget it! Get out!"

Without waiting for Vinnie to move on his own, the husband laid hands on him and pushed him towards the exit. Opening the door with one hand, the man shoved Vinnie out with the other. In the impact, Vinnie lost hold of his camera and it clattered to the sidewalk, a piece of plastic casing breaking off.

"Hey!" Vinnie protested.

"You've got ten seconds to get your hoodoo voodoo off my property or I'm calling the cops!"

The husband slammed the door, leaving Vinnie out in the cold with his busted equipment. He clenched his fist in rage, but forced himself to take a calming breath. Embarrassed and angry, he collected the pieces of his camera and skulked over to his paint-chipped Taurus.

The bell rang, and the wave of students flooding out of the doors carried Flynn to sea. After his incredibly long and stressful first day at school, he was absolutely exhausted and ready to go home.

Home in Wisconsin, that is.

But that was impossible. Instead a creaky, strange, new home waited for him.

And a mysterious phantom.

Suddenly the prospect of returning to his house filled him with almost uncontrollable panic. He prayed his dad would be home, but knew already that wouldn't be the case. Usually Mom was waiting for him, waiting to hear about his day...

Distracted by better times, Flynn wandered around the hall, lost once more. This time, though, there were no cute girls to help him along his way. He shuffled about, pushed aside by the other kids, completely disorientated.

Parents pulled up and accepted their noisy brood. School buses filled with more, but Flynn wasn't sure which bus was his. He looked around uncertainly, not wanting to board the wrong bus. He remained indecisive even as the buses pulled away. "No! Wait!"

Terrified of being left behind, he shoved his way through the mingling crowds outside, looking for his big yellow ride. Confusion overwhelmed him as the buses exited the parking lot without him.

He slumped, clutching his bookbag, fear settling in. A sob choked in his throat.

Vinnie entered the joint and took a seat at the bar. Removing his dark fedora, he waved down the jerk. "Line me up," he grumbled, making a line with his finger on the tabletop.

The tender went to work, eyeing Vinnie as he did so. "Rough day at the office?"

"Carl, it's always a rough day."

Carl was a good guy. He'd been running this establishment for thirty years. Before that he'd worked at the factory, where he lost his hand. Now the man had a prosthetic claw in its place and spent his time slinging drinks for the locals. Vinnie had been coming in here since he was a kid.

Carl finished off the drink and set Vinnie's chocolate malt on the counter. Vinnie stabbed it with a straw and took a pull off the frozen treat.

Propping an elbow on the counter, Carl leaned in. "Gettin' started a little early this afternoon."

Vinnie ignored the comment. "Keep 'em coming 'til I tell you to stop."

Carl sighed. "Suit yourself. Don't come to me when you can't fit in your britches no more."

Vinnie smiled at his old friend and scooped up a spoonful of malt to drown his sorrows. He was really counting on that two hundred dollars from the poltergeist-turned-sleepwalking case, too. He had rent to pay, and the landlord—as sweet as the old gal was—was done listening to empty promises. She, like most everyone Vinnie knew, thought he was chasing a pipedream by carrying on with his fledgling urban mythologist business.

But they didn't know the truth.

He hadn't known, either, once upon a time.

He thought of *her*, and felt a fresh pang of sorrow cramp his heart.

Flynn hurried down the strange side streets five blocks from the school. He was aimed in the general direction of his dad's office, but wasn't sure if he were any closer to it. Despite the winter chill, he was sweating profusely underneath his bulky coat, his breathing jagged and painful. Still he pressed on, too scared to stop moving.

All around him, shoddily-dressed grown-ups lounged about on the corners or brownstone steps. Most of them smelled and looked like they'd been dragged through the desert tied to a horse. Some of them cursed after Flynn to get off their block or hurry on his way. Their dead eyes were hungry and watched him steadily as they took swigs off bottle-shaped paper bags or long pulls off what he suspected weren't just regular cigarettes.

Paranoia rode on Flynn's back, turning his head sharply to regard every passerby, every car. Every face was a threat, every vehicle driven by some child molester looking to abduct him. Flynn put on his mental armor, kept his head down, and walked with purpose. Maybe no one would bother him. Maybe no one would notice—

A hand latched onto his bookbag and pulled it—and him—into an alley behind an auto garage. Flynn was thrown into stacks of old tires that lined the brick wall. He yelped and scrambled to his feet, adjusting his askew glasses to spot five youths surrounding him. They looked about Chigger's age. He wondered if he'd passed them in the hall today.

"Where you going?" one of them asked. This boy was older than the others. He didn't look like a student. His slimy acne-ridden face pulled back in a tight smile that revealed a shiny gold tooth.

Flynn kept his mouth closed and tried to move past the bullies, but Gold Tooth pushed him back down. "Whoa, whoa, you bein' rude? You disrespectin' me?"

"I just want to go home," Flynn said, his hands trembling, his voice quavering.

"Gotta pay the toll," Gold Tooth said. "These are Rufus' streets."

"I don't have any money."

"Got a nice lookin' coat, though. We'll take that."

Flynn's mom had bought him that coat, in preparation for a long winter. It was, perhaps, the last kind thing she'd been able to do for him before she went to the hospital that final time.

"No," Flynn said, his jaw taut.

Gold Tooth looked to his goons. "You just tell me 'no', small fry? Grab him."

Four pairs of hands reached out for him, but Flynn only saw their sneering faces. He wondered how God could take his mom, but leave these creeps behind. Mom believed in God. She always told Flynn that God was good and loving, but he didn't know how that could be true, given the current evidence to the contrary.

Anger fueled him, and Flynn swung a wild fist at the first kid to near him. He missed, and his desperate act elicited a laugh from Gold Tooth. "Check this kid out!"

Flynn kicked at them, trying to keep them back, but he was woefully underqualified for a fight. A fist came out of nowhere, bopping him in the side of the head. His glasses slipped to the cold pavement. He instinctively reached for them, then was pushed to the ground. He grabbed his glasses and started inching for the street outside the alley.

"Where you going?" Gold Tooth taunted him, and kicked him hard in the rear.

Flynn jolted forward, kissing concrete.

Please, Dad...where are you...?

"Will you look at that?" Carl muttered by the window. Vinnie looked up from his chocolate malt to see some kid in glasses getting harassed across the street by a bunch of older boys.

"Those guys new to the neighborhood?" Vinnie asked, watching as they pushed the boy against a wall, huddling around him like jackals, laughing, poking, and taunting him.

"Nah," Carl said, shaking his head as he wiped down the counter. "They were always there, but now they're unified under one banner."

Vinnie frowned. "Rufus?"

"Who else? I'll tell ya this, say what you will about Boss Marcon, but at least he had the decency to keep his business from spilling out onto the streets and affecting us regular folk."

Speak for yourself, Vinnie thought sourly, but knew that Carl didn't mean anything by the remark.

Carl shook his head. "Respect. That's what Marcon had. He was a decent guy, for a crook. Willowbrook ain't never been one of those Norman Rockwell paintings, but we used to be a nice enough town. Times are changing."

Vinnie's eyes narrowed as the kid across the street was pushed to the ground. He was scrambling to get away as his predators advanced, blocking off his chance of escape.

"Yeah, they are," Vinnie agreed, not liking it one bit.

Not one little bit.

He took a long drink of his malt and slammed the empty glass on the counter. Grabbing his fedora, he gave it a flick to restore its shape, and set it on his head.

"Hey, where you going?" Carl asked.

Vinnie slapped his money on the bar. "Keep the change, Carl. I got business to take care of."

Flynn winced as Gold Tooth hefted him by the coat and slammed him against a building.

"You gotta pay the toll!" Gold Tooth yelled. "Either in money or in blood. What's it going to be?"

Flynn whimpered, losing all hope, when suddenly a deep voice bellowed, "Neither."

The boys whirled around, and Flynn watched as a man crossed the street, wearing a dark coat and funny hat like out of an old black and white movie. The stranger was built like a linebacker with sandy blond hair and a round face that betrayed no sign of emotion.

Or fear.

Gold Tooth kept a tight grip on Flynn's collar, jerking his chin at the man. "Mind your own business!"

"This town is my business," the stranger said with a shrug, his hands in his pockets.

Gold Tooth finally let Flynn drop to his feet, then reached behind his back and pulled a gun from the waistband of his jeans, aiming it sideways at the stranger in black. Flynn backed away in horror, realizing now how close he'd come to being shot by that same gun.

"I said back off!" Gold Tooth demanded, his four friends bouncing on their haunches, ready to run or fight.

The man paused in his advance, but didn't look at all threatened. "Nice gun," he casually said. "But it ain't gonna do much good with the safety on."

Gold Tooth eyed the gun. "Safety's not—"

Before he could finish his sentence, the man in the trenchcoat took a large hand out of his pocket and wrapped it around the gun, wrenching it loose and pulling Gold Tooth off balance. The goon's friends hollered in panic, racing off, leaving their fearless leader to fend for himself.

Gold Tooth hurried to his feet as the stranger ejected the clip and the round in the chamber, then deftly disassembled the handgun into pieces, letting them clatter on the street. Gold Tooth brushed the seat of his pants, his face red, a little drool dribbling from his trembling lip. "Aw, man, you're gonna pay for that! Rufus will find you, man! He'll kill you!"

The stranger shrugged and stuffed his hands into his coat. "Better crooks than him have tried. Tell Rufus he don't own this town *yet*."

Gold Tooth took off, leaving a trail of obscenities in his wake. A balding man with an artificial hand poked his head out of a diner across the street and shouted, "Hey, Vinnie! Everything all right?"

The stranger—Vinnie—nodded and gave a little wave. "S'okay, Carl." Carl returned the nod and disappeared back inside his shop, while Vinnie faced Flynn. "You okay, kid?"

Flynn nodded, too stunned to speak.

"Need a lift?"

CHAPTER FOUR

Vinnie gave the kid a ride back to his house. The kid didn't say much—didn't even offer his name. Just sat stiff in the passenger seat, clutching his bookbag like he was afraid Vinnie was going to take it at any moment. Vinnie supposed that was smart. The world wasn't a safe place and kids were easy targets. For his part, Vinnie didn't say a whole lot, either, not wanting to make the kid any more uncomfortable than he already was.

After a while, they left downtown behind and headed towards the rural outskirts of Willowbrook. Vinnie wondered how in the world the kid thought he was going to hoof it all the way back out here on his own.

Vinnie turned his jalopy down Buckingham Road, feeling his skin prickle with remembrance.

"That's my house right there," the kid said, pointing across the train tracks. "My dad will be home. He'll be waiting for me."

Vinnie looked in the direction the kid had pointed and nearly jumped the curb. His heart stuttered in his chest. "*That's* your house?"

"Yeah. Why?"

It'd been a little over a year since Vinnie had laid eyes on it, but he'd never forget the house where a monster murdered Boss Marcon and a couple of his thugs.

Skullface...

"...No reason."

Vinnie pulled into the driveway and came to a halt.

"Thanks," the kid said, his head down, still hugging that bag. "Thanks for everything."

"Don't mention it, kid. Be careful out there."

The kid nodded and left. Vinnie watched the bespectacled boy unlock the door and enter the old house, and felt a knot growing heavy in the pit of his stomach. He gripped the steering wheel, his eyes narrowing on the house and its dark secrets, wondering if all its ghosts had been laid to rest.

The big house stood empty when Flynn entered. Despite what he'd told Mr. Caponi, he knew no one would be waiting for him, but he certainly wasn't about to admit that to a stranger. Even one who had saved him from those creeps.

Flynn was still shaken up over his ordeal. His old hometown had never been a dangerous place. Kids still rode their bikes down every street, and even his own house had remained unlocked some nights. Willowbrook, though, proved itself to be a lot different.

He debated on whether or not to tell his father about what happened, finally deciding against it. Dad didn't need to know. He'd just be worried, and Dad had enough worries right now. Flynn was wiser now. He'd be smarter next time.

Inside the creaking house, a simple note in his dad's sloppy handwriting told Flynn he'd be fending for himself for supper. There was food in the fridge, and Flynn had great practice in preparing supper-for-one since Mom got sick. A night spent without his father's company was the least of his concerns, however. Once he deposited his bag and new school books on the kitchen table, Flynn trekked outside, trudging through the four-inch snow.

He moved for the patch of yard where he'd seen the blue-skulled ghost the night before. The fear of investigating such macabre matters without having his father here for protection gnawed at Flynn's resolve, but he pushed forward, daring himself to be brave. Images entered his mind unbidden, that one terrible moment when he saw the ghastly face looking back at him playing again and again in his memory. His stomach heavy, Flynn struggled through his anxiety and finally came upon the very spot the "Blue Skull" had stood.

There were no footprints. The snow remained undisturbed. *But he was right here.*

Flynn reasoned that a fresh snow drift could have erased the proof he sought, but the weather had been clear since last night. He supposed it shouldn't surprise him that a ghost didn't leave footprints, but the Blue Skull had certainly looked solid. Solid and very, very strong.

You don't know what you saw. Maybe it wasn't a ghost. But what was the alternative? That a weirdo in a trenchcoat and glowing blue mask was stalking around his bedroom window at all hours of the night? That wasn't much better.

Without his dad, Flynn felt vulnerable and afraid, the sun's warm light doing little to banish the darkness of his thoughts. He didn't want to think about this anymore. Dad would be home soon, and he could begin to put all of this behind him.

Maybe it was a nightmare after all.

Flynn plodded through the snow, heading back for the safety of the house, determined to spend the rest of the afternoon unboxing and playing his video games until Dad returned to keep him safe from restless spirits and perverts alike. The snow sought to sabotage him, however, as a hardened lump of snow struck his foot. With an "oomph", Flynn stumbled forward, landing wrist deep in the white. The ice poked into his gloves, numbing his skin where contact was made. Flynn frowned in frustration and rolled over to a sitting position, the cold wetness of the snow seeping through the seat of his pants.

"Great…" he muttered.

To his left, he glimpsed a large, black Frankenstein boot pound the snow with a single, deliberate step. At his right, a matching behemoth foot sunk deep in the frost. Flynn's breath froze in his chest and he slowly craned his head up, up, up.

Into the face of the Blue Skull.

The monster peered down at him, regarding him with the same unnerving quiet of a stone statue. Just waited. Watched.

Flynn let out a shriek, his voice cracking with the onset of puberty, and he fumbled to his feet and hurried for the house. The snow might as well have been paste, sticking to him, fighting to hold him in place, to make him prey for the ghost or maniac or *whatever*. Flynn's legs burned with adrenaline until he managed to break free and crash through the back porch. He busted into the house, slamming the door tight behind him. Gasping for breath, he locked the door and peeked through the glass.

The Blue Skull was marching across the yard. Headed for him.

Flynn yanked the phone off its charger near the door. Dialing furiously, he waited with anticipation. *Dad will come. He'll know what to do.* But Dad didn't answer. Instead, the phone went right to his voice mail. In aggravation, Flynn hung up the phone, damming the tears that threatened to spill. He'd already been victimized once today. *Don't be a baby. You can deal with this.*

His mind sharpening, Flynn took a breath. He glanced back to the glass door. The Blue Skull was taking its first steps onto the back porch. Flynn whimpered and dialed again.

"9-1-1, what's your emergenc—"

"There's a monster outside my house!" Flynn screamed into the receiver. "He's trying to kill me!"

"Stay calm," the female operator said firmly. "What's happening?"

"There's someone in my yard! It's coming right for me! I-It has this skull head and it's—"

Black-gloved fingers reached for the door. Flynn's heart thudded as the thing twisted the knob. The lock held, but the monster rattled the handle, and Flynn doubted whether the door could prove sturdy against such a colossal figure.

"He's trying to get in!" Flynn cried. "Send help! I'm on Buckingham Road! I don't know the house number, we just moved! It's right next to some train tracks!"

"We have police on the way," the woman said. "Can you tell me who it is? Can you describe him?"

"I told you! He's huge and he's got a skull! I-I think it's a ghost!"

The Blue Skull banged on the door and Flynn slumped behind the counter, trembling as he held the phone close to his ear. "You have to help me! *Help me!*"

"Calm d—"

The back door exploded in a hail of wood and glass shrapnel. Flynn tucked his baggy coat over his head as shards of window pelted the countertop and rained down. He dropped the phone to the floor and peeked over the counter, where the Blue Skull stood in the ruined doorway, strong and impossibly large.

Flynn screamed.

The thing clomped across the hardwood floor for him, and Flynn raced, his shoes wet from the melting snow. He slipped, barely catching himself before he did the splits. He hurried down the narrow hall, ping-ponging against the walls in his haste. At last he barreled into his room, collapsing face first. Rushing to his feet, he clambered over his bed, clawing the blinds away, fumbling with the lock on the window. Weeping uncontrollably now, he struggled to undo the latch and open the window, but the frame wouldn't budge.

"*Help me!*" he screamed to no one in particular.

He chanced a look over his shoulder, his view suddenly filled by the cerulean skull face.

"No—don't!"

Ice-cold hands clamped Flynn's shoulders and wrenched him off the bed, flinging him across his room. He sailed on course and smashed into his open closet, ripping clothes off hangers. His back smacked the closet wall hard and something behind him broke loose.

The Blue Skull crossed the room in one stride, batting away the disheveled clothes, reaching once more for Flynn. The boy threw his hands in front of his face to defend himself, sobbing for the monster to stop. A solid arm, like wrought iron, smacked him sideways—

Then the Blue Skull probed deeper into the closet. Flynn pressed against the other wall in the cramped space, watching in stunned disbelief as the monster ignored him and removed a panel—the panel that Flynn had knocked loose.

Once the false wall was out of the way, a small hidden compartment was revealed.

In a flash, the Blue Skull flickered into static and vanished with a *pop*.

Flynn sat there for long minutes, his breathing slowly easing. Overwhelmed by adrenaline and fear, he draped his hands over his knees, bowed his head and cried. His tension released, he finally got control of himself and wiped his tears. Overcome by curiosity, he crawled on hands and knees towards the secret compartment. A dark square shape rested inside. Flynn's quaking fingers brushed against it and felt leather. A handle. He pulled it out of the closet, realizing, now, that it was a briefcase.

He tried the latch, but it was locked. What was inside? Why was the Blue Skull after it?

Excited, he ran back into the kitchen, shuffling through the drawers until he found Dad's screwdriver. Returning to his room, he worked at the lid with the tool, grunting in exertion until he finally tore open the box.

Inside lay stacks and stacks of bound cash. Flynn gasped.

"Flynn?" he heard his father's voice coming from the kitchen. He sounded concerned. Panicked. "Flynn!"

Flynn quickly closed the briefcase and tucked it inside the secret compartment in his closet. Trembling, he slid the paneling back in place and staggered out into the hallway. His father was home from work, examining the extensive damage to the back door, his mouth open in shock.

"Dad!"

His father spun. "Flynn! What happened? What's going on?"

Before he had a chance to answer, two uniformed police officers peeked into the cavity where once stood a back door, their guns raised, their eyes alert. They spotted Dad and aimed their weapons. "Police! Freeze!"

"Wait!" Flynn waved them back. "That's my dad!"

The police holstered their guns and swarmed in, grabbing his father and patting him down.

"What's going on?" Dad protested over the shouted commands of the officers. "What's happening?"

CHAPTER FIVE

About an hour later, the police were wrapping up their investigation. Flynn sat on the front porch steps and watched as the last of the units loaded up and returned to the station. One last cop remained, talking to Dad at the end of the drive. After a quick search and explanation cleared Dad of any wrong-doing, the cops had looked over the damage to the back door and asked Flynn a lot of questions. He had nervously answered them as truthfully as he could...

But he was careful to leave out any mention of the secret room in his closet and the load of money waiting inside. He wasn't sure what to think of that yet, but he knew it was somehow connected to the Blue Skull.

He *did* tell the police all about the Blue Skull, recounting for them his ghostly encounter the night before and how the thing faded out of sight, like a wisp of smoke vanishing on the wind. The cops rarely spoke during his confession, only exchanging wary glances between them. In the end, they quickly swept away Flynn's story and told his Dad it was probably just a burglar who got scared off. They even went to the trouble of bringing in someone to replace the door at this late hour—at no cost.

They seemed eager to smooth over the situation, leaving Flynn feeling empty and a bit suspicious. Dad shook hands with the officer, and the cop left in his patrol car. Dad hiked back up the driveway and Flynn stood anxiously to his feet.

As he neared, his father placed a hand on his son's shoulders. "Flynn, are you okay?"

Flynn nodded, warmed to see the concern and relief in his father's eyes. He'd not seen that kind of affection from his Dad in...well, it'd been a while.

"Dad, I know what I saw."

His father heaved an exasperated sigh. "Flynn, not now, okay? The cops said it was just some guy trying to get in—which is bad enough. We'll have to get a security system installed, and I don't know about leaving you home by yourself anymore."

While that thought excited him, and he hoped his father would suggest he come to work with him after school, Flynn pushed on. "It was a *ghost*. I watched it disappear."

Dad's double chin swelled like a bullfrog, his cheeks flushing. "Flynn—" Then he took a deep breath and clenched his teeth. "That's enough. No more."

Flynn chewed the inside of his lip in anger. "Mom would believe me," he muttered, headed for the front door.

"Flynn…" his father started, but the boy ignored him and pushed onward.

Just before he entered the house, however, Flynn noticed an old black Mustang parked across the tracks, aimed at his house. It was at a distance, but Flynn thought he detected someone watching him.

Billy Hart sat behind the wheel of the faded black 1968 Ford Mustang, watching the run-down house as the kid and his old man disappeared inside. He thought the little four-eyed boy might have spotted him, but Billy didn't let that bother him. He had to play this cool, despite his excitement.

With gloved hands, he reached into his jacket pocket and produced a cell phone. Dialed out. Waited.

His employer answered, "What?"

"Cops just left. Everything looks like it's calmed down."

"Good. Keep me posted if anything happens. And I mean *anything*."

"Sure thing." Billy's heart pounded as he thrilled at the thought of seeing the creature in the supernatural flesh. Sure, he'd heard the stories about the rampaging beast that had leveled Marcon's ranks, but he had yet to see the fabled blue-colored skull himself. "You really think this is it? That it's really him? It's been a year."

"You heard the 9-1-1 call yourself," his employer said. "It's him. And now it's time to bring him home. Don't screw this up, Billy."

"I understand."

Click.

Billy tucked the phone back in his pocket and resumed his watch on the house.

Vinnie sat alone in the darkened living room of his apartment that night, his flask in hand. Louis Armstrong played "Basin Street Blues" on the stereo, while Vinnie took another drink. It'd been a long time since he'd touched the stuff—not since it all happened, when the pain was fresh. But he found himself needing something stronger than a chocolate malt when his police scanner picked up the dispatch sending units to the old house on Buckingham Road. With that one call, all the pain and the fear and the anger came rushing back.

Vinnie played back the recording:

"Unit One, we have a home invasion in progress at 3507 Buckingham Road. Suspect is reported as being a large male wearing a skull mask. Consider armed and extremely dangerous."

"Dispatch, did you say a skull mask?"

"Roger that, Unit One." A pause. *"On Buckingham Road."*

The radio chatter went silent for a short moment, before the officer replied, *"What do you think the odds are it's the same house? We're en route, now, Dispatch. Over and out."*

Vinnie took another hard swig. He'd already followed up on the scanner call and checked in with Frank. The kid's dad and the cops had soon arrived, and the mysterious invader vanished. Frank said the boy was okay, which immediately relieved Vinnie. But the terrible truth remained.

Skullface was back.

It's not over.

Vinnie laid his head against the back of his recliner and thought of the girl, the one who had meant the world to him. Soon, Louis lulled him into a deep sleep.

CHAPTER SIX

Dinner was eaten in silence. Dad asked once, off-hand, how Flynn's first day at school went, to which Flynn shrugged and said "okay", leaving out Gold Tooth and Vinnie. That seemed to suffice, and Dad continued eating. Something screamed inside Flynn to tell his Dad about his close call with those older boys today, but he just didn't feel it was Dad's problem, somehow. The man was as much in his own world as Flynn was in his, a galaxy of empty space between them.

Flynn said nothing to his father about the money hidden in the briefcase in his closet. Not at supper that night. Not at their distant breakfast the next day. But he thought of nothing else *but* the money.

Images of big screen televisions, a new bike, mountains of video games, and lots and lots of chocolate tangoed through his thoughts all day, ruining his schoolwork and nearly obliterating such dark subjects as ghosts and goblins. When Flynn thought of the money, suddenly his world seemed a lot brighter. He'd never seen so much money in real life before, and he couldn't resist touching it and even smelling it whenever he had the chance. Eventually, his baser desires for spending the cash abated, and he thought of more noble pursuits. Maybe this would be enough to pay off the house, or Mom's leftover medical and funeral bills. Maybe this would be enough money to get his dad out of debt. Maybe his dad could stay home and relax, or maybe they could even go back to Wisconsin.

Suddenly big screen TVs didn't seem as important.

He would *have* to tell his dad about the money. No doubt. And he was prepared to do that, yet he understood that to do so would be to lose the cash. Dad would almost certainly turn it into the cops; he'd never just let them spend it. That was a disheartening thought, but perhaps the cops would let them keep a little bit as a sort of reward. Maybe it'd be enough to help out his dad.

But the question remained, where did the money come from? How was it connected to the Blue Skull? Flynn worried that money tied to something so frightening and supernatural might have horrible strings attached. He knew that before he could make one more move as far as the money was concerned, he needed to know the truth about what was haunting his house, and why.

After a couple days of fretting, Flynn skipped lunch one afternoon, hurrying to the school library. He searched the online database, scouring the catalog for books on ghosts. The unknown frightened him terribly, but he was focused on solving this riddle. Dad had no intention of leaving Willowbrook any time soon, so it was either fixing this problem or going nuts with fear, and Flynn wasn't about to submit to the latter option.

The boy was stunned to discover just how many books the school had on the subject of ghosts and the paranormal. Finally, he settled on a huge tome. At least a thousand pages, its solid black cover bore only one word in plain white bold text: GHOSTS. Flynn couldn't imagine anything *not* being covered in this book. He hefted it off the shelf and carried it with both hands to the nearest empty table. Letting it drop with a thunderous clap—louder than he'd anticipated—Flynn quietly slipped into his seat.

Time melted away as he lost himself in the pages of the macabre text. His eyes swooned over the dizzying display of ghostly accounts, foggy old-time photos of apparitions, and theory upon theory upon theory.

A cursory glance to the wall clock told Flynn he had stayed longer than he'd planned. Lunch was over, and the rest of his class would be returning to their seats. His teacher might even come looking for him. He had to make this quick.

His eyes scanned every page, desperate for something familiar to his case. However, he found no reference to ghosts in black trenchcoats with blue skulls. Once more he thought to talk to his father about the Blue Skull, but he knew it would be a fruitless conversation. If only his mom were here…She understood about these things.

Mom had been a spiritual woman. Some of his earliest memories were of his mother tucking him in at night, leading him in prayers. He hadn't understood much about it at the time, but his Mom spoke often about angels and God. He wondered if she were with God now. He hoped so. Maybe one day he'd be able to see her again.

Flynn glumly turned the pages, his eyes no longer seeing the words, but instead gazing deep into the pool of his memory, where things were so much better. He ended one chapter and turned to the next, the black words on white slapping his senses. The title of the next section read "PHOTOGRAPHING THE SPIRIT WORLD: GETTING YOUR PROOF".

"Proof…"

His eyes widened. Yes, *this* was what he needed.

Newly invigorated, his mind calculated the steps he'd need to take to capture the Blue Skull on film. He thought his mom had a camera—which his father probably still had in a box somewhere. It'd take some digging, but he knew he could find it.

Determined now, and happy to have a plan, Flynn closed the ghost text and slid it back on the shelf. He knew he really ought to return to class, but he figured he was already late—what were a few more minutes? After all, he still had one more piece of the mystery to tackle.

The money.

He found an out-of-the-way computer terminal and went online. Uncertain, Flynn simply googled his address, pulling up listings from when his new house had still been for sale. He scrolled through the search results, finding lots of partial matches, but nothing that—

Wait.

There was something.

A newspaper article. Dated a year ago.

Flynn frowned as he read. "Murders?"

"What are you doing here?" a voice startled him.

Flynn looked over his shoulder and spotted Chigger. Chigger grinned slyly, watching Flynn curiously. "What are you doing here, Spanger?"

"Just…looking something up. What are *you* doing here?"

Chigger nodded towards the nearby bathroom. "Takin' a smoke break. What's so important that's got *you* cutting class?"

Flynn blushed, but went back to the computer, preparing to close down the program window. "Nuthin'."

"Whoa, wait," Chigger interrupted, leaning over Flynn's shoulder. "You know that house?"

"Yeah. It's mine."

Chigger paused. Looked Flynn hard in the eye. "That's your house?"

"We just moved in, remember?" Flynn saw recognition in Chigger's petrified stare. "Do you know about what happened there?"

Chigger stood, his face paling. "Who *doesn't?*"

"Well, I don't, for starters."

The older boy looked over his shoulder, then pulled up a chair and hunkered low in it. He leaned in real close and whispered, "People got killed there. Hacked up *real* good. It happened last year."

Flynn gulped.

"Yeah, it was all over the news. Everybody was talking about it. One of the guys that got slaughtered was Boss Marcon. I heard he was totally dismembered. Like his body parts were all over the house and his guts were hanging from the ceiling."

Wide-eyed, Flynn turned back to the computer monitor. "I didn't know…"

"Oh, I'm just getting started," Chigger continued enthusiastically. "Some people say the house is haunted now. That Boss Marcon's ghost roams the halls, looking for his missing arms and legs—and if he sees you, he'll take off *yours* and use 'em!"

Flynn considered this. While Chigger's tale was starting to get out of control, the simple truth was that the house *was* haunted. But by whom? Was the Blue Skull really Boss Marcon?

"How do you know this?" Flynn asked tentatively. "I mean…has anyone…seen the ghost?"

Chigger glanced away, his face turning solemn. "Well, not me personally, but…yeah. There's this story about the house. Boss Marcon was meeting one of his hitmen there that night when he died. Way I heard it, there was some big fight and the hitman slasher-killed Marcon and his bodyguards. They were fighting over money or something, I guess. But the weird thing is, the hitman didn't take his pay. I heard he stashed it back at the house."

"Why?" Flynn asked, sitting upright, suddenly very curious.

Chigger relaxed and shrugged. "Dunno. I think it's bull, but…" He shuffled in his seat and rubbed at his arm, absently. "Eddie Spotnitz said he saw it. About four months ago. He worked for Rufus, like me. He was hiding out from the cops after a job, you know what I mean? He was hiding in *your* house. He said that, when the cops came looking, he hid in the closet and saw a briefcase full of money. He didn't have time to grab it, though, because the cops showed up and he had to keep moving. But he told us all about it and we knew it was the money from the story. Eddie swore he was going to go back and get that money."

Flynn adjusted his glasses, his mouth growing dry. "Did he?"

Chigger nodded, his eyes fixed on Flynn's. "Yeah. About two weeks later, when the real estate lady went to show a couple the house, they found Eddie. His chest had been torn open. All of his insides were on the outside. We all figured the ghost got 'im. After that, nobody went in for the money, but I guess it's still there. Guy that lived there before you apparently had a lot of secret hiding spaces in that house. Some doomsday prepper gun nut guy."

Flynn realized he'd been holding his breath and slowly released it. He caught Chigger eyeing him with a salacious grin. "*You* haven't seen the money, have you?"

"I'd better get back to class." Flynn stood abruptly, gathering himself.

Chigger rose with him, excited now. "Whoa, you have seen it!"

"You boys," a passing teacher called out, spotting the youths. "Where are you supposed to be?"

Chigger hurried down the hall, leaving Flynn alone in the woman's warpath.

"What are you doing out of class?" the woman demanded.

Flynn opened his mouth, but no sound came out.

She pursed her lips and yanked on his arm. "I think you need a trip to the principal's office."

After school, Flynn fidgeted on the bus—he'd figured out which one he was supposed to ride now—ready to get home. After his brief lecture from the principal on how "we don't tolerate rule-breaking here", Flynn wanted nothing more than to put school behind him. He was relieved when he finally had the chance to lock himself in his room and count his money.

The bills slipped easily through his hands, the answer to his father's problems. Once finished, Flynn sat back from his counting, amazed.

There's got to be thirty thousand dollars in here.

He wondered what Dad would say. If he'd be proud that his son had come through for the family. Or if even the sight of thirty thousand dollars wouldn't be enough to make his dad look up from his paperwork long enough to see him.

Flynn was prepared to take the chance. He had to show this to Dad.

The phone rang as though the universe had a plan. Flynn answered it, knowing who it'd be. "Hello?"

"Flynn," his dad began, apologetic. "I'm really sorry, pal. I'm stuck here."

Flynn frowned. "Okay…"

"It'll only be for a little while longer. There's some frozen meals in the freezer for supper, okay?"

"Sure."

"And call me if there's any sign of trouble, okay? I love you."

"All right…bye."

Flynn hung up, the thirty thousand dollars doing little to lift his spirits.

From somewhere in the house, he heard a shuffling. Floorboards creaking.

The ghost is back.

Flynn shut his eyes, a nervous shaking overtaking his hands. *Perfect timing.*

He was sick of being ignored, sick of being left alone, sick of being invisible. He was going to take that picture of the Blue Skull and make his dad see. He was going to tell him about the money and maybe—maybe after he'd done all that—he'd finally have the courage to tell his dad how he felt. He would tell him that he needed someone to make him feel like he mattered, and his dad would be there for him. They would be a real family again.

The temperature dropped in the room. Flynn saw his breath. The ghost book told him that was normal when ghosts were around. The situation suited Flynn just fine. He was ready for a confrontation. He slammed down the briefcase lid and stood, braced for war.

In a fit of fear and excitement he rummaged through his closet in all his boxed-up junk, looking for a means of protection. His search turned up an interesting assortment of odds and ends. He found a padded sparring helmet—a hand-me-down from his older cousin who used to take karate classes. Flynn slipped on the helmet, painfully squashing his glasses against his head. Next, he removed a wooden sword that he bought at an antique shoppe two years back on the family's last vacation with Mom. He wasn't sure if ghosts could suffer physical attack—especially not from a wooden sword—but Flynn wanted to have something in his hands, even if it was only a futile attempt at retaining some sort of control. But if a physical attack wouldn't do…

Flynn went to his bed and took down the cross that hung on the bedpost by a leather strap. His mother's cross.

He put the cross around his neck. Now he was ready.

Brimming with anticipation, he grabbed his mom's camera, that he now kept by his bed. The house grew ever colder, the electricity finally dying, plunging the entire house into black. With no electronic hums, the house was dead silent, save for the mad pounding of Flynn's heart.

Crouched low, he tiptoed through the darkened house, one hand on the hilt of his sword, the other on the camera. His mind worked against him, throwing phantom creatures in every shadow. Flynn struggled to adjust his eyes, trying to see past his own delusional fright to discern the truth. The boards groaned under his socked feet as he made his way into the kitchen. Groping in the dark, he retrieved the flashlight from a drawer and powered it on. His breathing became labored in the crippling cold of the house, but Flynn shone the light through the dark, seeking out his prey.

"Where are you?" he muttered between chattering teeth.

Pivoting from his stationary position, his flashlight penetrated the frigid gloom. Just as the light fell upon the hanging mirror in the hallway, Flynn caught sight of *him*.

The Blue Skull was standing right behind him.

Flynn yelped and brought the camera to bear—impossibly forgetting his own safety and overriding his fight-or-flight trigger—and flashed a picture at his and the monster's reflection. The beast roared as the dazzling light reflected off the glass.

Flynn grinned, feeling vindicated. Without warning, the Blue Skull firmly planted two black-gloved hands on Flynn's shoulders and squeezed.

"Wait!"

With primal speed, the beast hurled Flynn into the living room, where he bounced off the couch and collapsed onto the hardwood floor, shuddering the house. The monster clomped towards him.

Flynn was suddenly overwhelmed by a real, gripping fear, and screamed. He scurried backwards, grasping for the front door. The Blue Skull rose taller, its shoulders taut and menacing, and reached for Flynn.

Desperate to stay out of range of the iron-like claws that groped for him, Flynn strove to get the door open but failed. Tears blinded his vision, and he searched his chest until at last he gripped the ward around his neck. Just as the Blue Skull descended upon him, those thick fingers mere inches from curling around his throat, Flynn brandished his mother's cross.

In a blast of brilliant light, the beast was gone.

Flynn sat still, relieved and confused, as time ground to a halt.

At last he grinned, heavy breaths escaping. He'd done it. He'd really done it. "That...was...*awesome!*"

CHAPTER SEVEN

"It's a trick of light, Flynn. Don't read too much into it."

When Dad finally returned home, Flynn tackled him with the tale of his evening's encounter. But Dad was worn out and ready for bed, eager to dismiss his son's ramblings in favor of a good night's sleep, it seemed. Nevertheless, Flynn pointed at the image on the digital camera's screen.

"But, Dad! Look at it! It's right there!"

"All I see is a blur."

"There's a face! A big skull-face!"

Dad heaved a great sigh, then faced his son. "Does this have something to do with you ditching class?"

Flynn stiffened. "I—"

"Yeah. Your principal called me at work." Dad shook his head. "What's going on with you? You've always been responsible, Flynn. I could always trust you."

Flynn looked away, anger in his heart. "Forget it." He took the digital camera out of his father's hands and turned to walk back to his room.

Dad stood with a start and his tone turned sharp. "Don't you walk away from me. You get back here, right now."

Flynn faced his dad, his expression hardening. "You never listen to me! If you trust me, trust me *now*! This house—"

"Enough!" Dad's jowls flushed red and shook. "Enough about the house! This is where we live now! *This* is home! You just have to get used to it."

"I don't want to get used to it! I don't want any of this!" Flynn's vision blurred with hot tears.

Dad cooled. "Look, Flynn, I know what this is about. I know you miss your mother…"

Flynn deflated. "I don't want to talk about that."

He turned to leave, but Dad moved closer and gently pulled him back. "We need to talk about it. It's long overdue. I…I hear her, too, sometimes. I feel like she's everywhere and I… I wish she were."

Dad's eyes got watery and Flynn felt his own sinuses sting. "Dad, it's okay."

"No. I wish I could've done something. I wish I could give you your mom back, but I…"

"Dad."

Dad took a steadying breath. "It's perfectly natural to start talking about ghosts and the afterlife when someone close to us dies. But we've got to face facts. Your mom is gone, Flynn. Once someone dies…there's no coming back from that. No matter how much we want it to be different."

The boy felt like a hot iron had been plunged into his gut. "Mom believed in heaven," he muttered, seeing her face, hearing her laugh.

"People believe in a lot of things," Dad said. "But that doesn't make any of those things true. All right?"

Flynn nodded, his tears breaking free and bathing his cheeks.

"No more skipping class," Dad said, putting a hand on Flynn's shoulder and gently squeezing.

Once more, Flynn nodded. He still sniffled, but he managed to reel his emotions in.

"Is there anything else you want to talk about?"

Flynn considered the briefcase with thirty thousand dollars collecting dust in his closet. "No, sir."

Dad eyed him. "All right, then. Go get ready for bed."

Flynn entered his room and closed the door behind him. He dropped down on his bed, his mind and heart heavy. He seethed and feebly punched his mattress, releasing his feelings of rejection and betrayal. What or whom had betrayed him, he didn't really know. He just thought his dad would understand. That he *should* understand. Convincing his father to believe in ghosts was the last thing on his mind now. He felt stupid sitting there with the digital camera in his hand. What did he really expect to do tonight? What did he expect to prove? So, what if he *could* get evidence to show that their house was haunted? Who cared anyway? What did it matter? Mom was gone, and nothing he could do seemed to make anything right anymore.

He needed help.

But from who?

CHAPTER EIGHT

Across town, in the upstairs loft of Robert Cardiff, Sr., "Big Bob"—as his boys called him behind his back—sat at the stark black marble-topped table. To his side, the other heads of the racket families sat, all gentlemen who had, at one time or another, tried to kill each other. But here, they put aside their squabbling and claims to power to discuss the delicate equilibrium that kept the local crime running smoothly.

Recently, there had been an upset to this equilibrium. Adrian Marcon's murder had opened a power vacuum in his place. The fragile balance was shifting, and none felt the tension more than Adrian's daughter, Marcie.

The only woman seated at the table—and the only family head in the room under the age of fifty—the twenty-year-old criminal heiress appeared cold and passive, almost oblivious to the proceedings. Her dark eyes shone ever-apathetic from behind the tresses of long, luxurious ebony hair that framed her porcelain face. She crossed her legs, revealing most of her thigh in her too-short skirt. Anthony Brooks to her left took notice and blushed. Inside she grinned, though her face would not show it. Daddy had taught her how to deal with these people. She had to draw them in, make them look at her—desire her—but never return their attention. The game was all about power and, right now, Marcie commanded the room.

Every advantage was worth playing among this bunch, and Marcie knew it. So, she brought along one more status symbol—Darius Domingo, her late father's right-hand man. Domingo stood behind her, his thin frame draped in loose-fitting designer clothes. The young Englishman took no measures to hide his disregard for the Old World suits and ties surrounding them, fixing his pale blue eyes upon their company with a contemptible glare. With he dressed fit for a stroll on the beach, and she dressed like a trollop, the two of them looked young and carefree. Relaxed and removed from the decisions made in this room.

But to buy into that deception would be these men's downfall.

Robert casually reclined in his chair, as most of the men did, and chugged on a cigarette. "The truth is, we appreciate your situation, Marcie. You've done very well for your family during this time, given the circumstances. You have the respect of every man here."

Marcie tapped her manicured fingernails on the marble, unimpressed by his flattering remarks.

"However, our numbers are low all across the board and, I hate to admit it, but the Marcon Family is the weak link. Maybe it'd be best if you sold now to one of the other families. You're young. You have your whole life ahead of you to start something new."

Marcie sat quietly for a moment, her lips pursed in thought. One by one, the gathered men faced her. Once she had their attention, she pushed a few strands of smooth, shiny hair from her face and broke her silence. "My father built this business. Gave you all jobs. Purpose. You would have nothing if it weren't for him. Now that he's dead, you think I'm going to just give all that up?"

Robert withdrew the complaint, and Marcie caught Mr. Domingo grinning cruelly out of the corner of her eye. Domingo was maybe a decade older than she. He'd served her father faithfully and, after the Old Man's death, offered to be there for Marcie should she take up the Marcon Family mantle. The show of confidence had meant so much to her, as the only *other* person she wanted by her side after her father died had simply run away. Domingo's respect mattered to Marcie, and she was determined not to disappoint her father's memory, either.

At the other end of the table, a younger man, dressed in street clothes and obviously doped up on something, banged on the table. "Not *give it up*. Adrian's holdings would be in good hands with someone like Rufus."

Murmurs broke out among the men.

Marcie did not recognize the representative from Rufus' camp. Rufus was always sending his lackeys to speak for him. It showed a tremendous lack of respect, even more than Marcie's playful bending of the unspoken dress code at these meetings.

Robert seemed irritated as well. He regarded the representative, taking a long pull off the smoke. "And why is it that Rufus has yet to appear at one of our gatherings?"

Marcie chimed in, "Yes, if Rufus is so interested in my father's business, why isn't he here to represent himself instead of sending junkies?"

The acne-ridden man sneered, revealing a gold tooth. "Maybe he's waiting for someone worth his time to show up."

As one, the men eyed Marcie. She felt nervous under their gaze, her power threatened. Slowly she stood, smoothing her tiny skirt, and strolled around the table, her heels clicking on the floor. Behind her empty seat, Domingo remained standing, his hands behind his back, patiently waiting for Marcie to make her move.

Trailing her fingers along the corner of the table, careful to keep the men's attention, she addressed Gold Tooth, "He has a point. I know most of you feel that I am incapable of taking my father's place. But let me assure you that your loyalties to my family in this difficult time will be rewarded." Some whispers, nods. They were sizing her up, eager to see if she were only capable of strong words, or if she were like her father and able to handle any opposition to her goals.

Coming to a stop behind Gold Tooth, she said, "As for Rufus, if he has any issue with me, tell him to come and face me like a man and I'll tell him what I'm going to tell you."

Shuffling in seats. The men watched her. Gold Tooth looked up, still snarling, daring her to make a move.

With icy malice, Marcie took hold of the man's head and bashed it against the marble. Gasps from Robert and the other Bosses accompanied the thug's groans. His gold tooth shot out of his mouth, skittering across the table. Blood spewed from his newly broken nose and he cursed loudly. Still gripping his greasy hair, Marcie leaned down to hiss in his ear, "*Don't* make me angry."

Shoving his head away, Marcie marched back to Domingo, who offered her coat. She slid into it, her face not betraying the rush of exhilaration she felt. Maintaining her cool, Marcie simply turned and left the room, leaving Domingo to nod politely. "Pleasure doing business with you gentlemen."

Once they exited onto the street below into the cool winter air, away from the questioning eyes of her father's associates, Marcie fought even harder to resist the urge to shout or laugh or dance. Surely now those old codgers would know not to count out Adrian Marcon's daughter! *I'll make you proud, Daddy.*

Domingo stepped just behind her, slipping on his bowler, his pale blue eyes sparkling with mischief. Marcie relaxed in his presence, though careful not to drop her guard completely. Domingo was the closest thing she had to a friend, but she wouldn't hesitate to slit his throat should he threaten her father's legacy.

"You did well in there," he said, and she beamed inside.

Careful not to smile, she muttered, "Yeah…thanks."

Domingo reached over and opened the back door of the black-and-silver 1962 Bentley S-2 for his employer. Marcie slid onto the buttery custom leather seat.

"Your father would never have allowed it to go on that long, however."

"Well, as everyone is so fond of pointing out…I'm not my father."

"Not yet, my dear. But you're getting closer."

With a warmer grin than he'd ever offer the old men in the loft, Domingo tipped his hat, closed the door for her, and took his place behind the wheel. The drive was quiet, and Marcie took the moment's peace to stare out the window, watching the streets. Her father had grown up on those streets, forging an empire out of dirt. Marcie had never known a day of hunger or cold. She'd been given everything. Daddy had taken such good care of her.

But he's gone. It's up to you now.

Her doubts sought to betray her, but Marcie refused to give in.

I'm going to fix everything, Daddy. You'll see. I'll make you proud, I promise.

There was something soothing about driving balls down the range long after hours. By day, the exquisitely manicured golf course was occupied by retired grey-haired men in shorts and argyle knee socks, but after the country club closed, Rufus had the place all to himself. It gave him time to contemplate, to reflect on the stresses of the day. The moon overhead shone down on him, lighting his path, as he reared back with the nine iron and swung hard. He clipped the ball just right and watched with satisfaction as it spiraled four feet and hit its mark.

"Ack!" shouted the already beaten and bloodied shirtless youth, tied to the tree. Beside him, two of Rufus' henchmen hung back, wincing at the attack.

Rufus lined up another shot and regarded his target. "Hold still."

The man struggled against his ropes, weeping. "Please, I'm sorry..."

Ignoring the man's pleas, Rufus slapped another golf ball directly into the man's face, drawing more blood from his already busted lip. Had the goon still possessed his iconic gold tooth, Rufus was sure he would have knocked it out by now. But no. That Marcon brat had denied Rufus the pleasure of removing the tooth himself. Adrian's daughter seemed intent on humiliating him, refusing to cave to his offers.

Anger ripped through him and he was no longer content with the target practice. He raced forward and lashed out, swinging with all his might at the man's shins. Gold Tooth hollered, but Rufus still heard the satisfying crack of bone.

"I'm sorry..." the man whimpered. "Please..."

Rufus grabbed the pimply youth by his sweaty hair and jerked his chin up to face him. "You humiliated me tonight. You were *supposed* to be my liaison. Is *that* how you conduct yourself in front of the other family heads?"

"I was wrong...I'm sorry..."

Rufus raised the club but halted from bringing it down. He cooled and returned to his tee. Casually, he placed another ball on its marker and huddled over it, readying his swing. "You have no idea the kind of sacrifices I've made to get where I am today. You think the City is a place for failure? Do you have any clue what that place does to a human being? You think getting out was *easy*?"

When the bleeding man failed to answer his rhetorical question, Rufus swung again. The ball whizzed and smacked Gold Tooth right in the throat. He hacked up blood, struggling to breathe.

"But I did get out!" Rufus roared. "I clawed my way out of hell to be here, and I'm not letting some dopehead screw that up!"

"Rufus," another voice interrupted the scene.

He turned and beheld two more of his men marching his way, flanking a frightened-looking teen. Rufus rested the golf club on his shoulder and angled his head. "Who is this?"

One of the beefy escorts replied, "He said he moves product for you. Said his name was Chigger."

"No…" Gold Tooth wailed from his place at the tree. "Stay out of this…go home…"

Rufus regarded the exchange and addressed the boy. "Do you know this man?"

With a quivering look of terror, Chigger said, "He's my brother."

"He's about to be dead," Rufus told him. "If there's anything you'd like to say to him, now would be the time."

"*Wait.*" The boy took one step forward, but hesitated. "Let me make this up to you."

"Jeremy, no," Gold Tooth pleaded, his speech garbled by so much blood.

Rufus grinned. "I'm listening. Speak fast, boy. I bore very easily."

"What if I told you I know about the hidden money that Eddie Spotnitz died trying to get?"

"I'd say tell me another bedtime story." Rufus placed the ball on the tee and fired off a few practice swings.

Chigger stammered, "What if I told you it's *real*! It's in that old house on Buckingham Road. I-I know the new kid who lives there now. He's seen it!"

Rufus eyed the youth cautiously. "You don't say."

"I can get you that money."

"Hm. Better be sure, boy. Or you'll be my new caddie."

CHAPTER NINE

Flynn stepped off the school bus the next afternoon and jogged for his house. His mind had been occupied by planning all day, distracting him from his lessons. He had the visual evidence he needed to prove that the Blue Skull was real—now he just had to find someone to show it to.

He entered his house and dumped his bag beside the door. "Dad? Dad?"

No answer. A hiccup of disappointment hitched in his chest, but Flynn shoved it aside. It didn't matter. He had work to do. Filled with anticipation, he hopped into the computer chair and slid it closer to the monitor. With fervor he clacked at the keys, scouring the internet, this time narrowing his search to "WILLOWBROOK HAUNTING BLUE SKULL". A number of matches popped up, but nothing relevant. Willowbrook real estate. Random "haunted houses" from across the country. Skull tattoos.

Flynn chewed on his lip, cycling through the junk, feeling his hope slowly waning. He'd been sure he would turn up *something*.

There! A local community chat forum pinged in the results. The thread title read: IS WILLOWBROOK HAUNTED? Flynn eagerly clicked the link and followed it to pages of gossip and chatter from the folks who lived in his new town. Most of it was mud-hurling and trolling, but there seemed to be some legitimately curious people who had either seen strange sightings or simply repeated the kinds of ghost stories that Chigger had told him at school.

Flynn browsed through the endless pages of empty talk, until his eye caught something familiar: *Vinnie.*

Intrigued, Flynn scrolled back up and read closer. Some user named sxybeest2254 had typed, not quite articulately: THAT WIERD DOOD VINNIE CAPONI IS SUCH A TOOL. MY BROTHER SAYS HEEZ MADE UP THE WHOLE SKULL MAN STORY AS A HOAX. IF YOU ASK ME, HE PROLLY KILLED ALL THOS PEPOLE HISSELF. JUST LIKE HE KILLED HIS WIFE.

Flynn sat back and frowned. Vinnie? The man who had helped him the other day?

He adjusted his glasses, then opened a new window, starting a new search for "Vinnie Caponi". The very first listing led to a crudely made website advertising Vinnie Caponi: Urban Mythologist. It looked like it hadn't been updated in a year and was barebones content-wise at that. But it boasted of paranormal research-related services.

At the bottom of the homepage, a phone number.

Flynn copy-pasted the number into the search engine and pulled up a map locator. He grinned at the address displayed on the screen. "Bingo."

The apartment was a one-story red brick building in the nicer part of town. Surrounded by dead and twisted trees, Flynn stepped out of the cab. He hoped he had the right place. Judging by the elderly residents shuffling into and out of doors, it seemed he had wandered into a retirement village, but his information told him this was the street where he'd find the urban mythologist.

Flynn took a deep breath, put on his best ready-for-business expression, pushed his glasses onto his nose, and marched for the door. After ringing the doorbell, he waited, counting the seconds in his mind, running through a hundred different possible conversations. He had no idea how this meeting would go, but he knew everything was riding on it.

The front door swung open, revealing the familiar husky man with unkempt shaggy blond hair, round nose, drooping eyes, and jovial smile. The man looked to be in his thirties and was dressed in a white dress shirt—the sleeves rolled up to reveal big arms—and a black tie and slacks. He looked professional, but "off-duty" somehow. He stared down at his young visitor, curious.

Flynn pressed his lips into a thin line. "Mr. Caponi?"

Vinnie stiffened suddenly. Eyed Flynn closely. The smell of fresh baked goodies wafted from the open apartment. "It's *you*. Well...what can I do ya for, kid?"

"I need your help."

Before the man could reply, Flynn retrieved a color printout from his back pocket—his photo of the Blue Skull. He handed it to Vinnie. The man glanced at the photo, his eyes narrowing to intense slits.

Now very serious, Vinnie reached into his own pocket and offered something to Flynn. "Allow me to introduce myself. My card."

Flynn read the card. "*Fishy's Feed and Supply?*"

Vinnie continued studying the picture, mentioning off-hand, "On the back."

Flynn turned over the white cardstock. Etched in nearly indecipherable handwritten chicken scratch was a brief title he mumbled to himself as Vinnie narrated aloud, "Vinnie Caponi: Urban Mythologist, at yer service, kid. You got a name?"

The boy pocketed the card. "Flynn."

Vinnie held tight to the photo, nodding solemnly. He stepped aside. "Come on in. I think you and I got a lot to talk about."

Once inside the apartment, Vinnie stepped into the kitchenette and slipped on a pair of fuzzy oven mitts. "Ya caught me in the middle of baking cookies." He gestured toward the front room, his easy-going nature welcoming Flynn to make himself at home.

The place was a bachelor pad, all right. Dirty clothes collected in piles in the corners. A selection of ties—most of them either black or depicting a cartoon character—lay draped over a recliner that truly fit the phrase "moth-eaten". Flynn handled a blue tie bearing an animated caveman in an orange-fur shirt before laying it back with the others. Old big-band hits played from a stereo by the TV set, giving the pigsty a touch of class. The walls bore no pictures or plaques. But the bookshelf was lined with volumes of strange texts. Books on every facet of the paranormal stared back at Flynn. Guides on vampires, werewolves, demonic possession, rift-jumping to parallel dimensions, hauntings, and the like offered a peek into Vinnie Caponi's expertise.

I've come to the right place.

Feeling warmed by the affirmation, Flynn moseyed into the kitchen as Vinnie placed a hot sheet of perfect sugar cookies on a couple of trivets. Flynn noticed that his photo of the Blue Skull was lying on the table. Vinnie kept glancing back at it as he took a spatula and went to work relocating the cookies to a plate. "That's an amazing picture you got there. Where'd you get it?"

"I took it. My house."

Vinnie nodded to himself. "I was afraid of that." The man returned to his duties, setting out the cookies. Now that Flynn thought about it, they looked awfully tasty. "So how long have you had this problem?"

"Since me and my dad moved here a couple weeks ago. I've seen the Blue Skull around and I need to know why."

Vinnie mulled over the name. "The Blue Skull?"

"That's what I call him."

"Catchy name, kid. I like it. There a pattern to his visits?"

"No, not really."

Vinnie considered, staring long and hard at his plate of treats, lost in thought. "Why come to me?"

Flynn frowned. "Nobody believes me. My dad...he doesn't believe in this kind of stuff. I thought that maybe if I had some kind of proof—"

"Let me tell you somethin', kid," Vinnie interrupted, leaning on the counter and aggressively pointing a flower-patterned oven mitt at the boy. "Just because you can't see it, doesn't mean it don't exist, you catch my drift? There's a *whole* lot more to this ol' world than the stiffs would like us to believe."

Flynn nodded, dwarfed by the man's tirade, but feeling like he'd finally found a kindred spirit in his quest for the truth.

"Trust me," Vinnie leveled with him. "I should know. I've spent my life to trying to get people to see the truth, but they're blind. You gotta have the right kinda eyes, you hear what I'm saying? The Good Book calls it 'faith'. You got faith, kid?"

Flynn hesitated. "I don't know. I'm trying to find out what the truth is."

Vinnie crossed the kitchen and slid the oven mitts into a drawer. "Yeah? Well, you won't find the truth reading the papers, I tell you that much. You want the truth, you gotta go out there and find it. Just like I did."

"So what *is* the truth? Who is the Blue Skull?"

Vinnie paused. His eyes darkened and a weight seemed to settle over him before he faced the boy. "Follow me."

Flynn fell in step behind Vinnie as the large man trundled down the darkened hallway of the apartment to a closed door. "Lot of theories floating around about Big Blue. Could be a ghost or a phantasm. Could be the very embodiment of Death himself." Vinnie added, nonchalant, "Or, you know, it could just be an alien. That's what I've dedicated my life to finding out." The man wrapped a hand around the knob, then hesitated. He looked hard at Flynn. "How much do you know about your new house?"

Flynn shrugged. "I heard that people were killed there. Somebody named Boss Marcon."

Vinnie huffed. "Yeah. That about sums it up."

The urban mythologist opened the door, exposing Flynn to a room with no furnishings. Just piles of more arcane books, papers, boxes of receipts and hand-scrawled notes. On the wall, hundreds of photographs were linked by an elaborate spider's web of red yarn held onto the board by push pins.

Flynn gasped, overwhelmed.

Vinnie stood before his masterpiece. "Welcome to the truth."

Flynn stepped closer, marveling at the amount of information. He took a second to look at as many photos as he could comprehend in a single glance, noticing crime scene pictures, spots of blood, covered corpses. There were criminal mugshots and surveillance photographs and newspaper clippings with passages circled in yellow highlighter. At the center of it all was a picture of a beautiful young woman, smiling demurely at the camera. She was blonde with bright blue eyes and soft-looking skin. Flynn's heart thumped, feeling as though the woman was smiling at *him*. His face flushed, excited, but he snapped to attention when Vinnie said, "A little over a year ago, your house was the site of a major gangland killing. At least, that's what the police want the public to think. But the truth is, I believe, those bunch of good-for-nothings were murdered by your 'Blue Skull'. Since you're new, I'll give ya the rundown."

Vinnie tapped a black and white photo of a very ordinary-looking older man with a drooping grayed handlebar mustache, like out of a cowboy movie. The man, wearing a wide-brimmed fedora, was stepping out of a sedan, flanked by bruisers in street clothes.

"This is Boss Adrian Marcon. For decades, he owned this town. Everything legal and illegal went through him. Willowbrook's Favorite Son."

Flynn detected a healthy dose of spite in Vinnie's voice.

"No one could touch him. Cops eventually gave up and started working *for* him instead of against him. He kept things in order in Willowbrook, but times got tough a couple years ago. Some new pup named Rufus came to town, hoping to set up shop."

Flynn nodded. "I've heard of him. Some of the kids at school work for him."

"Yeah." Vinnie pursed his lips into a frown. "Those guys who roughed you up the other day run errands for him, too. He's like a virus, spreading through town, corrupting everything." The man sighed and looked to his wall of evidence. "And I always thought Adrian was bad…" Vinnie held up Flynn's Blue Skull photo. "Not long after Rufus showed up, Marcon's men started booking rooms in the county morgue. Most folks figured it was Rufus. Then I saw *this*. It was taken at one of the murder scenes."

Vinnie took the Blue Skull photo and held it up to a screenshot of a fuzzy video feed stuck to the wall. The image in the printout was blurry, but clearly the same creature that Flynn photographed.

"It's him," Flynn said.

"The Blue Skull. I think he's behind the killings."

"But why? Does he work for Rufus?"

"Could be. So far, none of Rufus' guys have bought the farm. It makes the most sense, but something just feels…different. I don't know how to describe it, but I think this goes deeper than that. I think the Blue Skull's working his own game, but I don't know what yet."

Flynn shuffled uncomfortably. "But he *is* a ghost. Right?"

"You could be right about that, kid. The stories I've heard—the things I've seen—he takes bullets like they're spit wads. And his strength is superhuman."

"I've seen him disappear."

Vinnie scratched his chin and nodded. "He's definitely supernatural, I'll give ya that. But a ghost? Not so sure."

"If he's not a ghost, then what is he?"

"After Boss Marcon died, the killings stopped. The Blue Skull vanished. There hasn't been a sighting in over a year. I thought maybe he'd moved on, but then you show up at my door, telling me he's still at that house. So, I'm asking myself, why? Did he leave and come back, or has he been there this whole time? Is he stuck there?"

"Stuck there?" Flynn said.

"I don't know what went on the night the Old Man died. There's only one person who does. Some hitman named Eli Ross, the Boss' number one guy. But Eli disappeared too. How'd he survive when everyone else who ever encountered the Blue Skull was killed? Whatever went on, it was a battle, all right. Battles, even supernatural ones, leave scars. Maybe your house was scarred in the process. Deep cuts like that? If they're not treated…they get infected."

Flynn worried. Was he in danger? Was Dad? A nervous guilt settled at the bottom of his gut. "But…what could be keeping him there? I mean…maybe he's looking for something or…you know, has unfinished business."

Vinnie turned on the boy, suspicious. "You got something specific in mind?"

Flynn looked to the floor, resisting the urge to wring his hands. "Well, I mean…what if you had something that the Blue Skull was interested in. Like…a briefcase."

"Brief—?"

Flynn met his inquisitive eyes. "Full of money. Like maybe a hitman's last payment. The same hitman who was there when all those people died. What if it was hidden and the Blue Skull seemed like he wanted it? Or needed it."

Eyes widening, Vinnie said, "Who knows about this? Does your pop?"

"No. Just you. And…" Flynn paused and rolled his eyes. "Crap…"

"*What*, kid?"

"Someone at school knows. Or, at least, he thinks he knows. Crap!"

Vinnie folded his arms. "But this kid wouldn't be one of those guys you were telling me about who works for Rufus, would he?"

Flynn hung his head. "Sorry."

The urban mythologist wasted no time, pushing past Flynn and entering the living room. Flynn followed and watched as the man donned his black coat and fedora. "What are we going to do?"

"That's a good question, kid. But we gotta work fast. If the Blue Skull is active again, it's only a matter of time before the body count starts rising."

CHAPTER TEN

The faded black 1968 Ford Mustang grumbled to a halt in front of the old country house on Buckingham Road. Billy Hart slipped on his black mask, concealing his features. He'd been watching this house for a couple of days, keeping track of who came and went, forming meticulous schedules, planning this heist. His employer had made it known in no uncertain terms that this job was a major loose end. Their "secret weapon" had been off the grid for over a year, but now that it was back, Billy saw this as his opportunity to move up in the ranks. He'd been too particular for bruiser work, unlike the two chuckleheads his employer insisted he bring with him for backup. They were thugs in masks, only good at getting in the way and being offered up as scapegoats should the boys in blue show up. But Billy was an artist.

He unsheathed his knife—a gruesomely crooked blade that he'd fashioned himself—and turned it over, catching the moonlight in the polished steel. This was his instrument—his brush—and he'd paint a masterpiece tonight. This job required finesse, and if he could show his talent to his employer, maybe his gifts would be put to better use.

The thug in the passenger seat, Stu, a thin crackhead with a wavering, whining voice, stuttered beneath his black mask, "Y-You sure this is going to work, Billy?"

In the backseat, the last of their trio—a man strangely called "Box"—hunkered, waiting for the violence to start. He hadn't said a word the whole way over, and for that, Billy was grateful. This dude beside him, though, hadn't shut up. "I told you not to worry. It's just one kid and his old man. How hard can that be?"

"Yeah, but you know what they say about what happened to Boss Marcon."

"Shut it. Those are just stories. Eli Ross was some pansy who couldn't handle this job anymore. He killed the Old Man and took off like a coward," Billy said, though he knew that was far from the truth. But, per his orders, he wasn't allowed to divulge their *true* target to these thugs.

Billy scoped out the house, the knife nearly pulsing in his hand, begging him to set it free on the canvas. While he was prepared for bloodletting should it come to that, as far as he could tell the kid and his father were gone. The dad was gone a lot, leaving the boy alone. But tonight, that kid took off in a cab, leaving the house easy pickings. Though his blade ached for another victim, Billy considered the true artistry might be slipping in and out of the house and fetching his prize completely undetected, leaving no one any the wiser. Any clown could murder and leave a mess—but Billy wanted to rise above such pettiness. "Now, you two know the plan. Split up. Cover the house. I'll go inside and get the money."

"But we splittin' the money three ways, just like you said. Right, Billy?"

The money. They still thought this was about the money.

Billy sighed under his mask, considering slitting the crackhead's throat. Were it not for the fact it'd ruin his upholstery, he would have. "I told you we would, didn't I? Now hurry up before anyone starts getting suspicious."

The three hoods stepped out of the car, flanking the house, preparing their siege.

Flynn sat in the passenger seat of Vinnie's battered Ford Taurus. Bobby Darin's "Beyond the Sea" played in the old tape deck and the urban mythologist lightly tapped along on the steering wheel. A cold darkness had replaced the sunlight of the afternoon, and Flynn watched as the first of the stars began to dot the ebon sky.

"All right, let's stick to the plan," Vinnie said, as they turned off the main road and started down Buckingham. "When we get to the house, you stay in the car and let me check it out."

"But what are you going to do?"

Vinnie took a hand off the wheel and fished around in his black trenchcoat, procuring a compass.

"What's that for?" Flynn said.

"It detects energy fields. Paranormal entities produce an electromagnetic disturbance. This thing should lead me to the disturbance and go haywire when I've found it. Your money *could* have something to do with your haunting. It's blood money. It's already tied to death and murder—just like the Blue Skull. Maybe it was enough to bond them together. If the money is the source of all of this, it should light the electromagnetic spectrum up like a Christmas tree."

Flynn nodded, only understanding half of that.

Vinnie added, "Have you, by any chance, felt any cold spots?"

"It's winter," Flynn said.

"No, I mean a strange kind of cold. Whenever you see the Blue Skull?"

Flynn frowned. "Yeah, I knew what you meant. I was just playing with you.

And, yeah, I've felt them."

Vinnie nodded, putting pieces together in his head.

"What if nothing turns up?" Flynn asked, growing fearful. He so longed to get his answers, to be rid of this strange presence haunting his house, and he didn't know where else to turn. If Mr. Caponi failed, well…there was no Plan B.

"If it's a ghost or poltergeist, the compass will work. If not…"

"What?"

"Then that means we're dealing with a different animal altogether."

"Like?"

Vinnie faced Flynn hesitantly, then turned back to navigating the winding country road. "This isn't the first time the Blue Skull has run rampant. I read an account of an American fighting overseas in World War II. He talked about encountering a 'blue giant' on the battlefield. He said he tore through men left and right like an 'avenging angel'. He said he was the Destroyer."

Flynn listened intently. "Who's the Destroyer?"

Vinnie furrowed his brow. "In Exodus—in the Bible—the Destroyer was God's own hitman, sweeping through Egypt as part of the plagues, slaying the firstborn in the land, only sparing God's chosen people, the Jews. They were instructed to write the mark of God in blood on their doorposts, and Death skipped them. The Passover."

"So…that thing could work for *God*?"

"Not sure. But now would not be a good time to be on God's bad side."

Flynn lowered his head, his heart hurting. He bit his lip anxiously.

Vinnie caught sight of him. "You okay, kid?"

"My mom. She…she used to believe in God. I wonder what she would have said if she'd seen the things that I have…"

Vinnie warmed and patted the boy's shoulder with his large hand. "Faith ain't easy, kid. Takes a lot of guts to believe in something, even when the whole world thinks you're off your rocker for it. Trust me."

"Do *you* believe in God, Mr. Caponi?"

Vinnie nodded, unfazed by the question. "Sure. You bet."

"But…*why*?"

"Because when you've seen as much darkness as I have, you gotta believe there's something out there greater than that. Otherwise, why bother with *any* of it?"

Flynn appreciated the man's certainty. Vinnie seemed certain about a lot of things that most people doubted, like ghosts and phantoms. Flynn looked up with a smile, but was surprised to find a terrible sadness covering Vinnie's normally jovial face. It was a sadness he recognized, for he'd seen it in the mirror every morning since his mom died. Flynn felt now was the time to brave the question that had been gnawing at the back of his mind ever since he read the gossip about the urban mythologist on the internet. "How did you get into the urban mythologist business anyway, Mr. Caponi?"

Vinnie's eyes never strayed from the road. "First off, call me 'Vinnie'. Second, that's a long story, kid. Full of a young boy's dreams, a harsh world's reality, and a lot of pretty faces who met with a grim and untimely demise. Maybe one day I'll let you buy me a drink and I'll tell you all about it."

Bobby Darin started another upbeat number and the two paranormal investigators rode the rest of the way in silence.

Billy crept across the back porch. His two partners were walking the perimeter, placing the brunt of this task on his shoulders. He preferred that. It only meant he'd receive more of the praise if the job went well. Forget the others.

An artist never shares credit.

If the job *didn't* go well...Well, that wasn't an option.

The house was dark. Billy secured his knife in its sheath, then went to the work of picking the backdoor lock. He knew he could break the glass, but, again, this was about pride. The lock took only thirty seconds to pop and Billy moved inside, slow and steady. Putting aside his lock-picking kit, he withdrew his knife, wrapping his gloved fingers around the handle. The blade was an extension of him—his dark half, always trying to rush the job, to cut straight to the butchery. Billy steadied his hand, skulking through the blackened house.

The hood known as Box trudged through the grass, stomping along the edge of the house. His gun drawn and his animal instincts on alert, the hulking bruiser maintained a steady vigil.

Unfortunately, he only noticed the strong hands reaching from behind and around his face at the last moment. By then, it was too late.

He dropped his gun in a spasm, as his head was rent from his torso.

Box died without a sound.

Vinnie cut the headlights as he came upon the railroad tracks and the creepy old house beyond, then sat forward in his seat. "Uh-oh."

It took Flynn a moment to pry himself from his thoughts. He peered through the windshield to see a faded black car in his driveway.

"Friends of yours?" Vinnie asked.

Flynn noticed that the lights were still out in the house. He frowned. "I saw that car the other day. Just sitting here on the other side of the tracks, like someone in there was watching me."

The soft glow of a flashlight passed by one of the windows.

"They're inside my house!" Flynn said, panicking.

Vinnie pulled over before he reached the tracks and parked the car a safe distance from the house. He stepped out of the car and, with a flourish, pushed aside his coat and whipped out a Colt M1911. "Better stay in the car, kid."

Flynn's breathing came out in jagged puffs. "Wait, what are you doing?"

Vinnie reached into another pocket and retrieved a cell phone. He tossed it to Flynn, who barely reacted fast enough to catch it. "If I'm not out in ten minutes, run as far from here as you can and call the cops. Ask for Lieutenant Frank Dutton. Tell him everything."

Flynn nodded dumbly. "Be careful."

Vinnie pursed his lips, cocked the gun, then headed for the house.

Stu had his mask lifted over his nose and was chewing anxiously on his fingernails. In his other hand, a pistol dangled. He was sweating under his layers of black clothing and felt a need for a fix. He didn't do well under stress in the best of circumstances. But this was even worse. He'd heard the stories. Old Man Marcon died in this house. Some said a monster took him out, even though Billy told him that was stupid. Nevertheless, the night pressed in on Stu, constricting his breathing. His movements. He pushed on, making his rounds, wondering if Billy had found the money yet. He briefly considered radioing in to Box, but that guy sort of weirded him out, with his constant silence and all. Stu fidgeted, trying to rub warmth back into his arms.

Something large and immovable stubbed his toe. Stu nearly fell over. He grabbed the flashlight clipped to his belt and aimed it down.

It was Box. Or…at least it used to be. Now it was just a body with a bloody stump where a head should be.

"Oh, man…" Stu gulped.

Fumbling for his radio, Stu dropped his flashlight into a pool of sticky, dark red blood. Squealing into the radio, he reported, "Man down! Man down! We got a problem out here, man! Aw, this is so bad…Billy? Man down!"

When Billy didn't immediately respond, Stu pulled his mask off, wiping the sweat from his brow with the back of his hand. His heart thundered within his scrawny chest and his breath turned visible as the temperature around him dropped to unnaturally frigid levels.

"This is so bad," he repeated to himself, wondering why he couldn't have just kicked the addiction and been a dentist like he'd always intended to be. "Billy!" he shouted into the night, forgoing his radio. "Billy? Help! We've got a problem—"

A twig snapped behind him. Stu whirled around and saw—

Billy was only dimly aware that Stu was freaking out about something outside. He was more focused on finding the money. However, when he heard Stu's shrill warbling scream suddenly cut to silence, he knew the trap was sprung. Was it one of the crime families? Or maybe…just maybe…it was *him*. The one he was searching for. The guy with the skull face and the long coat.

"Hold it right there, ya mook."

Billy had his knife out in an instant, about-facing to see, not a monster, but a large dumpy man in an overcoat and fedora. Wearing a Snoopy tie, but aiming a Colt M1911 with one sure hand, the round-faced man stood his ground, panting slightly.

"Who are *you?*" Billy snapped.

"I'm the guy with the gun," Fedora smirked, "Now get yer hands up."

Billy did not comply. Something was going on outside and he seriously doubted that this overgrown man-child with a gun could be responsible for besting his men. "Where's the money?" he growled.

"Boy, did *you* ever pick the wrong house. If you want an easy take, ya better go look somewhere else." Fedora flicked his wrist, reminding Billy that he had brought a knife to a gunfight.

Billy lowered his knife. "Then you know about *him*. The skull-man. Where is he?"

The dope in the fedora blinked rapidly, his outstretched gun arm slightly wavering. "How do you know about that?"

"Did you really think this was about money?" Billy felt an impatient anger simmering just below the surface. Outside, his men were probably getting picked off, and meanwhile he had to contend with this goofball in a cheap suit who had ruined his plans of ascension. The knife hummed in his hand and Billy thought to finally let it speak its mind. "This is so much bigger than you realize. You have no idea who you're messing with."

The other man smirked and holstered his gun. Next, he systematically stripped off his overcoat and tossed the fedora to the floor. "So why don't you show me, eh? I'd like to know what kinda guy steals from little kids."

Billy watched, bemused, as the man rolled up his sleeves, preparing for a fight. "Are you sure about this?"

"Come on," the large man waved him on, throwing a few harmless punches—warming up. "Come on!"

Billy grinned beneath his mask. This guy was an idiot, but Billy had to respect his honor. Billy slid his knife back into its sheath and flexed his fists, keeping loose and agile. "All right. You asked for it."

Rearing back, Billy hurled one fist, easily passing through the other man's lame defenses, and connecting on that bulbous nose.

One punch, and the man with the Snoopy tie was flat on his back, out cold. Billy chuckled. "Sucker."

He withdrew his blade and spent about half a second contemplating using it on the big doofus, but he realized it would only make the situation messier. Already his moment of glory was ruined, but maybe, if he was quick enough, he could regain it. Shaking his head at the chump on the floor, Billy left the house. Opening the screen door to the back porch, he stepped out into the frozen night air. His hot breath plumed out of his mask, and a chill set deep in his bones. The temperature had dropped considerably since he'd entered the house.

But the knife in his hand kept him warm.

"Hey!" he bellowed into the black. "Where are you guys? What's going on?"

He lifted his radio. "Stu? Where you at, you moron? Come back—"

Strangely, he heard an echo nearby. Stu was close, or his radio was. Billy tensed, speaking into the walkie-talkie while following the audio trail. "Stu? Stu, you there? Stu—"

A red light blinked on and off as the guardrails at the tracks lowered, a steady *ding ding ding* interrupting Billy's search. He did his best to shut out the noise of the oncoming train, though he felt the locomotive's power thundering in the ground, in his legs. The train flashed by with a throaty screech, and that's when Billy spotted Stu's radio dangling from a nearby tree…along with the upper half of Stu's body and his entrails.

Billy muffled a gag and stepped back, bumping into a shape. He turned, his blade held out before him defensively. The thing behind him was wrapped in a black coat, and for one ridiculous moment, Billy thought the guy with the Snoopy tie had returned for a rematch. But this guy wasn't a clown. He towered at least seven feet tall, and his face—it was a blue skull, faintly fluorescent in the night.

"You… I'm here to help you," Billy shouted over the roar of the passing train.

The Blue Skull did not move.

"I need you to come with me. We-we thought we lost you."

Billy tried to swallow, but his throat was tight. This thing, whatever it was, had torn Stu literally in half. *You're not going to make it out of this*, Billy told himself. But the knife in his hand made promises.

The creep with the skull face regarded the blade, then took a solid step forward.

"Whoa! I'm on your side!"

The skull-faced beast reached for him. Billy jumped back and flicked his blade, ignoring his instincts to run, and giving in to the will of the weapon. Forget what his employer wanted. He wasn't prepared to die for it. "This how you want to play it? Well, open wide, baby, 'cause here it comes."

Billy charged at the monstrosity, swinging, stabbing, slashing. The creature moved with impossible speed despite its gargantuan size, ducking every attack, backing away inch by inch, narrowly avoiding the blade's edge. Billy grunted with exertion, pushing his celebrated skills to the edge, but he was unable to touch this guy. "Stand still, you freak!"

The blade finally connected, tearing a strip in the monster's sleeve. Hope renewed, Billy lunged forward, his knife whistling as it cut through the frozen air.

Until the creature caught his hand.

Like an iron clamp, the monster's hand closed around Billy's knife hand, instantly turning his fingers to pulp. Billy screamed in agony, but could not drop the knife or retract his ruined hand. He'd made a living with that hand—that blade. It was his craft. What would he do without it? Though, in his heart, Billy knew he wouldn't have to worry about his future after tonight.

Still clutching Billy's hand and knife, the giant whirled him violently, bringing him into a chokehold. Billy's arm twisted painfully, and he felt the creature plunging his own knife into his back. Gagging as the blade severed muscles and nerves, Billy kicked and squirmed. But the monster pushed further until the smallest tip of the blade glinted through Billy's abdomen.

With a gurgle, Billy slumped, his eyes rolling into the back of his head.

The skull-faced killer discarded the body, tossing it with a hard bone-crunching thud against the side of the train cars that rocketed by, then stomped for the house.

CHAPTER ELEVEN

Flynn remained huddled in the floor of Vinnie's car, only the top of his head peeking out above the dashboard. He heard screams from the house, but he couldn't see anything for the speeding train blocking his path. He clutched Vinnie's cell phone in one hand, but the other was squeezed around his mother's cross that he wore around his neck.

Come on, Vinnie... Where are you?

At last, the train moved on, and now Flynn watched in terror as a familiar shape moved around the house. Flynn ducked down quickly, easing his eyes over the dash once he was sure he hadn't been spotted. There, tromping across his yard, headed for the front door, was the Blue Skull. The monster ascended the porch steps, reaching out for the door, then sizzled and vanished in a wisp of smoke.

Vinnie!

Despite his panic, Flynn couldn't abandon his new friend to the creature. His ears pounded with the sound of his terrified heart, but Flynn opened the car door and aimed himself for the house.

He only made it two steps before a grimy hand clamped over his mouth from behind and pulled him down into the snow and mud. Flynn squirmed against his captor, but settled once a secondary, recognizable figure filled his vision.

"Shh, quiet down, Chief."

The hand removed itself and Flynn asked, "Chigger?"

Whoever held Flynn released him and he turned to see Gold Tooth—sans the gold tooth. He looked from Chigger to Gold Tooth and back again, growing more frightened. "What are you—what do you want—what—"

"Easy," Chigger said, staying low behind Vinnie's parked car. "We were going to ask you the same thing."

Gold Tooth took Flynn by the arms and gripped hard. "What's going on? Where's the money? Who are those guys?"

"I don't know," Flynn shouted in a whisper.

"We *need* that money, Spanger," Chigger said.

"Don't you get it? The money's haunted!"

Gold Tooth sniggered and pulled a gun out of the waistband of his torn and dirtied jeans. "Yeah, right. Come on, let's go."

Chigger reached out and gripped his gun hand. "Hey, no, you don't need that."

"You think I'm gonna take the chance of this little punk ditching out on us? Our whole lives are riding on us gettin' this money!"

Chigger's expression sank. He turned to Flynn. "I'm sorry, man. He's right. We need the money."

Gold Tooth shoved Flynn forward. "Move."

Flynn obliged, wondering what bloody horrors would be waiting for him on the other side of the front door.

Vinnie's head hurt, though he couldn't be sure if it was due to that mook's incredible punch or the falling back and smacking himself unconscious on the hardwood floor. Either way, it'd been a long time since he'd been in a fight and he scolded himself for going so soft.

When the urban mythologist finally came to, his blade-wielding attacker was nowhere in sight. Groggy, Vinnie stood and braced himself against the kitchen counter. Something clicked in his pocket. Recognition flooded his mind, and he scrounged around in his coat until he brought out the compass. The needle was leading him somewhere like a dog on a leash. Vinnie followed its trail, slowly, drawing his Colt 1911 and keeping it ready.

Moonlight splashed on the floor, illuminating Vinnie's path in patches of white-blue. He crossed the kitchen, his boots creaking on the old floor, and headed down the darkened hall. Vinnie traced the compass around every nook and cranny, following wherever the supernatural cold spots took him. He neared a room at the end of the hall and eased the door open with his pistol. Inside he saw a clutter of video games and comic books and action figures—Flynn's room. The compass rattled in his hand, turning him around and aiming him at the closet.

He slipped his gun into its holster and reached a burly hand for the knob. With a slow creak, he opened the closet and bent low, almost crawling inside. As he neared the back wall, the compass spun at a fevered pitch until the glass face cracked audibly.

Smirking, he stuffed the ruined compass back in his pocket and felt along the wall. A portion of it gave way and he slid aside the paneling, laying eyes on the briefcase.

"Gotcha."

Vinnie grabbed the briefcase and hugged it to his bosom. Excited, he hurried

out of the room—

And froze.

At the end of the hallway, the giant with the blue skull stood. Watching him.

Vinnie's eyes narrowed, and he carefully drew his gun. "*You*," he whispered, forgetting about Flynn or blood money. His world fell away, and nothing mattered but this one moment. Grinding his teeth, hot tears welling in his eyes, Vinnie locked the Blue Skull in his iron sights. "I've waited a long time for this…"

He curled his finger around the trigger, thoughts of *her* flooding his mind.

Then the back door exploded in, and Flynn raced into the kitchen with two other guys.

"Flynn!" Vinnie shouted, faintly recognizing one of the others. It looked like the goon with the gold tooth who had harassed the kid the other day. What was *he* doing here?

The Blue Skull halted and slowly veered on its heel, facing the intruders. At the sight of it, Gold Tooth panicked, whimpering where he stood. He raised a gun and fired off two thunderous blasts, shrieking at the top of his lungs. Flynn covered his ears and ducked low, running out of the way.

The creature's shoulders rose, its head bent at a low and menacing angle, and it marched for Gold Tooth.

"Get out of the way!" Vinnie shouted, taking quick aim with his own gun and firing. His bullets dug harmlessly into the blue behemoth, but it was enough to annoy the giant. Its skull-head jerked sharply and pinned Vinnie with hollow dark sockets.

"That's right," Vinnie growled. "Let's end this!"

Flynn opened his eyes, his ears still ringing from gunshots, and saw the monster headed for his friend. By Flynn's side, Gold Tooth and Chigger remained frozen, trembling in pale-faced shock. Flynn hurried to them, shaking Chigger. "Go! Run!"

Chigger's eyes cleared, and he looked to Flynn. "But—"

Gold Tooth grabbed Chigger by the arm. "We have to go!"

"The money!"

"*Forget* the money!"

The two raced out the back door and Flynn watched them cut a line through the snow before slipping into the dark forest beyond the house. He warmed momentarily, glad that someone had made it out of here alive, but he knew he wasn't done yet.

The Blue Skull stormed towards Vinnie. Flynn reached into his shirt and ripped the cross off his neck. He raced ahead and slid to the creature's side, brandishing the holy symbol as a ward. "Get away from him, you monster!"

At the sight of the cross, the Blue Skull roared just like before—a terrible sound of rending metal—and batted away the boy's hand. With impossible speed, it thrust out its other hand and seized Flynn's throat.

"Kid, no!" Vinnie shouted, leaping forward, football tackling the Blue Skull from behind.

The creature teetered, but did not fall. With Flynn still in its grasp, the monster flexed its arms and bowed its back, thrusting Vinnie off of it. The urban mythologist hurtled through the air, landing on the edge of the kitchen table, flipping it over. Vinnie crumpled in a heap on the ground, dazed. "Run, kid…run…"

Then he lay still.

"Vinnie…" Flynn choked the words out, his breath cutting short. Anger pumped from his heart and he grit his teeth, glaring at the Blue Skull. "No…"

So many questions remained: Who was the Blue Skull? What did he want? Why was all of this madness happening?

Steel claws tightened around Flynn's throat, and he felt his shoes lift off the ground, squeaking against the wood.

Flynn worried he'd never have the answers to his questions. He'd never see his dad again, or tell him how much he loved him. He'd never grow up, meet a girl, and get married. He was only twelve, barely old enough to have lived at all, and now it was all gone, and he had no idea why.

He thought of his mother in heaven and wondered if he'd see her. A month ago, he hadn't known if he believed in heaven. But now, after the things he'd seen, after his talks with Vinnie, he was certain that something must exist beyond the veil.

Because when you've seen as much darkness as I have, you gotta believe there's something out there greater than that, Vinnie had told him. *Otherwise, why bother with any of it?*

Stars overtook his sight and Flynn felt his life ebbing away. Still, he had just enough strength to reach out in faith. Everything that he would have been suddenly came down to mere seconds. Flynn felt his body grow numb, no longer in pain. He was dying, but— "I'm not afraid," he wheezed, realizing he meant it. If he died today, he would be with his mom in heaven—he was sure of that now.

"I'm not afraid!" he coughed, determination setting in.

He felt a wave of heat flush his face, moving towards his forehead. There was a blast of light and the Blue Skull grunted in surprise, immediately loosening its hold. Flynn collapsed to the floor, gasping air back into his lungs, his chest and throat on fire. The bogeyman considered him, tilting its head from side to side, then backed away. Then the creature vanished in a burst of static, startling Flynn. Blinding light filled the house and Flynn shielded his eyes. The thing's terrible metallic shriek expanded like a sonic explosion, blowing out the windows in the kitchen in one tremendous blast.

Once the calm settled, Flynn blinked sight back into his eyes and saw Vinnie, still splayed out on the floor, but propped up on his elbows. In one hand, a silver Zippo lighter. At his side, a small bonfire of rainbow-colored flames emitted from the open briefcase. The flames flickered and danced and popped like firecrackers, filling the house with smoke. In a strange and unnaturally fast way, the colorful fire consumed the money, turning it to ash in little more than an instant.

Flynn stood and rushed to his friend's side. "You burned the money!"

Vinnie coughed up a little blood and grinned. "Figgered if it was anchoring the Blue Skull here, I'd remove the anchor."

"What if that hadn't worked?"

Vinnie chuckled and rolled over on his back, exhausted. "Yeah, ha ha. What if?"

Flynn grabbed the briefcase and dumped the smoking remains of the cash into the sink, then ran the water to douse the smoldering ruins. Once that was finished, he moved back to the urban mythologist.

Vinnie sat up, massaging his head. "I thought I told you to stay in the car."

Flynn offered a hand to his friend. Caponi took it, working his legs to wobble to a stand. "I saw him coming," Flynn said. "I had to do something. Then that guy from school showed up."

Vinnie rubbed his eyes, groaning. "But why didn't the Blue Skull kill you?"

Flynn crossed the dark room and turned on the light. "I have no idea."

When Flynn turned to face him, Vinnie's eyes opened wide. He gaped at the boy. "The Mark…"

Flynn stared back, confused. "What?"

Vinnie inched closer, took hold of the boy's shoulders, then angled him towards the hallway mirror. "Look, kid…"

Flynn froze. Emblazoned on his forehead was jagged writing, made of pure white light. Flynn didn't recognize the symbol, but it looked a bit like an upside down "u". The strange character glimmered there, bright as a star at first, then slowly dimming until it finally vanished. Vinnie spoke, barely above a whisper. "Just like the original Passover in Egypt…Those who bore the Mark of

God…Death skipped them."

Flynn didn't know what that meant. Was the Mark always on him, only visible when needed? Or was it a once-in-a-lifetime thing? He stood there speechless. *Unless…* "You said it took faith, remember?" A silly smile decorated his face. "I guess it worked."

Vinnie patted the boy on the shoulder. "Good job, kid."

Flynn leaned against the counter, his hands shaking. He'd faced a ghost—perhaps even the Destroyer himself—and proved victorious. He felt invincible, and also hungry for more. The rush of having looked into the face of fear and lived to tell about it was surging through him. Was this what Vinnie faced routinely as an urban mythologist? If so, Flynn was ready to sign up. "So," he began. "Where do we go from here? Is the Blue Skull gone?"

"Could be. Could be severing his tie to this world sent him back to the Hereafter. Or…" Vinnie grew quiet and scratched his chin.

"Or…what?"

Vinnie bit his lip. "Well… Things have been quiet for over a year because the Blue Skull was trapped here. Could be…we set him loose."

Flynn groaned. "Then it's not over."

"No, your house is clean. I'm sure of that. But…the Blue Skull might still be out there somewhere. Looks like I'm back on the case."

Flynn grinned. "Think you could use a partner?"

Vinnie returned the smirk with one of his own. "Could be. You ever considered applying for a job in the vastly increasing field of urban mythology?"

A new voice interrupted the triumphant moment. "Flynn?"

Flynn and Vinnie jerked towards the door. Dad stood there, mightily confused and surveying the mess that had once been his kitchen. "What's going on?"

Eyebrows perking, Flynn's voice cracked. "Uh…hi, Dad."

Dad's eyes zeroed in on the urban mythologist. "Who's *this*?"

Vinnie reached into his shirt pocket and retrieved a card, handing it over with the utmost professionalism. "My card."

Dad read it. Snarled in bewilderment. "Fishy's Feed and Supply?"

Flynn and his new partner both sighed and said in unison, "*On the back.*"

CHAPTER TWELVE

The starry heavens stretched into infinity above Vinnie, who leaned on the trunk of his paint-chipped Taurus. The cops had arrived and were making a thorough search of the grounds. Across the yard, bathed in the twirling red and blues of parked patrol cars, Flynn and his dad embraced in a long hug.

Vinnie grinned at the sight.

"You gonna tell me what this was all about?" Lt. Frank Dutton's raspy voice caught Vinnie's attention.

The lieutenant lit a cigarette and took a hard hit. Vinnie retrieved a strawberry Dum Dum sucker from his stash and joined in. "You *know* what happened here, Frank. I've given you all the evidence. You just refuse to believe it."

Frank shook his head and sighed. "Well, we can't find any bodies or any sign that anyone else was here. I can't even tell that there's been a crime, except for the damage to the windows."

Vinnie stood straighter, his face like stone. "He was here, Frank. And the sooner you start trusting me on that, the sooner we can catch him. *Stop* him."

Frank nodded and took a drag on his cig. "The kid's dad's not pressing charges on the mess. The kid says you're innocent, and his dad believes him. But I'm asking you, as a friend, stop pushing. Leave this ghost-hunting business to one of those shows on TV. Okay? Do it for me. Do it for Allison."

Vinnie's breath caught in his chest, his throat stinging. "I *am* doing this for Allison."

Frank exhaled loudly, shaking his head. He flicked his spent cigarette to the snow-covered ground and turned away.

"One more thing," Vinnie called after him. "The perp I fought sounded like he knew about the Blue Skull. Like maybe there was something bigger going on. Like maybe the Blue Skull's got help. You wouldn't know anything about that, would ya, Frank?"

Frank did not face him, but spoke into the dark. "No," he said after a long moment, then left the urban mythologist behind. Vinnie frowned, a deeper mystery calling to him.

Flynn parted from his father, as Dad faced his son eye-to-eye. "We have a lot to talk about," he said softly. "I'm ready to listen now, if you still want to talk?"

The boy grinned, tears burning his sinuses. "Yes, sir."

Dad kissed his son on the head and stood. His eyes scanned the yard until they stopped on Vinnie, who stood some distance away, by his car. "Strange friend you've made," Dad said.

"Yeah. But he's okay. I'll be right back."

Dad nodded, and Flynn crossed the distance to lean against the car beside Vinnie. The two stood in comfortable silence for a time. Vinnie seemed fairly confident that, with Flynn bearing "the Mark of God" and all, the Blue Skull wouldn't be lurking around his window at night anymore. Flynn hoped that were true, though he didn't know if he'd ever uncover the truth of what really happened tonight.

Still, with the evening's excitement over, Flynn felt the cold shrinking away. A lone deer wandered along the tree line at the edge of the lawn, no longer fearful of the specter of Death that had haunted Flynn's house. It seemed his quiet country home was just that. It felt good.

"Nice night," Flynn said at last, enjoying the calm.

Vinnie chewed on the last bit of his Dum Dum. "Yep."

"So, Vinnie, what do you think it all means? Who *is* the Blue Skull?"

Vinnie sighed wistfully, speaking to the stars. It was obvious he'd given a lot of thought to the Blue Skull's identity before Flynn showed up on his doorstep. Flynn wondered what Vinnie's history with the monster was and if the urban mythologist would ever trust him enough to say. He hoped so. "That I can't tell ya, kid. Could be some spirit of vengeance? God's own Angel of Death sent down here to punish the wicked? A secret police organization determined to weed out the dark underbelly of our society? Truth is, we may never know."

Flynn nodded, reflecting on the mystery. Life had seemed so small when he first moved here, but now the world was opening up to him, revealing the truth, and he knew there were still more unknowns out there. He understood that he could search for his entire life and still never grasp the unfathomable depths of the universe. It was a staggering notion, but somehow comforting at the same time. He considered the Blue Skull and all his possibilities. "Or it could just be an alien."

Vinnie tossed aside the stick from his sucker and gave the boy a sidelong glance. Flynn smiled.

PART III
THE SERPENT

CHAPTER ONE

He's in his old high school. He feels at once safe—surrounded by the familiar—but he understands that something is dreadfully wrong. The halls are empty, and an exit is open somewhere, but he can't find his way out. A slight breeze blows through the abandoned school, carrying a small parade of dried leaves. He inches down the hall, knowing he's been here before. He's faced the monster before. But he can't remember how this is supposed to unfold—only knows that it has before and it will again.

Children's crayon drawings line the hallway. Different scenes are depicted—houses, trees, cars…but the monster is there, drawn onto every single page. The beast is everywhere, watching as he pads down the hallway. Somewhere, he can hear a choir singing, but the tune is muted. Distorted.

He turns, thinking he's heard laughter, yet he finds no one. When he resumes his journey, he realizes that the walls are blue. The doors are blue. Even the very light permeating the lonely hallway is blue. It suffuses everything in his reality, in his clothes, his skin. He wants to scream and take off running, but knows that's not the way this will end. No matter how far he would run, the thing would always catch him eventually.

For reasons he cannot comprehend, he moves to a classroom and peers in. She sits there, alone, in the center of the room, wearing the pleated skirt and dark jacket that she was wearing when he first saw her. She's eighteen—just like he'll always remember her—her shapely legs crossed, dark hair draped over her face as she concentrates on her schoolwork.

She's the one bright star in his universe.

He opens his mouth, prepared to call out to her, hoping that she'll remember him. That she'll save him. But he knows that's not how this will end, either.

The lights in the hallway flicker and die, casting the corridor in empty blackness. He teeters on the edge of the classroom, debating whether he should go in and interrupt the girl from her studies.

"It's important," he says to himself. "She needs me."

Now the shadows that have overtaken the halls begin to seep into the classroom. He hovers over the abyss, watching the inky blackness slithering towards the girl at the desk. The Dark forms a lump in the room. The shape pulses and grows, membranous, like a cancer. Finally, the black thing metamorphoses into—

"No…"

The giant is cloaked in the very shadows, only its grotesque blue death's head visible and glowing with a steady, throbbing pulse—the thing from the drawings in the hall. It looms over the girl, who remains painfully unaware of Death approaching.

113

"Wait!" he shouts, reaching out for her, when he hears:

"At it again, lover boy?"

He hesitates. Turns. It's James. Wearing the same navy coat he had on the day he died. A small dot of blood ruins his white shirt—the entry wound of the bullet that ended his life.

"James…"

"Not going after her, are you?" James smirks, his face white, his skin cracking like dried mud.

"I have to. She needs my help."

"Don't you think you've done enough for her?"

The drop of blood expands on James' shirt, swelling across his front, oozing. James smiles.

"I'm sorry," he tells James. "I didn't mean to."

James nods towards the room. Following his gaze, he sees the dark-eyed girl struggling. Death has her in its hands, throttling her violently. She gags, her brown eyes rolling into the back of her head. She kicks at the table, blood beginning to ooze from her mouth.

"NO! STOP!"

But Death will not stop.

Not until the girl is dead.

Eli Ross sprang out of bed, trembling from head to toe. His face was wet with tears he hadn't realized he'd been crying. His stomach cramped, threatening to heave, and he hurried into the bathroom. He knelt before the commode, and when nothing came up, he went to the sink and ran cool water over his hands, splashing his face. For long moments he rested his head against the mirror, focusing on breathing.

The nightmare again. The same he'd been having since last December. Four months now of these night terrors, and they were getting worse.

She needs me. Eli's own words from his dream lingered in his mind.

I have to save her.

CHAPTER TWO

Eli always thought of his dad when he worked on cars, which he did almost every day now. He was well on his way to running his own garage. Jed Barker was the old curmudgeon who owned the place, a simple shack behind his house in Greensboro. The man rarely came outside to do a job himself anymore, seeming content to shout orders at his grunts through the screen door or appear long enough to inspect the work. It'd been years since Jed had done much more than drink coffee and flip through *Popular Mechanics*, but the man gave every job his stamp of approval, his reputation in town the only currency that meant anything to him.

Eli knew his dad would have liked ole Jed.

Eli—though people in Greensboro knew him as "Paul", a name he adopted, drawing from his own Damascus experience—was Jed's top mechanic and worked alongside Ralph Dyers, a fresh-faced college kid. Ralph was a goofy sort of guy, floppy brown hair with a strange skunk spot of grey on the left temple. He had a big nose and thick brows that he'd grow into in a couple more years, no doubt. Though the boy carried himself with a perpetual awkward wince—as if he suspected someone to punch him at any moment—he was amiable, honest, and a good guy.

The sun prepared its descent that late Friday afternoon. A cool breeze rustled the trees—the first sign of spring after an unusually cold winter—inviting the neighborhood to life. Dogs yipped and played in backyards, chasing little boys holding water guns. Couples took walks and a pair of young parents pushed their baby in a stroller. Eli was anxious for the work day to be done, to enjoy the pretty evening, though he understood he had graver places to visit. Old friends to see.

Last night's dream lingered in his mind.

The images of the blue-faced Death Angel had all but faded, but the feeling of helplessness remained. She was in danger. Time was running out.

Eli set down his wrench and poked his head out from under the truck's hood. "Try it now," he called to Ralph, who sat behind the wheel.

Ralph cranked the engine and the truck sputtered before purring with power. Eli nodded in approval and dropped the hood closed. Taking the filthy rag out of his back jeans pocket, he wiped at the grease on his coarse hands, rounding the truck as Ralph shut off the engine and hopped out.

"That about does it for this one," Eli said, knowing Jed would still have to come out and go over the work. But he had learned from the best—his dad—and knew the job was through.

"Good," Ralph said. "Now maybe ole Earl Canton will stop calling and harassing us. He's supposed to come by and pick it up this afternoon. He should have a check with him."

Eli bobbed his head as though he agreed, when in reality he had no idea what Ralph just said. The setting sun reminded him that night would fall soon, and if the increasing frequency of his dreams was any indication, tonight would be a night of horrors.

His stomach rumbled, and he felt nauseous. He'd not felt that sort of weight in his gut since he faced down the blue-skulled angel nearly two years ago in Willowbrook.

It's happening again. He's coming back.

"You think you can handle this?" Eli spoke over his shoulder, headed for the shed where his grey flannel overshirt waited. Jed made a big deal about his help staying until the second their shift ended, but Eli had enough sway with the grumpy old timer to convince him to let him clock out early today. "I need to get going."

Ralph lagged behind him. "Where you going?"

"I got some business to take care of."

"Where at?"

"Out in the country," Eli offered. "Out by Old Greenesboro."

"Old Greenesboro? Nothin' out there but sticks."

"That's where I'm headed."

Eli stepped inside the drafty shed, dodging the racks of tools and finding his worn shirt crumpled on the work table where he'd left it earlier. Ralph's voice trailed from outside, "You got family out there or something?"

"Ha, no."

"Friends?"

Eli considered. "Sort of. I guess."

"Goin' fishin?" Ralph asked with a laugh, running out of options.

When Eli ignored him, putting up the tools he'd dragged out over the course of the day, Ralph droned, "Y'know, Paul, we've been working over these trucks for a while now and I hardly know anything about ya. No friends stop by or call. You never mention any family. Can't find a soul in town who ever talked to you before you started working here at the garage. I mean, where did you come from? You just drop from the sky?"

At length, Eli sighed. "No."

"Then what were ya? I mean, *before?*"

116

Eli slid into his shirt, its familiar fuzziness warding off the chill that the approaching night brought. "There's not much to tell, man."

Ralph rambled on, "With all these secrets you been keeping, sometimes I wonder if you're with the Witness Protection Program or somethin'. What didja do, work for the mob?"

Ralph chortled over his own comment, but Eli hesitated, unwelcome memories flooding his mind.

CHAPTER THREE

AFGHANISTAN, THREE YEARS EARLIER

Sergeant Eli Ross sat in the cramped cab of the rumbling HEMMIT, gripping his M4 Carbine in his gloved hands. Specialist Cortez sat behind the wheel this time, shouting lame jokes over the noisy engine, trying to fill the silence with idle chatter. This was the second run their convoy had made in as many days and everyone was feeling the nerves. Already two transports from another platoon had been incapacitated by improvised explosive devices on this route and overwhelmed by insurgents. Only Booker and Cash lived through the last hit, Eli heard, but Booker lost the lower half of his right arm to a hand grenade.

The tangos were monitoring this route with extreme prejudice, but Command was unable to plot a different course to deliver their supplies. This was the only way in or out of the area—which made it a perfect kill box.

Yesterday Eli's squad had passed through without incident, and if he were a believing man, he would have thanked God for that. As it stood, he just felt lucky.

But he didn't feel like they'd be that lucky twice in a row. Especially since his tour ended in three weeks. If he could just last that long… Of course, he had no idea what he'd do once he returned to civilian life. He'd enlisted in the first place because he had no direction. His father was a veteran and praised the Army for giving him purpose, but Eli had yet to find that same kind of certainty as a soldier.

"What are you so jumpy for, Ross?" Cortez asked, chuckling.

Eli kept his eyes on the lead Humvee, his throat dry and tight. "Just doing the job, Cortez."

They were hauling parts for the motor pool this time out. Eli rode behind Lead in the HEMMIT with the supplies. Behind him, his commander Lt. Stokes rode in the Command vehicle with a fourth Humvee bringing up the rear. Eli worked radio while Cortez drove and insisted on sharing his obnoxious humor. Cortez was a little lax on regs, but a decent enough guy. Eli tolerated him, though he wouldn't say they were friends. Eli didn't make a lot of friends. He liked to keep to himself and do his job. However, despite whatever anti-social behavior he modeled, he had deeper reasons for his somber mood today. Tucked in one of the Velcro pouches of his body armor, he kept a note from his mother. He hadn't spoken to his mother in years. Even before that, their conversations were brief and perfunctory. He'd not forgiven her since she left Dad and that was over a decade ago. Eli couldn't imagine why she was writing him now. Since Dad passed away a couple years ago, the only person Eli ever heard from back home was Alex. Alex wrote nearly every week, keeping Eli posted on life in Willowbrook. Alex had two kids now and finally married Kylie. It seemed he was turning his life around, and Eli hoped he wasn't running with the same crowd he used to. Eli had actually expected a letter from Alex for several days now, but nothing.

Now a note from his estranged mother? Something was wrong. Eli felt it in his gut, but he refused to read the note when he received it that morning. He had a mission and if anyone could get him angry enough to turn irrational, it was his mother. Feeling it was safer to put it off, he stuffed the note in a pouch on his body armor to read later.

Supposing they survived this mission.

Eli fixed his stare on the road ahead, scanning the narrow streets, cluttered alleyways, and rooftops, a cold shadow passing over his heart. The rumble of the HEMMIT on the hard-packed dirt rattled his brain inside his helmet, and he struggled to focus. To breathe.

Cortez finished another zinger and burst out in gut-busting appreciation of his supposed hilarity just as Eli spotted a skinny youth standing alone on the side of the road. The kid, dressed in shabby rags, stared at the four-truck convoy and slowly raised a handheld video camera, aiming it right at them.

Eli's eyes widened in fear. Terrorist propaganda filmmakers loved footage of Americans—

Especially if they were Americans falling into an ambush.

He opened his mouth to warn Cortez when a bowel-jarring *foom* sounded ahead. The lead Humvee bucked as a white-hot flash seared off the engine block.

An EFP.

Explosive Formed Projectiles were nasty concoctions. A cone-shaped brass plate was fixed to the top of a coffee can filled with explosives. Usually remotely detonated, when the bomb went off, the brass plate became inverted and superheated into a giant bullet of melted metal moving at supersonic speeds.

Instantly the molten projectile demolished the front end of the lead Humvee, but just as Eli realized what had happened, a second blast—this one a concussive 155-millimeter Howitzer shell, he imagined, buried deep under the dirt—ignited on the passenger side of the ruined Humvee, rocking it onto its driver's side.

Once the dust cleared and the shock faded, Eli finally found his voice and used it. "Contact front!"

Just as Cortez slammed on the HEMMIT brakes, kicking up dust, Eli spotted a dozen insurgents racing forward from the right, wearing loose fitting shirts, shorts, and sandals. The street soldiers aimed AK-47s and lit up Eli's HEMMIT. He instinctively threw himself across the seat as bullets perforated the glass, chewing through Cortez's vest, hands, and face. Eli screamed himself hoarse, watching his buddy jerk and twist in the carnage, blood splattering the windows and seats.

Eli barked into the radio, "This is Bulldog Two Two Bravo! We're pinned down! We are taking small arms fire! Bulldog Two One is down! Crew status is unknown!"

Shattered glass pelted Eli's helmet, the staccato gunfire in the crowded space deafening. His ears rang from the blast and continuous insurgent fire, and Eli's mind wandered to the note in his pocket. Maybe he should have read it before he came out here to die in the sand, so far from home.

He screamed in rage and drew his Beretta M9 sidearm. As soon as tango clips ran dry, Eli bounced upright in his seat and returned shots. Firing blindly, he did little more than injure one man's thigh and send the others ducking behind parked cars for cover. But that was enough opening to allow Eli to crawl across poor Cortez's bloodied remains and out the driver's side door. Hurriedly, he yanked on Cortez and dragged him to the ground, propping him against the HEMMIT and checking for a pulse, but Cortez was cold dead.

Eli slipped his Beretta in its holster, transitioning to the M4 clipped to his body armor. He braced against the hood of the HEMMIT and fired in controlled bursts, laying down suppressive fire as he retreated towards the rear of the vehicle. The Command Truck floored the gas in response to the terrorists' attack, circling around Eli's vehicle to protect him from the brunt of the assault. The Humvee growled as it pushed the parked civilian cars out of the way, crunching their cheap frames, shoving them aside. Command's gunner, Williams, lit up the street with the almighty power of the 240-B mounted machine gun. Rear Vehicle swerved hard to the right and parked, blocking off an avenue of escape, and its gunner mowed downrange of the improvised kill zone.

Stokes exited Command and gestured towards his driver, Private Bentley, and Eli. He pointed in the direction of the Lead Humvee, hollering over the clatter. "Ross! You and Bentley snatch Two One! Two Three and Four will provide cover!"

Eli nodded and charged for the downed Humvee with Bentley at his side. The insurgents slung their rifle barrels out of their hiding places and popped off a seemingly endless supply of rounds. Eli kept his head down, bullets striking around his feet, zipping past him. One scraped his helmet enough to toss him off-balance, but he pressed on, his teeth grit in panic and anger. As soon as he neared the incapacitated vehicle, Eli slid behind cover and fired his M4, buying Bentley time. Bentley took a round to the calf and lost his footing, spinning sideways to the dirt.

Eli scurried for Bentley and dragged him by his straps to safety. Bentley shouted and cursed, his face marred by pain, but he continued to fire on his attackers relentlessly. Once he secured Bentley, Eli pulled the ring out of a fragmentation grenade and hurled it over the top of the vehicle. "Frag out!" The explosive went off with a sharp *clack* and the enemy gunfire ceased for brief, precious seconds. He glanced over and saw Stokes and the others pressing the attack on every quadrant, pushing back the insurgents.

His entire body shaking with pure adrenaline, Eli hurried to the gunner's seat. The doors would be impossible to open, but the occupants could climb out the top opening safely. The gunner, however, dangled lifelessly, his face blackened and bloodied by the 155 blast. The driver was either dead or unconscious, but the passenger coughed and wailed in pain. Shrapnel had pierced the side window and sliced his cheek open, but he was alive.

Eli reached inside and pulled the passenger out as rounds pinged off the ruined undercarriage of the Humvee. "Come on!"

The passenger half-fell, half-crawled out of the top hatch and collapsed in the dirt, weeping and screaming in misery. Eli tuned him out and reached for the driver. Checked for a pulse. It was faint, but there. Eli unbuckled the driver, wrapped his arms around him, and heaved. Bullets tore through the front windshield, lighting up all around Eli. He released his hold on the driver, aimed, and shot his M4, catching his attacker twice in the stomach, once in the shoulder, and again in the left eye. The tango stumbled backwards, and Eli finished pulling the driver safely from the vehicle.

Of the dozen insurgents that attacked, only three tangos remained. They retreated into the alleys, just as the rumble of a second convoy approached. Eli and the other beleaguered troops rejoiced that their back-up had arrived. Eli braced himself against the downed Humvee, surrounded by the busyness of a battle's aftermath. Soldiers reported to Stokes, and Eli knew he had his own reports to make. His entire body ached, overwhelmed by fatigue as his adrenaline levels stabilized. The medic was already seeing to Bentley, and the medic from the second convoy rushed in to assist the injured driver and passenger whom Eli had saved. In the meantime, he slid to the ground and sat, the sounds of chaos slowly dying away. He leaned his head against the Humvee, trying to get a grip on his breathing.

Soon, his ragged breaths eased into a steady rhythm. He'd made it. With any luck, it'd be his last spot of action before he went back home.

Eli finally brought out the letter from his pouch, needing some small taste of home, a welcome distraction from the nightmare he'd just survived—even if it was from his mother. Maybe he'd misjudged her all these years. Maybe none of the things they'd said to each other mattered anymore. Maybe he just needed to be home and away from this awful place.

He unfolded the letter and read. Yet, as his eyes pored over the words, his expression dropped. His eyes filled with tears and his heart dropped like a lead weight into his stomach.

His brother Alex was dead.

Three weeks later, Eli returned to the States, incomplete. He'd shipped off for his tour months ago, Alex punching him in the arm and telling him to "kill Bin Laden for him".

Now he was returning safe and sound, but his brother was dead.

The bus hissed to a stop and Eli looked up to see a fleet of cars waiting, yellow ribbons tied to antennae. A small mob of teary-eyed families eagerly awaited as, one by one, men and women wearing Army fatigues that matched Eli's own, stood, gathered their duffels, and stepped off the bus. Eli waited his turn, watching through the window as families were reunited. Parents scooped up their children, nuzzling their necks, weeping even as they kissed them. Wives fell into their husbands' arms, fathers gave firm bear grapples, and mothers nearly fainted. Even the coldest heart should have been melted by the sheer amount of joy that emanated from that parking lot, but Eli felt numb to all of it. There was only one face he wished he could see in that crowd.

Even now, he still half-expected to see Alex out there, waiting for him with that smug grin, ready to tell him that the letter was just a joke. That he was fine. Everything was fine. That magic was still alive.

The world, however, was not a place governed by miracles.

Eli stood and straightened his military cap and filed behind the other soldiers. One by one, the line grew shorter as men and women he'd fought alongside in the sandbox left behind the robotic façade that had been drilled into them since Basic and, once more, became flesh and blood. Eli didn't know if he could restore his humanity with a flip of the switch like that. Maybe his switch was broken.

Shouldering his duffel, Eli dodged the emotional outbursts around him like mortar shells, unsure of where he should be going.

"Eli?"

Hearing his own name startled him. Hearing *her* voice startled him more.

Eli about-faced and saw a woman slightly shorter than himself, her eyes flanked by crow's feet, her hair streaked by a little more grey than he remembered. She approached him hesitantly, her hands clasped together, a somewhat pained wince marring her manicured features.

"Hi, Mom," he said, aware of how cold he sounded to the woman who birthed him.

His mom edged closer, tears threatening to overtake her. At last she released a sob and hurried to him, wrapping her arms around his neck. Eli stiffened in her embrace, but forced himself to give her a friendly pat on the back.

"I missed you," she sobbed, but he had no reply to give.

Mom drove while Eli sat in the passenger seat, watching Willowbrook through new eyes. Everything looked the same, but somehow the soul of the place had been scooped out, leaving an empty husk behind.

Or maybe, Eli reflected, *I'm the husk.*

"How did it happen?" he asked, setting his gaze forward, clenching his jaw.

"I don't know what you want to hear that wasn't already in the letter. He was shot."

"Did they catch the guy who did it?"

Mom huffed, revealing a dash of anger. "With the kind of people that Alex always ran around with...I don't know if we'll ever found out. It could have been anyone."

Eli turned on her. "So, the police aren't looking, is that it? Alex was just another crook, so who cares if he gets murdered?"

"I hate to say this, but he brought it on himself. You know that," Mom trailed off, shaking her head with a quiet sob. "Such a waste."

Eli bit the inside of his lip in anger. He continued to watch the streets pass him by. Saw the hopeless look of the people stuck in dead-end lives, milling about dilapidated homes, toking up on front porches.

"I'm staying in Willowbrook," he muttered.

"What?" his Mom said, and the car veered a little onto the shoulder. "No, come home."

Eli couldn't take his eyes off the familiar streets, ridden as they were with vice and crime. He couldn't help seeing the ghost of his younger self pedaling on bikes with his brother. "Willowbrook *is* my home."

"Where will you stay?"

"In Dad's old house. He left it to me…and Alex."

"That place is falling apart, Eli."

Eli grimaced and narrowed his eyes on the road ahead. "Just because you walk out on lost causes, doesn't mean I do, Mom."

The rest of the drive was spent in silence.

The kids played outside. Two towheaded girls with his brother's eyes.

Eli watched through the window over the kitchen sink as his nieces bounced in a dingy inflatable bounce house. Their shrill laughter reached his ears and he smiled, praying they'd remember the day like this, but he knew what losing a parent felt like. It seemed every day was shadowed by death. Every happy memory tainted because someone who should be there wasn't. And he'd lost his father as an adult—he couldn't fathom what it would have been like to navigate his way through childhood without him.

Eli turned his gaze to his sister-in-law. Kylie stood at the back door, pulling back the sheer curtain just a bit, peeking out at her children. Kylie's bottle-dark Joan Jett hair was undone and not styled as he remembered seeing it. Her mascara was streaked just slightly, but Eli didn't bother telling her. To him, she looked as beautiful as ever. Kylie leaned her head against the glass, her green eyes vacant and drooping.

"How are they holding up?" Eli asked, shattering the quiet afternoon.

Kylie stared out the window, the sounds of her fatherless children's laughter echoing across the yard. The woman's voice was barely above a whisper. "Hannah cries a lot. Especially at night. Niah…she's too young to really understand, but… She knows that Daddy's not coming home."

Eli glanced back out the window. There was six-year-old Hannah, long blonde hair and tall for her age, and Niah—only just turned two. Niah was short and stocky and not afraid of anything, while Hannah was the sensitive one. What would they become in life? What could they accomplish?

Alex would never get to see any of it.

Eli took a deep breath and faced Kylie. "How are *you* holding up?"

Kylie was quiet for a long time before letting the curtain fall back into place. She grabbed a pack of smokes off the dinner table and lit one in a hurry. "What am I supposed to do?" she demanded, inhaling angrily. "Forget this ever happened? Move on and start a new life?"

"The cops haven't been by?"

"The cops don't care. They're probably grateful. One less bad guy on the street, right?" She sat down and ran her fingers through her short hair, blowing out a sharp hiss of smoke.

Eli joined her at the table. "Don't say that. Alex wasn't a bad guy."

She frowned. "But he worked for some really bad people, Eli."

"He was trapped, Kylie."

"We get ourselves into our own traps. And we can get out of them, if we choose to."

Outside the girls shrilled in excitement and their momentary joy cut like daggers into Eli's gut. He winced in fresh misery.

Kylie shook her head, her eyes vacant and faraway. "I thought that after Niah was born, he'd quit, but…"

An impossibly full silence descended until Eli reached over and brushed his knuckle against Kylie's. "If you guys need anything…"

She nodded in appreciation, wiping away a tear and taking an anxious drag on the smoke. "Actually, there's something I need to give you."

Kylie led Eli into her bedroom. Pictures of the girls decorated the walls. Eli couldn't help but look closer, seeing candid shots of Hannah sitting on her father's lap, watching TV, or Niah riding on his shoulders.

He felt sick.

Kylie dug around in the closet and pulled out a box, then set it on the bed. "The cops brought this over once they were done with it."

Then Eli understood. It was Alex's personal effects. The things he'd had on him the night he was gunned down. Resting at the top, folded into a bundle, was a familiar sight. A smile broke loose despite Eli's best efforts and he reached down, pulling the leather jacket free. His brother's coat. Even now, it smelled just like him, summoning his brother's spirit.

Kylie crossed her arms, smiling through tears. "Your brother loved that stupid thing. He always thought he looked so tough in it… so cool."

Eli resisted the urge to hug it to his chest—his last connection to Alex. Kylie warmed. "He'd want you to have it."

Eli's grip tightened, and he choked back a sob. "Thanks."

Kylie rested her head on Eli's shoulder and he found himself slipping an arm around her. "I think we're leaving," she said after a moment. "My mom lives in Ohio. I think we need a change in scenery."

Eli nodded, already missing her.

"What will you do?" she asked.

But he had no answer. Where did dead men go when they lived past their time?

CHAPTER FOUR

Over the next week, Eli loaded what few belongings he could find at his mom's that he cared to keep and returned to his dad's house in Willowbrook. Crossing the town limits was like stepping back in time. Every corner held a memory of Alex. The two of them riding their bikes down Main Street, headed to the baseball card shop. The shopkeeper kept nudie mags stashed behind the counter, and twelve-year-old Alex had managed to grab a *Playboy* while the man wasn't looking. The two boys had chased each other out the back with their ill-gotten loot and Alex had spent a good half hour poring over the foldouts. Eli had been too scared to look at the naked ladies for more than a second at a time, and finally convinced his brother to throw the book in the dumpster before they got caught. Alex had obliged, but he spent the rest of the day ragging on Eli for being such a wuss. That was Alex, though. Always looking to break the rules.

Eli spent this afternoon unloading the last of his belongings into his dad's house. As evening began to settle, he took a break to stand in the yard and give the place a once-over, lost in nostalgia. His father had left the house to his sons; Alex hadn't wanted it and Eli never felt right selling it. They'd spent the best times of Eli's life here. Once upon a time the house had been a sight to see, but over the years, as work piled up at the garage, Dad let the upkeep of the old place fall by the wayside. Now the yellow paint on the old two-story was chipped and fading, the wood was warping, causing the house to lean a little to the left, and the large oak that grew beside the house had breached the roof. Late at night, Eli could hear squirrels and other small critters scurrying about in the walls. Dad swore to his boys he'd fix up the joint—eventually—but something always took precedence.

Eli hoped to restore this place to its former luster.

Taking another box from the trunk, Eli crossed the weed-filled yard to the front brick steps. Some of his father's decorations remained, including the American flag he proudly displayed on the porch post.

Eli set the box on the porch and ran his fingers along the rough hem of Old Glory. How was it possible that *Alex* had been the one gunned down, instead of him—after all he'd been through? The irony tormented him.

"Hey, man," spoke a voice he'd not heard in a long time.

Eli turned, surprised, and saw none other than James Lenderman stepping through the yard in a long navy overcoat, headed his way. Eli warmed at the sight of a familiar face. Without even thinking, he stepped down and met his friend with a hug. The embrace tightened, and Eli finally felt like he'd returned home from the war.

James helped Eli move the last boxes inside, and together the two retreated to James' house on Buckingham Road for a beer. James dug around in his fridge and returned with a bottle for Eli and one for himself.

James popped the top and took a chug, but Eli smirked, holding his beer at arm's length. "You're still drinking this crappy brand?"

James snickered, a trademark irrepressible cocksure grin on his face. "Well, when you steal a truckload of it from the British military, you kinda develop a taste for it."

Lenderman had always been a boaster with a big mouth, even when they were kids. Growing up, James lived down the block and Eli sometimes ran around with him during those Willowbrook summers. He'd never really considered James a friend, since they only saw each other about three months out of the year, but, as it turned out, they both enlisted and crossed paths in the military. After that, the two had struck up a deeper friendship, sharing experiences that no one back home would understand.

James got an honorable discharge a little over a year ago. He'd seen some heavy combat and managed to live through it when a lot of his buddies hadn't. Rumor was that James had simply hidden instead of picking up his rifle. A lot of soldiers froze in combat, so Eli didn't think any less of James for it, if the locker room chatter *were* true. But that was something they didn't talk about.

"So, what's next for you?" James asked, setting down his beer.

Eli took a drink. "I honestly don't know. I can fire an M4 and fix an engine, but I'm not good for much else."

"You know…you could always hit up Marcon for work."

Eli stiffened. Looked long and hard into his drink. "I think you and I both know I've done enough for Adrian Marcon."

"I know, I know. And I kept your name out of it, just like you wanted." He sniggered. "But we've been supplying the guy guns for a while now. Might as well make it official."

Eli chuckled. "Technically, the Iraqi military was supplying the guns. I just *commandeered* them and diverted them to a private gun collector with a taste for under-the-table battlefield trophies."

James grinned wide and lifted his beer in a toast. "And I, in turn, 'diverted' those trophies to Adrian for a healthy fee."

The two clinked bottles and drank on it. Eli really did like James. The guy was nothing but trouble, but he'd been a good friend through the years.

James leaned on the kitchen counter. "Seriously, though, you should have some mad bank."

The man was right—Eli had a significant financial cushion that he had set aside for himself so that, post-enlistment, he'd never have to slave for minimum wage like his father. Nevertheless, he shook his head. "Nah, it's not about money. My dad… Ha, he always told us we needed to keep our hands busy. Good hard work." Eli grinned, but the expression was too hard to maintain. He let his smile fall and spoke into his beer. "Too bad that never got him very far."

"Hey," James laughed, "I've always been a fan of taking shortcuts to my financial freedom."

Eli couldn't return the laugh. "Yeah, well… My dad never took shortcuts."

James nodded respectfully.

"So, you're in with Adrian?" Eli said, deciding a subject change was in order.

James nearly spewed his drink. "Ha! Not hardly. I sell the guy guns, but I'm not exactly on the payroll."

"But you're trying?"

"Shyeah, I'm trying! Are you kidding me? Everybody's trying to get in with this guy. Marcon's got this *whole town* on lockdown. Practically nothing gets done in Willowbrook without Adrian's say-so."

Maybe it had always been that way. Maybe Willowbrook had been crooked Eli's whole life, and he just didn't notice it as a child. Still, it seemed the town had grown…darker somehow. Even Alex had turned to a life of crime, working for this boss, Adrian Marcon. Alex had always been a rebel, but this seemed like more serious stuff. Eli considered it all, the cheap beer souring his stomach. "If Marcon knows everything about everything around here, then who got to Alex? Did Adrian kill him?"

James paled, his usual smirk fading. He set his drink down and took a breath. "Look, man… I'm not exactly 'in' with Marcon, so they don't tell me much, but I hear things. There's talk of some new guy moving in, named Rufus. Word is he's been flipping some of Old Man Marcon's guys and…" James winced and shrugged, obviously trying to be delicate. "Those who *don't* flip…well, they don't last too long."

Eli nodded, absorbing the information. Carefully, he eyed his friend. "What about you? You thought about flipping?"

James sprang up, suddenly animated. "*Me*, flip? Forget about it. I may be a thief, but I'm loyal to my cashflow."

"What about Alex? Was he thinking about joining up with Rufus?"

James shook his head, simmering down again. "Alex? Nah, man. Your brother was Family, through and through. If I had to guess, I think Rufus couldn't get him, so he took him out."

"Have the cops done anything?"

"Are you kidding me?" James said emphatically, nearly going cross-eyed. "The cops don't do jack in Willowbrook. They leave it to Adrian and the other gangs to fight it out. Trust me, man. This stuff goes deep."

Eli stiffened, growing agitated, feeling tied down while his brother's blood cried out for justice. "If Adrian is the law around here, then why hasn't Adrian done anything? Doesn't he care that somebody's killing his people?"

"Who knows? The Old Man's got his reasons."

That's not good enough. Eli dug at his fingernails, feeling jittery, just like he always did on the eve of a mission. "Where can I find Rufus?"

James waved his arms, his eyes wide. "Uh, *no.* No, no. *No.*"

Eli snapped, "What?"

"I've seen that look. You're thinking about doing something really stupid."

"I just want to talk to him."

"First off, let me explain something to you. Nobody talks to Rufus. The guy's invisible. Second, this town doesn't work like that. There's a way things are done. If it really was Rufus who had Alex killed, Adrian will deal with it in *Adrian's* way."

Eli fumed and glared at his friend. "Well, you said it yourself. I don't work for Adrian. And this is *my* brother."

CHAPTER FIVE

"Can I just reiterate that this is a bad idea?"

James slumped behind the wheel of his car a couple nights later, downtown, Norman Greenbaum's "Spirit in the Sky" on the radio. He had on his navy overcoat, concealing all but the butt of the Beretta M9 holstered underneath. Eli sat in the passenger seat strapped down in a military-grade tactical vest, wearing his brother's leather jacket. He'd come with a complete loadout—spare clips, sidearm. But in his hands, he gripped the M4 Carbine that James had lent him from his own inventory, loaded with 556-millimeter NATO rounds and, as James put it, "enough of it to viva la revolución."

Sometimes it paid to have arms dealers for friends.

Eli surveyed the Laundromat across the street. The place was dimly lit and sparsely populated at this time of night. "That's where they hang out?"

"They run a game in the back. But I'm telling you, man, they might not be able to get you in to see Rufus. *Who knows* where that guy's at?"

"Doesn't matter." Eli bit the inside of his lower lip, seething. "If I make a big enough bang, he'll come to see what the noise is all about."

James heaved a great sigh and rested his head on the wheel. "Eli, man…"

"You don't have to come," Eli snapped, facing his friend.

"Are you *high*? No way you're walking in and out by yourself. No telling how many guys are in there."

Eli looked through the glass front of the Laundromat. Just a few disheveled folks shuffled about in various stages of undress, smoking cigs and waiting for their laundry to ding. Beyond the main room was a tacky curtain of multi-colored beads—presumably leading to the back area where Rufus' thugs resided.

"The place isn't that big. Can't be more than three or four," Eli replied automatically.

James reached into his coat and pulled out a flask. He took a couple hits and offered it to his partner, but Eli declined. Better to go in sober. Better to hold on to the mental images of his brother. Of Kylie, now a single mother piled under emotional and financial stress. Of Hannah and Niah, who would never get to dance and giggle with their father again.

No, Eli wanted the pain. The pain made him strong.

He brought down a skull-printed balaclava over his face. "Let's hit it."

Eli approached the Laundromat, the M4 raised in the "breach" position. Out of the corner of his eye, he spotted James scurrying around the back and throwing him one last, "are you suuuure about this?" glance. His face set like flint, Eli pushed open the door to the building, entering the dimly lit Laundromat. Instantly his presence incited gasps as the few bleary eyed customers hurried out of his way, shielding themselves as though he were about to shoot them. He hurried forward, regulating his breathing, sweating profusely under his gear. Instantly he was back in the sandbox, engaging insurgents, fearing for his life. If the Army had taught him anything, though, it was that his life was worthless unless he was risking it for a cause. He hadn't found much cause in Afghanistan, fighting simply because he was ordered to. Perhaps his only cause had been making his father proud. But Dad was long dead, and now Alex—

A skinhead burst out of the beaded curtain, no doubt investigating the commotion. His frightened eyes scanned the emptying store and landed on Eli— a specter of death dressed for war. The skinhead fumbled to pull a pistol out of a shoulder holster, but Eli was on him in an instant, bashing the stock of his M4 against the man's ear. Knocked cold, the thug collapsed, and Eli slipped through the curtain, traveling down a long, dark hallway, drawn by a muted thump-thump-thump of rhythmic bass. A single door rested at the end of the corridor with a simple chair parked in front for the guard—the skinhead he'd just clocked.

Eli double-timed his steps, hoping to get the drop on Skinhead's reinforcements. Taking one last deep breath, he hurled his foot through the door, splintering the frame. Immediately he scanned the room, spotting three guys smoking joints and kicking back tequila at a center card table. A pile of chips occupied the middle and each man had a hand of cards. They were caught in mid-laugh, scantily-clad skanks draped over their shoulders like cheap furs. Sickly sweet-smelling smoke filled the room and obscene rap music assaulted his ears, but Eli focused through the haze.

Overwhelmed by their intruder, the men stood out of their chairs, toppling over the table in the process, and pushed the women out of the way. Glasses shattered, and cards and chips flew to the floor. But Eli already had the thugs in his line of sight and hollered, "Don't move! Hands up! *Hands up!*"

The goons glared at him, but slowly raised their hands to the ceiling. Eli jerked his barrel to the women. "Get out."

They whimpered, collected their things, and raced past him back down the hall and through the beads. Eli leveled on the men, his heart throbbing so hard his head hurt.

"You have any idea who you're knocking over?" one of the thugs—a skinny youth in a basketball jersey, gold-rimmed sunglasses, and a sideways trucker cap—snarled.

"I'm not here to rob you," Eli told them evenly, never lowering his aim. "Alex Ross. You know him?"

The crooks eyed each other, then Trucker Cap sneered. "*Knew* him, you mean. He's worm food, now."

"I'm looking for the guy who killed him. You work for Rufus. I want a meeting."

Despite having a loaded automatic rifle aimed at them, the goons burst into laughter. Trucker Cap spoke for the group again. "C'mon, man, what makes you think *I* ever had a meeting with Rufus? He don't show his face to nobody."

Eli felt a bead of sweat trail down his temple behind his mask. He gritted his teeth, hands shaking. "How do you contact him? Tell him to make an exception."

Trucker Cap chuckled, lowering his hands. "There ain't no exceptions."

Then Eli heard a click and felt a cold weight settle on the back of his head. *Gun.*

Eli scolded himself for letting someone get the drop on him, but kept hold of his rifle. Trucker Cap eased forward, slipping under Eli's outstretched arms and casually relieving Eli of the SIG Sauer P229 James had lent him.

"Drop it," a burly voice from behind commanded.

Eli lowered the M4 and eased it to the floor, keeping his free hand up. Trucker Cap circled him, examining the SIG like it were a work of art. "I'm impressed, man. You really thought you could just roll up in here all by yourself and take us all out?"

"No," Eli said, grinding his teeth, counting down in his head. "I didn't."

The back door exploded open at the lock, James following close behind with his breaching shotgun. As the three thugs whirled towards the distraction, Eli flung his elbow up into the face of the man behind him, shattering the bald brute's nose—but not before the man fired off a round, grazing Eli's right temple. The man dropped his gun and Eli caught it mid-fall and brought it up under the man's chin, firing twice. Baldy's brains painted the ceiling and Eli turned to see Trucker Cap's flunkies reaching for guns. Adrenaline wiping out all thought and leaving him with only animal instinct, Eli pulled the trigger as fast as he could, emptying an entire clip in the left thug before running dry.

James was through the door by then and aimed his shotgun, firing off a swarm of pellets that turned Trucker Cap's remaining buddy's torso into red

133

pulp. The man collapsed backwards.

Trucker Cap raised his arms, shouting. "I surrender! I surrender! Whoa!"

James lowered his shotgun just a hair, as Eli coolly collected his M4 from the ground. He rose up, and yanked his SIG 229 out of the crook's hand, holstering it.

"Let's try this again." Eli yanked off his skull mask as Trucker Cap backed up, the inside seams of his khaki shorts turning dark with urine. "I want to talk to Rufus."

"I told you! He contacts *us* when he needs something! I have no idea how to get hold of him!"

Eli glanced at James who shook his head. *Give it up*, that shake said, but Eli grabbed Trucker Cap by the jersey instead. "Who shot Alex Ross?"

"B-Benny! Benny the Squeal! It was just an initiation, man! Benny had to prove himself to Rufus! It wasn't personal!"

"It was to *me*," Eli said, firing his M4 point blank into Trucker Cap's midsection. The man flinched and gurgled, and Eli pushed him to the ground like discarded trash.

When he looked up, James was staring at him, askance. "Eli, man..." He stepped closer, suddenly paling. "Whoa, you've been hit. You okay?"

Eli nodded absently, warm blood spreading down the side of his face, dripping off his chin.

Sirens cut through the settling silence and James bugged out. "Come on! We gotta go!"

Eli paused, surveying the death he'd wrought tonight. For the first time in a long time, he finally felt something.

Vindication.

A grin slipped out and he did not rebuke it.

"*Eli, come on!*"

Eli gathered his senses, slipped his mask back on, then made his retreat out the back door.

Eli sat on the edge of Kylie's bed, wincing as the needle lanced his flesh. "Ack!"

Kylie paused in her work, her brow furrowed in concentration. "Sorry."

He clenched his jaw and suffered in silence as Kylie finished sewing up the gash on his temple where the stray bullet struck. She'd not been happy when he'd arrived on her doorstep, bloodied, with news that he'd struck back at Rufus over Alex. She was in her pajamas, and the girls had fallen asleep in a heap on the living room floor, a Disney princess movie fading into the end credits on the television screen before them. With a sad sigh, Kylie ushered Eli into her bedroom and brought out rubbing alcohol, needle, and thread.

Eli wanted to tell her how sorry he was, but sorry for what, he didn't know. Sorry that he was gone while Alex was killed? Sorry that he'd done something stupid—just as James knew he would—and poked a sleeping dog with a stick? Sorry that he'd brought all his troubles on Kylie?

"You know," she began quietly, her hand steady, "I've done this more times than I care to admit."

"Thanks," Eli muttered.

Kylie nodded absently, until Eli carefully took her hand. "No," he said, looking her straight in the eye. "Thank you."

Comfortable silence settled in the gap left by unspoken words. Their gaze held, and Eli felt safe and welcome here. Something passed over Kylie's green eyes and Eli felt his heart flutter. He realized that, without thinking, he'd moved in closer to her. She must have sensed it too. Her cheeks flushed, and she stood abruptly, gathering her first aid kit. "That's the best I can do," she mumbled in a rush, walking into the bathroom.

Eli's heart slowed, and he cleared his throat, confused and overwhelmed.

Kylie tossed bloodied cotton swabs into her bathroom trashcan and faced him through the doorway, her face set. "So, is it over then?"

He stood, shaking his head. "No. A man named Benny killed Alex. It's not over until I…"

She huffed, but kept her voice down for the benefit of the girls slumbering peacefully in the other room. "Eli, don't do this. Isn't it bad enough that Alex is dead? It's not going to do any good. You're just going to end up dead too."

"It doesn't matter."

Her hand reached out and unexpectedly brushed his. "It matters."

Bright lights flooded the bedroom window, slashing through the partially closed blinds. Eli jerked to attention, shielding his eyes from the luminary onslaught.

"What is that?" Kylie asked, her voice rising.

From the other room, he heard Hannah cry in a half-asleep whine, "Mommy, what's going on?"

But Eli understood. "It's them!"

He hurried out of the bedroom, snatching the 229 he'd placed on Kylie's dresser upon his arrival. But he heard a crash and found the front door hanging by its hinges by time he made it there.

"No!"

Hannah stood in bare feet and a cupcake-patterned nightgown, her cries muffled, as a slim man wearing loose-fitting designer clothes and a bowler held her still. His hand clamped over the young girl's mouth, while his other hand aimed a pistol right at Eli.

Niah awoke and wailed in confusion from her place on the floor and Kylie screamed. "No, please!" She ran for Niah and scooped her to her chest, shielding her from the strange man. Eli immediately raised his hands, his eyes locked on Hannah's brilliant blue eyes. His brother's eyes. The child was crying and shaking, silently begging him to save her.

"Eli Ross, is it?" the gunman asked cheerfully in a British accent.

"What do you want?" Glancing over the Brit's shoulder, Eli spotted two sedans parked out front, their headlights targeting the house. Shadows moved in the light. Men with guns. He couldn't make out their faces.

"Mr. Marcon would like a word with you," the man said. The casual nature of his voice suggested a man chatting with an acquaintance, not holding a gun to a little girl, petrified stiff in his arms. "And believe me when I say, it would be most unwise for you to refuse."

Eli lowered his gun to the floor, his hands shaking. "O-Okay. J-Just please...let her go..."

The Brit regarded the child in his arms then grinned roguishly. "Of course. We're not barbarians, you know."

He simply released his grasp and Hannah wept uncontrollably, rushing forward into her mother's arms. Eli shared a look with Kylie and saw the fear there. At least Alex had kept *his* dirty work out of their home.

"I'm sorry," he said and stepped out into the light.

On the front porch, he got a better look at the men. On the left, a hulking bruiser with grown-in stubble stood. He wore a leather jacket and gloves and had a stocking cap pulled down, just above his beady eyes. On the right, a duo— one was taller and squeezed into a too-small tweed sportscoat and wore a too-big fedora; the other, shorter, in a baggy coat and dingy ball cap.

Standing between the hitmen was a gaunt man, hunkered over. He wore a long, expensive-looking dark suit coat and white scarf. On his head, a wide-brimmed fedora. The diamonds on his gnarled knuckles sparkled in the headlights. When the man lifted his face, Eli saw a gray handlebar mustache drooping past a wrinkled mouth.

But it was the man's eyes that pinned Eli in place with fear. They were empty of emotion, but spoke of terrible intellect and malicious cunning. He knew this must be Boss Adrian Marcon.

The Old Man had one hand behind his back and Eli feared it held a gun. Adrian stepped aside, but instead of a weapon, it was James behind the Old Man's back. His friend's face was busted, his clothes torn. Adrian shoved James to the dirt and Eli resisted the urge to help him up.

"I'm sorry, man…" James spat through bloodied teeth. "They made me talk."

The Brit circled Eli, nonchalantly, twirling his gun as he spoke. "Not very clever. The building across the street from the Laundromat had a security camera. It caught your little escape. Our friends on the police force were very helpful in passing along some rather incriminating photos."

"They recognized me," James said, weeping. "I'm so sorry, man…"

Eli hated his friend in that moment, but said, "No. I did this. This is on me."

Adrian pulled out a gold-plated Desert Eagle and pressed it to the back of James' head.

"Wait," Eli said, his heart stopping. "Please. What do you want? Can't we talk about this?"

The Old Man eyed his flunkies and gave a nod. Without a word, they piled into one of the black sedans. Then the Boss turned to Eli and gestured toward the other sedan. "Get in the car. We need to have a little talk."

After holstering his customized weapon, the criminal gathered the hem of his long coat and climbed into the car. The Brit followed behind, offering a smug look to James, but leaving him unharmed. The sedan door remained open, waiting for Eli, but he stopped by his friend's side, helping him to stand.

"Let me come with you," James said, clinging to Eli's shirt. "This is my fault."

"No, stay here," Eli said, looking back at the house. Kylie stood in the doorway, shielding her children behind her back. "Take the girls somewhere safe. Stay with them until…until I get back."

James said, "What if you don't come back?"

Eli lowered his eyes and slipped inside the sedan. He closed the door behind him, taking his place beside Adrian and behind the Brit in the bowler, who sat in the driver's seat.

Adrian had the gold-plated gun out again, resting it on his knee, and Eli couldn't help but stare at it. It looked familiar. In a dark moment of hilarity, Eli realized it was one of the guns he'd stolen from the insurgents and sold to James.

He supposed it was poetic.

The sedan pulled away from Kylie's house and, while Eli worried for his life, he felt a tremendous weight lifted knowing that his family was safe.

"I want to ask you a question," Adrian began at length, his voice a coarse timbre. "How did you *think* this was going to go tonight?"

He let the question linger, but Eli wasn't sure how to respond.

Adrian answered for him, "*You* thought you'd waltz through town, guns blazing, and then vanish into the night like you were the Lone Ranger or something. Am I right?"

Eli glanced up into the rearview mirror and spied the smirking Brit, who was apparently enjoying this one-sided conversation.

Adrian tapped his gun, drawing Eli's attention back to the imminent danger. "It doesn't work like that, kid. Every decision you make has a consequence. Not just for you, but for everyone around you. There's a way we do things in this town. I'm not above killing, but generally I like to make friends of my enemies because it's much more profitable that way."

Adrian lowered his head and removed his hat, revealing short gray hair. He spoke through his Wyatt Earp mustache, those gunslinger eyes never moving from Eli's own. "But, see, you've caused me some trouble. Take this new guy, Rufus. He's some punk from the City. He thinks it's all about the violence. But, see, I was trying to extend a little olive branch. Maybe form a mutually beneficial relationship. This Rufus has been trying to turn my guys. Worse, he murdered my *best* guy. I think you know him: Alex Ross."

Eli looked away, biting his lip. His vision blurred from the rush of blood to his head and he wished that, if Marcon were going to kill him, he'd just get it over with.

But Adrian sighed and glanced out the tinted window into the passing night. "That's not easy for me to overlook, but I've tried to, for the sake of civility." The Old Man focused on Eli again, his words carefully measured. Calm, but pregnant with threat. "Then I get this new problem. Some kid rolls up on one of Rufus' joints tonight and starts shooting up the place like he was the Grim Angel of Death. Naturally Rufus thinks *I* did it. So, I'm gonna let you piece together how that affected all our peace talks. You wanna figure that one out?"

"I'm sorry," Eli finally offered feebly, his throat dry.

"Oh, I *know* you're sorry. And I was prepared to make you a lot sorrier. But your brother wasn't just one of my boys. He was like a son to me. He stuck it out with me through a lot of tough times. Me *and* my business are gonna miss him."

The man grew quiet, rubbing his thumb and forefinger together, staring into space. Eli sensed real grief there and recognized it. He leaned forward, earnest. "Someone named Benny killed my brother."

Adrian nodded. "Benny the Squeal. I know. He used to be handy to have around. Gave me a lot of good information."

Eli sat back, his jaw tense. "If you knew, why didn't you do anything about it?"

Marcon cut hard, wizened eyes at Eli. "That's not the way the game is played. I've been in this business a long time, and I know what I'm doing. Benny will get his, but when *I* order it, and not a second before." Adrian cooled, then pointed a gnarled finger in Eli's face. "But this ain't about Benny. This is about you. You made a mess of things, and now I'm giving you an opportunity to make it right. You are going to work for me."

The Brit stifled a laugh. Eli directed his eyes at the driver again, then turned a softer, more careful expression on the old gangster before him. "Look, man, I appreciate the offer but—"

"It wasn't a question," Adrian said, stressing each word. "You *will* work for me. What you did tonight was stupid, but you were angry, and I get that. It also took a lot of guts. And whether you like it or not, you just started a war with Rufus. I'm already hearing that he's planning a retaliation against my operation. That's on *your* head. Frankly, we're not ready for open hostilities. My guys have had it soft for a long time. I don't need thugs and leg breakers, Eli, I need *hitmen*. Cold-blooded killers who will get the job done. It's the only way to survive out here. Your brother understood that. I'm thinking you understand that too."

Eli nodded, fear and disgust sitting heavy in his stomach. Suddenly, Kylie's words came back to him. *We get ourselves into our own traps.* "What if I refuse?" he asked.

Adrian hooked a thumb in the stoic Brit's direction. "Would it work better for you if my friend Mr. Domingo, here, set you up with a nice plot down in Shady Grove Cemetery?"

Mr. Domingo sneered. Eli hated that guy already.

"…No."

Adrian nodded and holstered his gold-plated gun. "I thought you'd see it my way." Then he extended a decorated hand, which Eli carefully took. "This is the part where I say 'welcome to the family'." Marcon squeezed Eli's hand and jerked him closer. "Don't disappoint me, kid."

Eli pressed his lips together in silence, hearing the doors of possibility slam shut. There was only one path for him now.

And he already knew where it would lead.

CHAPTER SIX

NOW

"Paul?"

Three years later, Eli shook off the memory of the night he sold his soul to Boss Marcon. Ralph stood in the doorway of the shop in Greensboro, scratching his head, that familiar awkward wince on his face. "You okay?"

Eli finished sliding into his flannel shirt and faced his co-worker. "I gotta get going."

Eli passed his friend, entering the blinding glare of sunset. He had places to go, promises to keep.

"Try not to burn the place down while I'm gone," Eli said in good humor, eager to escape the past's hold on his mind.

Ralph called out after him with a funny whine, "That only happened that one time. I don't see why you gotta keep bringing it up."

Eli laughed and climbed into his blue Jeep Renegade.

"Hey, uh, you be careful out there. Don't get yourself into any trouble," Ralph said.

"Yeah. Sure."

Ralph waved in the rearview mirror as Eli headed for Old Greenesboro and the North Woods.

Local folk in Greensboro told strange stories about the charred ruins of Old Greenesboro deep within the North Woods. Eli never used to put much stock in small town talk or ghost stories. Not until he met the blue-faced Angel of Death in the flesh.

That experience had left Eli changed. The veil separating the natural from the supernatural had been lifted from his eyes and he understood, now, that secret things waited in the dark. There were truths that might be better left unknown, but he had an inkling of them all the same. And with that knowledge came nightmares, as though part of his brain now existed in that strange space between worlds where monsters dwelled. His dreams told him things, warning him that darkness was falling in his life once more.

Darkness was coming for *her.*

Greensboro's KDZY played on the radio. Smooth-voiced DJ Daryl Baker cut in over the last chords of "99 Red Balloons", crooning, "If you've just tuned in, don't worry, you haven't reached eighty-eight miles per hour. You're just listening to our All Eighties Weekend. Coming up next is a little tune dedicated to all you fellas out there who have just been dumped. Or maybe you're in your car on your way to an ex-girlfriend's because you can't just man up and let it go, ha ha. You know who you are. It's Soft Cell's 1982 hit, 'Tainted Love'."

The synthesized beep of "Tainted Love" began, and Eli warmed. This day seemed to be *made* to go see her, as though the entire world was rearranging itself, paving the way for him. Destiny waited at the end of his drive, he knew, though whether or not it was a pleasant destiny…well, that remained unclear. But Eli determined to face it, all the same. He had to try. For her.

Reaching up to his visor, he retrieved the photo he kept stashed there, even after all this time. He was met by the familiar image, he and the brown-eyed girl.

THEN

Six months after Eli began working for Boss Marcon, his life had drastically changed. After the night Marcon and his men invaded her home, Kylie and the girls left for Ohio. Eli gave them a substantial amount of money that he'd made on the side overseas. They parted amiably, but Eli could tell that Kylie had lost a certain amount of respect for him. He simply stayed behind in his brother's stead, shouldering all of Alex's old burdens. Eli wondered what would have happened if he'd gone with Kylie, but that ship had sailed. He was locked in now, serving as Adrian's faithful son. He'd even managed to finagle James a couple jobs for the Old Man in the process.

One Friday evening, Eli was called to an unexpected meeting at *Jefferson Antique Furniture*—one of Adrian's many dummy companies sprinkled about Willowbrook. They rotated their command center on a regular basis, staying ahead of authorities, even though most cops in Willowbrook didn't care what Adrian did with his time or theirs. Mostly they were happy that he kept the town afloat, and occasionally cut them in on his business. But the Feds sniffed around every once in a while, and that called for discretion.

Eli smoothed out the dark suit Adrian had custom-fit for him and adjusted his tie, then slipped past the Old World stylings of *Jefferson's* inventory and entered the storeroom in back. He ascended the metal steps and pushed his way through the door, nodding once to the receptionist—a ginger beauty named Darla.

"He's expecting you," she said.

Eli gave a light rap on the office door with his knuckles.

Darius Domingo answered him from the other side of the door. "Come in."

Eli entered Domingo's office, a bland, unremarkable room. The walls were a dull beige and, though art adorned the walls, it reflected nothing of Domingo's character. It was a façade, uninspired prints and store-bought trinkets to give the illusion of class, like the store out front. Only a small wooden sign behind the desk that read "CHAOS, PANIC, DISORDER...MY WORK HERE IS DONE" gave any hint of genuine personality. Domingo himself leaned casually against his desk like he owned the world. Wearing a breezy, long sleeve gauze shirt and slacks, he looked like he'd just stepped off a beach in the Caribbean. All he needed was a fruity drink with an umbrella and the picture would be complete.

Domingo was alone, which was not surprising. With the war on Rufus turning hotter every day, Adrian rarely made public appearances. Most times, Eli dealt with Domingo. An okay guy, for a killer, but he had a definite superiority complex.

"You wanted to see me?" Eli said.

Domingo took his manicured hands out of his pockets and gestured towards a TV mounted above one of the filing cabinets. "There's something I want to show you."

Eli neared the TV and saw a young, beautiful blonde woman on the screen, tied to a chair in a familiar warehouse. The footage was grainy and amateurish, like a crude home movie.

In the footage, Eli heard Domingo's British accent, *"There, there. It's all right."*

The woman continued to struggle, weeping behind the gag in her mouth.

"I wager when you woke up this morning you never thought you'd end the day bound and gagged, did you?" Video Domingo asked. *"Funny how life throws you a curve ball, isn't it?"*

Some other stuff was said, but Eli had a hard time making it out. Then he heard a door close offscreen, but the camera remained on the girl squirming in her chair.

His stomach dropped at the pitiful sight. "Who's the girl?" he asked, holding back the bile rising in his throat. He'd been with Adrian for months now, but he usually dealt with smart-mouthed punks and, more often than not, he felt they actually deserved the punishment he showed up to administer. This innocent young woman, though…she only made him think of Kylie and the girls, of that horrible night when sweet little Hannah had been held captive by Domingo, too, however momentarily.

"An unfortunate casualty," Domingo said, without any hint of remorse.

The girl in the video froze, then jerked against her restraints even more violently. She squealed now, and Eli felt the hairs on his neck rise. Blind panic overtook her face as she wept fresh tears and nearly knocked her chair over, trying to get away. At just about the time Eli was going to ask Domingo what was happening, a new, hulkier figure entered the frame. Wearing a jacket and a stocking cap pulled down just above his eyes, the bearded man was instantly familiar. He'd been there that night Adrian came to Kylie's house to recruit Eli.

Eli looked to Domingo, surprised. "Is that Malcolm?"

"Keep watching."

Eli did, as Video Malcolm roughly asked the girl, "*What's your problem?*"

But the girl only twisted and scooted and screamed through her gag.

A black shape crossed the camera and Malcolm turned with a startled, "*Aaah!*" The goon pulled his gun and fired, but the shape was gone. Malcolm looked around, his gun at the ready, and the shape materialized again, this time behind him. The gunman whirled and blasted away, but the shape disappeared once more.

"What is this?" Eli asked, spellbound.

Again and again, some dark giant appeared in the video, but immediately flickered out of sight just as Malcolm was about to kill him. Finally, the gunman was so paranoid, he started hollering and shooting at everything, trying to hit his unseen attacker.

In the chaos, the girl was shot. Eli's heart broke.

He took one step closer to the TV, watching her chest, to see if she were still breathing. But her cries were silenced. Her life ended.

Video Malcolm cooled from his hysteria and saw the girl's still form. He instantly dropped his gun and rushed to her, shaking her shoulders. "*Hey! Hey, come on! Wake up! Wake up!*"

When she didn't, he stood, a weary hand to his head. "*Oh, man…*"

Then the black shape emerged from behind him. Eli involuntarily leaned forward to warn the man onscreen, though knew it was useless. The shape reached out with thick arms and wrapped two gigantic hands around Malcolm's neck. Without any visible effort, the giant twisted and removed Malcolm's head, spilling gore everywhere.

Eli backed away from the footage, repulsed.

With the carnage finished, the shape dropped Malcom's remains. Just as the killer turned around, the camera caught a fleeting glimpse of its face. Domingo hit pause and Eli bore witness to a strange, luminescent mask or helmet or *something*. Something obscured the killer's face—something in the shape of a skull.

Domingo switched off the TV. "Do you know anything about this?"

Eli turned, startled by the question. "What do you mean?"

"As far as I know, there's only one guy in town who likes to dress up in a Halloween mask and go around gunning down hitmen."

"You don't think that's *me?*" Eli protested in a panic.

Domingo studied him carefully, then smirked, only testing him. "No. Of course not. Still, we have a problem."

Eli considered what he had just seen, trying to shake the sights of the poor blonde girl and decapitated Malcolm from his mind. "Do you think it's someone working for Rufus?"

Rufus had turned into a mad dog since Eli shot up that Laundromat. In the right neighborhoods at the wrong time of day, Willowbrook was a warzone now—just as deadly as Afghanistan had been. *And I made it that way.* How many people were dead because he'd been looking for payback?

"We're not sure who it is," Domingo said, shaking Eli from his painful reflections. He chuckled and mentioned, "That crazy preacher, Loomis, thinks it's some sort of divine retribution headed our way." Domingo reached up with the remote control and clicked off the television set. "But Mr. Marcon can only assume that this hit is meant as a personal attack."

Eli nodded, assuming as much.

Domingo carried on, leaning over his desk, an ornately ringed finger reaching for the intercom button, "Therefore, he wants *you*, his best man, to take care of the most important thing in his life." He depressed the button and spoke. "You can come in now, darling."

The door opened behind Eli and he turned, curious as to what a man like Boss Marcon would consider "most important". What walked through the door, though, was the last thing he expected.

No older than eighteen, she stood five-foot-three, wearing a stuffy private school uniform. Smooth, shapely legs jutted from beneath her charcoal grey pleated skirt; knee-high socks made her toned thighs even more noticeable. Moving up, her sweater swelled at the bust, a nice full shape, and Eli felt heat rise under his skin. Long, straight dark hair hung over the right side of her bored-looking porcelain doll face. Heavy, dark eye makeup accentuated her chocolate-brown eyes. Eli's palms began to sweat.

"Eli, this is Mr. Marcon's daughter, Marcie."

"Hey," Eli greeted, his heartbeat filling his ears.

"Hey," she replied with barely an interest.

Domingo smiled at the introductions, no doubt amused. "Marcie wants to go to the library tonight, and you're going to escort her. Just the library and home. Nowhere else. Make sure nothing happens to her."

Marcie blew out a breath and crossed her arms. "I don't need a babysitter."

Domingo grinned slightly and faced her, speaking as though to a small child. "Mr. Marcon says you do, and around here we do what Mr. Marcon says."

The teenager rolled her eyes. Once Domingo was sure she was done pouting, he turned back to Eli. "Can you do this?"

"Of course."

"I knew I could count on you, Eli."

Eli stepped to the girl, offering his arm to show respect to the Boss' daughter, but Marcie leveled him with a withering glare and marched for the door on her own. Eli retracted his gesture, and Domingo muffled a snicker. Eli stepped in double-time to catch up to the girl, but Domingo called him back, "Oh, and Eli."

Eli paused halfway into opening the door for an impatient Marcie.

"Remember, this is a job. You can look, but don't touch."

Eli's face flushed, his very thoughts penetrated. "Yeah."

"And have her home by midnight. Mr. Marcon worries."

Marcie groaned and stormed outside. Eli followed as Domingo gave a little wave. "Have a good time, kids."

The library walls were tomato red, a strange color for rest and quiet reflection, Eli mused. Closing time was fast approaching and most of the patrons had left for the night. He had spent the last hour and a half shadowing Marcie while the girl tirelessly perused the shelves, looking up books in the computer system. She'd amassed a small stack, and he'd once again tried to play the gentleman and carry her books for her, but she refused without a word. She clearly didn't want him hanging around like an overprotective chaperone, and for his part, he didn't want to be here, himself. He kept a close eye on Marcie, occasionally walking down nearby aisles as if expecting Rufus' men to try to make a move.

Or this new terrifying character with the skull mask.

Who was it? Where did he come from? With strength like that, how could Eli stand up to him, even if he did show up?

Resigned to his fate, he trailed behind the girl in his charge. She was undeniably attractive, and when she bent over every so often to retrieve a book on the bottom shelf, he looked a little longer than he probably should have. He hadn't had a girlfriend in a long time—not since before enlisting in the Army. He missed a woman's touch, the smell of smooth female skin.

"What?" Marcie snapped, suddenly facing him, snarling.

"Huh?"

"What are you staring at?"

He blushed. "Nothing. Just…uh, thinking."

"Why don't you close your mouth? You look like a Neanderthal."

Eli bit off a retort, and followed the young woman to the table where the rest of her selection waited. Marcie took her seat and crossed her legs. Taking the top book, she thumbed through it, scanning.

Casually glancing at the small stack of books, Eli read the names on the spines. Some works by a guy named Lovecraft, and a few others on folklore and witchcraft. They were weird, to be sure, and he guessed Marcie to be one of those stifled Catholic school girls who moonlighted as Goths. It was so terribly *teenage*, but he himself had gone through an embarrassing earring phase not so many years ago, so he withheld judgment.

Long seconds ticked away, and Eli checked his watch, then the clock on the wall. Rubbed his eyes. Stretched. He finally leaned over and asked, "So…don't you think you should have some friends to hang around with or something?"

"I don't have any friends," she replied, not looking up from her book.

"Really? Why not?"

She glanced at him, her right eye still veiled behind her hair. "We're not in the business of getting attached."

Eli cracked a grin at her seriousness. "Now you're starting to sound like Adrian."

Marcie put the book down, looking at Eli through her brow. "I don't think it's so bad to sound like him. My father has a pretty good idea of how to run a business."

Eli waved his hands. "Don't get defensive, I'm just making an observation."

"I'm not being *defensive*. I just thought since you work for my father you'd agree with some of his business tactics. And one of the most important ones to agree with is not getting attached."

Looking finished with this conversation, Marcie picked up her book and turned a page.

Eli decided to keep his mouth shut. The last thing he needed was this spoiled brat heading back to her father and tattling that her babysitter was speaking treason. He slumped in his chair, determined to get through this night as painlessly as possible. He was surprised when Marcie looked up at him, her expression softening. Apprehensive.

"What's going on, anyway?" she asked, her voice nearly a whisper.

"What do you mean?"

"What are you baby-sitting *me* for? Shouldn't you be out killing this Rufus guy or something?"

It was a backhanded way of saying she was scared. Eli understood that. He was marked, but so was she. Even more so, as killing her would be the surest way to cripple Boss Marcon's resolve. Eli realized how important Marcie was, and this job of serving as her bodyguard suddenly felt weightier. He'd chosen this life for reasons that seemed beyond him now, but she was born into it.

He pitied her. Attitude and all.

"There's been some weird things happening," Eli said, thinking of that bizarre shape in the video with Malcolm. "Your dad just wants to make sure you're okay."

Marcie exhaled slowly, uncomfortably shifting in her seat, ever so slightly. If Eli didn't know better, he'd have thought that she was starting to tolerate him. A bit encouraged at seeing the Ice Queen thaw, Eli commented, "To tell you the truth, I didn't even know Adrian had a daughter. It must be weird growing up in that kind of family."

Eli thought of his own family. A good home, even after the divorce. A god-fearing father who'd taught him about life. A brother he'd loved like himself. Funny how something so good went downhill so fast. But Marcie never even had a chance.

"What does your mom think about it?" Eli asked.

Marcie's face hardened. She parted the curtain of her hair, tucking it behind her ear. Her eyes fell back on her book. "I don't know. I've never met her."

Eli faltered, feeling the sting of his tumultuous relationship with his own mother. "Sorry."

"Well, I mean, not really," Marcie explained. "She left when I was a baby."

He wondered why Marcie was telling him something so personal, but he didn't press it. Just listened. Marcie's voice dropped low and she kept her chin down, talking into the book. "Sometimes I wonder why she didn't take me with her. But I can't blame her."

That surprised Eli, since he blamed his mother for plenty. "Why's that?"

A flicker of sadness passed over her face, then Marcie turned solid once more. "She didn't get too attached."

The day long over, darkness overtook the Willowbrook landscape. Frank Black's lazy and seductive "Dark End of the Street" played on the radio as Eli pulled past the gate to Adrian's estate. He'd only been to Adrian's house a few times. Usually he just met with Domingo or Adrian in their business fronts around town. The grounds were well-lit and constantly watched by security cameras. Adrian's private security detail casually moved about the perimeter, dressed in fitted suits like Eli's. The place looked more like a prison than a home, and now Eli thought he understood why Marcie wanted to stay at the library until they were finally asked to leave by the tired librarians ready to go home for the night. She didn't check out a single book, just read through them all there, trying to draw out the moments, he assumed, until she had to return to her actual life.

Now Marcie sat in the passenger seat of Eli's silver 2002 Porsche 911 Carrera 4S, nursing a blue Icee she bought when they stopped for gas. Eli noticed how she stared up at the imposing mansion, a forlorn resignation in her chestnut-colored eyes.

He pulled to a stop in the driveway. A couple of the guards watched him warily, but moved on once they recognized him.

"Thanks for the ride," Marcie said.

"No problem."

"So," she began, slowly turning his way, bringing the drink to her mouth. "You wanna come in or something?"

She slurped on the straw, long and purposeful.

Eli flushed. He'd hardly been able to take his eyes off her all night, but she was off-limits. "No, better not," he chuckled, unnerved. "Besides, what happened to not getting attached?"

Marcie did not smile, but her eyes betrayed a playfulness he'd not seen in her tonight. It was quite charming. The girl unbuckled her seatbelt and climbed out of the car, a sly smile now forming. "Just because you don't get too attached doesn't mean you can't have any fun."

She closed the car door, offered a flirty wave, and jogged up the front steps to the door. Eli just sat in the car, watching her, a bewildered grin plastered on his face.

Quite charming, indeed.

CHAPTER SEVEN

In the following weeks, Eli and Marcie were inseparable. Per Adrian's orders, he dropped her off and picked her up from her parochial school, took her to the library and wherever else she wanted to go. Marcie had loosened up since their initial encounter and even joked occasionally with her bodyguard. They had a mutual respect for each other, but never crossed from the professional to personal. Still, Eli enjoyed her company and found himself counting the hours until school let out so that he could escort Marcie all over town as she spent her father's money. He'd hold her bags while she went shopping and offer his opinion on outfits when asked. He'd tried hard to keep his growing attraction for her in check, but Marcie sensed it like a shark in bloody waters. At clothing stores, she'd parade lingerie or bathing suits in front of her bodyguard, asking which one she should buy. He dutifully spurned her playful advances, which only seemed to make her try harder.

One warm spring night, Eli pulled up to Adrian's estate. He offered a nod to the guards who now recognized him—even expected him. Without knocking, Eli entered the lavish home, struck, as always, by the ornate gold-inlaid design. Adrian began his life as a bottom-feeder back in the old days and, through cunning and perseverance, had risen to the top of the Willowbrook food chain. He certainly didn't mind parading his hard-earned wealth, though the extravagance was a little much for Eli's taste. Just having a house that didn't fall apart and enough money to cover a lifetime of bills would be enough for his contentment.

He poked his head into the foyer, and heard voices coming from the adjoining study. Adrian was in there, hovering over his mahogany desk, muttering to others. Eli stepped closer and entered the office. Mr. Domingo rested casually in a wingback chair in the corner, a pretend king on his throne. Stan and Lee were there, shuffling about awkwardly, as was Ian, who stood like a shadow off to the side. Stan and Lee were morons, and the more Eli got to know Adrian's "bodyguards" in the tweed coat and dumpy jacket the less he cared for them. Ian, though, was a good guy. A Texas-born good ol' boy, Ian fancied himself right out of the Old West. He wore jeans, boots, a duster in the winter, and a cowboy hat. He spoke little, his stoic face always sporting his trademark sunglasses. He had a cattle-hand approach to the job—keep your head down and get it done. Eli respected him for his work ethic, even though he didn't exactly think of Ian as a friend. But, of all of Adrian's goons, Eli figured he got along with Ian the best.

Adrian looked up from his desk, spotting Eli, startled.

"What's going on?" Eli asked when all eyes slowly turned on him.

"What are you doing here?" Adrian snapped, his eyes squinting suspiciously. The Old Man was getting paranoid these days, no doubt feeling the pressure of having Rufus constantly circling his operation.

"I'm here for Marcie. It's prom night. Remember?"

Adrian nodded, but his eyes were glassy, as though he still didn't understand. He gestured to his desk, and now Eli saw it was covered in black and white crime scene photos. He moved in for a closer look. Saw blood and body parts strewn about everywhere.

"The guy with the skull mask again?" Eli asked tentatively.

Adrian rubbed at his whiskers, his face ashen. Domingo spoke from his place in the corner of the study. "The police haven't turned up any leads. Our friend on the force, Lt. Dutton, is keeping us apprised, but so far we have nothing but more corpses."

Adrian mashed the side of his fist on the desk. "I want this sicko found!"

Eli clasped his hands behind his back. "Do you need me to do something?"

Adrian shook his head. "You're doing it. Keep Marcie safe. She's all that matters now."

It was perhaps the first time he'd ever seen Adrian express any kind of affection for his daughter, and Eli thought for a second that maybe his employer wasn't such a monster after all.

"She's my legacy," Adrian added coldly, and Eli's heart slowly sank. "This will all be hers one day. Provided I can keep it running long enough to pass it down to her. I worked too hard for my name—I'm not going to lose it over some freak in a mask."

"Daddy?"

The men in the room faced the doorway, where Marcie stood in a beautiful lavender prom dress. The strapless gown exposed her slender shoulders and barely hinted at her ample bosom. Her hair was pinned back into a loose knot, save a few tiny ringlets hanging in delicate curls that framed her face. She was positively effulgent, her radiant smile rivaling the power of a sunset. Eli felt his breath hitch at the sight of her and hoped he wasn't grinning as wide as he imagined.

"What do you think?" she asked her father, twirling slowly to show off her designer dress.

Adrian stiffened and walked forward. "Marcie, you shouldn't be here. Eli, take her out."

Even Eli hesitated at the curt order, but Adrian practically pushed him away. "Stay out of trouble," he mumbled. Once he had personally escorted Eli and Marcie out of the study, the Old Man swiftly closed the door.

Marcie stood in the hallway, her head lowered, fondling the handle of a large matching handbag she carried. "I hate this dress," she spoke quietly.

Eli tugged at her elbow, just slightly. "I think you look really nice."

He offered his arm to her. This time, she took it.

Eli drove the Porsche towards the school while Marcie sat in the cramped backseat, staring out the back window.

"What are you looking for?" Eli asked, amused by her odd behavior.

She paused a moment more, just as Eli turned the corner, leaving Adrian's palace behind, then quickly slid her dress down past her arms, exposing a flesh-toned strapless Victoria Secret push-up bra.

Eli nearly lost control of the car. "What are you doing?"

Marcie ignored him, laying on the seat, her gorgeous legs extended as she tugged off the dress. When she righted herself, she grinned savagely at him. "Please. Did you really think I was going to spend all night laughing and smiling with people from school? I make a point of not having friends, remember?"

Eli divided his attention between the road and the rearview mirror, watching as Marcie dug around in her massive handbag and retrieved street clothes. She shimmied into a pair of tight jeans and pulled a sheer black turtleneck over her head. Her hair mussed, but her face full of mischief and excitement, she draped her arms over the back of Eli's seat.

"Let's do something *exciting*."

Now he was curious. "Like what?"

"Let's rob a liquor store."

Eli parked in front of a downtown liquor store in nearby Russellville. The trip had cost them half an hour, but Marcie deduced that they'd be too easily spotted committing such a brazen crime in their own town. Only one other car—

a beige Plymouth—rested outside. Inside, the place was well-lit as the lone customer grazed. Behind the counter, a large woman sat on a stool, her face relaying a severe case of boredom.

Eli supposed they were here to change that.

He turned to Marcie, who had since climbed into the passenger seat. She dug around in her handy bag. He couldn't remove the humored grin from his face. "You're serious?"

She pulled out a scrap of pantyhose and offered it to him, even as she slipped one over her head, squishing her nose. "Hurry."

"What about cameras—"

Before he could finish, she handed him a can of black spray paint. "That's your job."

"You're really not kidding."

"Not even a little bit. Come on, don't tell me you're 'above' this sort of thing. We're young. We should act like it."

He chuckled and shook his head. "All right. But no one gets hurt." To further demonstrate his intent, Eli slid out his SIG 229 and dumped the clip into his hand, feeding it to his inside suit jacket pocket. Making sure the chamber was empty, he handed the gun to her, butt first.

She gladly accepted the gun, nearly bouncing in her seat. "Ready?"

He groaned, feigning aggravation. "Sure."

Marcie shoved the door open and practically skipped for the store, flinging the glass door open and waving Eli's gun around like a wild savage.

Eli swore and struggled to keep up with her, nearly tripping out of the car, trying to reach her. By time he got inside, she had the gun pointed at the customer, the clerk, then back again, letting zip a string of colorful obscenities— using phraseology that Eli had never heard, even in the military. He was mightily impressed by her show of force, and nearly forgot his own part to play in this heist. Quickly, he popped the top off his spray can and blew a cloud of black mist over the cameras.

Marcie shoved the gun in the clerk's mouth, screaming at the top of her lungs. "Give me the money or I'll blow your teeth out the back of your head!"

The hefty cashier wailed, her bulk trembling as she opened the cash register. The customer kept his distance, but his eyes were cagey, like he was thinking of being a hero. Eli pointed at him, and hollered, "Turn around! On the ground! Don't look at us!"

The man moved to comply, but not fast enough. Eli gripped his shoulder and forced him to his knees. Marcie waved on the cashier, raging, "Hurry! *Hurry!*"

Her task completed, the woman handed over a plastic sack of money and Marcie hollered over her shoulder, "Romeo, we got it! Let's go!" She grabbed a bottle of cheap wine from a display near the counter and rushed out the door.

Eli was startled at first by her choice of codename, but came to his senses and followed her outside. The two jumped into the car and Eli floored the engine, backing out and squalling away.

"*Romeo?*" he asked her, adrenaline flaming in his veins.

Marcie ripped off her mask, looking as proud as a kindergartner on graduation day. She beamed splendidly, out of breath. "I thought it added something." She lay back in the seat, pumping her fists and the stolen bottle in the air, tossing her hair from side to side, hollering at the top of her lungs, "Woooo!"

Eli laughed and drove on.

Eli wound around the North Woods for the next hour. He was only vaguely familiar with the Maribel County backroads from long Sunday afternoon drives with his father in his youth, but he always found the quiet woods peaceful and reassuring. Marcie took a few occasional swigs from the bottle before declaring it disgusting and tossing it out the window. At last, Eli parked the car on a cliff down the gravel road from a worn-out old church. A faded, weed-covered sign out front read "Good Church of the Faithful". The rickety church looked more abandoned and creepy than good or faithful, but it seemed to fit the moment. The old building was like he and Marcie, forgotten by the good people but hanging on just the same. And tonight, it felt, for the first time in a long time, like maybe he was doing more than just hanging on—maybe he was actually living again.

He lay on the hood of the car, gazing out over the cliff at the small town of Greensboro. Nighttime bugs chirped pleasantly in the distance, and a cool breeze tickled the back of his neck. Marcie twirled her arms under the starlight, dancing in the wind.

"Isn't it amazing?"

He could only look at her and grin.

"Oh! Almost forgot." She reached through the rolled-down passenger window and brought out their catch for the night. Sixty-three dollars. She thumbed through the cash and took a big sniff of it, releasing a pleased sigh.

Then she procured a lighter from her back pocket and touched the flame to the corner of the cash.

Eli sprang upright, startled. "You're not keeping it?"

She snickered, watching the money burn. "Eli, I don't *need* the money." She faced him, raising a coy eyebrow. "Do you?"

He chuckled. "No."

"Then let it burn," she spoke into the flame, dropping the wad of cash to the ground, where it slowly dissolved to ash.

Eli eased back on the car, still watching her. Still in absolute awe of her.

Once the burning was complete, Marcie stamped out the embers and moved closer to the edge of the cliff, watching the sleeping town below. She tucked her hands in her pockets and swayed slightly. "You won't tell my father what we did tonight, will you?"

"No."

She nodded. "I wonder if he'd be proud. He's stolen from Willowbrook for years, and people just sit by and let him do it."

She would not face him, but he heard the hurt that crept into her voice when she began to talk about her father. Eli thought of earlier that evening, of the cold reception her stunning dress had garnered from the Old Man. Eli sat up. "I'm sure he loves you very much."

Marcie turned on him, a wild grin stretched across her face, though her eyes were red and just a tad puffy. "Loves me? I'm just his 'legacy'. Has he given you that speech yet? I'm just his lame bid for immortality. I'm just here to ensure that some part of all that he worked for lives on."

Eli frowned and looked away.

Marcie kicked at some loose gravel on the road. She snickered after a time and said, "You know, when I was little, I would always catch him in his study, talking with his guys. I have this really clear memory of being four or five, and the door was open. I always wondered what he was looking at in there…what kept him so interested. I remember walking down the hall, wanting to see for myself, but he caught me and closed the door. I used to stare at that door, wanting to be in there with him. That's where the power was. And I wanted it, too. To see if it was worth him always being gone."

Eli asked with a genuine curiosity, "What was he like growing up?"

Marcie considered, and a ghost of a grin escaped. "He wasn't cruel, if that's what you're asking. He rarely raised his voice to me and *never* harmed me. If anything, he treated me more like an adult than a child. He'd talk to me, teach me things, but it wasn't like he was imparting some great wisdom, you know? It was like he was just preparing me for adulthood, no bells or whistles about it. I always felt like I had Daddy's respect, if not his affection."

"Respect is important."

"Not when a hug would suffice," Marcie said coldly, facing him with dead, dark eyes. She seemed to catch herself and chuckled. "I used to have these nannies, growing up. Daddy was always so busy... They were usually older women and seemed to dote on me even more than what was required of them. I think they felt sorry for me. No mom, hardly a dad. They'd shower me with extra hugs, or read me bedtime stories, teach me to bake. 'Womanly things', they said."

Eli warmed. "That's nice."

She stared hard at the ground. "But I was still watching that door to Daddy's study. I was learning more about what he did, and I wanted his kind of power for myself. I...ha, I used to steal something valuable but totally inconsequential from my father's stuff, and I would plant the evidence on my nannies."

Eli frowned, surprised by the confession. Marcie faced him, a mad, tragic glint in her eye.

She said, "I would watch as they broke down in tears, pleading for Daddy to believe they were innocent. I would just grin as they lost their jobs. It's funny... Thinking back, I have to believe that my father suspected I was the culprit. He's too smart to have thought that he was that poor a judge of character in nannies. But Daddy never even asked me about it. I guess I thought that was his way of approving. I thought he was testing me. To see if I was strong enough to be his daughter."

"Marcie..."

"The weak get abused," she said firmly. "That's what he always told me. The weak get abused... And they're all weak. Everyone but Daddy."

Eli considered sliding off the hood and giving her a hug. He felt it was strangely appropriate after she'd been so honest with him. But he kept a respectable distance.

Marcie dried her eyes and faced him, smiling. "So, there's my sob story. What's yours? I bet you came from a perfect family, right?"

He smiled. "Ah, *no*. I thought it was perfect for a while. We lived in Willowbrook. Mom used to clean hotel rooms. Dad had a garage. He was...he was great. Never short-changed anyone. Always treated people better than they deserved. He was a quiet guy, but, man...he'd look at you and you felt like you were untouchable. Like, no matter what happened, he would be there for you."

Eli rubbed at his hands, still smiling, seeing his father's grizzled face, full of warmth and strength. But the happy memories stopped there. "Mom left Dad when I was ten. For all of Dad's noble qualities, Mom wanted more than he could give her, I guess. Well, *money*," he corrected himself. "She wanted more *money* than he could give her. It was a big custody battle and she took me and my brother from our dad. We moved around all over the country. She got re-married a few times. I don't know what she was ever looking for, but she never found it. Me and Alex would stay with Dad during the summers. Work on cars with him. He was always broke after they got divorced. Man…he'd stay at the garage 'til three in the morning some nights, but he never got ahead. He looked so tired all the time, but he'd always say that God would 'see him through'. I didn't think Dad had a very good god if he was such a great man but had such a crappy hand dealt him. I swore that I wouldn't be like that. What good is it to be a decent guy if people just walk all over you?"

"Your mom's an idiot," Marcie interjected hotly.

Eli couldn't argue with her there. "She was really unhappy. Still is, I think, but I don't talk to her very much. The thing is, though, Dad never said one bad word about her. Never. Alex and me…we knew Dad still missed her, so we just didn't talk about her while we were with him. It was like she didn't exist during the summer. All I ever wanted was to make Dad happy again."

Eli supposed Marcie could relate.

"It's why I enlisted," he said.

"So, you were, like, a Marine, or something, right?"

Eli smirked. "Army. Sergeant."

Marcie watched him out of the corner of her eye. "Did you shoot anybody?"

It was a common question asked by people who didn't know what war was like. It rankled Eli, but he'd grown accustomed to the wary looks of civilians who worried he was some traumatized vet with a grudge and a hair trigger. "Yeah."

Marcie regarded him more closely, morbidly fascinated. "What's war like?"

Eli rubbed a knuckle, finding it weirdly awkward to be sharing his war memories with a rich schoolgirl. "It's not like it is in the movies. It's…chaos. Our convoy got hit one time. IED. The vehicle in front of us took the worst of it, but we were stalled in the road. Insurgents started coming out of the woodwork, firing at us. You just… You hunker down or run and you *shoot*. Most of the time, you're not even looking where you're aiming, you're just trying to get away."

His heart pounded, and he felt a sheen of sweat cover his forehead. He'd not shared that with anyone—not even James, who'd seen his share of combat, as well.

In the quiet that followed, Marcie moved closer to him and climbed back onto the hood of the car. She kept climbing until she straddled his lap. He straightened his back, startled. She leaned in, her mouth parted just slightly, her warm, sweet-smelling breath on his face. "Why won't you kiss me?"

156

Oh, how many times Eli had thought about it. Especially tonight. She *was* eighteen and graduation was just around the corner.

"We can't," he said, looking away.

"We don't have to tell Daddy. It'll be our little secret."

She leaned in, and Eli grabbed her, nearly throwing her off him. He hopped off the hood of the car, his body trembling with the fury of unspent hormones. "It's time to get you back home."

Marcie glared at him, then slid off the hood, herself. She passed him on the way to the passenger side, purposefully bumping into him.

"Marcie—" he began, but she ignored him, getting into the Porsche and slamming the door behind her. He sighed, took his place behind the wheel, and headed back to Willowbrook.

CHAPTER EIGHT

After their night on the cliff, Eli and Marcie's relationship stayed friendly over the next few weeks, though a bit strained. He had rebuffed her advances, and was beginning to understand that Marcie did not like being told "no".

While he played babysitter, however, Eli kept hearing the reports from Domingo—more guys were falling victim to that freak in the skull mask. The town was growing colder, despite summer being just around the corner, and within the chill, Eli felt the certainty of his own demise. Death walked the streets, and there was no way he was going to dodge its touch.

But Marcie…Marcie was a welcome distraction.

"Come on," she pleaded in the passenger seat, nearly bouncing up and down.

Eli craned his head to look past her to the brightly lit night club. "No."

"But I graduated! I'm an *adult* now!"

"Drinking age is twenty-one."

"Whatever," she said, looking at him through the brow as she often did in her most petulant of moods. "That didn't stop me from taking a drink when we robbed that liquor store in Russellville. Anyway, my father *owns* this dive. They'll let me in."

"I'm supposed to be taking you to the library."

"But don't you want to celebrate? I just graduated today! This is a *big deal.* Please? Pretty please?"

"I don't know…"

She laughed and leaned over and kissed him on the cheek. "Ha! You're the best. Park the car around back. I'll see you inside."

"But—"

Marcie leapt out of the car, marching to the front door of the exclusive club. Eli leaned over to get a better look as she pushed her way through the line, to much protest, and approached the doorman. He gave her some gesture that looked like "buzz off", but Marcie propped her hands on her hips, tilted her head, and said something. Eli couldn't follow her lips, but whatever she said, when she was done, the doorman tripped over himself to get out of the way. He unlatched the velvet rope, wiping sweat from his brow. Marcie waved at Eli back in the car, then danced her way inside.

He grinned. "Unbelievable."

Eli parked the car as instructed and made his way into the club. The doorman still seemed shaken when Eli pronounced his own introductions. As he entered, strobe lights and loud dance music ruthlessly assaulted his senses. A headache slowly swelled in his mind, his eyes hurting from the noise. Young, half-dressed twenty-somethings danced together, slinging their red plastic cups everywhere. Nothing but spray tan and hair gel as far as the eye could see. It was obnoxious and petty and so not the kind of place Eli would have ever pictured himself.

But this was Marcie's day and Marcie usually got her way.

Then he spotted her over by the bar. Marcie was actually *on* the bar, sitting with her legs crossed, drinking a beer and apparently entertaining three beefcakes with a humorous story. Jealousy stabbed Eli's heart, but he shrugged it off. She wasn't his to possess, though…in a way she was. Somehow, they had grown close, he realized, and she was giving someone else the attention he'd come to expect—no, *crave*—from her.

It wasn't until that moment that Eli realized how much he'd fallen for her already.

He buried all that deep in his gut and made his way through the sweaty crowd to the bar.

"There he is!" Marcie yelled for her new fan club to hear. "My hero! Have a beer, Romeo. Want me to buy?"

"I'll buy my own," Eli grumbled, sliding onto a stool. He motioned for the bartender and got a brown bottle in return.

"Isn't this great?" she shouted over the music. "Forget the library! We're coming here every night!"

"I think your father would have something to say about that."

Marcie frowned, grew deadly serious, and turned to her men. "You guys better take off."

They did, shooting Eli ugly looks. He smirked to himself and took a drink. Marcie climbed down from the bar and sat next to him, her face devoid of the carefree glow it possessed only a second ago. "What's your problem?"

"It's too loud, too crowded. It's not safe."

Angry, Marcie said, "You're ruining my fun."

"You think it's fun for me seeing you with those guys?"

Whoa. That just slipped out.

Marcie blinked back at him in surprise. She smiled. "Are you jealous?"

"You've got five more minutes and then we're out of here."

Eli returned to his beer and Marcie leaned over him, resting her chin on his shoulder. Her defenses lowered, she whispered, "Dance with me."

He shrugged her off. "I can't. Stop doing that."

"Doing what?" she cooed.

"You *know* what."

Marcie stepped back, rigid and tense. "Fine."

Eli saw her out of the corner of his eye. She charged onto the dance floor and he swiveled in his seat to watch her. His conflicted feelings towards her were only complicated by the fact that this wasn't a good place to keep her safe from Rufus' men. The club was wall-to-wall people and noise, and he had to lean and stretch to keep an eye on her.

Marcie caught up with the boys from the bar and danced with the one with the most muscles. He took her in his arms, a big stupid grin on his fake-tanned face, as they gyrated on the dance floor. Marcie turned her back to him, grinding on him, but keeping her eyes focused on Eli.

She grinned, an evil glint in her eye.

Eli glowered at her, but refused to play her games. Instead, he showed her his back and casually drank his beer.

"Hey!" he heard a shout pierce the cacophony.

Fearing an attack, he whirled around and saw Marcie pummeling her dance partner with her fists. He was hunkered over as she beat at him, full of rage. Eli stood, unsure of what had happened. One of the other guys moved in and grabbed Marcie's wrists, pulling her back.

"What's your problem?" the Good Samaritan screamed at her.

Marcie kicked him in the groin, then in the face once he doubled over. Marcie's dance partner rose up behind her and punched her full on in the mouth.

Eli's blood hit boiling point. Still holding his beer, he stormed into the melee and cold-cocked the guy on the skull. The bottle didn't bust, but the man's forehead did. Blood spilled out of a cut on his brow and he went down on the ground, clutching his wound.

Two more guys came at Eli, swinging fists. Eli took one punch square to the jaw and saw Marcie, still holding her busted lip, slipping away in the crowd, sneering with red teeth.

What the—?

Marcie headed for the exit, and Eli moved to follow but was intercepted by more men. He sidestepped a kick and punched the nearest man in the nose, breaking it. A beer bottle clanked him on the back of the head—that one broke—and he instantly saw stars slipping in and out of black space. Another punch to his stomach and he lost his breath. He saw a foot coming for his face, but was able to twist out of the way in time and came up with an uppercut to the man's inner thigh. The guy groaned and went down, and Eli stood, dazed, and tasting copper in his mouth.

The meatheads advanced, but Eli reached under his suit coat and brought out his SIG. Wavering, he pushed it against the nose of the man nearest him and everyone froze.

"Back off," Eli said, his lip swelling.

His attackers lifted their hands in surrender, their eyes wide with mortal dread. Eli stepped backwards, his gun still aimed, his vision hazy. Once he was sure no one would follow him, he chased after Marcie out the back exit.

Eli banged open the door, fearing that anything could have happened to her while he was getting the crap kicked out of him inside. Outside, the back alley was deserted. His head still spinning, Eli staggered, searching. "Marcie! Marcie!"

"Ha, ha!" she growled playfully, leaping from behind, pinning him to the wall. She kissed him hard on the mouth, her tongue pushing past his teeth. She tasted warm and sweet and Eli wanted to—

He pushed her away violently and eyed her in rage. She just smiled, seductive and wild. "What was that in there?" he demanded.

"I was just having fun. Didn't you have fun?"

"*No!*" Eli hollered after a moment's pause. "My brain hurts, my face is bleeding, and I almost shot some guy for no good reason!"

Marcie pressed against him, tugging on his jacket, bringing him closer. "Come on, admit it. It was a little fun."

He just stared at her. His heart beat harder and he shouted, "You're crazy, you know that? What's *wrong* with you?"

Then he suddenly kissed her. He didn't plan to do it, but his body overtook his mind and without warning he was all over her, reckless and free. Marcie jumped up in his arms, wrapping her legs around his waist, running her fingers through his short hair, pulling him in.

That night, when Marcie invited Eli inside after he took her home, he accepted.

CHAPTER NINE

NOW

Eli remembered that night as he drove down Highway 65. Up ahead, he spotted an E-Z Mart and pulled in. Greensboro was going through some changes lately. The highway that cut straight through the heart of town was in the process of being moved. Construction crews and detours were everywhere, as if these backroads weren't winding enough without the makeover. Somewhere out here in the North Woods outside of town, she waited for him. Was it coincidence that she'd moved so close to where he'd hidden?

Or was it fate?

Climbing out of his Jeep, he entered the store and the squat woman behind the counter pushed her thick glasses back over her round nose. "Can I help ya?"

"Yeah," he said. "I think I'm a little lost."

"Oh," she groaned, shaking her head. "You don't want to get lost in *these* woods."

Eli flashed a grin and pulled out his map. "Why's that?"

"Ah, well, you always hear stories about the woods, you know? Folks get bored. But there's some new stories out there now. Some kinda psycho or something, like outta one of those Jason Voorhees movies, stomping through the woods. Tore right through a bunch of campers last week."

He raised an eyebrow. "Really."

"But you probably didn't want all the gory details," she giggled. "Sorry about that."

Laughing respectfully, Eli shook off the eerie story and turned back to the map. "I'm trying to find County Road 90."

The woman leaned over, taking a gander at the map, and started giving directions.

Eli left the E-Z Mart behind, a soda in hand and a better sense of where he was headed. He crossed the distance to his Jeep and felt eyes on him. A strange sense of danger wrapped around him like a wet blanket, chilling his skin. Eli paused and gave the gas station a once-over. He saw nothing in the tree line, and he was the only customer around.

It was an altogether unpleasant feeling, but not an unfamiliar one. The discomfort was unique and the only other time he'd felt it before had been right after he murdered James. He'd felt it then—felt like retribution was coming. That his sins were about to be judged.

He felt that again, the presence of Death. It watched him.

As quickly as the fear overtook him, it vanished, leaving nary a trace. Eli blinked back his nerves and stepped into his Jeep. DJ Daryl Baker spun another tune from the '80s, and Eli soon drifted back into his memories, as they became more vivid each step he drew nearer to *her*.

THEN

Four months had passed since the night their relationship blossomed into something much more than professional. Marcie celebrated a birthday, turning nineteen. In a short amount of time, she grew up so much. She put aside some of her more revealing and childish clothes and her Goth makeup. Now she dressed respectably, though still as alluring as ever, and had even taken to styling her hair back out of her face, revealing the beauty beneath all that angst. She smiled more these days and so did Eli.

Passion burned bright and they had many late-night romantic rendezvous. The first time they were together after that ruckus at the club, Eli had to sneak into Adrian's compound to be with her. He couldn't lie—the thrill of breaking the rules certainly added to the experience. He felt invincible that night, above Adrian's influence. It felt like he had his life back. That he could be with whoever he wanted.

He wanted to be with Marcie.

As exhilarating as that night was, though, Eli's rational sense quickly returned and the next time they met in secret would mark the beginning of what they jokingly referred to as "The Motel Tour". It became a game, then. Playing hide-and-seek all over town, one waiting for the other to find and claim their prize.

Bodies were adding up in the morgue downtown. Adrian's army was dwindling and rumors of Rufus' consolidation were on everyone's lips. Things were coming to a head, but Eli shoved that aside. He had something in his life now that dwarfed his anxieties.

The Smiths' "Please, Please, Please, Let Me Get What I Want" played on the small alarm clock in the cheap motel room as Eli and Marcie lay in bed, pleasantly exhausted after their latest tryst. Eli traced Marcie's arm, both staring at the ceiling, enjoying the moment. She felt like home in his arms, a return to a simpler life. He felt like any other young man, lying with a beautiful lover.

But in the back of his mind, a dark feeling loomed. As electrified as he felt when he was with Marcie, soon they would be apart, and all the doubts would return. And that awful emptiness.

This isn't right, that voice told him, no matter how hard he tried to ignore it.

Maybe this wasn't right, for a million different reasons, but Eli wanted it—*needed* it—to be right. He was going to die, just like everyone else on Adrian's side. Rufus would make sure of it. Couldn't he have this one thing go right before then? He was angry, but didn't know with whom. Himself? His father's God? Did God exist? Was that the persistent voice weighing on his conscious? *Why can't you let me have this, God? I've never asked you for anything.*

Marcie nuzzled Eli's chest, then glanced at the clock. She swore and rose from the bed. "I gotta get home. I didn't realize how late it was."

Eli watched her, taking in the magnificent glow of her smooth, perfect body. Marcie hurried around the room, hastily redressing. Eli slid out of bed, as well, reaching for his own clothes, slow and deliberate, feeling sick and lonely inside already. The void enveloped him more quickly each time he and Marcie parted. He hated leaving her.

"You know," he said, putting on his jeans and socks, then tying his sneakers, "protecting you has been the best job I ever had."

"Yeah," she smiled, bent over into the mirror, trying to smooth out her tussled hair. "It's been great."

Eli stood, shirtless, and moved to her. His soul ached, and he faced her reflection, seeing his own turn grim and dark. "But you know we can't keep doing this. We're gonna get caught."

Marcie hesitated. She looked his way, then returned her attention to her own face, putting on a fresh touch of lipstick. She smiled, but it seemed insincere. "No, we won't. Don't worry."

He reached for her, interrupting her primp session, and turned her to face him. Her confident grin faltered under his stare. "Marcie, you *know* this can't go on forever."

She jerked from him, crossing the room in a huff and stepping into her shoes. "Where's all this coming from? Aren't you having fun?"

"Yeah," Eli defended, sensing her anger. "But running around and keeping 'us' a secret…it doesn't feel right."

Marcie slipped her jangly earrings into their holes, her face hard. "Keeping secrets doesn't feel right. Funny viewpoint for a hitman."

That hurt, and Eli knew it was meant to. He grabbed his shirt off the floor and put it on. "You know what I mean. If your dad ever found out about us, he'd kill me."

She considered, then moved closer to him, touching his chest and staring into his eyes, restoring his invincibility with a single glance. "But Daddy won't find out."

Oh, how he wanted to believe that. He had no idea how long their relationship would last. He wasn't even sure they'd be involved with one another at all if it *weren't* for the danger. Did Marcie feel the same way about him that he did about her, or was this another one of her games, designed to amuse her and give her a moment's distraction from her dreary existence?

"I'm just having my doubts these days," he spoke, soft and uncertain.

"What do you mean?" she asked, sincere. No games.

Maybe she *did* feel the same. *Please, God, can't I just have this one thing?*

Eli sat on the bed and Marcie joined him, leaning close, listening intently. Ready to help. There was so much he'd kept bottled inside this past year running with Adrian. Secret things that he'd not spoken aloud to anyone. Profound silence settled until Eli finally confessed, "After my parents split, I stopped wanting things."

"What do you mean?"

Eli shook his head. "I was completely empty. I turned into a 'yes' man. I did whatever my Dad wanted, then when I enlisted, I did whatever the Army wanted. Then with your dad… I've never wanted anything for *myself*." He faced her. "Except now. I want *you*."

She grinned.

He touched her face. "And that scares me. Because now I have something to lose. I've made a lot of mistakes, and I'm starting to see how my actions can affect the people I lov— uh, care about."

Marcie stiffened beside him and Eli hated himself for letting that slip. Marcie wasn't looking for love. She was still looking for fun.

But to his surprise, Marcie snuggled closer to him, her cheeks blushing. "I…care about you too."

Eli faced her, and their eyes met. There, in her gaze, he saw the truth. She *did* feel for him. Somewhere in all of the games and lust she had fallen for him just as hard. "Maybe you were right," he grinned, testing her resolve, just to be sure before he finally gave his heart to her fully. "Don't get too attached."

She drank of his eyes, her countenance relaxing. "But I was wrong, Eli. I *am* attached, and it's okay." Marcie paused, but relented. "I love you."

Years of anger, bitterness, and guilt melted away with those three simple words, and Eli kissed her, soft and tender, and he felt afraid and fearless at once. Marcie was shaking in his arms and he admitted he was trembling a little, as well. His future was wrapped up in this girl—his heart would live or die by her command now.

They parted, both smiling, looking the other way. Marcie stifled an embarrassed giggle.

"I'd better go," Eli said, still grinning like an idiot. "I'll pick you up tomorrow."

She nodded, her fingertips brushing against her lips, fondly recalling their kiss.

Eli stood and made to leave. He opened the door, feeling the cool night air meet him, reinvigorating him. He was ready to take on the world now, no matter what came. "By the way," he called over his shoulder, turning back to Marcie, "I love you, too."

Eli left the motel behind, every atom in his body singing. As he made his way to his car, parked some distance off in the shadows, all he could think about was how his life was on track again. It wasn't without its problems, no. He was still seeing Adrian's daughter behind the Old Man's back and that *would* have to be dealt with. But maybe he could just explain it all to Adrian. Eli had been faithful to the family for a while now, had earned his place with hard work and quiet servitude. Adrian might be *glad* that his daughter had chosen Eli over someone like Justin or Joey or any of the trigger-happy apes Adrian had in his army. Eli was determined to take care of Marcie, just as he'd been doing, and Adrian would no doubt see that. Maybe he'd even offer his blessing and suggest that the safest place for Marcie would be out of Willowbrook and away from whatever plans Rufus had cooking and the killer with the skull face. Eli and Marcie could run away, settle down, start a life together.

Free.

Eli hadn't had a dream in a long time, and it felt good. Like purpose. Like providence. Perhaps the God his dad had relied on really *was* looking out for him after all.

A snap sounded in the bushes, and Eli had his hand around his back, under his brother's leather jacket, where his SIG 229 waited for him. He listened for more noises. Heard a strange gurgle. A dark shadow crossed his soul, dampening Eli's spirit.

"Who's there?" he asked, but the noises had stopped.

The cold presence passed by, too, and Eli relaxed his grip on his gun.

Jumping at shadows, Eli. Relax. Probably just a cat or something.

He unlocked his car, calm returning, and headed home.

When Eli arrived home that night, he discovered James sitting on Dad's porch swing, headphones on. He had his eyes closed, immersed in his music, bobbing his head and singing along, "We are the world…we are the children…"

Eli raised an eyebrow. Cleared his throat and stomped lightly on the floor of the porch.

James opened an eye and jumped clear out of the swing. "Oh! Shoot, dude."

Eli passed him, headed for the door, amused. Regaining his cool, James straightened the camo cargo pants he wore and took his headphones off. "Gettin' in kinda late for a school night, don't you think?"

"I've been busy."

"*I'll* say. Ever since Adrian put you on 'babysitting detail', I hardly ever see ya."

It was a good-natured complaint, but Eli understood the truth behind it. Marcie had taken up so much of his life for the last few months, he'd shoved everything else aside—including his best friend. He huffed, trying to play it cool, "Jealous?"

"Shyeah! Of *you*! She's a hottie." James traced the outline of an hourglass figure in the air, and Eli groaned. Then, wiggling his brow, James leaned in, his voice low and salacious. "So…you two done the…uh—"

"Stop," Eli interrupted. "Right there."

James laughed, "Hey, aren't best friends supposed to know the dirty details of each other's love lives?"

"Not when said details can get one or more of them killed."

Eli turned for the door, ready to be done with the conversation. He had missed James—no matter how obnoxious he could be sometimes—and was having fun with this playful banter, but James was cutting closer to the truth than he realized. If word got back to Adrian—

"You don't honestly believe all that crap about Adrian killing anyone who touches his daughter, do you?" James chuckled as Eli pulled his keys from his pocket. "I think every father in *the world* uses that line. Theresa's dad was always like—" James puffed out his chest and did his best gruff drill sergeant impersonation, for that's what Theresa's dad was. "*—Boy, I will peel your eyeballs like grapes if you ever touch my little girl.*"

Eli smiled. With his dramatic reenactment finished, James snorted, "Of course, that never stopped me."

"It's late. I'm going to bed."

"I was gonna head down to *Charley's* for a drink. Come with. We can talk woman troubles."

"Nah, I'm spent."

"All right, fine," James sighed, as though his heart were broken. "Keep the good stuff to yourself." Turning serious for a moment—a rare feat for James Lenderman—the man faced Eli, his look betraying a hint of fear. "Look, personally, I don't care if you're dating the Boss' daughter or not. But just be careful in case half of what they're saying about Marcon is true."

But it won't be like that, Eli thought. *Adrian will understand. I've got this in the bag.*

"I will," he replied, serious as well.

With that business out of the way, James resumed his jovial tone. "Oh, and try not to get me killed in the process, if you don't mind. Theresa's got the kid on the way and we're still fighting over what to name it."

"Deal." Eli grinned and opened the door to his house. "Good night."

"Good night, lover boy," James saluted and jogged down the porch steps.

Eli closed the door behind him and rested his head against the frame. Things were worse than he thought. He had to make his move soon or else word would get out before he had a chance to explain. The thought of facing Adrian and telling him that he loved his daughter was petrifying, but one thing was clear now: Eli couldn't keep living in secrecy anymore.

It's time this ended.

CHAPTER TEN

The day after their declaration of love, Eli was tasked with going to the morgue.

Ian had been brutally murdered the night before.

The coroner, a husky, hairy man who seemed to be gnawing on a sandwich whenever Eli saw him, opened the door to the back room and stood aside. Chill refrigeration splashed against Eli's face and he pulled his suit coat a little tighter around him.

"Go on in," the coroner invited in between chews, dribbling a little lettuce on the floor.

Two lines of sheet-covered bodies waited for him, and Eli moved into their midst, slow and cautious, eyeing each corpse as if it were going to rise up and lash out at him. Adrian had many friends on the police force—some of them had even gotten their start as teenagers making money drops or serving as muscle for the Old Man. The coroner was on Adrian's payroll, too, and placed a call first thing this morning when Ian turned up.

Eli had been to the morgue only a handful of times before today—each time summoned to take a look at one of their own, to draw his own conclusions for the family instead of exclusively relying on what the police wanted the public to know. Most times Adrian took the word of his boys in blue, but *Ian's* death… Well, Adrian thought it warranted a personal investigation.

The bodies at his right and left brought the reality of his life into perspective for Eli. Soon, he feared, he'd be another anonymous stiff, draped in a white sheet. Another cold slab of meat.

It suddenly struck him that Alex and Dad had both been through here.

I'll be with them soon. Rufus will see to it.

"It's that one down there," the coroner called out in his raspy voice, closing the door behind him.

Carefully, Eli approached the body.

"Cops brought him in this morning," the coroner explained loudly, sidling up to the body. He continued munching on the sandwich. "Go on. Lift it up."

Eli's palms began to sweat. Gently, he pinched the edge of the white sheet at Ian's head and pulled down.

Eli jumped, a gut response, but he centered himself, fighting to calm his rapid breathing.

"Yeah," the portly man next to him sighed. "Pretty bad, I know."

Pretty bad didn't cover it. Ian's head was twisted at a 230° angle, his spine snapped and grotesquely protruding underneath bruised skin. Below his neck was even more carnage—a hole about the size of a silver dollar punched clean through the man's chest, splintering his sternum. As soon as the information registered, Eli draped the cloth back over the body, shaken.

"What did that?" he asked, resisting the urge to vomit.

The coroner finished a mouthful of sandwich and swallowed. "The puncture wound we've ID'd as being inflicted with a rifle that we found at the scene."

"A bullet couldn't have torn through him like that," Eli hotly protested. "Not unless it was, like, an elephant gun—"

The coroner laughed gruffly. "No, no. He wasn't shot. He was *stabbed* with the rifle."

Eli paled, and the man continued, "Yep. The thing was shoved right through him. Like I said, we found a rifle by the body, covered in blood with some of this guy's inside stuck down the barrel. You know, like if you jab a straw through a potato?"

Eli's knees felt weak and he thought he might need to sit down. Ian wasn't a good man, but he didn't deserve this.

Is this what's going to happen to me?

"Did...did you find his hat?" Seeing Ian's bald head naked like that, he thought the man would have wanted his dignity. Would have wanted his cowboy hat with him, to ride off with him to wherever it was he had gone.

The coroner blinked back at him. "No. Didn't see a hat."

Eli looked down at the lump under the sheet, imagining his own face beneath it.

"Only thing is," the coroner said, "Can't tell if the chest wound was inflicted before or after he nearly got his head torn off his shoulders. Still trying to figure *that* out."

Rufus couldn't have done this, Eli reasoned. For one thing, it wasn't the guy's M.O. He just would've had Ian shot, not mangled like some animal. He thought of the weirdo with the skull face in Malcolm's death video. Who was he? What did he want, other than wanton destruction?

Or was that it?

Adrian's men were dying by the truckload. *He's getting closer. I'm not going to get away...*

"Where did you find him?" Eli asked.

"In the parking lot at that one motel, what is it, the Ultra 8? Off Bannister."

Eli froze. That was the place he and Marcie had met last night.

The gurgle in the bushes. The snap.

He'd heard Ian die.

What was Ian doing there with a rifle? Did he see Eli and Marcie together? *Did he know?* And did he tell anyone, or did he take that secret to the grave?

Worse, if the "skull man" was responsible for this, that meant he had stood mere feet from Eli. He was moving in.

"I've seen enough." He walked for the door.

"Hey, kid," the coroner called him back. For the first time, the cavalier corpse dealer stopped chomping on his sandwich, and his expression turned grim. "Pretty nasty business you boys are wrapped up in. I know we aren't supposed to say much, seeing as how Mr. Marcon takes care of a lot of us, but…you sure there's not something *else* you could be doing with your life?"

Eli thought about that, but did not have an answer.

His cell phone beeped with a text message. Eli checked it. It was from Domingo and read: WE HAVE TO TALK. NOW. WE KNOW ABOUT MARCIE.

Oh no…

Stan escorted Eli into Domingo's drab office, then excused himself and closed the door with a malicious sneer. Eli glared at him, then faced Domingo. The stylish man stood with his back to the entrance, looking out the window. The silence was thick and palpable, coating Eli's tongue.

Yet, Eli did not see Adrian.

Long seconds passed, and he considered clearing his throat or giving some other indication that he had arrived, but he knew better. Domingo knew he was here—he was just letting him stew.

"Are you nervous, Eli?" the man finally probed, reflective, still not facing him.

Eli considered telling the truth, but he didn't know how much Domingo knew of his relationship with Marcie. Perhaps there was some way of salvaging this situation if he played it cool. Without invitation, he took a seat in one of the chairs facing Domingo's desk. "No. Why?"

Domingo remained standing with his hands clasped behind his back, watching the traffic outside. "Your friend James. He has a big mouth."

Eli couldn't argue. It was James' big mouth that brought Adrian to Kylie's doorstep in the first place nearly a year ago. In some way, it was only thanks to James' big mouth that he was in this trap at all.

"I know," Eli said at length.

"He also can't hold his liquor. Funny thing, Stan and Lee were at *Charley's* last night. They tell me your friend was getting properly squiffed. He starts divulging things, things that maybe he ought to keep to himself."

Eli felt a sinking feeling in his stomach, like the bottom of his boat had just fallen out.

"What...what did Adrian say?" he asked.

Domingo lifted his head, watching the sun-bathed sky. "I've not told him."

"What?"

At last Domingo regarded the young man, his demeanor relaxing. He circled his desk and took a seat, reclining and crossing his fingers over his stomach. "This family has a lot of respect for you, Eli, so I'll cut to the chase. Your good friend James claims you and Marcie are...*more than friends*, shall we say. I heard it from Stan and Lee, myself. When James told them, they laughed. They couldn't believe you would be so stupid. But, see, I know better."

"Look, I—"

"It's my job to protect Mr. Marcon and his interests, and I think this development couldn't have come at a worse time. He has enough to worry about without your indiscretions. Truth is, what's past is past, and I understand that. Nothing you can do about that now. What we have here, though, is a problem. While you've been off lollygagging with the Boss' daughter, our boys have been dropping like flies and, so far, no one has found the man responsible. Mr. Marcon's resolve is crumbling, and the last thing he needs is a reason to take out his most loyal man. We need you out there, trying to find the guys doing this. So, whatever you are or *are not* doing with Marcie is just going to have to wait."

Eli's heart rate slowed. "I understand."

"To be honest, it doesn't matter to me if you're dating Marcie, but just in case you're wondering about all the talk of Mr. Marcon breaking the kneecaps of any man who'd lay a hand on his sweet, pure, innocent little girl..." Domingo grinned, a hint of mischief in his eye. "It's all true. Therefore, think of this as your one and only warning. Whatever you're doing with Marcie, stop it. Don't see her, don't talk to her, stay away from her. We've got a war here—one you helped start, by the way—and we don't need our best man with his head in the clouds over some puppy love affair. You do that for me, and Mr. Marcon will never have to know. Are you reading me?"

Eli nodded quickly.

"Now get out of here. And let's not have this conversation again."

Marcie waited for Eli in the alley behind the club where they'd shared their first kiss. When Eli arrived, she was staring at the full moon above, lost in thought. Eli hung back for a moment, admiring her beauty in the soft blue hues of night. He'd arranged this meeting for one purpose, but his heart rebelled against him at the last moment.

Still, Domingo was right. There were things going on in the shadows of Willowbrook that required his full concentration if he wanted to survive. Maybe after this freak was found and hung by his toes, maybe then things could be different.

Yeah, Eli reasoned. *That's all this is. We're not ending things, just putting them on hold.*

He stepped closer to her, prepared to say something, but stopped short when he saw Marcie's uplifted face. She looked different tonight than he'd ever seen her. She looked haunted and small, like she was in serious trouble and had no idea how to save herself. Eli had seen Marcie in a number of lights—he'd seen her at her best and her worst, he believed. But now, he saw something new in her. He couldn't name it, but he pitied her and felt suddenly worried about what the future held for her. He wanted to hold her and shelter her from the world, to rescue her from whatever trap she'd walked into.

What is it?

"Hey!" she beamed, suddenly catching sight of him. "There you are!"

Instantly, her moment of truth shattered, and her happy plastic mask was back on. As much as he felt he knew her, Eli now understood just how much she kept hidden from him.

She raced forward, throwing her arms up to catch him in an embrace, but he gently lowered them to her side.

"What's wrong?" She searched him, her eyes relaying hurt.

"I can't see you anymore."

"*What?*"

"They know, Marcie."

Realization sunk in. Tentatively, she asked, "Does…Daddy?"

Eli shook his head. "Domingo said he wouldn't tell as long as I broke things off."

Marcie nodded, mulling the news over. Anger slowly kindled in her eyes. "How did he find out?"

"James."

"But I thought he was supposed to be your best friend!" Marcie shouted at him. The anger in her eyes burst into full flame, lighting up her face. "Why would he go and tell on us like that?"

"I don't know. It doesn't really matter anymore."

"So, what?" she snapped, crossing her arms. "So, you can give me up just like that?"

"That's not fair. I love you. But I don't know what else I can *do*."

Marcie lowered her head, slowing her breathing, calming. After a moment, she lifted her eyes, quiet and strange. "Do you really love me? Do you really want to be with me?"

"Of course. Why would you even ask me that?"

"Then we have to save ourselves," Marcie declared, cold and professional. "We have to eliminate the problem."

Eli blanched. "What's *that* supposed to mean?"

Marcie touched his chest, sympathetic. "I know he's your best friend, but he double-crossed you. James is the only thing standing in our way. If Domingo doesn't have an informant, he won't know if you don't stop seeing me. I know you won't like the idea but..."

She trailed off, but her expression told him everything.

Eli flinched, snarling at her. "What? You want me to—" he lowered his voice, casting paranoid glances down the alley entrance, "—*kill James?*"

"He'll kill *us*, Eli, if you don't."

He took a step back, glaring at her. He'd seen Marcie in some twisted moments, it was true, but this...*This?*

She's nuts.

Disgusted, Eli laughed. "That's just great. You want me to kill Stan and Lee while I'm at it? How about Domingo? We can just take on the whole family, you want that?"

"I don't want that," she protested matter-of-factly. "Domingo's a valuable asset, but James—"

"How can you *talk* like that?"

Marcie turned away, refusing to face him. Muttering, she said, "Why would you have to kill Stan and Lee?"

"That's not even the point!"

She faced him, all business. "Did James tell them too?"

Eli sighed, giving up. "Yes."

Marcie hurried to him, clinging to his leather jacket and staring up at him, her eyes begging him to kiss her. Despite the madness she was speaking, he wanted to. "We have to eliminate our obstacles," she pleaded. "I can't lose you *now*."

A war waged within Eli, with a part of him focused on nothing more than keeping Marcie close to him, and another part replaying memory after memory of his younger years, running around and getting into good-natured trouble with Alex and James. Ricocheting images flashed through his brain, of Alex, of Marcie, of his dad, of Kylie, a whirlwind of events that had led him to this moment. He had already given up, already realized that he'd never be one of the good guys, but double-crossing a friend for no more than the sin of being a sloppy drunk was a line he couldn't cross. Even without James' loose lips, his affair with Marcie had been leading to an eventual end from the moment it began. And much as he cared about her, when he looked at her now, he could see no more than a confused, broken tangle of a person who needed help.

Help that he was not in a position to give.

He pulled her off him. "Enough. It's over."

Fed up, Eli tromped out of the alley, his heart burdened.

"Eli!" Marcie screamed, but he did not reply.

CHAPTER ELEVEN

The Marshall Tucker Band's "Can't You See" played on the jukebox at *Charley's*. Eli sat alone at the bar—his suit coat unbuttoned, his tie undone—nursing his second beer of the night. He'd really done it. He'd broken up with Marcie. Leaving her had opened up a black hole in his heart, and it scared him to realize that she'd become his reason for waking up in the morning. Maybe the separation was good. It was time that he finally figured out who he was. Away from Dad, his brother, Marcie—all of them. He needed to be Eli for once. Just Eli.

"Hey, man," a voice greeted him softly.

Eli looked up and saw James taking a seat next to him. Frowning, he returned to his drink.

James ordered a beer and dug at the bar with a fingernail. "Man, I'm sorry. I didn't know Stan would say anything. We were just sharing drinks and talking, and it… I should never have opened my big mouth."

"I don't want to talk about it."

James shifted on the stool uncomfortably. "Listen, that's not the only reason I came. Domingo's been trying to get in touch with you all night."

Eli swigged his beer and answered in a bitter tone, "I turned off my phone."

"Sorry, pal, but we're on the clock. There's been another hit."

Eli turned sharply, immediately fearing it was Marcie. *I should have been there. I should have protected her. I never should have left.* "Who?"

"Justin."

Eli cooled, his heart rate returning to a steady beat. "What happened?"

"His arm was torn off. His chest caved in, like a cement block landed on it from two stories up."

Eli turned back to the bar, gazing into his beer bottle. In his mind's eye, he replayed Malcolm's video and saw the brutal slayer with the skull face. Saw poor Ian in the morgue. "Same guy did it?"

"I'm thinking it has to be. It fits his style. But there's more."

Turning, Eli eyed him. "I'm listening."

"It happened in one of Rufus' loading bays across town. The cops responded pretty fast. Made one arrest. Someone else was there, but managed to skip out unharmed. Cops let him go, though, because they couldn't find anything on him. Adrian wants us to go question him ourselves."

"Who is it?" Eli said.

James took a breath and leveled Eli with a powerful stare. "Eli, it's…Benny."

Eli stiffened.

Benny the Squeal. The guy who killed Alex.

James said somberly, "I'm supposed to come with you. You know, to make sure you don't do anything stupid again."

Eli huffed and took a long drink from the bottle. "Why send me at all? Why not Stan and Lee?"

"You kidding me?" James laughed.

Eli shrugged. "Okay. See your point."

"If…if you can't do this, I'll go by myself."

Eli finished off his beer and sat the empty bottle down noisily on the counter. "No." He rubbed his eyes, willing himself back into hitman mode. "I'm good. Let's go have a talk with Benny."

Eli sat in the darkened parked Porsche, fixing his tie, then tapping his gloved hands against the steering wheel. He took note of the time, his stomach flip-flopping. Not yet ready to leave the safety of the vehicle, Eli just continued to stew and watch the house through his windshield. The place wasn't much to look at, just a house that matched all its neighbors in a nice-enough part of Willowbrook. There were families on this street, middle-class types that had no idea what kind of scum shared their block with them.

Inside was Benny the Squeal—a small player with a big mouth. Adrian had made it clear that Eli wasn't to make a move against Benny, but that didn't mean he hadn't done his homework on the guy over the last year. Benny was barely into his twenties and never worked a day in his life. He had always lived with his ailing grandma, selling drugs in the back room while she watched *Judge Judy*, oblivious to her grandson's illegal activities. When the old girl passed a couple months ago, she left Benny the house and her savings. From everything Eli could dig up, the guy just loafed about, eating pizza, watching TV, and offering his home to other unsavory types.

The way Eli heard it from Stan and some of the other guys who had been with Adrian for a long time, there was a time when the Squeal was an informant for Marcon. An earthworm who "knew" things, at a price. The kid had an ego the size of Atlanta, and he was just plain annoying to boot. Adrian only tolerated him because, every now and again, the kid came through.

Except, that was before Benny flopped sides. Before he killed Alex.

"You sure you're okay with this?" James asked for the umpteenth time.

"Of course I am."

"Then…why are we just sitting out here? Shouldn't we go in? No offense, but I kinda need to get this show rolling. I told Theresa I'd meet her for Lamaze class tonight."

Eli fixed him with a sidelong glance. "Lamaze class?"

James chuckled. "Yeah, she says she wants me to play a more 'active role' in the birth of our child."

"You are so whipped." Eli rubbed his tired eyes, a headache looming somewhere inside his skull. Amiable silence followed, until Eli spoke. "Well, I guess you got what you wanted."

"How's that?"

"Here we are. Working for Boss Marcon."

"Yeah," James said quietly. He frowned and looked out the window at Benny's house.

"Is it everything you hoped for?"

"Is anything?"

Eli supposed not. James looked at him, that same earnest expression he wore at *Charley's* back on his face. "I really *am* sorry, dude. About everything."

"I know you are." Eli let that settle in the air, perhaps the closest he'd ever come to forgiving James for the times he'd blabbed and brought trouble down on him. "We'd better go."

Eli and James left the car behind and scurried for the house, shaded by darkness. Eli felt the weight of the gun underneath his jacket. He shivered off his nerves and kept careful watch on the surrounding night. He nodded to James. James returned the gesture, drew his Beretta, and stacked up against the side of the door, sticking to their military training.

It was an odd moment, but Eli felt himself suddenly waxing philosophical. Other than the adrenaline pumping through his veins, he felt nothing—just a cold, mechanical drive that kept him moving through the task at hand. He recalled that his father had fought in Vietnam, but never told his boys any war stories. The brothers would stay up long past their bedtime, dreaming up heroic adventures of Dad fighting a one-man war against Charlie, but the elder Ross didn't like to speak about Vietnam, except to say that he had to shut off a part of himself to get through. Eli understood now what his father meant.

Keeping his gun holstered, Eli stepped to the side door of Benny's house and rapped with a black-gloved fist.

"Who is it?" Benny's muffled voice sounded suspicious from the other side.

"Pizza," Eli sang, trading preparatory glances with James.

Two beats later, the door opened, revealing Benny—a thick guy with a dark Beatles-style mop top. The confusion on his face was quickly replaced by startled fear when he locked eyes with Eli. "*Holy*—"

Benny turned tail and retreated deep into his late grandmother's house. Eli entered without invitation, and James followed, gun drawn, sights lined up. Eli sauntered through the place, noticing Benny had kept all his deceased grandmother's decorations in the kitchen—except for the pile of smack on the table. That was probably new.

"Benny, Benny, Benny," Eli droned, projecting his voice across the house, relishing the youth's fear. Crossing into the living room, he spotted a glass bowl filled with M&Ms. Eli took the dish and dug around for a red one. "Y'know, Adrian's got a problem and I hear you're the guy who might have the solution."

Eli and James followed Benny into the back bedroom, entering a haze of pot smoke. Benny knocked over a small center table, spilling an ash tray and a pile of joint butts onto the stained carpet. The youth crawled on his knees, plunging his hand deep under the bed's mattress and pulling out a .38 Special. Whirling, with fear in his eyes, he wagged the revolver at Eli.

It'd been a while since Eli had a gun pointed at him and he felt simultaneously afraid and outraged. Instinctively, he used the bowl to knock the gun away, then brought the dish down hard on Benny's face.

The glass did not break, though the same could not be said for Benny's nose. Blood exploded out of his nostrils, covering his lips, and he let out a surprised yelp before collapsing backwards on the bed. M&Ms rained everywhere and Eli raised the glass bowl and hit him again, his adrenaline surging. Benny's .38 dropped to the floor and Eli's fear slowly subsided.

James shrunk back, lowering his gun just a bit. "Eli…"

Benny rose off the bed, clutching his broken proboscis. "I don't owe you or Adrian *anything!*"

Discarding the bloodied candy dish, Eli forced himself to calm. He was the clear-headed one. That was what Adrian liked; that was what had kept him alive this long.

Through clenched teeth, Eli said, "Somebody is killing off Adrian's lieutenants, and I'm thinking your buddy Rufus is behind it."

"But he didn't do it!"

Eli hit him again with a tight right fist, then grabbed the kid by the collar, thinking of all the ways he could murder this boy for killing Alex. "Help me out here, Benny. You don't have to die unless you want to. We all know you were there when Justin died. Did *you* kill him?"

"What? What, no! I swear!"

Another punch, this one knocking loose Benny's front tooth.

"I'm telling you the truth!" Benny blubbered, his face smashed. "It's not Rufus!" Despite his hatred for Benny, Eli was beginning to believe him. "...But I know who did it."

Eli let go of the youth and straightened. "Name."

"He doesn't *have* a name! He's a shadow—*a phantom!*"

James stepped forward, entering the conversation. "What were you doing with Justin tonight?"

"H-He asked to meet me! He wanted to throw in with Rufus. I met him to talk business, but then this thing shows up! Y-You wouldn't believe it! He was like a giant and he had a blue skull face! He got to Justin, and I barely made it out! I don't know who he was, but I swear it wasn't Rufus."

Eli backed away and Benny scrambled further onto the bed like the frightened child he was.

"He's like the bogeyman," Benny said.

Eli tightened his jaw and stepped forward, burning with rage. This was the man who killed his brother? Some punk dopehead?

James reached out and touched Eli's arm. "Eli, come on. We got all we're gonna get."

Eli turned his back on the frightened boy and headed for the door, but Benny called after him. "Eli? *You're* Eli? Alex's brother?"

Eli slowly pivoted. James looked between Eli and Benny, his eyes wide with fearful expectation.

Sweat formed on Benny's head. "Man, I heard you were looking for me a while back. Dude, I just want to say that I'm sorry about your brother. It wasn't personal. You gotta believe me! Alex was a friend of mine."

Eli faced the kid, his anger boiling. "Friends don't turn on each other."

Benny retreated an inch back on his bed. "He wanted to flip. He came to me—"

"Liar! Alex would never sell out Adrian."

"I swear! We talked about it for months. But he got cold feet at the last minute. I had orders! If I didn't kill him, Rufus would have killed *me*! You gotta beli—"

Eli put two slugs in Benny's head before the youth could finish his sentence.

The kid slumped forward, then tumbled to the floor, so much dead meat.

James screamed, *"Are you out of your mind?"*

But Eli tuned his friend out. He stepped up to Benny's corpse and regarded the body coolly, though his blood was hot fire in his veins. His hand trembled at the sight of what he'd done. If Adrian found out...

I'm going to die, he realized.

James paced across the room, frantic. "I can't believe you did that! What are we going to do? Do you know what Adrian is going to do to you? To *us?*"

Eli holstered his gun. "We'll take care of the body."

James ran his fingers through his short hair, tears welling in his manic eyes. "Dude... *What are we gonna do?!*"

Eli gripped his friend and forced him to meet his eyes. "James. Are you with me?"

"What? You ask me if—" He cooled. "Yeah. Yeah, dude, I'm with you. But, Eli...Man..."

CHAPTER TWELVE

Weeks passed. Eli and James properly disposed of the body, but did it in silence. After the grim deed was done, James told Eli that he thought they should keep their distance from each other for a while. After all, James had a family to think about.

And Eli, well, Eli had nothing. No one. Not anymore.

He desperately wanted to tell Marcie what had happened with Benny, but he wasn't even sure he could explain it. Maybe it was the pain of breaking up, maybe it was a redirection of his anger towards James. Maybe it was just the disgust he felt when he saw what a worthless punk had gotten the jump on Alex. Or, he considered, maybe he just wanted to do something so desperate—unpredictable, just like Marcie—to force Adrian's hand. Eli wanted to die. His life didn't matter anymore. What did he have to live for?

Nevertheless, he ignored Marcie's calls and tried not to feel hurt and betrayed when she left angry messages damning him for being a coward and giving up on the best thing either of them had. It was hell not seeing her, but he needed time to think.

Eli spent a weary Tuesday morning "on tour", visiting Adrian's investments, convincing them that, in spite of the recent murders, Adrian was still in charge and they had no reason to jump ship and run to Rufus for protection. Eli did his best to appeal to their sense of loyalty and nostalgia, bringing to recollection all the good Adrian had done for their business and the town, in general. In keeping with Adrian's preferences, Eli had a partner during his meetings. Unable to bring himself to call James, though, Eli brought Joey on board for this assignment. Joey was a skinny crackhead with wild Albert Einstein hair, dyed blond. He had a major Sid Vicious obsession and shot his mouth off too much. But even a guy like Joey knew when to stay silent and let Eli do the talking. Eli's presence carried a lot of weight in Willowbrook's underworld. That little Laundromat incident back in the day had garnered him a reputation for being a guy who got things done. Adrian's partners knew him as the brave one, the devout company man whom Adrian trusted explicitly.

Joey served his purpose during their meetings, and Eli believed the two of them had relieved a lot of minds that morning. Which was good, he supposed, though he, himself, had no such guarantees. Adrian's empire was crumbling fast, and cops and criminals alike were not a step closer to discovering Benny's "phantom".

Eli couldn't help but think of Marcie and wonder what would happen to her if the killer finally reached Adrian.

"I'm hungry," Joey grumbled in the passenger seat of Eli's Porsche on their way back from the last stop of the morning's tour. "Pull over."

Eli spotted a donut café and parked on the curb. Joey got out, slipping into his tattered coat to conceal the Magnums holstered to his chest. He stretched. "Man, I'm glad that's over. This junk is boring."

Eli stepped out and entered the shoppe behind Joey. A young woman and a little boy, maybe four or five years old, were the only patrons. Eli took a seat, facing the window, as he never put his back to a window or door, another leftover trait from Afghanistan. Joey, meanwhile, headed for the counter, calling out his order, buying a large and colorful assortment of donuts.

Eli watched the traffic pass by, the soft strumming of acoustic coffeehouse music floating down from speakers overhead. He and his partner were getting some uneasy looks from the young mother, and he couldn't blame her. Joey's coat was adorned with fire-breathing topless women, and his earlobes were stretched around rings so large that a Buick could fit in them. Plus, the guy had no "inside voice". Eli tried to smile at the woman, to ease her worries, but she averted his glance and told her son to hurry and finish his sprinkled cream-filled donut.

Eli frowned.

From the street, tires squalled, and Eli's eyes cut hard to the front glass. A suped-up Caddy screeched to a stop. The dark-tinted windows rolled down low enough to allow the barrels of two submachine guns to peek out.

"Joey!" Eli shouted, falling backwards in his chair and bringing up his table to use as a shield.

Bullets shattered the glass, chewing up the shoppe. Eli flinched against the bang and glanced towards the counter. Joey hurled himself over the top, but the skinny man at the cash register took two rounds to the chest and neck. He gurgled in a spray of blood and collapsed.

Lead rained down, and Eli knew he needed to reach for his gun, but fear and shock kept him frozen. Through squinting eyes, he saw the mother across the café. She'd been hit in the shoulder and was on the floor, bleeding heavily. Her little boy huddled behind their booth, his hands over his ears, screaming in blind terror at the top of his lungs.

"Stay there!" Eli hollered to the kid, though his words were drowned out in the bedlam.

At last, the shooting stopped, and the boy cried hysterically.

Joey shouted from his hiding place behind the counter. "Eli? You still alive?"

"Yeah! The woman's been hit!"

"Clerk, too," Joey called back. "He's a stiff."

"Call an ambulance."

"Uh...are you sure that's—?"

"*Do it!*"

Eli heard the soft electronic beep of Joey's phone. Heard him muttering the basic outline of the incident to the 9-1-1 operator. He hung up before the operator had a chance to ask too many questions.

"You're going to be okay," Eli told the woman, preparing to move to her side, when he heard crunching glass.

A man's baritone voice cut in through the woman's sobbing. "Eli Ross."

Eli peeked through a hole in the table, saw three guys standing just inside the ruined glass wall, wearing stocking masks over their faces. In their hands, they carried AK-47s.

"How many?" Joey shouted. "Two or three?"

Eli did not answer. Just watched the gunmen and prayed that they didn't shoot the mother out of pure spite.

"Rufus has a message for you," the leader with the deep, booming voice relayed. "He said Benny was pond scum. Why don't you pick on someone your own size?"

"What's he talking about?" Joey again.

No way. Eli panicked. Killing Benny had been out of line and completely unprofessional, but Eli's sloppiness had ended there. He *hid* that body. Rubbed down Benny's grandma's house and left it clean of fingerprints. There was simply no way anyone could have learned about that.

The mother on the ground wept, her blood everywhere, her son traumatized.

I did this. I keep doing this...

"Three!" Eli finally hollered to Joey.

Without hesitating, Eli pulled out his SIG 229 and stood, firing at the center shooter, while, simultaneously, Joey rose out of hiding, dual .44 Magnums in his hands. In tandem with Eli's precision, Joey fired on the flanking goons. Rufus' three messengers hit the tile floor together.

"Woo!" Joey shrilled, holstering his revolvers and clapping his hands. He hopped over the counter, exhilarated. "Money shot, sucka! That was awesome!"

Eli half-crawled, half-slid to the woman and put his hand over her entry wound, pressing down hard. She'd lost a lot of blood, and her skin was paling.

"Come on, man!" Joey said, stepping over the bodies and heading for the car as sounds of sirens emerged in the distance. "We gotta go!"

The woman stared up at Eli, her mouth open in a soundless plea, her eyes expressing uncertainty and horror. Eli had no idea if she'd make it. With emergency responders almost here, she had as good a shot as any, unless the bullet had hit a major artery, in which case, her little boy would never go out for donuts with her again.

"Come *on*!" Joey shouted and cursed.

Eli waved the boy over. "Come here."

The boy did, still sobbing. Eli gently took his dimpled hands and placed them over his mother's wound. "Press as hard as you can right here, okay?" Eli said. "Don't take your hands off her until the doctors come get her. Okay?"

The boy did not nod, but did as he was told. Eli looked one last time at the mother. "I'm sorry."

Joey was jumping up and down, banging on the top of the car. "They're almost here! Hurry it up or I'm leaving you behind!"

Eli holstered his gun and raced outside. As he and Joey sped away, he saw the ambulance arriving at the café.

Eli burst through the door to Domingo's office without invitation, catching the Englishman in the middle of a phone call. Domingo put a finger to his earpiece, said, "Listen, Robert, I'll have to call you back," and disconnected the line.

Domingo's receptionist followed Eli close behind, exasperated. "I'm sorry, sir—"

"It's all right, dear," he said, waving her back.

Darla fumed, but looked relieved not to be in trouble. Exiting, she shut the door behind her, leaving Eli and Domingo alone.

Eli still had the mother's blood on his hands and shirt.

"What's going on?" Eli shouted, but Domingo just placed his hands in his pockets, relaxed. "Rufus' guys just shot at me—in broad daylight!"

"Eli," he gestured to the chair. "Please, have a seat."

Eli landed in the seat, bouncing the ball of his foot. Domingo circled him, patient and collected as ever. Eli didn't have time for his middle management games. Domingo was a mouthpiece, locked up in his stuffy little office, making calls and balancing books all day. He didn't know what it was like out there. He didn't have people shooting at him.

"We've hit a bit of snag," Domingo said, coming to a stand in front of Eli.

Standing over him. "Our little friend Benny was found face-up in the river with a bullet in his head."

Then it's true. Scenarios raced through Eli's mind. What had gone wrong? How did they find out? *Who* found out? *What do I do now?*

For the moment, he remained silent.

Domingo continued, "Word's got out to Rufus, too, and he's not too happy, as you are already painfully aware."

"Yeah," Eli muttered, thinking of the small boy he may have well left motherless. "I picked up on that."

Slowly, as though he were mulling over some puzzling conundrum, Domingo paced back to the other side of his desk, his back to Eli. He allowed a heavy silence to fill to the very corners of the room, until, at length, he turned again to face him. Placing a hand on the back of his plush leather chair, Domingo cocked his head, inquisitive. Domingo never raised his voice or gave any indication of anger, but his tone was definitely one of *displeasure.* "Now maybe you can clarify something for me. We sent you to Benny's to investigate. Murder was not part of the job."

Eli hung his head. So, this was how it was going to end. He wondered if Domingo would shoot him, himself, or if the well-dressed man would consider that distasteful.

"Marcie," Domingo began, and Eli's ears perked up at the sound of her name. His heart ached with the knowledge that he'd never get to be with her again. Now he hated himself for bowing down to Domingo's wishes and staying away from her these last few weeks. If he'd only known he had mere weeks to live, anyway, he would have lived them to the fullest with her.

"Marcie tells me that *James* shot him."

Eli's breath caught. *Marcie, what are you doing?* He saw her hand in this now, and understood that she was giving him an opportunity to save himself and return to her. After all the hateful things she'd said, she was still fighting for their love, in her own way.

"So, which is it, Eli?" Domingo asked gently, coaxing him, as Dad had done in his childhood when Eli had broken something but was too afraid to confess. "What happened?"

Sweat formed on Eli's brow, his heart pulsing so hard his stomach felt sore. *This is it,* he heard Marcie screaming in his ear. *Here's your shot! Don't throw your life away! James betrayed you first. Save yourself!*

"It was…"

Eli saw his dad in his mind's eye. That good hardworking man who never complained about his lot in life but believed in earning his keep and taking his lumps. He'd been screwed over by life or God or whoever, but he held his own and died with dignity. His dad wasn't a coward and certainly wouldn't have thrown his best friend under the bus to save himself from the repercussions of his own mistakes.

What would his dad say?

He didn't know. His dad was dead. Alex was dead. Everyone was dead, but Eli didn't *want* to die.

"James," he lied, nearly blurting out his friend's name. Stammering now, he rambled, "J-James shot him. Things got heated with Benny and James pulled the trigger. H-He didn't mean to. It just…happened."

Domingo sighed, as though sincerely grieved, and Eli felt ready to vomit. "That's what I was afraid of."

The man dialed his phone and held a finger to the piece in his ear, turning away from his guest. Eli waited in the silence, deaf from the blood rushing in his ears. After a second, Domingo responded into the receiver mike, "Yes, it's me, sir. Yes. No, he said it was James. Yes, sir, just like Marcie said. I understand. I know, sir."

Domingo hung up the phone and took a seat behind his desk, leaning back, steepling his long, manicured fingers together. "Mr. Marcon has come to a decision. He hates to do this, what with our numbers being shortened as of late, but James has to be disciplined."

"…You mean *kill* him."

Of course he means that. What did you think? Did you think they were just going to talk to him?

"Your friend's not very reliable, Eli. He slips up a lot. He needs to be let go."

Desperate, Eli leaned in, pleading, "Mr. Domingo, you can't do this. He's about to be a father! He's just starting out. I know he messed up, but he won't mess up again."

"I understand he's your friend, and I would have Joey do it. But the truth is, we can't find Joey."

"But I just left him a half hour ago."

"That may be true, but he's not returning our calls or texts. Mr. Marcon wants a speedy resolution to this—a sort of goodwill offering to Rufus. If we can't find Joey—"

Eli bit his lip, furious that no matter where he ran, death and misery were waiting for him. "*I'll* have to do it."

"Can you?"

Eli's breathing slowed. He felt dead inside. There was no going back now. "Yeah."

Domingo grinned, pleased. "I knew you could do it, Eli. Now for the details. I'll send James on a sort of 'redeeming' mission. He'll be going to Vinnie Caponi's house. That bumbling P.I. has been sticking his nose in Mr. Marcon's business for far too long now."

"I thought Caponi quit the private investigator business and moved out after what we did to his—"

"Ah, right." Domingo's smile widened, revealing a conniving streak in the man. Eli absently wondered if Adrian knew how scheming his right hand man was. "See, you and I know that. James doesn't. You will wait for him at Vinnie's old house and you will kill him. Do you understand?"

"Yes," Eli said, his voice no longer sounding like his own. It sounded cold. Mechanical. *I'm just a gun. That's all I've ever been.*

"Don't look so grim, Eli," Domingo beamed, propping his arms up on the table. "Mr. Marcon knows this is hard for you and he's willing to pay you thirty thousand dollars for your trouble."

Thirty thousand dollars. That's how much James' life meant to him.

"Now you'd better get going. You've got a lot of work to do."

Eli sat in his parked car, white-knuckling the steering wheel.

He'd parked away from the house, towards the tree line, where he could keep a clear view of the gravel road that led to the old Caponi place. Eli tapped the wheel impatiently, his insides squishy and trembling. James should have been here by now, and this horrible, damnable business should have been behind him. But James…even until the end, late to his own funeral.

Unless James never showed at all. Maybe Theresa had called him away on another errand for the baby.

Man, he's going to have a kid…

Maybe he'd bail on Adrian. Maybe Eli would never have to go through with this.

Stay home, James. Don't come here.

He checked his phone. Thought about calling James. Telling him everything.

Eli cursed himself for not telling Domingo the truth. For not standing up to Marcie and her machinations. Love wasn't supposed to be like this. This was just…it was tainted. All wrong.

Please, stay home, James. Don't come this way.

He wanted to call James. To tell him he was sorry. To confess everything that had been going on and be his friend again. They were such good friends. They'd laughed and watched movies at each other's houses. They'd drunk beers together and talked about growing up. *Why can't I just do what I want to do and stop being so afraid all the time?*

Fear had led him here. Fear of living life without Alex, fear of what Adrian would do to him if he ever disappointed the Old Man, fear of looking less of a man, fear of losing, losing, losing. But the tighter Eli gripped on to things, the more he feared losing them. The more he found himself here—right here—ready to do unthinkable things to hold on.

Why can't I just let Marcie go?

A white car turned onto the road up ahead.

Eli's throat tightened. *No, it's not him. It's not—*

It was.

Eli sobbed in despair, laying his head on the steering wheel. He looked up again. Saw that it was indeed James' car, headed his way. Getting closer.

He banged his forehead on the steering wheel. Again. *Again.* He cried, cursed, begged, and smacked his head over and over, watching James pull up into Caponi's driveway. He wept, his chest heaving, bile rising in his throat. At last he screamed, the sound deafening in the cab.

James stepped out of the car, putting on his best tough guy face. He was doing this. The kid was here to kill somebody, and he wasn't playing around.

Through agonizing tears, Eli was proud of his friend.

Then, taking the SIG 229 that silently waited for him in the passenger seat, Eli opened the door and marched forward, his heart full of fear.

It's time to end this.

Moments later, a single gunshot echoed in the clearing skies.

CHAPTER THIRTEEN

NOW

Two years had passed since that day Eli murdered James, but as he drove through the backroads in the countryside north of Greensboro, the pain was fresh. Some days he felt distant from the memory—like it had been a part of someone else's life. In a way, it had. He was a different person than he'd been. But when he remembered that, out there somewhere, Theresa was raising James' child without him...

He'd taken away that kid's father, and the pain of losing a father was something with which Eli was all too familiar.

Eli focused on the road ahead, still listening to KDZY's All Eighties Weekend. Crowded House's "Don't Dream It's Over" played while Eli stuck to the directions he'd gotten from the woman at the E-Z Mart. Dark was almost upon him now, with the sun fighting for every last second that it stayed in the sky. The cashier had said he didn't want to be out in the woods after sundown, and he felt he knew why.

The Death Angel had returned; that's what the dreams told him. God had loosed the Destroyer once more, and Eli knew there was little he could do to stand in its way. His only hope was to convince Marcie to surrender—as *he* had done. Giving himself to God had saved him from the Grim Reaper, and he believed Marcie could be spared as well, if she'd only give in.

He just hoped she was ready to listen this time.

THEN

James was dead. Eli's hands were still shaking.

He sat on a park bench, the nearby sound of children's laughter haunting him. Reminding him of a little kid who'd be born without a father now. Birds mocked him in song above, and life tormented him by playing out before his eyes, oblivious to the terrible thing he'd just done.

The first place Eli went after shooting his best friend was to his father's grave. He sat there, cross-legged in the grass, slumped over and bawling his eyes out until he puked. He pleaded with his father to forgive him, but the cold stone of the grave marker did not respond. No voice from the Great Beyond rose to soothe him, and facts smacked him like an icy slap in the face. Everyone was dead, and Eli felt he was as good as dead. Life had been drained of color, of hope.

For whatever reason, after he'd collected himself, Eli called Marcie. He hated her now for everything she'd put him through. But he missed her. Some part of him thought maybe she'd know what he was going through. No doubt she was plagued by guilt, too—they'd conspired to *kill* a man, for no other reason than so that they could continue to sneak around to motels all over town and sleep together. That was all their relationship really was. Not *love*.

Why did I get so attached?

Eli was not surprised when Marcie agreed to meet him.

"Are you okay?" she asked, approaching him on the bench ten minutes later.

Of course he wasn't okay. He wanted to throttle her. Shoot her dead, right here under the sun. He'd done it to a guy who'd never harmed him, why not? Today was Eli's day for killing.

"No," he finally answered curtly, in response to her dumb question.

Marcie sat next to him. He hadn't been this close to her in weeks. He smelled her perfume, felt her brush against him. He'd missed her so much. Even now, as he seethed against her, his mind was flooded with memories of their private moments in the dark, her caress, her laugh.

"You did what you *had* to do," she whispered sympathetically. "For us."

"Us?" Bouncing his knee up and down, he whirled on her, unleashed. "What's so great about us? What's so great that people's lives don't even matter anymore?"

"I want to be with you." Marcie's brow furrowed. She faced him as though he were a beloved pet who couldn't understand her emotions.

"But at what cost? James is already dead! Who else? Marcie, we can't see each other! Just because James is dead doesn't mean your dad won't still find out. Stan and Lee are already suspicious, and they hate me enough as it is! If they even suspect anything's still going on, they'll go straight to Domingo!"

Marcie bit her lip, a little girl playing at being a crime boss. "I can take care of it."

"How? Are you going to talk to Adrian? You going to tell him about us? You know he'd kill me."

She looked away, that same strange unreadable expression on her face that

191

Eli had seen under the moonlight the night he broke things off with her. Once again, he wondered what she was thinking, what she was dealing with. "I don't want you to worry," she muttered darkly. "I can handle this. We'll be safe. We'll be free."

"Free…" Eli shook his head, chuckling. "I don't think we'll ever be free," he said. "Even if by some miracle we ran away from here and could stay two steps ahead of your father, we'd still have to live with the things we've done. I'd still have to live with the things…"

He absently wiped at his puffy eyes, while children at play ran past, laughing and chasing each other. Eli shut his eyes, trying to drown out their joy, but unable.

Marcie slid closer, hooking her arms in his. She leaned her head against his shoulder. "I forgive you."

"It's not your forgiveness I need," he replied automatically, appalled that she thought so highly of herself. But he'd lost the strength to hate her now. Marcie was damaged goods. She had more crap going on in that head of hers than Eli could ever guess at. He felt sorry for her, that even now with James' blood on their hands, she still didn't see how strange, how wrong their union was.

It was then that he wanted to tell her it was over. For good this time. Marcie was a dead end for him and he was ready to step out of her trap. To loose fear's grip on him and live life out in the sun again, unburdened by his sins. He didn't need Marcie's forgiveness, he needed his dad's. He wanted to find that man he was so close to becoming once upon a time. The hardworking, god-fearing man that his father always believed he could be.

God-fearing…God had always meant so much to his dad.

Eli stood, preparing himself to take the first step into his new life.

"What are you doing?" Marcie asked uncertainly, still seated at the bench, beckoning him to sit beside her again. To stay confined to this hell of their making.

But he was done with that. "I have to go."

"Where?"

"To church."

Despite the small part of his heart that longed to be accepted in Marcie's arms, Eli turned his back on her and walked away, sluggish at first, as his past fought to hold him. But with each step, Eli felt more and more sure of himself and this decision. He had nothing to lose anymore.

He would go to the church. Get some things right with God.

Then he'd find Adrian, and tell him he was done.

I'm going to do it. Tonight, I'm taking my life back.

The next couple of hours blurred by for Eli. Looking back on that time, he would remember his visit with Pastor Loomis—learning that his subconscious suspicions were not as far-fetched as he had hoped. That, perhaps, the Angel of Death *was* stalking the streets of Willowbrook, eliminating those in opposition to goodness and decency. Adrian was a noble man of evil actions, and it seemed God's mercy had reached its limit. Now, discipline was called for. Adrian was facing the wrath of God, and Eli, just as the other butchered hitmen, was condemned for his part in Adrian's empire. That was how the pastor explained it all, more or less.

After that, Eli did all that he knew to do. He offered a simple prayer to God, recalling the times his father had prayed by his bedside in his youth. He asked for forgiveness, mercy, but most of all, to be made *right* again. To start over. He made a call to Marcie—but got her voicemail instead—and told her that he was ready for a change.

He was ready to leave the family. For real, and forever.

Then he went to James' house, where Adrian was waiting. The monster with the cerulean skull-face was there, too, and tore through Adrian and Stan and Lee, butchering them before Eli's eyes.

Next, it moved for Eli, but it seemed that his prayers had been heard.

The Angel passed over him, moving on, God's vengeance sated at last.

He had his second chance. He promptly ditched the money he'd been paid for his last hit in one of James' secret crawlspaces in a bedroom closet where he often kept some of his "off the market" weaponry. Eli stuffed the briefcase in there, determined to leave behind the thirty thousand and all it represented. Those were the wages of a killer—a monster—and Eli only prayed that God would bind that monster to the stacks of bills and leave Eli well enough alone.

After months of bloodshed and misery, his life was his own once more. Immediately he knew he'd leave town, go far from this terrible place where danger lurked in the night, and face his future without the shackles of his past.

But there was one stop he had to make first.

Eli left James' house on Buckingham Road behind, driving down the darkened Willowbrook streets headed for Adrian's mansion, his breathing still hurried, his heart dancing excitedly in his chest. He followed the familiar route to the Marcon estate, knowing in his heart he'd never come this way again. Adrian was dead and soon his legacy would crumble. The FBI would no doubt swoop in like vultures, picking clean the remains of the beast they'd failed to kill on their own. However, maybe the Feds wouldn't have the opportunity. Eli could only assume that Adrian's death was the beginning—that God's agent of destruction would fall upon this house, too, tearing down every last shred of Adrian's evil. He would burn this empire to the ground and salt the earth.

But I won't be here, Eli thought with confidence.

He'd be long gone by then. He'd sell his father's house, take what little money he had, and leave. Start over. *Get it right this time.*

Eli spotted the bright lights of Adrian's gated sprawl, feeling drunk on his newfound freedom. He nodded to the guard at the gate, fighting against his exhilaration, and was let through. Guards wandered the grounds, just as they'd always done. The news hadn't reached them yet. They had no idea that the Old Man was dead—that the shady life that had brought them so much material comfort was at its end. Eli's secret knowledge of their fate filled him with power, but not as much as the realization that he wouldn't be here to share it with them.

He pulled around the driveway and parked. Guards eyed him, no doubt having heard the decree that he should not be fraternizing with Marcie. Even if they *had* heard, they wouldn't do anything to him except report him to Domingo or Adrian. Eli didn't like that idea, on second thought. As soon as one of them tried to call Adrian, they'd be alerted to the Old Man's absence. Maybe even suspect Eli had something to do with it, given his brazen visit, but Eli didn't have time to second-guess his actions. He had a few minutes to spare before the heat came down, and he was only planning on staying long enough to say what needed to be said.

He wiped away the blood on his hands where he'd handled Adrian's disembodied head, then stepped out of the car. He kept his eyes forward and clenched his jaw, hoping his tense posture would deter the guards' intervention.

Sure enough, no one moved to stop him. The one nearest the door dipped his chin in greeting. Eli returned the gesture, then stepped inside.

After passing the first hurtle, Eli dropped his stoic charade and raced up the steps to Marcie's room, taking two steps at a time. Frantic, Eli nearly burst through her door to find her sitting in the dark, on her bed, sobbing in the moonlight.

"Marcie!" he whispered harshly, relieved to see her, to know she was okay.

Marcie gaped at him, her mascara staining her face in purplish-black rivulets. She leapt off her bed and threw herself around him, burying her face in his chest, bawling. "I thought I'd lost you! I thought I'd never see you again!"

Eli paused, caught off guard by her reaction. She couldn't possibly know what he'd just survived. Then he remembered he'd phoned her, left a message. He'd told her that he was going to see her father, to quit the family.

"Hey, hey, it's okay," he soothed, pulling her away to face her. He stroked her hair. "I'm here. Listen, we gotta go. I saw him."

"Who?"

Eli let go of her and moved toward the window, peeking through the drapes to make sure Death had not yet arrived. "The guy that got Ian and Malcolm and Justin and Joey. I saw him, and he was *huge* and he had this, like this, like a blue skull for a face! He came right after me. He killed Stan, Lee, and Adrian, and he came after me, but I got away."

"*What?*" Marcie's shrill reply shook him from his reverie. "Daddy's dead?"

Eli halted, realizing what he'd just rambled. "Marcie…"

Marcie cried, shocked and devastated. She slumped down on the bed, her whole body shaking, and Eli's heart felt sick. Sick that he'd divulged something so important so flippantly. He'd never seen Marcie so upset, but there she was, curled into a fetal position, her icy quasi-psychotic shell cracked and slipping, revealing the girl beneath.

The girl Eli wanted to be with. The real Marcie.

"This is all wrong…" she moaned, her face in her hands. "It wasn't supposed to happen like this. Daddy's dead…I don't understand."

Eli knelt before her, speaking tenderly, "I went and talked to the preacher and he told me things. It's God, Marcie. He's doing this. But we don't have to die. We can surrender, and He'll forgive us. That's what *I* did, and it worked! Death skipped me."

Marcie looked at him, hurt and confused. "This isn't making any sense."

Eli sighed, lacking the time he needed for a full explanation. "It will. But we have to get out of here. This thing is still out there, and I don't know what kind of pattern it's working, but I know the only way you can be safe is if you come with me. We have to leave. Tonight."

But Marcie just stared, unmoving. "I'm not going anywhere."

"Marcie, you have to!"

"But…" she shook her head, the light in her eyes dimming. "I can't."

Eli took her hands in his, squeezing them, urgent. "I love you, okay? I've tried not to, and I know it's not right, but I do. Maybe we're not supposed to be together, I don't know. But this is more important than that. I'm trying to save your life. You have to come with me. Marcie, *please*."

"I...can't. I won't."

Eli blinked at her, stunned.

Biting her lip, Marcie struggled to speak. "I have to stay. Daddy's gone, and I have to stay here and put things back together."

"Your father's dead," Eli stated as gently as he could. "The family's through."

"But I'm still here..." she whispered, her voice small and lonely.

"That doesn't mean you have to be like your father."

"It's my fault..." She cried fresh tears. "I have to fix it."

He knew that look in her eye, for he'd seen it in the mirror every day for years. It was fear. She was its prisoner now. But he didn't understand. "What are you afraid of?"

"Go," she snapped. Marcie stood, outraged, and unleashed a tidal wave of fury. "Get out! If you want to pretend like none of this ever happened and start your new life with a clean conscience, then *fine*. Go! Have a great life! But don't expect me just to give up everything my father worked for and my whole world. This is my life, Eli! This is who I am! And if it's too much of a burden on you and your new holy standing, well...I'm just sorry."

"I didn't say that."

Marcie cooled, putting on her mask again, becoming the same distant young woman he'd first met. *Don't get too attached,* she'd told him. "You didn't have to," she said evenly. "Everyone's dead and you want to leave. But I have to stay behind and pick up the pieces. If you can't do that with me...then I don't want you here. So, go."

She turned her back to him and stood staring out the window, barring him out of her life, now. Whatever trust he'd gained from her was gone. They were strangers once more.

"I'm sorry," he told her. He wanted to say that he'd face this fear with her, by her side, that he'd never leave, but that was a lie. As much as he cared for her, he had his own path now. "I can't do this anymore. Please come with me, Marcie. I love you."

"Enough to stay?" she asked him. Testing him.

In the silence he wanted to lie to her. Make her a million promises, just so she would love him. But a new resolve within him refused to let him speak words to her that he didn't mean.

Marcie whirled on him, her hair whipping about. She came at him like an angered beast and beat at his chest wildly. "Go!" she shrieked, hitting him again and again as he backed towards the door. "Get out! And if I ever see you again I'll kill you myself!"

She pushed him out of her room and slammed the door in his face.

NOW

That was the last time Eli saw Marcie.

Now, two years later, he was preparing to visit her again.

His Jeep rumbled down County Road 90, and Eli steered his way over the bumps and dips in the rain-washed gravel. Low hanging branches canopied over his vehicle, the trees inching closer to the road the deeper he went. It was untamed country out here, and he supposed that suited Marcie. No one lived this far out in the North Woods except people who wanted to stay hidden.

At last, the trees broke, and Eli spotted a house in the clearing. Immediately he felt a sense of déjà vu. It was a lavish home, though more rustic than Adrian's impersonal architecture. A wrought iron gate barred intruders, and if that didn't do the trick, the guards in tactical vests and cargo pants roaming the grounds would. Eli didn't instantly recognize the guards nearest the path, but they had the familiar stoic look that Adrian's men always wore. What's more, the guards now moved with Dobermans, which was a new addition to the program. By the cut of their short-cropped hair, their predatory watch, and their stiff march, he knew they were soldiers. Probably ex-military. *Mercenaries.* Despite its unassuming locale, this place was a fortress.

Turning off the radio, he pulled his Jeep to the front gate, where a single merc in full tac gear and shades sat in a tiny box of a security checkpoint. The man was a dark giant, his face cut from onyx. Eli got out of the car and approached, still wearing his grungy flannel and T-shirt from his day at the garage. With a lift of his chin, Eli said, "Hey, man, what's up? I'm here to see Marcie."

The Terminator slowly looked up from the magazine he was reading—*Guns and Ammo*, Eli thought—and eyed him. "No, you're not. Get back in your car and turn around."

Eli smirked. He'd almost forgotten how the "tough guy" thing worked. This was the part where he should respond with an equally macho threat, but the posturing seemed so silly to him now.

"I'm a friend," he said, ignoring the man's order. "She'll want to see me."

The human mountain rose from his seat and exited the little building, the earth trembling at his footfall. "No visitors. Do yourself a favor and turn around."

Eli chuckled.

Then punched the guy right in the throat.

The guard gagged, gripped his bruised Adam's apple, and slumped to his knees. Eli brought up his knee and smashed the large man's nose, laying him out on his back, immediately rummaging around the guard's vest and securing the sidearm holstered there. Eli brought out the gun and racked the slide, keeping it trained on the coughing man.

The yard came to life with barking Dobermans and yelling guards, all rushing for Eli at the gate, raising their guns at him and demanding his immediate surrender. Eli raised his hands, letting the gun dangle on his trigger finger by the loop.

"I'm just here to see Marcie," he announced. "I don't want any trouble."

Mercs spilled out of the gate, surrounding him, shoving their barrels into his face and reaching for his hands. He did not struggle as they slapped him in plastic ties and forced him to his knees. He wasn't sure if he was being taken prisoner or about to be executed.

"What are you doing here?" a woman's voice cut through the commotion.

The men—including Eli—froze and looked up at the new arrival.

Her hair was longer, and her eyes seemed older. Sadder. She looked entirely too grown-up, hardened by the years since he'd last seen her, and something about her just distressed him.

Still, it was good to see her again.

He warmed in spite of the assault rifle barrel pressed against the back of his head. "Hey, Marcie."

CHAPTER FOURTEEN

Eli Ross was the last person Marcie expected to see that spring morning. But now that he was here, a part of her realized he was always going to come. He was *meant* to come.

Especially today.

"Let him up," she ordered. Her men cut Eli loose and backed away, bringing their dogs to heel.

Eli straightened, adjusting his grungy overshirt and dusting off his jeans, a cocksure grin floating over his five o'clock shadow. Daddy had always tolerated his hitmen's quirks, like Stan's mismatched suits and Joey's punk rock fetish, but with Eli, Daddy always insisted he keep himself manicured in expensive suits. "*When you're out there,*" she'd heard Daddy tell Eli more than once, "*you represent me.*" Marcie had wondered if maybe he were grooming Eli to take Domingo's place one day. Now, seeing Eli's dark hair overgrown and his beard coming in, was like looking at a stranger. It was a sad reminder that her father was gone, and her old life was no more. Yet, it also showed her that Eli had attained something that she never could: He had escaped his fate.

The other bodyguards offered a hand to their wounded compatriot, but he pushed them away, defiantly standing on his own. Eli faced him with earnest eyes. "Sorry about that. No hard feelings, bud?"

The man rubbed his sore throat, muttered a curse, and lumbered off. Marcie approached her visitor, crossing her arms and hardening her face, lest he think this was all a joke to her.

"What are you doing here?" she demanded.

"How are you?" he asked conversationally, avoiding her question completely. The sunset behind him afforded Eli an obnoxious halo effect. He *was* quite beautiful. She'd missed his face, his strong, rough hands, his arms around her.

"How did you find me?"

He laughed, quiet and warm, as though they were the only two people on the property and weren't being watched by two dozen trained killers.

"Give me a little credit. I'm rusty, but not that far gone." Eli scanned the grounds over his shoulder. "You think we could talk for a second?"

Marcie spotted the dirty looks her men were throwing her visitor, noticed them mumbling to one another. Eli was upsetting the balance here, threatening to reveal her weakness. Marcie stiffened. "Let's go inside."

"Wow, this place is really nice."

Eli stood in the great expanse of her foyer, admiring the wooden vaulted ceilings and ornate chandelier, his dark blue eyes traveling to the stone-laid walls and polished hardwood floors. He had his hands in his jeans pockets, his shoulders cocked in a defensive posture. She recalled he had that same high set in his broad shoulders upon their first meeting, when he felt it best to keep his distance and not disturb her wrath. It'd been cute then—annoyingly so—and it was cute now. There was so much Marcie wanted to say to him. To ask him about his life now, without her. Most of all she wanted to know why he was here—today of all days, when she needed him most. How had he known? Was there hope for her after all?

No. Don't be an idiot. It's just a coincidence.

"It's home," she finally replied.

"So…you, uh, live here all by yourself?"

He was careful not to face her, his voice soft and casual.

"Yes."

He did not fully turn in her direction, but Marcie swore she saw the hint of a relieved grin twitching at the corner of his lips. "Must be lonely."

"Domingo's off on an errand," she informed him. "And I have my men outside."

"Right," he nodded, choosing to continue absently surveying her house rather than look at her.

She wondered how long they were going to dance around the issue. They had been crazy, passionate lovers once. They'd tempted the law, her family, maybe even destiny, to be together, but here, in her country home, they spoke as little more than formal acquaintances. She wanted to spin him around and demand his full attention. She wanted to shout and fight. Oh, they had such great fights. Violent and wild and hateful. And then they'd make up just as intensely. Marcie wanted to curse him for showing up on her doorstep.

Save me, Eli, she silently pleaded instead. *Save me from all of this.*

Marcie finally stepped in front of Eli, forcing him to acknowledge her. She craved his attention, just as she had back then. No one had ever paid attention to her the way Eli did—not her father, not the men assigned to watch over her before Eli got the job. Sure, her various protectors desired her, and some were even dumb enough to make advances. Though, that wasn't entirely their fault. Marcie had done her fair share of flirting, lulling her bodyguards into a promise of conquest, then reporting them to Daddy. Adrian always saw to their immediate dismissal and punishment. It was a game, just like the game she played with her nannies as a child. But Eli…Eli was the only one who had refused to play.

It had driven her feral. She always did love a challenge. Little did she know the affect he'd have on her. How hard she would fall for him.

"What are you doing here?" she raged for the third time, hoping to put him on the defensive. He'd been a man of fire before, underneath that deceptively cool exterior. Marcie hoped he hadn't lost that.

"I came to warn you," he said evenly, and Marcie felt disappointed.

"Warn me?" she snapped, ridiculing him. Provoking him. *Fight with me. Show me you still care.*

But he only stood there, his hands still in his pockets, at perfect peace. "I've been having nightmares lately. Nightmares about something coming after you. I think God is trying to tell me something. I thought maybe it was time to look you up again, and to get some things right."

The way that Eli just name-dropped the Almighty like the two of them were frat brothers infuriated her. Reminded her that *He* was the reason why Eli left. Out of some misguided sense of "finding God".

"God told you, huh? I see you're still into all of that."

Marcie stared out the glass patio door, overlooking the darkening woods beyond the house, hoping that her cold shoulder had hurt him in some small way.

"I've changed," he said, without coming after her. Not touching her or begging her. He still wasn't playing her game. She didn't know if that made her feel better or worse. "After I left, I traveled around a lot. I had to get some things straight. I knew that God had forgiven me…but I hadn't forgiven myself. I had to get that right. A year ago, I settled down, got a legit job fixing cars, and an apartment in Greensboro. Things are going good for me—"

Marcie turned on him, Eli's happiness a barb in her side. Didn't he know what she was facing? Wasn't that why he was here? "So, what? You decided you'd come back, look up some old friends, and show off your shiny new life? Sorry, lover, I'm not impressed."

But she was. He'd done it. He'd really made it out and was living a normal life now.

He stepped toward her, still keeping his distance, still not removing his hands from his pockets. "I always wanted to come back for you."

"Funny you waited *two years* to tell me that."

"But I wasn't prepared to do something like that before. I was afraid that, if

I stayed, I wouldn't be strong enough, and I'd just go back to the person I used to be."

"I liked that person." Marcie crossed her arms indignantly.

"I hated him," Eli said, coming alive. His Jedi Zen was cracked, only slightly, letting some of that former, passionate man through. His anger, however short-lived, was a ray of sunlight in her gloom. "I just wanted Death to come for me."

Marcie saw where the conversation was leading. It had to come here. They had to talk about *him*. That was what all of this was about, after all. "And it did," she said, studying him, wondering how he did it. How he'd beaten the accursed thing.

"Exactly! But I was spared! Don't you see, I had my second chance. I couldn't waste it."

"Waste it with me, you mean," she spat. It was a petty response, and not befitting a woman of her stature. They had more important things to discuss than their failed romance. But still, on some level, his words stung. Despite what Eli might have imagined in the prime of their romance, Marcie had never entertained thoughts of settling down with him. Or *anyone* for that matter, though if she had ever considered getting married and doing the "normal life" thing, she would have wanted it to be with Eli. They probably weren't good for each other, but he'd always talked to her like a person and not like Boss Marcon's daughter. But she had always known that, like her father, she would be married to her business, to dark deeds and a darker heart. There was no room for the tenderness of true love in all of that.

"*No,*" he defended hotly, and Marcie's heart fluttered, praying they were coming to it. They would fight. Throw things and scream and it'd be *spectacular.* But again, Eli's anger dissolved. He just looked concerned. "I wasn't ready for you."

That declaration caught Marcie unprepared.

Eli continued, "Something was broken inside me ever since my dad died. I was so messed up, and then I joined the Army and then Alex was killed…"

A bolt of sympathy stung her heart, but she held her high ground, concentrating hard to keep her stoic expression.

Eli shook his head, wandering in his own memories. He stepped by her, approaching the patio glass, taking a moment for himself. For what was not the first time, Marcie felt guilty for what she'd done to him. He never would have killed James on his own, not without her influence. At the time, it had seemed…Well, she didn't know how it seemed. She was broken too, and saw the world through a cracked glass.

Did she want to apologize? That would be admitting to a mistake, and Marcie didn't make mistakes. She made choices. Some of them turned out better, others worse. But a choice was a choice. No looking back.

Seeing Eli so fractured, though, and knowing she'd done that to him, at least in part...

Eli turned his chin, offering her his profile. The sun had finally fled the woods and blue twilight was falling outside. "Look, I didn't come here to win you back," he said, without hate or condemnation. "I just wanted to make sure you were okay."

Her moment had come. She'd been dreading this day, beseeching any deity she thought might listen, and God had sent His champion, all for her. *Don't waste it, Marcie. Tell him.*

Impossibly, though, her pride refused to dissipate. "Well, as you can see, I'm doing just fine." Rambling now, not even listening to the lies she spoke, Marcie continued, "Business is a little slow right now, but—"

"Are you happy?" Eli stepped forward, cutting through her defenses with ease.

She started, blinked once. *He does love me. He can help. Tell him!* "What does that have to do with anything?"

"I see you have a great house and power and money, but are you happy?"

His face was so gorgeous, his searching eyes powerful and smoldering.

No. I'm not happy. I don't think I've ever been happier than when I was with you.

"Yes. Of course I'm happy."

"That's not very convincing," he countered.

"No," she defended, jabbing a finger in his scruffy face. "You can't do that! You don't have the right to do that. You can't just show up on your white horse after all you did and expect me to hop on and ride off with you into the sunset."

There could still be a fight. If nothing else, maybe they could at least have one last great fight.

"I'm trying to help—"

"I don't need your help. I'm not the same little girl you knew."

Yes, you are, you liar, she scolded herself. *You are such a liar.*

"That's right!" Eli hollered back at her, then laughed, bringing her low. "You're the new boss in town, is that it? Daddy's Little Girl, all grown up. But to me, you're still Marcie. You're still someone I care about."

"You don't even know me anymore." She had to keep it coming, keep the angry words flowing or she might give in.

"It doesn't matter." He moved in, his words a whisper. His lips inches from hers. "I still want to take care of you."

Caught in his gravity, she edged closer, feeling on the verge of blissful tears.

But she could not allow him to best her. "Why? Because it's in your newfound Christian credo?"

"No. Because I love you." He winked with a warm, silly grin. "Duh."

Time slowed. Outside, birds sang in the distance. Marcie heard wind rustling through the treetops, nighttime's gentle lullaby. The world fell away, only the two of them drifting in empty space. They alone were Creation in that moment. They alone were God. Giving in, Marcie leaned close, ready to ascend—

Then Eli pulled away, awkwardly.

Time and space resumed. Creation returned. God was back, too, with all His cruelties, and Marcie dipped her head, her fate closing in on her.

Eli clenched his jaw. "About these dreams…I've been seeing that guy with the big, blue skull. He's different now, though. Stronger, somehow, and I think he's coming to finish what he started two years ago. He's coming after *you*."

Surprisingly her temper was gone, and Marcie felt only grim resolve. Whatever she and Eli were, whatever they could have been, that was gone now. She had things to face, and he'd come all this way. It was time he knew.

"I'm not worried about it," she muttered, her eyes on the floor.

"Marcie, this is *Death*. You can't stop it. Only God can take away its power and give you eternal lif—"

"Would you stop with the sermon, choir boy? He's not Death."

"…What?"

Marcie turned away, taking a deep breath, ready to divulge the greatest secret of her life. "The guy with the big, blue skull. He's not Death. He's…something else."

"What do you mean?"

It's time, Marcie. No more lies.

"Come with me," she said. "I'll show you everything."

204

CHAPTER FIFTEEN

Thanks to James Lenderman's late night drunken babbling at *Charley's*, Eli had been taken from her. It had been a couple weeks since Eli officially ended the relationship, and Marcie was furious at him for reasons she didn't fully understand. He had been her boyfriend, yes, and now he was not. They had a dynamic physical relationship and he was great to love. But there were more, deeper reasons that fueled Marcie's anger. Eli was, perhaps, the closest thing to a real friend she'd ever had. There were so many things she hadn't told him—didn't know if she ever would—but still she'd told him more than anyone else in her life. He knew her secrets, and that left her vulnerable. He also factored into her aspirations of breaking away from her father. She had believed that Eli was loyal to *her*, now, and should she ever choose to leave, he'd follow along obediently.

But in the end, Eli was too much a coward to stand up to her father and caved at Domingo's request, ending their affair and setting Marcie's machinations back a considerable distance. *Of course* she called him. Bullied him, threatened him, demanded he grow a pair and love her again. Yet her calls went unanswered.

After a lifetime of waging a secret campaign against her father, however juvenile, events finally came to head, and Marcie's schoolgirl antics escalated past the point of no return.

She sat in her pajamas at the vanity in her spacious bedroom one night, her wet hair up in a towel. She was applying her usual evening facial cream, stewing over Eli, when she spotted a dark shape enter her field of vision. Startled, she spun and saw the familiar aged face of Adrian Marcon.

"Oh! Daddy. You scared me."

"Where were you tonight?" he asked, his voice monotone, his drooping mustache twitching.

Marcie cooled and returned to her facial. "I was at a club with friends."

"Was Eli there?"

No, he hadn't been there, because Domingo had scared him off. But to tell Daddy that might cause him to question why the man he had hired to protect his daughter wasn't around.

It was a trick question, and Marcie knew she must be careful not to let her hand show.

Finally, she settled on the truth, to see how far that would get her. "No."

"I'm a busy man, Marcie, but I'm not blind. I know you two are seeing each other."

A finger coated with cream hovered a centimeter from her face. She froze for only a fraction of a second, but feared her father had already noticed. "What would make you think that?"

"Ian told me. I had Domingo send him to watch after you and he said he saw you and Eli together behaving less than professionally."

No. Marcie shivered, her rage and fear nearly uncontrollable. *That's not possible.* There was no way Ian could have told anyone in time—

"And you believe him?" she forced a snicker, rubbing her face down. Groaning, she said, "Ian would tell you anything to try and impress you. Where is he now? I bet if we found him and talked to him together—"

"See, that's the thing," Adrian cut in. "Ian's dead. Mr. Domingo and I fear he's become the latest casualty."

Marcie watched in the mirror as her face fell slightly.

"Oh."

Adrian maintained his distance, his voice a steady rhythm, devoid of passion or fire. "Marcie, I understand. You're young. I was young once, too. We all make mistakes. We fall in love and we think it'll last forever. But it doesn't. Love only makes us vulnerable and leaves us humiliated and heartsick. Trust me."

Marcie stared at her father's reflection in the mirror. He was vigilant to never expose himself to his enemies. He rarely even allowed his own men to gaze on his face. Everything about him was guarded and secretive and impenetrable. But seeing him now, as he spoke of love and heartbreak, Marcie saw something in his weathered face. A soft sadness was buried deep in his dark eyes. Though his voice did not betray a soul, Marcie felt as though, for the first time in her life, Boss Marcon was talking to her as a dad.

Suddenly, all her schemes were washed away. She never wanted to rebel against him again, just so long as he'd look at her like that forever. Marcie craved that connection, desperate to sit at the feet of her Daddy and learn all that he'd been through. All the things that had happened to him in his boyhood that had forged him into the calculated killer he'd become. Maybe she could heal that broken part of his heart, if he'd let her.

Let me love you, Daddy.

"It doesn't have to be that way, does it?" she whispered tentatively, facing his eyes in the mirror even as he averted her glance.

"I never dreamed your mother would leave, but she did. People change, Marcie. They don't stay the same people you fell in love with. You're the best thing to come out of…my time with your mother."

Nineteen years of tears threatened to escape the hardened wall around her heart. Marcie turned to her father, beseeching his approval. His love. "Well…doesn't that make everything worth it?"

"No," her father said, without missing a beat.

Marcie felt as though she might die. An unwatered flower, unable to blossom in the sun, she would wither and fade.

Worse, her father would not even care.

Her head dipped and swiveled, her brown eyes locking on their reflection in the mirror. She was cleaning herself up, beautifying herself, but it was useless. She'd never be beautiful or loved or special. Eli had left her. Daddy didn't want her. That settled it.

Tonight, after Daddy went to sleep, she would take the .38 revolver he'd given her for protection, put it to her temple, and squeeze the trigger.

"One day, everything I have will be yours," Adrian promised, without pride. "Eli, though, will always be a grunt. Don't let him drag you down. You have greater things in store for you. Besides, Eli might not be around much longer."

Marcie's thoughts of suicide halted, Eli's safety becoming paramount in her mind. "What do you mean?"

"He's slipping up. We sent him and James to talk to Benny the Squeal. Now we find Benny. Dead."

What? Eli had never said anything about that. What was he keeping from her? Was he in trouble? "Oh, is that what this is about?" she said, eagerly applying the cream once more, her mind working fast. "'Cause Eli didn't do it."

"No?"

"No," she answered, a devilish plan forming. Eli did love her. He was only away from her now because he was afraid of her father. Because James had to open his big, dumb mouth. *But I'll fix it, baby. You can come back to me.*

I won't be alone.

"It was James." She shrugged. "You know how much of a screw-up he is. He's a trigger-happy gun nut. Eli tried to stop him, but things got out of control. Eli wanted to cover it up because James is his best friend. Ask Eli." She beamed. "He wouldn't lie to you."

I'll take care of you, Eli. We'll be together.

"And what about you?" Adrian said after a moment's pause. "Would *you*…lie to me?"

"Of course not, Daddy," Marcie squeaked, smiling up at her dad.

"Not even to protect your 'boyfriend'?"

She laughed, casual, priding herself in her skill. "He's not my boyfriend, I promise. Maybe I thought he was a little cute, but I know better than to get attached."

Adrian reached out in an uncharacteristic moment of affection, and stroked the back of Marcie's neck. A flicker of doubt shrieked inside her and she wondered if she'd made the right decision. "I'm proud of you, Marcie. Good night."

"Good night, Daddy." She grinned until the man left her room.

Her eyes fell on the mirror for the last time, allowing her a good look at who she was. What she'd become. *I'm my father's daughter*, she resolved.

NOW

Two years later, James was murdered by Eli's hand, Daddy was dead, and Marcie was alone, after all.

Marcie led Eli up the stairs to her attic, the boards creaking beneath their feet. The dimly lit room was musty and hot. Candles were situated here and there atop the sheet-covered old furniture and boxes of old junk. Marcie lit each one with a silver cigarette lighter as she passed them, and their tiny flames struggled against the dark. Bric-a-brac was shoved against the walls, clearing a space in the middle of the floor, where still more candles created a circle, surrounding an intricate red chalk pattern that took Marcie the better part of an hour to construct every time she made it. Everything had to be mathematically perfect or there would be dire consequences.

She stood against the boxes lining her ceremony room, unable to look at her guest. Eli was as stiff as stone beside her, his hands no longer in his pockets. He took two steps in front of her, looking at everything, taking it all in.

"What is this?"

Marcie seized a deep breath, feeling naked before him. "It's…a conjuring circle. It's how I brought him here."

He looked to her, quiet horror dawning on his face. "Who?"

She bit her lip. "The Blue Skull guy."

His eyes screwed up in tears and he chortled, hard and bitter. Turning from her, he put his hands on his hips like a disappointed parent and surveyed the mess she'd made. Marcie couldn't imagine what he was feeling. He had believed that the Blue Skull was Death—God's left hand of retribution. His encounter with the beast had prompted him to have some sort of spiritual awakening. Everything he held to about God, whatever faith he had, was wrapped up in the identity of the Blue Skull.

To reveal the truth to him…Marcie understood that she had finally killed Eli where it mattered. She hated herself for that.

"I'm sorry," she offered, and meant it.

He was quiet for a long time, and Marcie shriveled in the silence. It swallowed her and she was terrified to hear what he might say next. Before he had a chance to speak, she filled the empty space with emptier words, praying he'd understand. "Daddy always taught me about power. How you have to command it. But all my life I felt so powerless." She shut her eyes, remembering a life of seclusion. "Living in that house, his thumb over me all the time…no one allowed to touch me or talk to me… He had me holed up in his tower; I felt like I'd never be free."

Marcie hated her father for what he'd done, but also missed him terribly.

"After Rufus showed up, about the only place Daddy would ever let me go was to the library. Domingo would take me, and I used to spend hours there. Not because I liked books, necessarily, but just because it was the only place I could be free." Nearly smiling at those memories of her first real taste of independence, Marcie's fondness was quickly overtaken by darkness. "We found some books on magick one night. It sounded pretty cool, you know? About empowerment and finding your inner strength. It was just a joke, at first, but then I goofed around and tried a couple spells. They *worked*, Eli. It was incredible, and I felt like I could do anything! I read more and more and pushed myself. I wanted to see how far I could take it. Once I got a taste for it, I went deeper. Experimented more. I couldn't stop."

Eli remained quiet, still standing apart from her in his disappointed father pose, his posture rigid and his face obscured from her. He looked frightening in the dark, but she felt safe with him. Safer still that he was finding out everything she'd worked so hard to hide. *He'll know what to do. He can fix this.*

On a cathartic roll, she moved towards him, barely able to stop herself from reaching out to him, holding him, begging his forgiveness. "I found a spell that would summon a 'great enforcer' from the Other Side. Daddy used to move people around like they were chess pieces in some little game of his. I wanted that, too." Hanging her head, Marcie cursed her own immaturity. Her motives had sounded noble in her mind, but voicing them—to Eli, most of all—revealed them to be so trivial. "I just wanted someone to control," she admitted. "I didn't know what I would be bringing, though…"

"All the murders…" Eli said at last, his voice little more than a croak. When Marcie rounded to face him, she saw he'd been crying. "Malcolm, Justin, and Joey…it was *you*."

She wept too, and touched his arm, not caring about propriety anymore. "Eli—"

He jerked his sleeve out of her grip and crossed the room, pacing around the circle, glaring at it like *it* had done all of this. *But it's me. I did this. On my own. I'm the one you hate.*

"But why?" he asked her.

Marcie looked to the floor, grave. "Daddy loved you all like sons. Sometimes I think he would have been happier with sons… But he only got me." She faced him, desperate. "You were wrong, Eli. He never loved me. He loved *them*. He loved his 'empire'. So, I took it all away from him." She exhaled, biting down on her lip. "I thought… I don't know what I thought. I thought if I was the only one left then he'd see how important I was." Eli shook his head, and Marcie felt her face flush with embarrassment. "It was stupid, all right? I know that. But I was angry—"

"What about Rufus?" he demanded.

Marcie shook her head. "He's still around. He's trying to take over where my dad left off, but he doesn't have anything to do with this. This was all my doing. Since all this happened, I've tried sending it after Rufus, but it won't work. Rufus…there's something about him. It's like he's magick, too, and his is canceling out mine."

Now Eli glowered at her. "It came after *me*," he hissed, betrayed. "It…you…you tried to kill me."

"*No!*" she shouted, tears ruining her carefully made-up face. She stepped closer to him, but he kept the tiny flames of her candles between them. His eyes were alight in the fire, burning with anger. "You don't understand! *Please!* Daddy was always so tied up in his business. I tried to pretend I didn't care, but…I wanted to get back at him. Then I met you and it changed, Eli. I *swear* I changed."

"Don't," he snapped.

"I tried to protect you from finding out. Then Domingo started getting suspicious of us. I overhead him sending Ian to kill you if the rumors were true. So, I had to use the Blue Skull to protect you."

Eli looked like he might be sick. "I heard him," he said, his eyes vacant, lost in time. "That last night that we were together…I left the motel, and I heard something in the bushes. The next morning, Ian was dead. He died right next to me and I didn't even…" He paced again, fuming. "That was you! That thing shoved a rifle through Ian's *stomach*, Marcie! Did you know that?"

She hung her head. "I don't tell it what to do. Just who to go after."

"It's the same thing!"

"I didn't want to. I wanted to stop."

"But then James found out…"

Eli was shaking, reaching hysteria. Marcie rounded the circle to be near him, but he backed away. "I would've taken care of it," she said. "I didn't realize Daddy would make *you* kill him. I know what that did to you."

Marcie blubbered now, crying harder and freer than she had in years. Not since she was a little girl and didn't understand why her daddy was never there to tuck her in. But her nannies would tuck her in, kiss her, read bedtime stories, and tell her they loved her.

I betrayed them, too. I betray everyone who cares about me.

"But Stan and Lee knew about us, too," she wept. "It was all getting out of hand. I was afraid of what Daddy would do to you if he found out. I was afraid he'd take you away from me!"

Eli slumped, his fight dying. Now there was only sad resignation in its place. He ran his fingers through his thick hair, his eyes haunted by truth behind all the evil that couldn't be undone.

Marcie recalled the afternoon she drew the circle and recited the incantation that summoned the Blue Skull to kill Stan and Lee. The monster had arrived in a blast of rainbow-colored light as it always did, silent and ready to do her bidding. She had placed the order without regret, "*Find Stan and Lee, they're with my father. Kill them and anyone else who gets in your way.*" If only she'd known how literally the beast took orders, that, by naming her father in the list of targets, she'd made him one as well. And Eli, who was "in the way"—

"I never meant for you to be there," she told Eli. "When I got your message that day, that you were going to see Daddy, to quit, I was so scared that it would get you, too. *Please*, Eli. I never meant for it to kill you. Not you…"

Eli cooled, staring blankly at the circle. "It *didn't* kill me," he muttered, almost to himself.

Marcie relaxed, seeing him begin to calm. "I never accounted for that. I didn't know how you could have survived."

Recognition flashed across the man's hard-cut features and he faced her, a sense of peace about him again, like the gentle confidence he wore when he first arrived. Solidly, he declared, "It was God. He saved me."

"Oh, Eli." Marcie warmed at the sentiment. She had just crushed everything he believed in, and he still found the strength to struggle through and reclaim his faith. He really was unbeatable. But his indomitable will didn't change the fact that his faith was misplaced. "You were wrong, Eli," she said, pitying him, and at the same time wishing she were able to muster such blind devotion to a silent God. "The monster doesn't work for God. It didn't spare you because you were on the same side."

"I know, but don't you see?" He hurried to her, new life washing over him. "That only proves how powerful God *is*. He has authority over some thing from hell!"

She paced back, away from his convicting eyes. "It's getting worse, Eli. The monster is changing. I'm losing my power over it."

He halted, his face open to her once more. Ready to listen. To help. He was Eli again.

"Last year I sent Billy and some of my men to collect the money you left behind after James' hit." She felt a sad smile creep onto her lips. "I don't know how it happened, but when you left the money behind, the Blue Skull got stuck. For over a year, it was gone, and I thought it had returned to the Other Side. Then some little boy moved into the house and we intercepted a 9-1-1 call. The Blue Skull was still there, in James' house. We tried to get it back, but it killed Billy and the others. What's worse, that kid and an annoying 'urban mythologist' burned the money. It freed the Blue Skull, but now I can't bind it anymore. It's on its own and there's nothing I can do to rein it in."

Eli considered. "Who knows about this? Domingo?"

Marcie nodded. "It took a lot of convincing, but he finally came around. He's been trying to help me get it back under control. We've looked all over the world for psychics, mediums, shamans, *anything*. That's where he is now. But every time we find someone who might know something, they die. It's the Blue Skull, Eli."

"He's trying to survive," Eli countered, looking thoughtful and intense. "Trying to protect himself by killing anyone who could stop him."

Marcie agreed. "The North Woods are a convergence of spiritual rhythms. It's been this way ever since the time of Old Greenesboro. That's why I moved out here. I've been able to draw from the woods' convergence to build up a barrier around me to keep him out. So far, my spells have held, but it gets harder every day. I can feel *it* circling the woods, trying to get in. My strength is weakening, and I know it's going to come for me. I can't control it anymore. It's too powerful. I don't know what it wants."

"I do," Eli said. "To be free." He shook his head. "You had no right to do this, Marcie. The forces you're playing with…"

"Don't you think I know that?" she snapped back. "Don't think I haven't lost things, too! I didn't ask for this!"

They stood, neither one speaking for a moment, the distant sounds of barking dogs a soothing white noise. "I prayed," Marcie whispered. "Domingo said it was stupid, but we've tried so many other things. Last night I just…I asked God to help. And," she looked up at him, her lover. "He sent me you."

A ghost of a smile brightened his face in the darkness, but he quelled it. "I can't save you, Marcie."

The breath left her body. "Wh-what?"

"I couldn't even save myself. It was God. I still believe that. You want salvation, you'll have to go to Him."

She laughed in disbelief. "I don't believe this. I ask for help and I get a sermon."

"Maybe that's exactly the help you need."

Marcie gestured to the candles, the occult trappings. "Look around. This isn't religion to me, this is *practical*. I want something, and if some 'dark spirit', or whatever, is offering, we'll cut a deal. You can't cut deals with your God. You either sell out or go home."

"Exactly."

"Yeah! Exactly! I'm not doing that, Eli. I don't belong to *anybody*. I never have. I'm not going to start now."

Marcie railed against him in her heart, tearing him apart and wishing he'd die. This was the help she'd prayed for? *I take it back, God. I don't need you. Forget it.*

"You should go," she said, remembering their last break-up all too clearly.

But Eli did not budge this time. "You can't scare me away, Marcie. It doesn't work like that. I—"

Gunfire from inside the house below.

Marcie froze, her heart jumping a beat, and Eli's eyes widened. *No.* She cried inside. *No, it's not time. I'm not ready. No, no, no, no!*

"It's him," Eli said, even as the sounds of screams drifted up through the floor boards. "The Blue Skull is here."

CHAPTER SIXTEEN

Marcie and Eli hurried down the stairs and it felt to her as though they'd descended into hell. The lights flickered sporadically, casting a strobe effect on the art that adorned the walls even as bulbs popped from supernatural energy. Frigid air turned her breath to white plumes and prickled her flesh. Her men squealed like women as they died, and the walls were painted in blood. Near the bottom steps, she and Eli stopped to take in the scene.

At the center of the grisly masterpiece stood the Blue Skull.

Presently the beast held a dead guard dog by its broken hind leg and swung it like a bat, slapping away firing guns and knocking men off balance. Disoriented, Marcie's soldiers fell to swift death as the monster tore off their limbs, snapped their necks, or impaled them with its black-gloved fists. Her stomach churned as she spotted arms and legs scattered about the blood-drenched floor. Bodies draped over her expensive imported furniture, her vases and knick-knacks shattered on the hardwood floor and plush rugs.

The Blue Skull itself was covered in gore, its long black coat glistening wet with dark blood as though it had stomped through a winepress. The uncaring thing paid no regard to the death it delivered, as though it were as natural as breathing. Perhaps it was. To its kind, to murder was to be alive.

"The iron gate should have kept it out!" Marcie shrieked. "Those idiots must have left it open or— This can't be happening!"

Eli jerked on her arm, his voice shrill and shaky. "We have to go!"

Marcie could not move from the staircase. She watched helplessly as the capable soldiers she'd hired to protect her from this very creature were consumed like dry kindling by its blue fire. They didn't stand a chance. They never did. She and Domingo were wasting their time thinking they could save themselves from the monster. Eli was right—the beast was revolting, breaking the mystical chains she'd used to enslave it, and rising against its master.

I'm going to die, Marcie understood. *And there's nothing I can do about it.*

As if sensing her fear, the beast stopped in its blitz of destruction for a moment, taking a bullet to the skull without seeming to notice, and looked straight at her. Through the chaos, they shared a reflective moment. Her son of hell had returned to its mother.

"Welcome home," she whispered.

Eli pulled her again, taking a few steps down the stairs. "Marcie! Come on!"

Marcie allowed him to drag her, but pulled from his sweaty grip once they touched the floor. He slipped on blood, nearly losing his footing, and confronted her. "What are you doing?"

She sidestepped him, her eyes locked on the vacant sockets of the blue skull. The beast tore the head off a nearby mercenary and hurled it like a baseball, knocking two more men to the ground. Then the thing marched for her, sustaining gunfire from the few remaining mercs, but suffering no damage. Bullets coughed up dust instead of blood, and still the demon marched, impervious to physical harm.

Marcie held her ground as Eli shuffled beside her. "Come on!"

Shutting out his shouting, Marcie opened herself up to the dark forces she'd used to conjure the accursed thing. Raising her hands, she drew concentric circles in the air—a binding pattern she'd learned—and recited her summoning spell, "Thou evil from ages past, Thou darkness yet untold, Thou cold blue head of death, Appear now and be controlled."

An explosion of green light rippled from her body, expanding outward. The Blue Skull was caught in the wave and struggled against it until its gore-encrusted boots mystically fused to the floor. It twisted and pulled but was bound by invisible straps, stuck.

Marcie let out a slow breath, her face flushed, and grinned. She'd done it, without any divine help.

Take that, God.

The Blue Skull snorted and grunted, working with all its weight, but still its chains held until—

They snapped.

Marcie fell back as a blast of magick hit her like broken elastic. Eli caught her, saving her from falling in a pool of spilled blood. She staggered to a stand, amazed as the beast moved one foot, then the other. It was literally *breaking* her spell.

"No," she whimpered.

The devil picked up speed, unhindered now, and filled Marcie's vision with its impossible bulk. It looked like it had grown since she'd last commanded it, and its cerulean visage was even more frightening. Its skull burned brighter with blue fire, spewing out a plume of dark charcoal smoke like a chimney. It was mutating, but into what? Had it only been an infant when she first conjured it? Perhaps that was why she'd been able to control it all this time. But now, it was maturing into an adult and, like all teenagers, was rebelling against authority. Only, Marcie would not survive its adolescence.

"It's okay," she said, warm tears dropping from her lashes to her flushed cheeks. "I won't fight anymore."

"No!" Eli shouted. She'd all but forgotten he was still here and wondered why he hadn't fled with the last of her useless guards. Instead, he clamped his hand painfully over her arm and yanked with all his might.

Marcie jogged to keep up as Eli raced through the house, dragging her with him. "It's pointless, Eli," she called in hurried breaths, watching as the Blue Skull stormed after them, the mounted wall lights shattering in sparks as it passed. "It's okay to die."

"If you die now, you'll go to straight to hell!" he shrieked at her, frantic and out of breath. Like a caged animal desperate for escape, his head pivoted madly, looking in every room. "I've got to buy you more time! There's time to come to God. He can save you!"

She laughed, careless and free, ready to greet hell. Ready to see her father again. To stop the pain of living.

The Blue Skull was persistent, toppling over any obstacle in its way, marching after her. "Come and get me!" she squealed in delight to her killer. "Come on! Finish it!"

"Shut up!" Eli paused long enough to slap her across the face. "I'm not letting you die."

She recoiled in shock, then faced him. His eyes were red and swollen and filled with tears. "I'm not losing you," he muttered, a cry mixed with his words.

Marcie touched his face. "It's okay, Eli. Really, it's okay. After everything I've done…I deserve to go to hell."

Eli hung his head, then looked to his left, staring down the beast closing in on them. Her lover struggled against tears, fixing his jaw in anger, glaring at the devil. With one hand, Eli kept a tight grip on Marcie's arm, refusing to release her to her doom.

"You've got to let me go," she whispered to him, weeping now, but unafraid. "I was never yours…no matter how much I wanted to be."

Eli shook his head furiously.

"Don't get too attached," she said, cracking a smile, hoping to alleviate his fears. The Blue Skull was nearly on top of them. It would be over soon.

With his free hand, Eli reached into his back pocket and pulled out a pocket knife—the kind she assumed most handy men always carried with them. He flicked it open, his eyes boring into the blue-flamed beast.

"Eli, what are you—?"

Eli dug the blade into the inside meat of his forearm. Blood ran out of the wound, splashing on the floor.

"Eli!"

Stifling a curse through bared teeth, Eli brought the knife up, slicing through his flesh and muscle, opening up his veins. Marcie pulled against his restraint, confused and upset.

Growing weak, Eli dropped the knife, then reached into his oozing wound, gathering a handful of reddish purple blood. Marcie gasped as Eli smeared the blood on her forehead, and down her cheeks.

"Eli!" she screamed, but he faced her again, the color draining from his face. Then, just above his eyes, a faint white light pulsed, illuminating a single character—a letter. She knew it, but she never thought she'd see it.

"You…" she breathed. "You're one of them?"

"Listen," he slurred. "His blood for me…mine for you…"

His eyes rolled into the back of his head, and Eli collapsed to the floor, loosing her. Marcie stood shaking, watching him bleeding on the floor at her feet, his system teetering on the edge of shock. "No! *No!*"

Hot air ruffled her hair and Marcie looked up, right into the Blue Skull's fiery face.

The demon hunkered over her, dwarfing her in its terrible size. But it did not move against her. Instead, it craned its head this way and that, studying her. It drew its skull face closer to her, sniffing her neck, her face, like an animal. Marcie shut her eyes, her body rigid. The thing snarled, snorted, then backed away. Turned.

Walked off.

Marcie blinked one eye open, then both.

The beast was gone, taking the cold with it.

I'm alive. Eli did it. He saved me.

She stooped down to her savior and cradled his head in her lap. Smoothing his locks out of his face, she watched over him.

CHAPTER SEVENTEEN

Eli opened his eyes into a blinding bright light. For a split second he hoped he might be in heaven, reunited with Dad, but then he heard beeping equipment to his side. Felt the pinch of an IV in his hand. He gurgled and sat up, his eyes taking in a hospital room, the soft blankets covering him, and his arm wrapped in bloody gauze.

"Welcome back," a familiar voice greeted.

Woozy, Eli lay back in bed, blinking sight back into his eyes. "Where am I?"

"A hospital in Greensboro."

"What are you doing here?" he groaned.

Darius Domingo stepped closer to the bed, a sportscoat draped over his arm. He held his trademark bowler in his hand. Domingo offered a cocky grin. "What you did was very brave. And foolish. But then again, that's your style, as I recall."

Eli sprang up, his memory returning. "Marcie?"

"She's fine," Domingo said. "Thanks to you. Speaking of which, what *did* you do?"

Eli pursed his lips and looked out the window. "Hebrews 9:22. 'Without the shedding of blood, there can be no forgiveness of sins.'" He shook his head, his words quiet. "Christ shed his blood for me. I hoped maybe I could extend that grace to Marcie for a second." Firm, Eli eyed Domingo. "But all I did was buy her time. If she wants to stop this thing, she knows what she's got to do."

The man raised a haughty eyebrow. "At any rate, I wanted to thank you for looking out for her when I couldn't."

Domingo slid into his coat, sat the bowler on his head, and walked out the door. "He's all yours," he commented casually to someone standing just out of view in the hallway.

As soon as Domingo was gone, Marcie walked in, wearing stiletto heels and a form-fitting red dress, a hole strategically cut across her chest, revealing a tantalizing hint of cleavage. Eli hardly recognized her as the simple schoolgirl he'd fallen for. "Hey," he said.

She kept her distance, remaining by the door, ready to bolt at any moment. "You're alive."

"Yeah. Guess so."

She nodded, cold. "You're lucky. You survived the worst cougar attack Maribel County's ever seen."

Eli sighed. "Cougar attack? The cops really bought that?"

"Did you forget who I am? The cops buy anything I sell them."

He grinned. She was flexing her authority, overcompensating for last night. Her extravagant dress was a part of that façade. Marcie was afraid, even if she didn't want to admit it. *Same old Marcie.*

The brown-eyed girl approached, her heels clicking on the hospital tile. "Why did you do it?"

"Shouldn't that be obvious by now?"

She stood over him, her steely veneer making way for real anger. "Why can't you understand? I don't *want* to be saved. I deserve whatever hell wants to give me. I murdered my own father, Eli. You don't just tell God you're sorry for something like that and expect to live a great life."

"But God will forgive you," he interrupted, wishing she could believe that.

Marcie softened, shaking her head. "But I don't forgive me."

He hung his head, the same old silence moving in as the third party in their relationship. They could fill planets with the words not spoken in that void. Eli decided to cross the great chasm to her. "I asked you before: Come with me." He chuckled and held up his bandaged wrist. "Well, you know, as soon as I get out of here."

She grinned. "You can't save me, choir boy."

"Yeah. Figured you'd say that."

Marcie turned on her heel, strolling for the door, hesitant.

"Where will you hide?" he asked her.

She didn't answer.

"Your demon is still out there," he told her. "It's only a matter of time before it comes for you again. When that happens, I may not be there to protect you. Be careful, okay? I love you."

Marcie stepped to the door, her back to him. "By the way," she offered before looking him over one last time. "I love you, too."

Then she was gone.

Eli laid his head back on the pillow and drifted to sleep.

PART IV

THE SLEUTH

CHAPTER ONE

Lenore Patterson was *smoking* hot. Douglas Ritchie couldn't believe he'd snared her, though he didn't think his girlfriend Trish would be very happy about it.

"Is this it?" Lenore asked, shouldering her camping gear as they came to the clearing.

Douglas gestured to the woods around them—green leaves with golden highlights thanks to the late afternoon summer sun. "Beautiful, isn't it?"

Lenore dropped her bag to the forest floor and did a slow 360°, surveying the dense copse. Douglas slid off his own pack, feeling instantly lighter, and dropped to a knee to undo the straps on the rolled-up tent he'd brought along. *Tonight's the night.* He could barely contain his anticipation. Or his libido.

He gawked, nearly salivating, as Lenore unscrewed the top off her water bottle and took a long swig. A few drops sprinkled onto her revealing tank top. Douglas gulped then grinned. His hands numb with excitement, he fumbled to construct the tent as fast as possible, ready for Lenore.

He'd met her at a bar after a fight with Trish one night. Trish, with all her nagging. Wanting to move in together. He needed to be his own man for *at least* another ten years. Sow some wild oats. Sleep with as many chicks as possible before he finally settled on one.

One. He couldn't imagine sleeping with the same woman for the next fifty years.

Lenore knew the score. He'd seen her at the bar a few times, usually on a different man's arm every couple weeks. She liked the party life, and that suited Douglas just fine. She didn't want commitment from him—she just wanted to be surprised. To be entertained. That's when he decided on camping.

He felt a little bad about their secret rendezvous. Trish loved camping. In fact, she'd turned Douglas—who was a happy couch potato, by and large—on to the whole outdoor scene. Having Lenore out here in the very same spot he and Trish had camped *last* summer seemed like a different sort of betrayal. But Trish wouldn't know any better. Douglas had enjoyed many flings behind Trish's back, but so far, she hadn't caught on. He was sure she didn't suspect a thing—something that was certain to change if they moved in together.

"Need any help?" Lenore asked as he assembled the tent.

"No, thanks. It won't take me long."

She shrugged and sat on a downed log, crossing one leg over the other. Douglas palpitated. *Come on, tent! Let's get this show rolling.*

"You've been out here before?" she asked, glancing around the forest, looking a little apprehensive.

"Yeah," he laughed. "Why? Spooked?"

"Well, this is the North Woods, right?"

"Actually, that's south to us, but yeah, I guess it is."

Lenore rubbed the back of her neck, frowning. "I used to hear stories growing up about the North Woods. Ghost stories, you know?"

"Oooh," Douglas sang, wiggling his fingers like the Wicked Witch of the West. He even went so far as to cackle, "I'll get you, my pretty."

"Stop," she giggled. "I'm serious. You never heard them?"

"No."

"I heard a lot of really weird stuff happened in Greensboro a hundred years ago or something. Whole town went nuts. Started killing each other. They say the ghosts are still out here…"

"Well, we're nowhere near Greensboro." Douglas abandoned the tent for a moment, needing a fix. He stood and moved to Lenore, taking her hand and leading her to her feet. Wrapping his arms around her curvaceous hips, he pulled her close. "Besides, I'll protect you."

They kissed lewdly, untamed and sloppy. Trish was always such a boring kisser. That was what happened when you stayed with one woman too long.

Douglas parted from their kiss, wanting more, but making himself wait. If he could just get the tent up, they could do this right. Lenore brought out a compact mirror, wiping at her smeared lipstick, while Douglas went back to work. "So, what kind of stories did you hear?" he asked, making small talk. After all, a little danger made for great romance.

But Lenore didn't seem to want to play along. She sat down, keeping a careful eye on the looming trees. "I don't know. Just that there are *things* out here."

"Like monsters?"

She nodded, firm.

"Aw, come on, Lenore. These are big woods. Why get so spooked? It's not like it is in the movies. Even if there were such a thing as monsters—which there aren't—what are the chances they'd be right where *we* are?"

He laughed, but Lenore stood and screamed. Before he could ask what was wrong, Douglas felt two cold hands gripping each side of his head. There was a terrible pulling and the muscles in his neck went taut, then relaxed. His ears rang, and he felt weightless, but no pain. Suddenly he was falling and landed hard on the earth on his right ear. *Lenore?* he wanted to ask, but couldn't. Just felt warmth spreading, oozing on his cheek. He saw a man standing over him, wearing his clothes. In fact, the man looked just like him, only it didn't have a head. The body took a step, then collapsed sideways.

Is that my body? he dimly thought before another shape stepped over him. This one was clothed all in black with a long black cloak or coat. The shape's head was like a skull lit with blue fire.

Lenore continued to scream, but stood stock still. Just as the blue-headed thing reached out for her, gloved hands encircling her throat, Douglas' sight faded to black.

In his last moments, he wondered what Trish would say.

Four days later, the bodies of Douglas Ritchie and Lenore Patterson, formerly of Russellville, were discovered. Douglas was found with his head pulled off, while Lenore had her heart ripped out and dark bruises around her neck, as though she'd been strangled. Police from Russellville and sister town Greensboro formed a joint investigation, and the whispers began that monsters were once more in the North Woods. Officer Dale Sharpton with Russellville P.D. had never seen anything so gruesome, and had gone behind his superiors' back to call in a "professional".

Urban mythologist Vinnie Caponi arrived at the crime scene forty minutes later.

Vinnie trudged through the thick woods, the edges of his trenchcoat getting tangled in the foliage. Now he realized he probably should have left the coat in the car, especially with the sweltering July heat, but the coat pockets were bulging with tools of the trade. Things he might need out here, investigating a monster attack. It'd been a long time since Vinnie had officially been part of a police investigation. Up ahead he spotted the yellow tape wrapped around trees, where the mutilated bodies lay scattered. Police photographers milled about, flashing photos of the severed head, the removed heart. Other investigators theorized, wrote notes, or knelt to examine the gory pieces. Vinnie felt an electric charge in the air, and his hackles rose. Despite the buzz of activity, a hush permeated the scene—a reverent fear of this place that even Vinnie sensed.

The North Woods were the subject of many area legends. To hear it told by the locals, the place was home to a bogle-king. No urban mythologist worth his salt would miss a chance to investigate such a claim, and Vinnie had been out here a few times in his career. He'd never found anything, just more tall tales from the folks in Greensboro. It seemed today he'd get his wish, though he couldn't say he felt good about that, given the circumstances.

Vinnie lifted a strip of yellow tape and climbed in like a wrestler into the ring. He spotted Officer Sharpton talking with a plain clothes detective in low tones. The white-haired detective had a long chin and drooping scowl. When he spotted Vinnie, the detective grimaced, spat once with a snarl, and walked off. Sharpton already looked apologetic as he approached.

"Hey, Vinnie," he said quietly, as though they were speaking in the back of a church service. Or a funeral.

"Dale." Vinnie nodded. "Bad time?"

Sharpton glanced at the detective who kept a steady, nasty watch on Vinnie. "Ah, local dicks, you know? Don't want anyone all up in their jurisdiction. You remember the type."

"I remember."

Sharpton was good people. Vinnie had thought so since back when they served together on the force in Willowbrook. Dale was Russellville P.D. now, but he and Vinnie were still friendly, though Vinnie had little time for friends these days.

"So, you ready for the gross stuff?" Sharpton asked, scuffling through the leafy floor toward the bodies. Vinnie followed, his stomach tightening. He hadn't seen a dead body up close in ages. He thought he'd be used to it by now, but he wasn't. Not even close.

He hunkered over the headless corpse of Douglas Ritchie, just as the angry detective shouted across the yard, shattering the carefully constructed quiet, "Don't touch anything."

Vinnie held up his hands, offering his surrender, then went back to a hands-off inspection.

After a moment, Sharpton leaned over his shoulder. "Crazy, huh? Ripped right off. What could do something like that?"

Vinnie didn't know for certain, but he was pretty sure that, whatever it was, it wasn't human.

"See why I brought you in now?" Dale said. "It's gotta be one of those monsters you hunt, right? What do you think? Bigfoot or something?"

He chortled a bit, but Vinnie remained grim. "I don't think so. Generally speaking, Bigfoot are gentle creatures."

"Vinnie, I was kidding."

Vinnie stood, brushing off his pants. "No claw or bite marks. Rules out a lot of feral creatures. The blood's everywhere—if it were a vampire, it'd be all gone."

Sharpton interrupted him, "Man, you're really serious."

"Isn't that why you called me out?"

The cop shifted, wincing. "Well, yeah. But, I don't know...I was sorta hoping you'd just tell me I was overreacting. Some of the old timers in Greensboro are all riled up, way I hear it. They think it's the demons from those old stories."

"Hm. Demons are rare. But they might be right. How many attacks?"

"This is the first one that Russellville's come in on, but I hear there's been others over the last few months. Maribel County Sheriff's got this place off-limits for the time being, but I guess some people just don't listen."

Vinnie reached into his pocket and pulled out a Dum Dum sucker. He unwrapped it and popped the candy in his mouth. After taking a hit off the tart, cherry-flavored orb, he withdrew it. "Most folks don't. If they did, maybe they'd stay alive longer."

"Got something," the white-haired detective announced. He bent over the ground, touching the dirt with gloved hands. The cops, along with Vinnie, converged on him, forming a football huddle around his discovery.

Vinnie spotted a boot print in the earth. Large and sunken deep.

"Think that belongs to our killer?" a Greensboro deputy named Adams asked.

The detective made a special point to look up at Vinnie. "It sure ain't a werewolf's paw, now is it, Mr. Caponi?"

Eyes turned on the urban mythologist, but he didn't let the comment faze him. He'd dealt with cops before who didn't understand the supernatural and scoffed at those who did. Instead, Vinnie took a drag off his sucker. "No. You're right about that. Congratulations, detective. But look at the indention of that print. Guy had to be four hundred pounds to make a crater like that."

"So?" the detective snapped. "We're looking for a fat guy, then."

Vinnie scoured the nearby area. Found another print. He placed one boot near the first, then stretched to reach the next. "Look at this gait. I'm a big guy myself, but this is unreal. Guy's gotta be a giant."

The detective stood, his face reddening at the challenge. "Doesn't change the fact that it's a man. Not a monster. Which means your 'services' aren't required out here."

"Come on, Halbreck," Sharpton said. "Vinnie knows his stuff."

"This isn't the time for ghost stories," Detective Halbreck shot back. "This is a serious police investigation. We got two dead young folks here, and I'm not goin' to their mothers and telling them the Bogeyman got them. Greensboro can be as superstitious as it wants, but that's not how we do things in Russellville."

Vinnie cut in, "You know, we've seen this kind of thing before in Willowbrook. A couple years back. A whole string of murders, the poor schmucks all tore up just like this."

Sharpton eyed him suspiciously. "You mean that Boss Marcon thing?"

"Boss Marcon?" The detective snarled. "What's that?"

"There was a gang war going on between Boss Adrian Marcon and some new player from the City. Nearly all of Marcon's gang were killed in horrible ways. The Boss himself got his…" Sharpton looked to the severed head on the ground.

Vinnie finished for him, having already pieced together the puzzle. "Got his head tore right off. Sound familiar, Detective?"

"But I heard it was one of Old Man Marcon's own hitmen that did it," Sharpton told Vinnie. "Some guy named Eli snapped and killed everybody, right?"

Vinnie shrugged. "That's what they say. But I happen to believe it was something else. A creature I've been chasing called 'the Blue Skull'. I thought I took care of him last December, but…"

The crime scene erupted in laughter. None laughed harder than Detective Halbreck. "That's rich. Where'd you dig this nutcase up, Dale?"

Officer Sharpton blushed while Vinnie just munched on his sucker. They didn't want his help, but he wasn't out here for them. He wasn't looking to solve any crimes, or get any cops big promotions. He was here for one reason only.

Find the Blue Skull.

That was all that mattered now. These mooks could laugh all they wanted, Vinnie had things to do. Turning, he left the crime scene behind, still observing the grounds, laughter echoing behind him. At last he spotted what he thought he might and called out over the din of hilarity, "Detective. Let me ask you this: If we're just dealin' with a flesh and blood killer, then how come his tracks disappear right here? Guy that big would leave a trail all the way back to his hideout. Unless you think he just climbed a tree like a monkey and swung on a vine all the way home."

Halbreck's laughter faded, but a cocky smirk remained. He nodded to his boys. "Move out. He's gotta have tracks somewhere."

Vinnie nibbled on his sucker, waiting as the cops formed an expanding circle, investigating the terrain. At last, Sharpton looked up from his search, smiling in Vinnie's direction. "Sorry, Halbreck. Can't find anything."

"Me, neither," Deputy Adams called.

"Nothing here," another.

Halbreck looked to Vinnie, his face turning white. Vinnie just grinned and crunched the head off his sucker. He tipped his black fedora and strolled away. "See you around, Detective."

CHAPTER TWO

Flynn Spanger checked his watch again and heaved a great sigh. Leaning on his bicycle, he craned his neck to either side of the road, but no sign of Vinnie.

Where is he?

Curiosity had become aggravation fifteen minutes ago, motivating Flynn to dig around in the pockets of his cargo-style jeans for his cell phone. He dialed Vinnie's number and waited until the computerized voice told him his party was unreachable. He groaned and slid the cell back in his pocket.

"Hey, boy, we gonna do this, or what?"

Flynn regarded the man in his company—Leland O'Dell, twenty-seven years of age, dressed in a dingy sleeveless undershirt, a dirt-encrusted pair of jeans and boots, and a straw hat. O'Dell winced against the late Saturday afternoon sun, leaned against his shed, waiting for an answer. In one hand he dangled a beer bottle, in the other he clutched a piece of straw that he chewed periodically. "Gettin' kinda late, idn't it?"

Flynn checked one more time, praying he'd spot Vinnie's beat-up Taurus rounding the curb at any moment, but the street continued to taunt him with emptiness. He huffed but quickly recovered. "Yeah," he squeaked, his voice doing that more and more since he turned thirteen back in April. "Okay." Nervous now that he'd have to do this on his own, Flynn rummaged through his pockets, momentarily forgetting which one held the small digital camera.

O'Dell spit once into the dirt and scuffed his boot over the spot.

Grinning sheepishly, Flynn procured the camera and took a deep breath to get his bearings.

"So what do I gotta do?" O'Dell asked, squinting at the boy, bored.

"Just tell me your story," Flynn said. "Just like it happened."

"I can do that," the man chuckled. "I won't forget it, I'll tell ya that."

Flynn lined up his shot and hit RECORD. O'Dell stared blankly at the camera, prompting Flynn to formally inquire, "What can you tell me about the Blue Skull?"

"Well, I seen 'im," O'Dell acknowledged, gnawing on the straw tip.

Flynn nodded appreciatively, though he already knew as much. Now that he'd updated Vinnie's urban mythology website, they were developing a regular following on the fringe. Flynn had buried himself in the arduous task of cataloging all of Vinnie's previous cases, along with any photos, videos, or firsthand account the private detective had accumulated over the years. Pretty soon, Vinnie's phone rang a little more often, and it seemed everyone had a spooky encounter to relay.

It was unusual, though, for someone from Willowbrook to call. Even more unusual that it was someone who claimed to have seen the Blue Skull, itself, following its disappearance from Flynn's house last Christmas.

Excitement tempted him to rush the interview—to find the monster. But Vinnie had taught him better than that. "Just start at the beginning, Mr. O'Dell."

O'Dell brightened. "Well, it happened about six weeks ago. I was over there workin' on one of my pick-up trucks. I'd just been by old Dodger Store up there 'n picked me up a twelve-pack of some Budweiser. And I was jus' sittin' out, y'know. Jus' havin' a cold one on a nice warm day, as it is today. I was out there doin' some work, and all a'sudden I heard some rustlin' over there in them bushes. I thought it was my hound down here."

Flynn kept the camera trained on his subject but glanced down at a charcoal-colored furball that must have been the dog in question. The dog perked up at Flynn's glance, as if waiting to be addressed, then whined and laid its head back on its paws, disinterested. O'Dell continued, "I looked up there and I said 'Hey, Pepper! Hey, Pepper, come o'er here'." He paused and shrugged. "Well she didn't do nuthin', so I walked over there, 'n all a'sudden I saw the most hideous face I ever seen in my life."

The man raised his skinny arms, splashing a few drops of beer on Flynn's shirt. At just the moment Flynn expected O'Dell to explode in a hair-raising supernatural account, the skinny man quieted and raised a defensive hand. "Now, I only had a few, y'know, but I know what I saw. This was 'im…it was crazy." O'Dell paused and looked around the camera, facing Flynn directly with an eager gap-toothed grin. "So, is this gonna be on the *tee-vee*? One of them reality shows? How much money am I gettin' for this anyway?"

Flynn's hopes plummeted, and he knew they'd have to file this one under "Unconfirmed". Another dead end.

Following his close call with the Blue Skull, Flynn thought of little else but encountering the beast again. After Vinnie burned the money that was mystically keeping the creature trapped on Buckingham Road, the thing had vanished. Was it really gone? Vinnie seemed to think so, but Flynn feared in his gut that it was only biding its time.

But for what?

For politeness' sake, he continued filming as O'Dell finished, the straw bobbing up and down in his mouth. "Anyway, he run on outta them bushes. Well, I run in the house and grabbed my shotgun. That's all I knew how to do.

He lit a shuck outta there. It was horrible. Absolutely horrible."

Lowering the camera, Flynn grinned, though feared it came off as more of a flinch. "Uh…thanks, Mr. O'Dell. That's good."

"Call me Leland," the man nodded, taking a swig of his beer.

Flynn offered a wave and headed back to his bike, with Leland calling out in a drawl, "Come on back anytime, now. Let me know when this shows up on the *tee-vee!*"

The sun had set on the afternoon, deepening purples stretching to blot out its light. Flynn pedaled his bike to the old folks' apartment complex that Vinnie called home. He'd cooled down considerably on the long bike ride over, but seeing the familiar paint-chipped Taurus sitting out front stoked his irritation all over again.

He hopped the curb like usual and slid to his regular stop on the front porch. As he kicked the stand in place, he was already fishing the apartment key out of one of his pockets.

Flynn turned the lock and entered the apartment to find only the kitchenette light on. Walking into Vinnie's, especially at this time of the evening, he usually found himself greeted by the pleasant smell of fried, fatty foods and the sight of the burly urban mythologist playing chef, dancing a little jig to one of his jazz standards as he cooked up the chow of the day. Tonight, however, the kitchen was empty, and no warm smells assaulted his nose.

"Vinnie?" Flynn called into the darkness, keeping the front door open a crack to allow the early evening moonlight to further illuminate his path. "You home?"

Straining to listen, he caught the faint sounds of one of Vinnie's old records playing in the other room. Over the months he'd been working with Vinnie, he'd come to learn the tunes—or at least the urban mythologist's favorites. Relieved at the sign of life, Flynn shut the door and followed the music to the back room that held what he had always thought of as, the "Wall of Truth"—Vinnie's ode to his Blue Skull obsession.

Flynn eased open the door, Duke Ellington's rendition of "Stormy Weather" growing louder. There stood Vinnie, his back to the door, pacing in front of the wall of pictures and notes he'd taken over the years; the evidence of his hunt for the monster that had touched both their lives.

Presently, Vinnie mumbled to himself, running his finger along the various threads of red yarn that connected one lead to the next. As he puzzled it out, the urban mythologist smacked on a Dum Dum sucker, and Flynn noticed that the ashtray in the room was littered with crumpled Dum Dum wrappers and spent sticks.

"Hey," Flynn began softly, not wanting to startle his friend from his intense reasoning.

Vinnie didn't bother facing him, leaning closer to the board, studying a number of photos. "Hey, kid."

Flynn huffed an annoyed laugh, expecting at least an apology. "Where were you today? We were supposed to meet at that guy's house for the interview."

Vinnie shrugged, still concentrating. "Had other things to take care of."

"Other things?" Flynn said, growing angry.

"Find anything useful?"

He sighed, shifting his agitation to O'Dell. "No."

"Told you it wasn't going to pan out."

"But it was worth a shot, wasn't it?"

Vinnie shrugged again, indifferent. When he didn't immediately offer a further answer, Flynn relaxed and took to looking around the room. He'd been here with Vinnie nearly every day this summer, but there was always something new to spot in the cluttered mess of collected occult trappings in this pigsty. He rustled through a stack of books, sifted through pictures and strewn documents. Among them he spotted the framed photo of Vinnie and his old partner. Flynn had asked him about it a couple times, but Vinnie didn't say much except to identify the skinny guy in the baggy coat and dumpy newsboy hat as "Josh". In the photo, Vinnie and Josh stood with their arms across each other's shoulders, big smiles on their faces. They looked younger and untouchable, and Flynn wondered what Vinnie was like back in the early days. It seemed odd to him that his friend had a whole other life before they met.

A life he rarely spoke of.

"You need something, kid?" Vinnie finally asked, startling him.

Flynn set the picture down. "I don't guess so. Just wanted to make sure you were okay."

"I'm fine," he said, more distant than usual.

Flynn stepped up to the bulletin board to see what had captivated Vinnie's attention. It was then that he noticed a couple of new pictures on the Wall of Truth. Vinnie's bulk obscured most of the material, but Flynn recognized woods. Blood.

"What's this one? This new?"

Vinnie went rigid and pressed his back to the wall, blocking the new evidence from Flynn's sight. "Don't worry about it."

Burning hot, Flynn said, "What's going on? Where were you today? Why aren't you answering my calls or my texts? I thought we were partners."

Vinnie exhaled and rubbed his puffy eyes. He appeared terribly tired, Flynn noticed now that he'd stopped ranting long enough to get a good look at him.

Quieting, the boy asked, "Are you okay?"

"Nothing for you to worry about, kid. An old friend of mine from back in the day gave me a call. Needed me to come out and take a look at a case he was working on."

Flynn's eyes returned to the photos Vinnie didn't want him to see. All he saw was more blood. Was that a human heart lying on the ground?

He gulped, wondering if he'd just turned paler.

"Is it bad?" he asked.

Vinnie's face remained expressionless. "Still working on it."

Flynn's heart beat faster. "Is it…is it *him*?"

The question, and all its implications, lingered in the silence that followed. Flynn rubbed his arms, his stomach souring. "Did we… We did that, didn't we? The Blue Skull was stuck in my house and we let it out. Now it's killing…" He couldn't bear to finish the sentence.

Vinnie faced him, stern and sympathetic. "We don't know that. There are no hard and fast rules when you're facing the preternatural, Flynn. But we'll find him. We'll stop him. It just takes time to hunt down an elusive creature of myth."

Flynn nodded mutely, terrible guilt weighing on him.

The urban mythologist planted a firm hand on his shoulder and gave it a gentle squeeze. He offered a smile. "C'mon, kid. You look like you could use a drink."

They parked the Taurus on the curb, Flynn's bike stuffed haphazardly in the trunk. Vinnie stepped out of the old clunker, then reached into the backseat for his rumpled fedora. He led the way into the diner, Flynn trailing behind. They hadn't spoken on the ride into town, but Flynn knew Vinnie was troubled about whatever he found out in the woods earlier that day. A part of him desperately wanted to know what had happened, but when Flynn remembered the image of that heart, discarded like trash in the dirt, he considered that maybe he didn't want to know, after all. Especially not if the Blue Skull did that.

Is it our fault?

Inside, the diner was packed with people—young and old alike—eating the supper specials and treating themselves to a frosty dessert. The bell over the door signaled Vinnie's entrance and the one-handed man behind the counter perked up and gave an affable wave with his prosthetic claw.

"Hey, Vinnie," he greeted over the noisy bustle of the supper-time rush.

Vinnie tipped his hat. "Carl. Chocolate malt for me and my partner, here."

"You got it." Carl grinned wide and jerked a nod to the back of the diner. "Your booth's empty, but it won't stay that way for long tonight."

Vinnie shuffled his way to the back of the diner, careful to dodge the waitresses that zipped back and forth, trays precariously balanced in upraised hands. Flynn stayed close, his mind elsewhere. Still on that removed heart. Who had it belonged to?

"Oof!" he gasped, nearly toppling a passing stranger. He glanced up and saw a tall, slender girl, her long straight blonde hair done up in a messy ponytail. A handful of strands hung down in her freckled face, but were unable to hide her wide brown eyes. He'd met her before, when he first moved here and she, working as an office aide, helped him find his way to class on that first terrible day in a new school. He'd been struck by her beauty then, as well.

Flynn gulped and blushed.

"Sorry," the girl said, her earlobes reddening.

"No, it's my fault," he stammered, stepping past her, a silly grin slowly spreading warmth to his entire body.

The girl grinned, rolled her eyes in amused embarrassment, tucked a few loose strands behind her ear, and hurried off. He watched her move across the diner until she finally took a seat with a couple who must have been her parents and a little brother who looked maybe seven or eight. The family was in mid-conversation and the girl easily slipped back into her place…but not before sparing Flynn another glance. Another smile.

He felt like laughing, but didn't know why.

"You all right?" Vinnie asked him.

Flynn blinked the stars out of his eyes and sat across from Vinnie. He furrowed his brow, doing his best not to steal another peek at the girl. "Yeah."

Vinnie smirked. "You know her?"

He looked up, caught in his private thoughts, then quickly shook his head. "I've seen her around at school, but I don't know her name or anything."

Vinnie patted the table and made to stand. "Well, we can fix that—"

"No!" Flynn shrieked, his voice cracking, and reached across the table to put a kung-fu death grip on Vinnie's thick arm.

The big man laughed—the first time he'd really laughed in a long while, Flynn realized—and sat back down. "Easy there, *kemosabe.*"

One of Carl's girls appeared at the table, sporting a tray with their malts, thankfully bringing an end to the awkwardness. Flynn dove headfirst into his malt, hoping to cool the flush in his cheeks. A chuckle lingered over Vinnie's end of the table before the man poked around a bit at his drink.

"I'm just saying," Vinnie carried on, right when Flynn thought he was in the clear. "Never hurts to make a new friend."

Flynn grimaced, a spoonful of ice cream halted in front of his mouth. "Can we just talk about something else?" Lowering his voice, he muttered, "Besides, we've got Big Blue to worry about."

He finished his bite and Vinnie suddenly frowned, his drooping eyes sad and serious.

Tentatively, the urban mythologist nursed his malt, his heart clearly not in it anymore. Suddenly Flynn didn't feel much in the mood for ice cream, either. The two of them sucked absently at their malts, saying little for a time, before Vinnie asked, friendly enough, "How's it goin' with your dad these days?"

The question caught Flynn by surprise. They rarely spoke of their off-duty lives to each other, content to spend their time discussing their latest cases. Despite his frustration with Vinnie's no-show today, Flynn warmed. "A lot better. He got switched to a different department, so he's able to be at home a lot more."

"That's good." Vinnie nodded, taking a sip of his drink. "It's good to have more than work. Family's important."

The urban mythologist withdrew, and Flynn suspected now was his moment to probe the secretive man a little harder. He still knew so little about him. "What about *your* family, Vinnie? You don't really talk much about them."

Vinnie slowly stirred his malt with his straw. "I suppose I don't have a family anymore."

Flynn dipped his spoon in for another bite, listening intently.

"I did," Vinnie said, staring into his glass. "Once, I was married. My Allison. She was beautiful. Made great pie too."

Flynn recalled the photo of the blonde woman at the center of Vinnie's Wall of Truth. He'd asked Vinnie several times about that woman in the picture, but Vinnie always changed the subject. *Was that Allison?* "What happened to her?"

Vinnie's eyes glassed over, and the usual mischievous shine there dulled. "I guess that's the grim story I'll have to tell you sometime."

Vinnie arrived home after ten that night. He dropped Flynn and his bike off at the kid's house on Buckingham Road, then took a little drive, hoping to clear the cobwebs out of the attic. But no matter how hard he tried, he couldn't stop seeing those twisted bodies in the North Woods. A head missing. A heart torn out of a pretty girl's chest. Big Blue was on the move again and Vinnie didn't know what it all meant. Willowbrook had been the creature's private hunting ground for years now—why the relocation? What was out in the woods? Those sticks were full of old stories. Maybe they were true, at least in part. Could it be some dark energy was brewing out there, drawing the Blue Skull?

All just theories now. He understood Flynn's impatience. He'd been hunting the monster a lot longer than the kid, and he had a lot more on the line. But Flynn was eager—a little too eager for his own good. The kid was still under the impression that they were hunting some phantom that would only attack if provoked. The boy didn't really understand. They were after a *killer*. It wasn't safe, a fact to which Douglas Ritchie and Lenore Patterson could attest, and it wasn't something a thirteen-year-old should see.

Vinnie had hunted Blue for a long time, for reasons he wasn't ready to share with his young partner. It had been mostly cold leads and false alarms for years now, but lately things had turned a corner. Something was stirring in the shadows, and Vinnie felt the cold hand of fate encircling him. He'd almost had his monster that night in Flynn's kitchen last Christmas, but the creature had slipped away. In his heart, Vinnie felt he was about to get his second chance to confront the Blue Skull. After all this time hunting the beast, what would he do when the time came to finally face it?

Vinnie meandered towards his front door, rummaging around for his keys. This late at night, most of his elderly neighbors were in bed, giving the apartment complex an eerie loneliness after dark. Vinnie had gotten accustomed to the solitude—craved it even—before one cold December afternoon when young Flynn Spanger showed up at his door. The kid had brought purpose to his life again, but what had Vinnie given the kid in return? Finding Blue was *his* problem. Flynn should be a kid, right now. He should be riding bikes with his friends and worrying about girls and first kisses. *I'm taking away that kid's childhood.*

He thought of Flynn's comment earlier about being too busy worrying about finding Big Blue to bother with making a friend his own age. Maybe it was a fib told to conceal his shyness, but Vinnie feared that, at least in part, what Flynn said was true. The thought saddened him. The kid's shoulders were too small to carry such a load.

Burdened and confused, Vinnie unlocked his door and entered the darkened apartment. He removed his fedora and plopped it on the coat rack by the door, then climbed out of his coat and hooked it as well. He—

A shadow crossed him. His stomach dropped. Vinnie felt a dark presence in the room with him, somewhere in the shade. Without turning on the light, he reached for the secondary holster he kept draped on the coat rack and pulled out his Colt M1911. He racked the slide and spun, pointing the weapon at a man-sized shape silhouetted by moonlight from the front window.

"Hello, Mr. Caponi," the man spoke in a British accent.

"Can I help ya?" Vinnie asked casually, the pistol trained at the unknown man's head.

"Perhaps. Perhaps we can help each other." The man reached towards the end table and switched on a lamp, casting the room in a pale glow, revealing his features. He was pretty—not handsome—with ghostly blue eyes, high cheekbones, and a soul patch. He wore a dark button-down shirt, loosely tucked into his khakis. The man grinned, introducing himself. "Darius Domingo."

"Yeah…" Vinnie snarled, still aiming the .45. "I know who you are."

He'd never forget *that* face. That smug, untouchable grin.

Domingo's lips spread into a smirk. "Riiiight."

For a flicker of an instant, Vinnie considered pulling the trigger and getting his revenge here, but…that wasn't right. Besides, it was the Blue Skull he was after, not common street trash. "I ain't got nothin' to discuss with Adrian Marcon's men. You can show yourself out."

"Oh, but Adrian's long been removed from the picture. There's a *new* Boss now."

"Yeah, well, I don't want anything to do with him, either."

Domingo took a seat on Vinnie's couch, reclining comfortably. He examined his nails, cleaning some grit beneath them. "I think you might reconsider it once you hear my offer."

"What offer?"

Finished with his grooming, Domingo looked straight at him. "I've got two words for you: 'Blue' and 'Skull'."

"What do you know about that?"

"Quite a bit, actually. And I'm willing to pass that information on to you."

Vinnie holstered his gun, then faced Domingo, crossing his meaty arms. "Yeah. Well, where are the strings and what do you want in return?"

"Why, Mr. Caponi…" Domingo leaned in, grinning devilishly. "I want you to kill it."

CHAPTER THREE

Vinnie steered his car down the long, gravel back road, inching past ominous trees and tangled brush. Flynn sat in the passenger seat, gripping his digital camera tightly. Vinnie feared he'd showed a severe lapse in judgment by letting the wide-eyed youth accompany him to interview the head of an infamous crime family, but Domingo knew something about the Blue Skull and was willing to divulge that information. This was an interview, same as with Leland O'Dell yesterday, Vinnie told himself.

But it's not the same. Domingo wanted him to kill the monster. Vinnie wanted the same thing. He'd wanted to kill it the moment he learned of its existence. Years of tears, of struggle—it came down to this moment. So why did he bring Flynn?

Maybe he needed Flynn more than he was ready to admit. The boy was a straight arrow. He could trust the kid to keep him honest, to make sure he didn't lose his head.

Like last time…

Vinnie maneuvered around a bend in the road and spotted a house in the clearing. The stately home emanated rustic charm, but any glory it had once possessed had long since faded. Cold, dark windows overlooked the overgrown yard of waist-high weeds and wildflowers. Even the boards themselves looked drained of color and life. No cars dotted the driveway, no guards on the grounds. Nothing.

"Wow…" Flynn marveled in a reverent hush. "This is it? You sure anyone lives here? Looks empty."

Vinnie chewed on his lip, puzzling out the scene, his eyes tracing the wrought iron gate that barricaded the rest of the world out of this decaying shack. "Look. Up there."

Flynn did and noticed what Vinnie had already seen. Security cameras at tight intervals, pivoting back and forth as they kept constant watch over every square inch of the property.

"Looks like a prison," Flynn muttered.

Vinnie shrugged, still watching the house beyond the iron gate. Could it be coincidence that Marcon's house was in the North Woods? A different spot than the Blue Skull's latest victims, yes, but in the same woods. Was that an ironic twist of fate, or part of the mystery as to why Big Blue had left Willowbrook?

Vinnie parked his jalopy in the driveway, in front of the closed gate, and climbed out. He slipped his coat on despite the heat, concealing the holstered Colt .45 under his arm. He grabbed his trusty fedora and gave it a pop to restore its shape, before placing the hat on his round head, taking comfort in its familiar feel. Flynn clambered out of the car, camera in nervous hands.

"Are you sure we're doing the right thing?" Flynn asked in a whisper, keeping step as the two made their way towards the iron entrance and the speaker box Vinnie now saw placed there. "I mean, do we really want to get mixed up with organized crime?"

"If it gives us answers as to who our blue-faced bogeyman is, I'll attend a meetin' or two."

Flynn's steps slowed as they neared the front gate. "Maybe no one's home."

As Vinnie reached out to push the call button on the speaker, a series of automated locks noisily popped, and the gate grated open on a track buried in the tall grass. Vinnie retracted his hand, ignoring a small, unsettling rumble in his gut, and gave his companion a pressed grin. "Guess they know we're here."

The two crossed the threshold and the gate slipped closed behind them, locks slapping back in place. Flynn sighed, quiet. "That really can't be good."

Vinnie grimaced, his nerves on high alert, taking cold comfort in the gun under his coat. *I shouldn't have brought the kid.*

The front door opened before them, and Domingo stepped out onto the stone porch, a GQ model with the sneer of the devil. "Mr. Caponi," he greeted professionally. "Glad you could come." The Englishman cut hard eyes on Flynn. "Who's the boy?"

Vinnie took some small pleasure in seeing the calm, manicured man at a disadvantage. Bringing Flynn along might have been unwise, but seeing that momentary look of confusion shattering Domingo's perfect control made it worth it, at least for now. "He's with me."

"The invitation was for you alone."

Vinnie repressed a satisfied grin. "If the kid's out, I'm out."

Domingo considered it, scratching his chin, his icy eyes studying the two of them. "Very well. But the camera stays with me."

Flynn dutifully handed over the contraband and Domingo's wolf-grin returned as he stepped aside, allowing Vinnie access to the inner chamber—and the answers he'd sought for so long.

"Please, gentlemen, this way."

Flynn felt his heart beat in his throat, a steady throb, as the sounds muted around him. Vinnie was as unflappable as ever at his side, as though he could not be impressed by anything, and Flynn drew strength from that. Vinnie probably didn't feel anxious at all, after all he'd seen and done, but Flynn figured he'd sweat enough for the both of them.

He wasn't sure what he expected upon entering the home. Signs of wealth and power—a life lived to the fullest. Instead, the inside of the place was as dead as the outside. Only a sparse bit of furniture filled the emptiness, but the meager furnishings were not such a shock as the sight of the walls. There was not a picture, not a painting. Rather, every free inch of wall space was covered in strange glyphs. Crude and hand-painted in black, the eerie markings began at the floor and reached all the way to the ceiling—where even a few more waited to be discovered by curious eyes.

Flynn stared at the abundance of sigils, feeling as if they were staring back at him. He expected some sort of break in the pattern, but noticed them down the entire length of the hallway and in every partially revealed room they passed. Vinnie seemed interested in the markings, too, observing them, taking mental notes. He wanted to ask Vinnie what they meant, but he figured now wasn't the time.

Mr. Domingo opened a set of double doors into an office and entered first, announcing, "Here they are, darling."

Vinnie and Flynn stepped in next and stood side by side. Immediately Flynn felt a real presence. Whoever lived here spent more time in the study than anywhere else, as the place exuded personality. Books were everywhere, their spines reading a lot like the ones on Vinnie's bookshelf. The occult, magick, monsters—it was all here. Mounted above the fireplace that sat cold and empty on the far wall was a silver battle axe, by all appearances not just a piece of décor, but a threatening weapon.

At a messy desk sat a figure in a high-backed leather office chair. The chair swiveled upon their introduction, and Flynn gaped at the occupant. It was a girl, for starters, with the most knockout legs he'd ever seen, protruding from a thigh-length skirt. The woman wore a low-cut blouse, her cleavage visible, and Flynn felt his face grow hot. She was shockingly attractive, with long, dark hair, bright red lips, and wide, brown eyes that invited danger.

"Whoa," his budding hormones spoke before he had a chance to refuse them.

"Expecting someone else?" the woman asked, cocking an amused eyebrow in his direction. She exuded a sort of animal cunning and Flynn felt very exposed in her presence. He looked away, embarrassed.

Vinnie said, "I thought the boss would have been a...*man*."

"He is. Or *was*. Adrian Marcon was my father." The woman stood, smoothing out her skirt, and extended a manicured hand for Vinnie to shake. "I'm Marcie. Welcome to the team."

Vinnie looked down at her hand, his face impassive. "We ain't part of any team. We just came to hear the offer straight from the horse's mouth."

The girl—Marcie—shrugged, indifferent. "Fair enough." Crossing the room, she stood with Mr. Domingo by the dark fireplace. Together the two looked like a formidable pair. *We can't underestimate them*, Flynn warned himself.

"I want the beast dead," she said at last.

"That might be a little hard since we don't know anything about it," Flynn said.

Marcie reached for a worn and oversized leather-bound book that was lying on the mantle above the fireplace. She hefted it, her smile mischievous. "It's all in here. Page 458."

Before Flynn could begin to question what type of book would provide all the information they ever needed to know about the Blue Skull, or why Vinnie wouldn't already own it, Vinnie asked in a reverent hush, "Is that...?"

"The Malitivar Codex," she sneered coyly. "Yes."

Flynn turned aside to his mentor. "You've heard of it?"

"Yeah," Vinnie replied with a grimace. "It's a tome of ancient dark magick. Never thought I'd *see* it, though."

"It wasn't really that hard to come by," Marcie chimed in, casually. "For the right price, you can find almost anything. Turns out evil's a profitable business."

Vinnie's eyes narrowed, his tone seething. "You would know."

"That's right. I would. But that's beside the point."

Flynn observed the verbal sparring, wondering if Vinnie and Marcie somehow knew each other. "So," he began, drawing their attention, "who *is* the Blue Skull?"

"First off, his name is Molok," Marcie said, carefully placing the tattered book back on the mantle and moving to sit on an ottoman. She crossed her legs, all business, and explained, "He was one of the fallen angels of heaven, worshipped by the Ammonites, before he was sentenced to live in the gloomy claves of hell for all eternity. At least, that was the plan. Thanks to the Codex, I got him an early release."

Flynn felt instantly exhilarated to hear the secret of Big Blue's identity, but then a bit deflated upon realizing that all of his and Vinnie's speculations had proved inaccurate. "So much for the alien theory…"

"Hold on a minute," Vinnie cut in, sharp. "You mean *you* summoned it?"

"And controlled it," Marcie divulged easily. "For a while, at any rate. Long story short, I wanted power; Molok was available. So, I lit a couple candles, said a pretty little chant, and Molok appeared to do my every bidding."

"So, it was *you* who killed Boss Marcon's crime network," Flynn said, piecing it all together. This was going to look great on the website.

"Well, yes and no. I wrote up the order, Molok made the delivery."

"You had your own father killed?" Vinnie asked, his tone harsh.

At that, Marcie faltered. "That…was an accident. The rest is a long story."

Flynn was curious. "If he's so handy, why do you want him dead?"

Marcie's patience waned. Her pitch turned crisp, her dark eyes hard. "Because he's out of control. Apparently the 'faithful dog' routine was all an act. He was biding his time until his full power returned. Now that it has, he's a free agent. And everyone—including me—is fair game. I can't have a loose end like that running around town."

"So, you hid," Vinnie accused. He gestured to the hallway from where they'd just come. "The iron around your perimeter—iron is a deterrent to spirits. Those symbols out there on the walls? Let me guess—Enochian? You're lookin' to stay invisible to some supernatural creature. Molok, am I right?"

Marcie tensed, on the defensive. "Yes. It appears he has a score to settle."

Vinnie huffed and crossed his arms. "Gee, you lasso an ancient Ammonite god into being your private little cabana boy and you wonder why maybe he's got it out for you."

The beautiful woman remained unflinching in the face of his sarcasm. "It's true. I may have been able to bring him into this world, but I can't send him back to hell. Believe me, I've tried. But I know you have more experience with the supernatural and—"

"Sorry, kitten. Not interested."

Flynn snapped to his friend so fast his neck popped. "Vinnie?"

"Let's go, kid." Vinnie jerked his chin toward the door and was already headed that way before Marcie stood, her steely calm shattered. She looked frantic. Desperate.

"Mr. Caponi, I'm prepared to pay you a very large sum of money."

He turned to her, cold. "I don't want your money."

"I've been watching you. I know the urban mythologist business doesn't pay very well."

"Doesn't matter. It's honest work." Vinnie brushed aside his coat and placed meaty hands on his hips, his voice hard. Mean. "Way I see it, he's after *you*. Just you. All those campers in the North Woods he's been cutting up, that's just him blowing off steam while he's waiting for you to slip up, so he can make his move."

Flynn saw Marcie's expression drop—only momentarily—and he realized that she was in very deep trouble. Sure, she was a criminal, but Vinnie was a hero. Heroes were supposed to help everyone, including those who didn't deserve it.

But Vinnie seemed in no mood to play the hero today.

"What's your point?" Marcie snapped, face devoid of the playfulness of earlier. The show was over, and now she was engaging in an all-out fight to get what she needed.

"My point, Miss Marcon, is that I see you sitting here, all gussied up in your nice clothes and makeup for our benefit—to *impress* us—but the truth is, by the look of the place, you probably haven't left this house for months out of fear of that infernal thing."

Marcie flinched as if slapped, but kept the man's gaze.

Vinnie towered over her. "My *point* is that you're a prisoner here, princess, and the way I see it, that's better than you deserve for what you've brought into this world. You can rot out here, surrounded by your fancy magick words for all I care. Rot, or do the rest of us a favor and just step out past that front gate and let him take you already."

Marcie glowered at him, tears threatening to build in the corner of her eyes, but she did not break eye contact. The two of them stared each other down in perfect silence. Flynn realized he'd been holding his breath and slowly exhaled.

"We'll show ourselves out." Vinnie finally said, then adjusted his fedora and marched out of the study. Flynn offered one last apologetic look to their dejected hosts, then hurried to catch up to his friend.

Outside, Vinnie stomped for the front gate, his face pensive. The gate opened with an abrasive scraping noise and Vinnie stormed past without missing a beat. Flynn raced to keep step, slipping out just as the gate sealed behind him. "Vinnie, *wait*. I can't believe you just said all of that!"

"It's the truth," he grumbled over his shoulder, his big boots crunching on the gravel. "It's all her fault. Don't you get that? She has this coming. *Has* had it for a long time."

"But she knows so much!" Flynn protested. "If we put our heads together, we might actually be able to kill the Blue Skull once and for all!"

"Not interested."

Flynn watched, flabbergasted, as Vinnie opened the car door to get in and abandon Marcie—and their one shot at stopping the monster—forever. Flynn forcefully grabbed Vinnie's shoulder and turned him around, his anger flaring. "Hey! What's wrong with you?"

"This ain't no normal spook, Flynn. This is a real, live demon. That's Major Leagues, right there, and I ain't risking our lives for *her.*"

Flynn laughed, beside himself with bewilderment. "Are you kidding me? This is all we've talked about for months! The wall in your apartment! All you wanted was to hunt this thing!"

Vinnie soured, his eyes becoming hooded and secretive. "Things change, kid."

"But we could do some *real good* here! We can't just let Big Blue keep hurting people. We have to do something."

"Fine," Vinnie barked, taking off his fedora and hurling it into the backseat. He jabbed a finger at Flynn's chest, a rare moment of rage for the urban mythologist. "You wanna go make a deal with that witch and hunt down a demon from hell, you go ahead and do it. But you can cut your good pal Vinnie out of it. Now get in the car. I'm takin' you home."

Flynn stared in disbelief as Vinnie climbed in and slammed the door. The engine turned over, rumbling to life, and Flynn finally obeyed and took his place in the passenger seat.

"This isn't the way I wanted this to turn out. I had this all planned."

Marcie watched the car leave, taking all of her hopes with it. She felt doubly damned now and, not for the first time, wondered why she'd brought that *thing* into this world. It had caused her only grief.

"The plan's changed," the ever-opportunistic Domingo spoke at her side, joining in her watch out the window. She cherished his friendship, though she would never tell him. That would be crossing a professional line. Though they were like siblings, he was still just a hired man. A servant. *Don't get too attached.*

"No," she said, bracing herself for what lay ahead. "It doesn't matter," she lied. "I don't need them. The players have changed, but the plan is the same." She poured ice into her voice, resolved now. "We *will* kill Molok. I'll do it myself if I have to. I'll find a way."

CHAPTER FOUR

Marcie had acquired the battle axe on a trip to Scotland six months ago. Domingo had escorted her there as the two of them charted Rannoch Moor, looking for a certain man. The man was hailed as the latest in a long line of warriors whose bloodline was dedicated to defending neighboring lands against the strange bogle-folk that rose in the Scottish mist. He was a man who dealt with legends, and Marcie was looking for such. She made him an offer—similar to the offer she'd later make to Vinnie. Like the difficult urban mythologist, he turned it down. Marcie understood, of course. He was a coward, she told him, hoping her cruel words would stoke the fire in his gut—would goad him into helping her, if only for his own typical desire to prove himself a man.

But the Scotsman didn't take the bait.

In the end, Marcie believed all she really needed was the man's axe. An instrument of supernatural slaying, it'd been passed down in his family for generations, used on the front lines in their devilish battles. She offered to pay handsomely for it, though in reality money was something much more scarce for her now. When he refused even that, Marcie resorted to what she was best at. Taking.

Domingo put two slugs in the man's chest and Marcie had her weapon.

Now the Scotsman's axe lay on her kitchen table beside a duffel bag. Domingo stood to her side, watching as she stuffed another black candle into the bag.

"So, what's the plan?" he asked casually.

Marcie wondered if Domingo were ever afraid. She certainly was, though she would never show it to him. That was weakness. Daddy had burned that out of her.

She grabbed a pouch of powder and put it in the bag with the candles. "Simple. We make a break for the Conduit. Hope he stays off as long as possible. I'll establish my connection, and that should give me the extra juice I need."

"Do you really think this will work?"

"We have to try something," she replied, all business, pulling her hair back in a rough ponytail. For all of Vinnie's abuses, the brute had been right about her recent living conditions. Today, like most days, she wore no makeup and only a simple pair of jeans and a meager blouse. She'd sold off all of her family's finer possessions since that disaster a few months ago when Molok slipped through her barriers and slaughtered her men. She had used all that money hoping to acquire the magic bullet she needed to put that blue-faced devil in the ground, but nothing had worked. Then, as the urban mythologist had pointed out so acutely, she'd hidden here. She hadn't been beyond her front gate in so long. Only Domingo had come and gone, bringing her food, water, the bare necessities.

This *was* her prison, a hell of her own making. She was ready to claw her way out now.

Reaching for the Maltivar Codex, she said, "This spell's the last one I could find that might do the trick. If not, well…" She shook aside her fears. "It'll work. I'm sure of it."

With her mystical ammunition tucked in the bag, Marcie zipped up the duffel, feeling a fool. Powders, candles, magick tomes, enchanted axes? *Ridiculous.* She trafficked in the world of superstition now, and she believed absolutely in the real power of spells and amulets and such, but none of these wards had done a bit of good when Molok came for her last time. Only Eli's infuriating sacrifice had spared her from Molok's wrath. She'd thought to contact her valiant protector to come to her aid once again—but no. Eli had already made it clear what *he* thought she ought to do, but the last thing she wanted was help from Eli's Almighty. She could do this. She *would* do this. Eli and all of his sanctimonious beliefs be damned.

Marcie handed the heavy bag to Domingo and gripped her axe, hoping that whatever heroic exploits this weapon had championed, a fraction of that power and reputation would still be bound to its steel.

Flynn sat in the passenger seat, bouncing his knee. He chewed on his fingernails, keeping careful watch on the passing North Woods. Beside him, the older boy drove—his long, unwashed hair frizzy and wild. Chigger smelled like pot most days, and his car was no different. Flynn hoped he wouldn't catch a buzz just by being near him.

Chigger steered his older brother's car down the tumultuous gravel road, leaving a trail of black exhaust behind. The derelict vehicle coughed and sputtered, bucking as it hit every dip in the path. Flynn braced himself as best he could, staying focused.

"I'm not staying," Chigger declared through gritted teeth. "I'm dropping you off, then I'm outta there."

"That's fine."

"I'm only giving you a ride because I owed you one."

Chigger was referring to the night last Christmas when Flynn had hurried the teenager and his brother off to safety while he stayed behind to fight the Blue Skull. Flynn didn't see much of Chigger after that night, only occasionally in the halls at school. Chigger was always quick to turn and head off in the opposite direction whenever Flynn happened across his path. Flynn didn't take it personal—he was the freak who fought monsters. Not everybody accepted that. Vinnie had prepared him for that eventuality.

Thus, Flynn hadn't spoken to Chigger in months, but he had managed to hunt down his phone number and ask him to give him a lift today. Vinnie wouldn't understand, which was precisely why Flynn didn't tell him.

Flynn said, "You know, I never really asked you before…what did Rufus do when you didn't bring back that money?"

Chigger's mood darkened, his face slackening to a slight frown. "We told him about the ghost and…he let it slide."

Flynn eyed him. "Just like that?"

Chigger shrugged. "Yeah. Looks like. Me and my brother have been staying quiet ever since, just to be safe. If Rufus knew where I was taking you, though, I'm sure he wouldn't let *that* slide."

Flynn hung his head. "I'm sorry. I didn't have anyone else to call."

"Yeah… Just be sure you keep your distance from me from now on, you got that, Spanger? This makes us even and I don't want to know any more about this crap you're all up in."

"Okay. Deal."

Chigger nodded up ahead. "Is that it?" He pulled the car to the iron gate. While the engine idled, Flynn opened his door, readying to leave, but his driver called him back, "Spanger."

Flynn paused. "Yeah?"

"You really shouldn't do this. You don't know these types like I do. You're not cut out for this."

Pursing his lips into a line, Flynn furrowed his brow. "It doesn't matter. I have to stop this."

Chigger shook his unruly mane, snickering. "You really are a goody-goody."

Flynn smiled weakly and shut the door, off to meet his destiny.

Marcie took the lead as she and Domingo headed for the front door. Her breathing became shallow and her fingertips grew cold. It was then that she realized she was walking out that door to die. Domingo, too. The fact that her faithful companion showed such utter confidence in her decision did not embolden her; rather, it only reinforced the tragedy of their situation. She wasn't a hero. She wasn't doing this to save anyone from the devil she'd summoned. This was pure, base survival.

Perhaps the worst realization was that Eli would know that, too. Maybe he'd read about her death tomorrow in the paper. Maybe he'd even grieve. But in his heart, her lover would know her last act had been a selfish one. That thought hurt her more than she wanted to admit. But it didn't matter. She was locked into Fate's roller coaster. There was nothing to do but hold on and wait for the ride to end, and end bloody.

She stepped outside and felt the sun's warm rays on her for the first time in weeks. She stifled tears stemming from emotions that she couldn't quite describe, then suddenly beheld a visitor down the driveway at her front gate. Flynn Spanger stood on the other side of the iron bars, a hand poised over the speaker box at the security checkpoint.

Behind the boy, Marcie glimpsed a clunker retreating down the dusty gravel road, leaving behind a noxious cloud of black exhaust. Flynn looked determined, his jaw clenched, his young eyes like steel. For a brief moment she saw Eli in those eyes as she approached.

"What are *you* doing here?" she queried, making her voice harsh. "I was under the impression you and your friend had already made your decision."

"Vinnie's out. But I want to kill the Blue Skull."

Marcie considered this development. How old was this kid? Fourteen? Fifteen? She'd hoped for a white knight like Eli, or at least a competent occult detective like Vinnie Caponi. She needed men, not this *boy*. If he came along, he'd just be more meat for the grinder. If anything happened to him, Eli would doubly curse her death, knowing she'd taken some eager kid from the world for her own egocentric pursuits.

Eli isn't here. Eli left you.

She *had* to stop caring what Eli thought. Eli had made his choice long ago, and now she had to make hers.

"Looks like you're in, kid," Marcie said through a sneer.

CHAPTER FIVE

What am I doing? Flynn thought as he trudged deeper into the North Woods. Mr. Domingo followed close behind with a Heckler and Koch MP7A1, complete with an extended clip, suppressor, and reflex sight. His pressed and starched shirt and slacks stood out absurdly in the overgrown forest. Marcie pushed onward, a bulging duffel bag slung over her shoulder, her slender fingers wrapped around the menacing axe Flynn had first glimpsed upon entering her study yesterday. A long midnight blue cloak concealed her attractive features, the expanse of its fabric hand-embroidered in gold with the same Enochian scribbles he saw in her house. Big Blue Camouflage, he assumed. Neither of the criminals spoke to him, except Mr. Domingo's casual warnings to watch his step over this or that tree root.

Criminals. These were real criminals. They'd killed people.

Will they kill me?

There was no reason why they would; Flynn wasn't a threat to them. But who knew what went through the minds of people like this? Flynn had horrible flashes of being shot in the back by Mr. Domingo, his body left to fester out here in the brush. What would his dad think? Would his dad ever know?

"Here," Mr. Domingo barked, startling Flynn like the gunshot he imagined was due him any moment.

Flynn's stomach lurched, and his steps grew clumsy. The assassin simply pulled a slim rectangle out of his pocket and handed it to the boy.

It was his camera.

Flynn brightened. He'd forgotten that he turned it over to Mr. Domingo to gain admittance into Marcie's estate and had failed to retrieve it when he and Vinnie left.

"You'll need this," Domingo said. "Document everything you see."

Flynn palmed the camera, feeling a newfound sense of purpose. Maybe they wouldn't kill him, after all. He was their cameraman.

Domingo carried on, "The next time you and your friend storm off in a righteous huff, be sure to get your things."

"Thanks." Flynn blushed.

Mr. Domingo cracked a wry smile that hinted at the cruelty he was capable of inflicting. "Wouldn't want to be accused of being a crook, now would I?"

Marcie pushed through into a clearing and halted, Flynn nearly tripping over her. Their feet had found a narrow asphalt path that traced the outline of Greensboro Park Lake. A tall stone and wood pavilion faced them at the opposite end, overlooking colorful playground equipment. This time of day, during the hottest part of July, this place should have been packed with families barbecuing, paddle-boating or swimming. Instead, the park was barren, with only a light breeze stirring the swing set.

Marcie gauged the lake and nodded once, firm. "We'll do it here," she announced. It was the first time she'd said anything since they entered the woods. Her face was a granite mask, immovable and tense, her eyes wide and apprehensive as she scanned the surrounding trees. Flynn wondered if she felt remorse for all that had happened because of her dabbling in the dark side, or just scared that she was in line to get her comeuppance. He supposed it didn't matter anymore. What mattered was that they stopped Molok.

Marcie knelt in the wild grass at the sparkling lake's edge, unzipping the duffel and procuring a number of fat candles. Methodically she placed them in a triangle around her at even breaks, every once in a while muttering something in a language Flynn did not understand.

It gave him the creeps.

She set the Malitivar Codex beside her, then turned her attention to the battle axe resting across her lap. Laying her hand on it, she muttered more strange words. From time to time, she glanced back at the grimoire, consulting its pages before intoning further syllables over her axe, making slow and deliberate motions with her hands.

Flynn leaned into Mr. Domingo and whispered, "What is she doing?"

"Blessing her axe. Marcie doesn't believe in guns." Domingo grinned, patting his machine gun. "But *I* do." He reached behind his back and pulled out a snub-nosed .38 revolver. He handed it to Flynn, handle out. "You know how to use one of these things?"

Flynn took it gingerly. It was such a tiny thing, no bigger than a toy. His hand froze around the handle, for fear the gun would accidently go off. "I-I've never—"

Mr. Domingo released his grip on his machine gun, letting it hang by its strap, in order to clamp his manicured hand around Flynn's, forcing him to get the feel of the gun. "Look, you point this end at the bad guy and squeeze—don't pull—the trigger. Got it?"

Flynn nodded, but it was a lie. He understood the principle, but didn't think he'd be able to use it. Mr. Domingo toggled something on the gun. "Safety's on. Be sure to take it off before you start shooting, yeh?"

"I'm almost ready," Marcie said, her voice quiet and concentrating.

Flynn watched as she dug in the folds of her cloak and pulled out a small dagger, no bigger than a letter opener. Periodically consulting her text, she etched symbols in the dirt, uttering eerie incantations.

The boy gulped, unsure if he'd made the right call in accompanying them. It seemed to him that witchcraft had gotten everyone into this mess to begin with—was it really wise to throw gasoline on an already-out-of-control fire?

Vinnie would be so disappointed in him.

Anxiously rubbing the sudden gooseflesh on his arm, Flynn ventured to disturb Marcie's ritual. "So…where did you find that book, anyway?"

"Domingo found it for me, actually," she said.

"Yes," Domingo interjected quickly but politely, "A severe lapse in judgment on my part, darling. Had I known the trouble it would cause, I certainly would have refused."

She looked up to him, a sincere softness in her expression that spoke of their bond. It was the first sign of humanity Flynn had seen in the woman, and now he realized she couldn't be all bad. "Don't kid yourself," she spoke to the Englishman. "I always get what I want."

Domingo snickered. "Indeed."

Flynn watched the two and couldn't help but be warmed by their banter. They both played it cool, but Flynn wondered what they were like in private. Were they friends? Something more? A part of him wanted to talk to them, to get to know them. Maybe they didn't have to be criminals anymore. Maybe they just needed someone to show them there was another way.

Marcie stood, now, rubbing the dirtied blade against the cloak before putting it to the palm of her hand. Without a wince or a cry—Flynn believed he had that part covered—she plunged the tip of the silver into her flesh, drawing blood. Flynn looked askance at Domingo, who appeared unbothered by the act. Feeling his face whiten, the boy asked, "What are you doing?"

Marcie narrated as she dangled her bleeding hand over the water, dotting its face with red. "Opening a small window to the Other Side. If I can use this lake as a conduit, I should be able to siphon from What Is Yet To Come to destroy Molok. Or, at the very least, banish him back to whatever hellish dimension I pulled him out of."

Flynn blinked once, then fumbled to readjust his glasses on his nose. "*What?*"

She eyed him haughtily, her pretty lips pulling into a devilish smirk. "What, didn't Caponi teach you all of this? I thought you were supposed to be his apprentice."

Flynn frowned and looked away, the tips of his ears burning.

Marcie chuckled. "History lesson, kid: Ivan Malitivar was a Russian poet, artist, mystic, and madman. In his writings, he claimed to have received a 'divine revelation' that ours is but one world in a series of parallel realities. It was Malitivar's belief that one could connect to those other planes of existences through water, mirrors—our reflections. Even blank canvas, parchment, or paper could potentially be used as gateways, since to an artist or writer, they symbolize limitless possibilities. In his Codex, Malitivar chronicled his journeys through the worlds. It was during this time that he learned the secret names of many demons, Molok included, and how to bind them for his own purposes. He also speaks of a Voice in the dark spaces between the worlds that he called 'What Is Yet To Come'—something even the demons fear."

Taking a bandage from a back pocket, Marcie tended to her wound as she faced Flynn. "Of course, even among occultists, Malitivar was considered a hack and charlatan. Malitivarian Magick is almost backwards from traditional spellcasting. Counter-intuitive. *Gibberish*, in fact. In 1569, Malitivar was burned at the stake by his own followers for heresy. Despite all of that, his writings lived on, and the Cult of the Onyx Forever, the Infernal Lodge, and—more locally— the Esoteric Brotherhood of the Sun, all draw from his Codex for the basis of their beliefs."

Flynn stared dumbfounded at the sorceress, struggling to take in her nefarious truths. "No...Vinnie never told me any of this."

"That's surprising," she said with a taunting, though faintly seductive, shrug. "I'm sure he knew all of it. Your mentor was a major player in the occult not too long ago."

When Flynn didn't respond, she continued, "He and that partner of his—the one before you—they hunted their fair share of monsters and cultists alike. In the world of magick, Vinnie definitely made some waves. Then, almost as fast as he started, he went into a sort of retirement. His old partner got out and Caponi just wasted away in that apartment, piddling on his silly little website, *chronicling* rather than killing. A shame. As much as he knew about the occult, he could have had *real* power. Now he's just a has-been 'urban mythologist' with some little kid as his only friend." She sighed. "Kinda funny, really. Sad, but funny."

Flynn took a step forward, propelled by righteous anger. "Don't talk about him like that. Vinnie's a better person than you'll ever be. He helps people. All you care about is yourself."

"You're right," she said, without the slightest hint of apology, and left it at that.

Secretly, though, Flynn wondered at her words. How much had Vinnie not told him about his past? What secrets was he keeping? Maybe he didn't know his friend at all.

The car rocked from side to side as Vinnie eased over the railroad tracks on Buckingham Road. He turned at the driveway and parked in front of Flynn's house, but hesitated to get out. He shouldn't have yelled at the kid. A part of him knew Flynn was right. It didn't matter where the Blue Skull came from or who brought it here. The thing was here all the same, and as long as it remained, there'd be more bodies piling up in the North Woods. Demons never tired, never faded. They just persisted until they accomplished their goal. Eventually Marcie would be dead, and then what? What would Molok be able to achieve once he was truly free of the only person who had any sort of control over him?

Vinnie had told Flynn the partial truth. It'd been a long time since he'd strapped on his Colt and driven into the shadows, looking to face down the legions of hell. Not since he rode with Josh. Those had been dark days, and Vinnie had hoped to leave that behind him. Better to study monsters, to follow along behind their carnage and record them. Maybe others could fight them without falling into all the same traps Vinnie had. Despite what the kid believed, Vinnie wasn't hero material. He was just a common joe. An investigator, not a warrior. Not anymore.

As he sat in Flynn's driveway, he thought to tell the kid that. To apologize for being too afraid to face the Blue Skull. Bogeymen, ghosts—that was one thing. But a demon... That was the blackest kind of magick.

The kind that called to Vinnie like a drug.

Groaning, he heaved his bulk out of the car and adjusted his fedora. Even as his big boots clunked on the creaky porch, he still didn't know what he was going to say. But he owed Flynn an apology at least, for snapping at him.

Jittery with uncertainty, he rang the bell and waited. The kid's dad answered the door, a big guy in a polo shirt and slacks, a bit of grey poking through his short dark hair. Flynn favored him in the face, but he had to have his mother's eyes.

"Vinnie," Ed Spanger greeted him, caught off guard. "Something I can help you with?"

Vinnie shrugged, tucking his hands in his trenchcoat pockets. "I, uh, brought by the kid's payment for last month for the website."

Ed gauged him awkwardly. "Sure. He'll appreciate that. I know he works hard on it."

"Yeah, I couldn't do it without him."

"Well, you're more than welcome to leave it here for him. He's not home right now."

"Oh." Vinnie's brow cinched together. Flynn was always home, unless he was with Vinnie. Maybe the boy was meeting new people. *Good for you, kid.*

"He took off a couple hours ago with a friend from school." Ed squinted, searching his brain for a name. "Jeremy."

Vinnie's face hardened. "Jeremy. You mean 'Chigger'?"

Ed shrugged. "Could be. He left in a hurry."

Vinnie's hands tightened to fists in his coat. What was Flynn doing socializing with Rufus' goons? The kid knew better than to make friends with a dope peddler like Chigger. Flynn was up to something, and whatever it was, it wasn't good.

Offering a tip of his hat, Vinnie turned and jogged down the steps. "I'll get the money to him some other time. Thanks."

"Vinnie?" Ed called after him, his voice strange and apprehensive.

The urban mythologist slowed and faced the father.

Ed stepped out on the porch in his socked feet and gently closed the door behind him. "Look, I, uh… Flynn thinks an awful lot of you."

Vinnie nodded, unsure where the conversation was headed. "Yeah. He's a good kid."

"He is," Ed echoed immediately. "And you've been a good friend to him. You were there for him after my wife died and…" the man scratched his nose absently. "You were there for him like I *should've* been, and I'll have to live with that. But now…"

Vinnie set his jaw, feeling the weight of the man's words before they even left his mouth.

Ed continued, shaky but determined, "Flynn's going through an important time right now. He's figuring out what kind of man he's going to be. You've given him a job, and I appreciate that, but he's suffocating. I think it might be best if he had a little space."

Vinnie nodded, but felt a sharp pain pierce his chest. "Sure."

"You understand," Ed said, but Vinnie knew that what he meant was, *Stay away from my son. You're trouble.*

"Yeah. I understand."

"What makes you think he'll show anyway?" Flynn asked, sweat trickling down his brow as he kept his digital camera steady on his female subject.

Marcie knelt in the grass once more. She took a handful of the powder out of her satchel and sprinkled it over the flames. The particles danced and popped like firecrackers. "This cloak is keeping me invisible, but as soon as I take it off, I'll show up on his radar." She leveled him a withering glare through his lens. "Trust me. He'll be here. You just be ready."

Flynn considered the pistol in his possession, but felt little comfort in its potential. Thoughtfully he reached into his shirt and brought out his mother's cross that'd he'd been wearing since that night in his kitchen.

"Your faith won't do you any good here, boy." Mr. Domingo snarled, total disdain dripping off his words.

Flynn regarded his mother's pendant. "My faith is what saved my butt the last time I ran into Big Blue. No offense, but God is the only One I'm counting on to get me through this."

Mr. Domingo eyed him. "Suit yourself." The assassin faced forward, ever the faithful protector to the woman in the grass constructing her magick circle. Flynn's eyes fell on the MP7 and he frowned.

"How come you got the big gun, anyway?"

With a smirk, Domingo replied, "Because I look good holding it."

"Are you two finished?" Marcie interrupted. "I'd really like to avoid dying today, if we can help it."

They quieted obediently, as Marcie drew a circle in the air above the candle to her left, reciting, "Ominus reparon." Once completed, she brought that candle to her lips and blew out the flame. She repeated the ceremony with the candle on her right. "Ominus secaron." Out went the second flame.

Overhead, charcoal clouds gathered above the lake. A flock of birds took flight from their once-peaceful perch in the treetops, and Flynn shivered. A stronger, frigid breeze stirred the waters, rustling his hair. He did his best to keep the camera focused on Marcie, but his sight lingered on the natural disruptions around him.

"It's happening, isn't it?" he asked, nauseous and shuddering. All at once, the reality of the situation asserted itself. He should have told his dad *something*. Instead, he'd lied to him. He'd given his dad a big hug, told him he loved him. But he should have said more. Wrote a long letter or something. Now he'd never get the chance.

Mr. Domingo had his game face on, staring up into the darkening skies. "All right, boy," he said without facing Flynn. "Time to earn your keep."

All that remained was the candle directly in front of Marcie. *No turning back now.* Flynn watched in mounting dread as she traced lines with both hands over the final candle, then closed her hands into fists. "Ominus di nae." Lifting the candle, considering it for a moment, she blew out the flame.

A weight dropped in Flynn's stomach like a stone hurled into the ocean as Marcie set the candle back on the grass. At last she stood, hesitated, then removed the cloak and let it drop to the windswept grass.

"Here we go," she said, unable to hide the quaver in her voice. "The Conduit to the Other Side is open."

Head held high, wind whipping her long dark ponytail about haphazardly, Marcie stretched her arms over the waters and shouted into the rising wintry gale, "I beseech you, O Beast! I beseech you, Chaos! I beseech you, Keeper of the Void! I beseech you in the name of Malitivar, my master! Accept my offering, my blood, and grant me a taste of your exceeding power! Bestow on me your blessings that I might return to you your lost child, Molok, god-king of the eternal blue fire!"

Ferocious straight-line winds buffeted against her slight frame, rocking her back and forth. Flynn felt light on his feet, his camera threatening to slip from his hands. His glasses rattled against the bridge of his nose and his eyes watered in the onslaught. Trees leaned to their sides, small branches snapping off and swirling away.

"No," he thought he heard himself say, but the cold storm stole his voice.

At his side, Domingo kept his gun at the ready, scanning the trees. Even in the midst of the tempest he looked collected, and Flynn envied him that.

At the same time, Domingo's calm stirred in Flynn a new breed of anxiety. What type of people must these be, to so brazenly call upon this kind of evil? Panic seized his heart when he realized that he was right there, a willing participant with them. He had known this was wrong from the beginning, but here he stood, just letting it unfold around him.

The wind whipped his mother's cross into his field of vision.

No. I can't let this happen.

Flynn stepped forward, screaming hoarsely over the roaring gusts, "No! This isn't right! You have to stop! *Please*, stop!"

Marcie did not turn to him, but remained with her fingers splayed to the heavens. The waters at her feet churned violently, sloshing waves along the bank. In the shallow depths of the lake, a rainbow-colored light shimmered and pulsed.

Flynn took one look at it and retched.

He staggered to the side, totally off balance, and wiped the corners of his mouth with his sleeve. The wind battered him relentlessly, nearly toppling him to the earth. His mother's cross flapped wildly until, at last, the leather knot snapped. Flynn groped empty air trying to catch it, but watched helplessly as the cross vanished in the encroaching darkness. He stared after it for a time, fearing God had left him as well.

Please, God… Please don't leave me here.

Shaking uncontrollably now, he reached out for Marcie once more. "Stop! Marcie, you have to *stop!*"

It was then that he realized she was floating. She pivoted, inches off the ground, to face him—her eyes solid black, blood trickling from her nose.

Flynn jerked his hand back, screaming.

Domingo's hand clamped over his arm painfully and pulled him close. "Quiet, boy!" The assassin pointed off to the distant tree line, his pale eyes narrowing. "He's here."

Flynn snapped out of his terror. There, breaching the woods, its chest and shoulders heaving with each great breath, stood the black-clad giant, its skull face radiant with a cerulean blaze that flared brighter as its dark eye sockets settled on Marcie.

The Blue Skull charged.

CHAPTER SIX

Chigger's car rested in the Ultra 8 Motel's half-empty lot. The stoner boy, himself, lounged on the hood, chatting it up with two older boys—one without a shirt who sat propped up on a bicycle and the other wearing a ball cap turned sideways. While the three carried on a monotone conversation, their cunning gazes not-so-casually scanned the streets and the lot around the motel.

Lookouts.

When Vinnie slammed on his brakes and swerved across two lanes of honking traffic to bump over the curb and settle to a rubber-burning halt next to Chigger's car, Shirtless grew wide-eyed and lit off on his bike, never looking back.

Chigger slid off the hood of his own ride, hands raised, trading "save me" looks with Ball Cap. Vinnie kicked open the door of his Taurus and stomped for the youth, grabbing the collar of his oversized Bob Marley tie-dye t-shirt. "Where's Flynn?" he asked, anger and fear building within him.

Chigger waved his hands, laughing, "*Who*, man? I don't know no—"

"Cut the crap," Vinnie barked. "Where is he? Where did you take him?"

Vinnie sensed movement behind him and turned his head just as Ball Cap was pulling a Glock out from under his shirt. Before the kid could breach his waistband, Vinnie released Chigger with a hard shove and slipped his hand inside his trenchcoat, drawing his Colt 1911. He didn't bother putting one in the chamber—didn't think he'd need it for this demonstration.

"Don't," he simply said, the gun leveled at the thug.

Ball Cap froze, his hand still halfway in his pants, his face a picture of deer-meets-headlight fright.

Vinnie jerked his chin over his shoulder. "Leave the piece. Scram."

The lookout slowly revealed his gun and lowered it to the ground, his eyes fixed on Vinnie's barrel. Then, as soon as metal touched concrete, the kid was off like a gazelle.

Chigger scrambled on the ground as Vinnie easily slid his gun back in its holster. Turning, he hoisted Chigger to an abrupt stand.

"Let me go!" Chigger cried. "You know what Rufus will do to me if he sees me talking to you?"

"If I were you, then," Vinnie said through gnashed teeth, "I'd talk fast." Lowering his voice to a deep growl, he rumbled, "Now, where's Flynn?"

Flynn aimed his camera at the supernatural monstrosity stalking across the windblown park grounds. Despite every instinct commanding him to the contrary, the boy found he could not move his legs or his hands, and even his mouth remained gaping open to dry out. Tears froze in his eyes as the terrible storm slapped his face with grit, dirt, and impossible flakes of snow. "What do we do?" he finally shouted to his two companions, but Domingo was already on it.

Mr. Domingo—back straight, gun raised at waist level—sidestepped closer to the woman in charge of their company. The man's face remained casual and impassive as always, and Flynn drew a little courage from the killer's blasé.

"Marcie, darling," Domingo called out with barely a tremble in his cultured voice, "Perhaps now would be a good time to do something."

The witch, still hovering above the swaying grass, extended one hand over the lake—the Conduit—and reached out with her other hand, palm out and aimed at the creature. Over the roaring squall, she screeched, "*Kalae sic-tahae!*"

Invisible force detonated from her, the ripples of it tossing Flynn onto his backside. On the ground, he adjusted his glasses in astonishment and watched as an undulating ring of pinkish-orange lightning crackled from Marcie's outstretched hand and hurtled for the Blue Skull. Flynn held his breath, a smile dawning on his face. *It's going to work.* The spiritual energy spiraled about the demon, forming a mystical net. Molok raced into it, either oblivious to its purpose or too stupid to dodge out of the way. The ring of light reached the target, wrapping tight around the hulking monster.

Flynn found the presence of mind to film the sight, clutching his camera as his excitement grew. *Yes, yes—*

Molok flexed, and the energy dissipated without fanfare.

The demon kept moving. Right for them.

"*No!*" Marcie screamed from her station near the water, dropping suddenly to her knees.

Just like that, the storm was over. The wind stopped, the cold dissipated, and the dark clouds dissolved on fast-forward to reveal the glaring hot sun once more. The rainbow-colored lights at the bottom of the lake sank into a fathomless abyss, abandoning the trio of would-be victors.

Marcie clutched at the grass on the shore, shouting into the water. "No! Wait! I need more—" Shaking and crying, she lifted her hands to the heavens as before. "I beseech you, O Beast! I beseech you! *Don't leave me!*"

Domingo was on her in an instant, yanking her to her feet even as she wept in hopeless desperation.

"It didn't work," she cried, lost and broken. "Why didn't it work...?"

The Englishman fixed her with his cold stare. "Run."

She looked to him, tears painting her face. "No... I won't leave you..."

"Run!" he roared, shoving her away, spinning around, his machine gun at the ready.

Before Flynn could react, the Blue Skull was at their side.

Domingo fired his gun from the hip as Marcie screamed and retreated into the tree line. Flynn watched after her, still on the grass, still defenseless, his heart sinking. *She left us... She left me.*

Bullets from Domingo's MP7 chewed through the foliage surrounding the rampaging Blue Skull. Muzzle flashes dazzled Flynn's eyes and he flinched in alarm, nearly dropping his camera in the process. Domingo fired for what seemed like an eternity, spraying relentlessly, cutting down branches and Swiss-cheesing nearby trees. At last, when his ammo was spent, he ejected the clip and regarded his path of destruction.

Flynn's ears rang, but he could open his eyes now. Molok was nowhere in sight.

Domingo pressed his lips together in slight consternation. "Hmm."

"Where did he go?" Flynn whispered, finally getting to his feet. With his camera, he scanned the perimeter.

Alert but calm, Domingo coolly withdrew another clip from behind his waist and slapped it into the gun. Cocked it.

"Watch out!" Flynn screamed.

The air beside Domingo shimmered and the Blue Skull suddenly appeared, knocking the assassin's gun away with one hand while simultaneously gripping the man by the throat. The monster lifted his prey as Domingo's feet kicked at the felled leaves on the ground.

"Wait!" Domingo hacked through strained breath. "Wait!"

But the monster only squeezed.

"Run...boy..." Domingo wheezed, and Flynn tore out of there, dropping his camera in the process. He huffed and puffed, crying a little, as he stumbled through the woods at a breakneck pace, twigs and brambles tearing his shirt, his pants. He lost track of how far he'd run—only knew that it wasn't far enough.

Behind him, a scream ended in a gargle. *Domingo. I left him to die.*

Flynn spun around, nearly losing his balance, and withdrew the .38 the criminal had given him. The revolver trembled in his loose grip as he swung it in a wide arc, ready to fire, but he saw no sign of the monster. No sign of

Domingo.

I left him to die…

The boy wept, ashamed.

Domingo's scream echoed through the pretty day. Marcie slid to a stop and choked through tears, looking back the way she'd come, but seeing nothing. "Domingo? *Domingo!*"

He was gone. *I'm next.*

Marcie wept for him, clutching the stitch in her side. She thought to go back for him but instead ran further into the woods, abandoning Domingo to whatever hell Molok had in store for him. She wiped her wet face, heartsick. She had to get out. Survive, just like she always did. Get back to her house, her protective symbols. Hide.

Flynn was back there at the park, too, she remembered. The sudden realization struck her, but she did not hesitate. He'd volunteered to come here, she told herself. No one put a gun to his head.

You'd really leave a child behind to fight your battles for you?

"Shut up!" she shouted, running harder.

She felt her neck hairs rise, a chill snaking up her moving legs to her arms. The air crackled ahead, and her worst fears materialized before her.

Its glowing skull dimmed to a simmering blue as it watched her. Waited for her. Marcie slowed before it, weeping anew. It had come to this at last.

Just as she deserved.

Molok broke out in a run, coming straight for her, its gigantic boots punching into the earth. Shoulders arched high, its skull dipped low and threatening, its head burst into a ferocious blue as it picked up speed; it was set on its task and would not stop.

The devil was mere feet from her and Marcie wondered if her death would hurt. *I love you, Eli. I'm sorry.*

Just as she surrendered to her own murder, however, a fire flared in her belly, filling her legs with strength and her heart with courage.

"No," she whispered, shaking her head fiercely. She couldn't die. Not like this. "No!"

She loosed a shriek and ran away. "Flynn!" she screamed into the sky, hoping he'd save her even though she had been prepared to abandon him. "Flynn!"

In perhaps the stupidest move of the century, Flynn retraced his steps once the sounds of struggle had faded. He found his camera on the ground beside his mother's discarded cross. His gun tucked in the waist of his pants, the teen knelt, gingerly taking up his cross. He dusted it off, penitent.

God, I'm so sorry.

Domingo was gone. No trace of a body or blood. He'd simply vanished. The Blue Skull had since fled, as well.

We blew it...

What would he tell Vinnie? What would he tell his dad?

Guilt buried him beneath its weight and he felt like crying, but had no more tears to shed over the matter. He'd sacrificed everything he believed in to come out here, and now... Everything was lost.

Then he heard Marcie's voice, faint, some distance away. *"Flynn!"*

She was out there, alone in the woods. Alive.

Flynn rose to his feet with new purpose, clutching the cross tightly, determined now to never to let it go again. Setting his face like steel, the boy ran towards the woman's voice.

Marcie shoved branches out of her way, her sight foggy with tears. She pushed deeper into the North Woods, now completely lost. Somewhere around here was the old highway—civilization—but she had no clue which way to turn. The demon behind her did not relent in its pursuit, clunking through the forest in a steady rhythm like a freight train. Marcie cursed herself for leaving behind the axe, but reasoned it'd be useless, just like everything else she'd tried.

Why won't you die?

"Flynn!" she hollered again, controlling her fear now, resolute that she would not be a victim. Adrian didn't raise victims. The boy did not answer, however. Was he already dead? He was just a kid. She knew nothing about him. About his parents. His mother would weep over her son's grave and it'd all be Marcie's fault.

"Flynn, don't you be dead!" she shouted, furious. "Answer me *right now!*"

Gnarled fingers of ice clutched her hair and yanked backwards. Her feet slipped out from under her as she collapsed into the Blue Skull's massive arms. In blind panic, she squirmed and beat at its grip. "Let me go! No! *No!*"

The thing hefted her high over its fiery head and hurled her through the air. She spun sideways, clipping a tree against her ribs, sure that she felt bone snap. Twirling, she landed on the hard-packed dirt, busting her lip and nose. Blood poured down the bottom half of her face like a red waterfall, and her vision refused to focus. Clumsy, she dug her nails into the earth, pulling herself along on her stomach, her breathing shallow. Eyesight dimming. She was about to pass out, she feared, and after that she'd be easy prey.

Molok walked towards her, slower now, savoring the kill. With each step, the ground beneath Marcie rumbled and her newly loosened teeth rattled. But she dragged her tingly legs, arms shaking in fatigue. Ahead, she spotted the narrow road that wound through the park grounds. If she could just get to it...get help...

Her head throbbed, her thoughts swam. She just wanted to take a nap. Sleep for a while...

Hands wrapped around her arms, hoisting her to her feet. Her mind cleared and she realized Flynn held her. "Come on!"

Behind her, the Blue Skull was almost on top of them, but Flynn dragged her away, hurrying towards the road. "Flynn?" she muttered, coughing up blood.

They stepped onto the road, with Marcie slipping in the boy's grip. He struggled to lead her, and she knew she was dead weight. "Run..."

Flynn spared one hand to reach around his back and returned with a cross. He waved it at the advancing monster. "Stay back!"

Impossibly, Marcie glimpsed a white light burning just beneath the surface of Flynn's forehead, growing hotter—*brighter*—until finally a shimmering symbol emerged from his skin. The boy didn't appear to be in pain, didn't even appear to notice the transformation, and she worried that she was slipping into delirium. It was the same sign. The one Eli wore when he saved her...

"Stay back," the boy pronounced again, inching away with Marcie in his arms. The Blue Skull took tentative steps forward, like a lion circling a campfire, careful not to touch the blaze.

"Flynn..."

He ignored her, holding the devil at bay. "*Back.*"

The thing snorted in frustration, stamping its feet. Still advancing, but forced to keep its distance as Flynn crossed the road. Marcie smiled in relief, in vindication. "You're...doing it..."

A screech of tires startled her, and a white paint-chipped Ford Taurus crashed headlong into the Blue Skull, crumpling the hood of the car and sending Molok catapulting through the air. Marcie watched the creature fly backwards, its long coat billowing in the wind, then land on the pavement, skidding its glowing face along the road. Bright blue sparks shot out as the devil slid to a slow stop. Dazed, Marcie looked to the car as the driver stepped out.

"Get in!" Vinnie Caponi ordered, brandishing a gun.

Marcie gaped in astonishment. *On his forehead...*

"Vinnie!" Flynn gasped, looking like his lost puppy had returned home.

"Now!" Vinnie demanded, using his door as a shield and taking aim with a M1911. Flynn pulled Marcie to the car just as the Blue Skull rose again to its full stature. Its coat was tattered now, its face burning hotter. Marcie climbed into the backseat and Flynn rounded to ride shotgun.

Vinnie fired repeatedly at the advancing creature, bullets burrowing into the thing's thick hide, dissolving in its mystical face. Once the gun ran empty, Vinnie twirled it, slid it in his holster, and took his seat behind the wheel in one effortless move. The detective was built like an ox, but proved himself surprisingly spry. Vinnie jerked the car into reverse and punched the gas, squalling tires in dark plumes of burnt rubber.

Molok, however, leapt.

Its tremendous bulk sailed forward, landing hard on the car, further crushing the hood. The beast punched black-gloved fingers into the metal and pulled itself up to the windshield. Marcie wanted to scream, but didn't have the strength anymore. Flynn shouted in fright as the blue-faced terror braced itself, then reared back one stony fist and punched. Glass exploded in, bathing them in sharp chiclets. Molok reached into the vehicle, wildly groping for purchase. Flynn batted at his arm with his cross, perhaps too stunned now to conjure up his "Power of Christ compels you" routine. Vinnie struggled for his holster one-handed, but failed to draw his weapon.

"Steer!" he ordered the boy.

"*What?*"

Without waiting for Flynn to catch on, Vinnie took his hands off the wheel, freed his gun from the holster, and reloaded it. Unmanned, the car swerved violently to the right, until Flynn threw himself on the wheel and turned. Vinnie's fat foot floored the engine while Flynn dodged the monster's attacks while steering from the passenger seat. With his gun ready, Vinnie aimed over the kid and fired point-blank in the devil's empty eye socket. Its head snapped back, and it squealed in earsplitting rage. Vinnie didn't let up. Again and again, he pulled the trigger, filling the car with the acrid smell of gunpowder and deafening Marcie in the process.

At last the relentless barrage of bullets managed to pry the beast loose from the car. Vinnie shoved Flynn out of the way, took the wheel, and cranked it hard.

The car swerved, the North Woods spinning by them, and Molok was finally dislodged. It hurtled to the pavement, rolling end over end before landing in a heap. Vinnie slipped the gear into DRIVE and shot forward.

"Ram him!" Flynn said in adrenaline-fueled excitement.

Vinnie's shoulders tensed, both hands swallowing the tiny steering wheel. Marcie felt the car rumble beneath her as they accelerated. The Blue Skull was already climbing to a stand and managed to look up just as Vinnie plowed through it. Marcie watched as the creature bounced off the hood and twirled to the side, passing by her window. Vinnie didn't stop, but barreled forward, heading for the park exit, leaving the accursed woods behind.

Marcie righted herself in the seat, glancing out the back window. Molok stood on the street, silently watching them in stewing fury. Feeling the nightmare was over for now, she collapsed in the seat, a pain in her side now screaming at her.

"What do you think you were doing?" Vinnie shouted at his partner.

"We were trying to kill it."

"You don't know nuthin!"

Flynn slouched in his seat, and Marcie's anger flared despite her body's trauma. "Lay off. We had to try something. Your boy did good. Must've had bigger stones than *you* did to come out here."

The detective's glaring eyes flicked to the rearview mirror. "You. Shut up. I'm dropping you off at the hospital in Russellville as a final courtesy. You come near me or my friend again and I'll kill you myself. Capisce?"

"Vinnie," Flynn eased, but his friend wasn't having it.

It had been a long time since someone had threatened her, but Marcie hadn't the energy to retort. Blackness crouched at the edge of her vision and she felt sweet oblivion overtake her. "Yeah…" she said, slipping out of consciousness, "…I got it."

CHAPTER SEVEN

Marcie woke in a strange bed, hooked to wires. Blue moonlight slipped in through the blinds, cutting hard abstract lines on the wall. A nurse stood over her, checking her vitals.

"Good, you're awake," she greeted cheerily enough.

Marcie shoved the woman aside, sitting, scanning the room, instantly on red alert. "Where is it?"

"What are you talking about?"

Marcie jerked the wires off her arm, out of her nose. Swung her legs over the edge of the bed and discovered she wore a flimsy paper gown. "Where am I?"

"Y-You're in Russellville Methodist. You need to—"

"Where are my clothes?" she demanded, already spotting her pants folded neatly on the couch across the room with her shoes sitting on top. Marcie moved for them even as the woman tugged on her. "Wait, you can't. You need to lie down. Doctor! We need the doctor in here!"

Marcie easily broke the nurse's grip and started pulling her pants on. "Where's my shirt?"

"We had to cut it off. It was ruined with bloo—"

Two more nurses hurried into the room, along with a white-haired man in a beige trenchcoat. He smelled like a cop. Everyone looked stern, but Marcie ignored them, putting on her shoes. "You owe me a shirt."

"Ma'am, why don't you lay back down?" the cop said. It didn't sound like a request.

It wasn't safe here. Molok was still out there, looking for her, and she didn't have her protective symbols. Domingo was gone and—

Domingo's gone.

She heard him screaming all over again in her mind. Felt the dagger in her heart, knowing this was all her fault. Her entire family was dead, and it was all because of her. She was alone now, and a demon had her scent.

Why did I do this? It seemed she had a thousand good reasons in the beginning, but when she thought of all the damage that had been done...the countless lives that had been lost, all because she wanted to get back at Daddy...

"My name is Detective Simon Halbreck with Russellville P.D. I need you to tell me what happened to you," the man carefully phrased as though he were talking to a child. "Do you remember?"

"Of course I remember," Marcie hissed. Reaching into her jeans pocket, she found her cell was still there. She breathed in relief—first good news all day.

"Ma'am," the detective again, raising his voice but trying to remain professional. "You suffered a mild concussion and a fractured rib. You really need to lie down."

"And *you* need to get out of my way."

The three nurses looked to the officer, unsure of how he'd respond. Under the gaze of the women, the cop flushed, but kept his cool. "If you don't lie down, you'll be restrained."

"Oooh." Marcie cooed, affecting a crooked grin. "I'd like to see you try it, handsome."

Halbreck slipped a pair of handcuffs off his belt and took a tentative step forward.

Then the room went dark.

A heart-stopping beat later, the emergency lights blinked on. The nurses gasped in surprise, looking at each other, at the cop. "What is that?"

Marcie felt her flesh tingle with goosebumps. *No, no, no…*

"Let me out of here!" she roared, pushing forward. The detective caught her in a bear hug from behind. She struggled against him as one of the nurses eased into the hallway, looking confused.

"I'll go check," the nurse said, disappearing around the doorframe.

Silence followed before Marcie heard a wet slap.

The others in the room froze. Distracted, the cop's hold loosened, but Marcie couldn't command her legs to move.

Another wet gurgle. The hiss of arterial spray.

"What *is* that?" another nurse said in an awed hush.

The nurse who had gone to investigate returned, walking stiffly into the room. The front of her uniform was now red and clung to her body.

Her throat was missing.

Pale and blank-faced, she reached for Detective Halbreck as though seeking a good roll of duct tape to put her back together. She extended her hands, her own blood dripping from her fingers, then collapsed face-first onto the tile in a crunchy splat. The women screamed—but not Marcie—while the cop fumbled for his gun.

From the dimly lit hallway, it entered. Clad in black, its coat glistening with sticky blood, the giant strode in, slow and deliberate. Its fire had smoldered; now its skull face emitted a soft, steady blue glow.

The nurses screamed again, backing into the corner. The detective raised his gun, barely keeping his wits in the presence of something so unworldly. He fired.

The bullet melted in the face of the blue skull. Marcie knew the cop would keep trying, and she also knew he'd fail. Molok blocked the doorway and a quick glance told her the windows were caged, which meant they were high up.

Nowhere to go, little girl, her guilty conscience taunted her. *Gotta pay the piper now.*

For a split second, she wondered if that were for the best. With her dead, would the Blue Skull finally give up its relentless pursuit? Maybe it would return to the Other Side, finally satisfied. If so, she'd almost come to the point where she would be glad to give her life, if it meant putting this sucker in the ground.

But what if I'm wrong? What if it still keeps killing?

Marcie stepped behind Halbreck as he fired again, but Molok advanced. The beast lunged, wrapping impossibly large hands around the man's hands and gun, then lifted up. The detective let out a scream as his fingers were crushed, then fell silent when the demon punched a hole right through his chest, spraying Marcie in gore. She shrieked involuntarily and collapsed on the bed, but the creature reached for her through the dead man's chest cavity. She crab-walked over the mattress before toppling to the floor on the other side, dashing a small bedside table to the ground.

A drawer slid opened, and a Gideon Bible spilled out. *Fine, God. I can take a hint. You win.*

The nearby nurses screamed so hard that one of them fainted. Marcie shut out their terror, her mind working. Trembling, she reached for the Bible mere milliseconds before the Blue Skull discarded Halbreck's body, took hold of the bed and hurled it across the room, knocking the remaining nurse over. In her panic, Marcie couldn't grasp the Bible. Fingertips brushed along the surface, her fear mounting. She began to weep.

Molok reached into its coat. Withdrew something that shimmered in the moonlight.

The Scot's axe.

Tears filled her view as Marcie watched in dumb fright while the demon raised the axe high like a guillotine—

—and brought it down.

Marcie raised her hands, screaming as the nurses had before her, and hid her face from the strike. The axe stuck into the wall above her head, sprinkling plaster dust on her hair. The Blue Skull snorted, tugging at the weapon.

Head clearing, Marcie yanked the Bible off the floor and crawled out from under the axe's shadow, scurrying on the blood-soaked floor. At last, the monster ripped the blade clear from the obstruction and chased after her. Marcie slipped on the detective's remains and fell, smacking her chin hard on the tile. She shrieked in fear and pain, feeling blood fill her mouth. Desperately, she clutched the Bible close to her chest as Molok descended upon her once more, axe poised in the air.

With nothing else to do, Marcie shoved the Bible before her like a shield, remembering Flynn's move in the park. A blinding pulse of light detonated from the book, suffusing the room in a white glow. The devil dropped the axe to the ground, where it pierced the grout between two tiles an inch away from Marcie's right thigh. Roaring, the creature batted away at the light, grabbing at its face as though it'd just been hosed with mace. While it staggered about, Marcie slipped in the blood and stood, losing the Bible in the process. Too terrified to retrieve it, Marcie tore free from the room and hurried down the hall—

Then skidded to a stop, her toes soaked in fresh blood.

She gasped, taking in the grisly sight.

Everywhere... They're everywhere.

Forgetting Molok, Marcie tiptoed barefoot down the hallway, new tears spilling down her face. Her chest heaved with deep, shuddering sobs as she glanced from side to side. The floor was a river of blood, leading to the exit. Gory red Rorschach patterns flash-painted the walls. Overhead lights flickered, strobing her vision.

And the bodies...

An arm, torn from the socket. A string of uncoiled intestines, leading into one of the rooms.

The hallway was littered with the bodies of the hospital staff. Patients. The beast had cut a bloody swath to reach her.

At last, Marcie could take no more. She broke down, crying and shaking uncontrollably at the sight of such carnage. A jaw bone, flesh dangling from the ends. Orderlies torn in half. Patients in wheelchairs, chests pried open, organs spilling out.

Marcie clamped a hand to her mouth, gagging. Weeping.

The demon had killed all of them without making a sound. All to get to her. All because of her.

"God, I'm so sorry," she whimpered.

She stepped over bodies, easing for the exit, still softly crying. A cold chill snaked around her naked feet, slithering about the floor. She remembered that cold. Remembered the monster who created it.

As if on cue, she heard a shuffle in the hallway from which she'd come, followed by a low grating noise. Dragging. Getting closer.

Screeee

She yelped and picked up the pace, but the *clomp-clomp-clomp* of boots grew louder. Nearer.

269

Panicked, she scurried to the nearby nurse's station and slid to hide beneath the countertop, out of sight. The grating turned maddeningly loud and she braved a peek around the corner, just glimpsing Molok emerging from around a corner, dragging the Scot's axe on the floor behind him as it searched for her.

Marcie's teeth chattered, and her heart felt as though it might burst from her chest, but she stifled the scream that threatened to give her away by clamping both hands over her mouth. Shutting her eyes tight, she begged God to spare her. Still Molok moved closer, a steady *clomp-clomp-clomp-screee*, that awful grating racket trailing behind.

Opening her eyes, Marcie realized she was right next to a nurse, dead and cold. The young girl looked to be about her age and was doubled over the counter, her neck bent unnaturally, her cheek pressed to the blood-drenched floor. Her unblinking eyes, dilated and dull, stared at Marcie in condemnation.

Marcie flinched in revulsion, but snapped her attention back to the sound of Molok's approach.

Clomp-clomp-clomp-screeeeee

She winced and dipped her finger into a pool of the slaughtered woman's blood, scooping up the cooling sticky substance and frantically scribbling on the floor.

Screee-clomp-clomp

She worked at a fevered pace, her heart fluttering like a bird in a cage, scrawling a sequence of Enochian symbols on the floor about her in a circle, praying it'd be enough to render her invisible to the creature's supernatural radar. On hands and knees, she cried silent tears as she finished writing her enchantment, then tucked her knees to her chest and huddled within the mystical circumference.

Clomp-clomp-clomp-screeeeeee

Marcie pressed her head to her knees, trying to be small, her body trembling violently in abject terror.

Screeeeeeeeeeee

PleaseGoddon'tlethimgetmePleaseGoddon'tlethimgetme

Clomp-clomp-scree—

At just the moment Marcie thought her anxiety would overtake her, the emergency door slapped open and the thunderous footfalls faded outside.

She raised her head, only slightly, and eased her eyes open. Molok's movements could no longer be heard, and warmth had returned to the room. The lights blinked back on and she felt safe again. Leaning her head back against the underside of the counter, she cried openly, unashamed. With blood-soaked fingers, she reached into her pocket and withdrew her cell phone.

CHAPTER EIGHT

Eli Ross was sound asleep in nearby Greensboro when the phone rang.

The noise startled him, and he sprang up, reaching for the familiar SIG Sauer P229 tucked beneath his pillow. He cast hard eyes across the darkness, adjusting to the low levels of light, looking for intruders—fearing his enemies had finally caught up with him.

The phone rang again.

Cooling, Eli answered. "Hello?"

"Eli!" It was Marcie. She was crying. "They're all dead...all of them..."

Laying his gun aside, Eli pressed the phone to his ear and rummaged for his discarded jeans on the floor. "Where are you? What happened?"

"I'm at Russellville Methodist Hospital," she wept. He'd never heard her cry like that before. She didn't even sound like the same Marcie. "He's after me...please...save me, Eli."

"I'm on my way."

Back in Willowbrook, Flynn sat in Vinnie's apartment office amidst the man's collection of comics and real-life books on the occult. He'd endured the ride over here under Vinnie's single-minded tirade. Now that they were back, the urban mythologist paced the room, his sleeves rolled up, his cartoon-patterned tie loosened. In his large hands he clutched Flynn's digital camera, playing back the footage the boy had recorded. Flynn couldn't see. Didn't *want* to see. Not yet, anyway. It was too fresh, and he'd already survived it once today.

Once the eerie scene had played itself through, Vinnie shut off the camera and tossed it back to the kid, shaking his head.

Flynn slumped. "I'm sorry."

"What were ya thinkin' going back to them?" Vinnie shouted. "You coulda been killed!"

"I was trying to help."

Vinnie whirled on the boy, pointing a finger at him. "Her life ain't worth yours, do you hear me?"

Flynn stood, shouting now too. "I don't get you! Before, you wanted to find out who the Blue Skull was as much as I did. It didn't matter to you that it was the mob who had the information! But ever since you found out Marcie was the one who summoned him, it's like you don't care what happens!"

Vinnie didn't reply. He seemed lost inside himself, unwilling to express whatever emotion he was feeling.

Flynn stepped forward, impassioned. "We could stop this thing. Marcie needs our help."

At length, the burly man lowered his head. "Marcie…killed my wife."

Rain pounded against his windshield, soaking the city. Eli leaned over the steering wheel of his Jeep Renegade, the wiper blades barely working fast enough to clear his line of sight. He followed Marcie's directions, driving seventy miles an hour to reach Russellville in fifteen minutes, but he had yet to spot her. Instead, he watched as a parade of speeding police cruisers—lights and sirens blaring—zoomed past him, headed in the opposite direction. Somehow, he knew Marcie was involved in whatever call they were answering.

He pulled down a darkened side street, parking in front of the corner liquor store he and Marcie had robbed a few years ago. Eli stepped into the rain just as the girl emerged from the alley shadows. She had on jeans and shoes and a soaked hospital gown clinging to her form. Her cocoa-colored hair lay matted to her face and she shivered pitifully.

"Hey, Romeo…" she said, trying to smile.

Immediately he took off his jacket and draped it over Marcie like a blanket. Carefully he led her to the passenger seat and helped her inside. Checking once to make sure they weren't being followed, Eli took his place behind the wheel. He cranked up the heat in the Jeep, aiming the vents her way. Still she shook, eyes shut, head dipped forward. Rubbing her shoulders, he asked, "You okay?"

"My place isn't safe anymore. Can I stay with you?"

He nodded, feeling an almost uncontrollable urge to hug her, to hold her. But that wasn't his job anymore. Instead, he shifted gears and drove home in silence.

Vinnie figured he should begin the long, sordid tale at Josh Banks.

"I remember when I first met the string bean," Vinnie said over a glass of milk in his kitchen. Flynn listened without interruption. Vinnie appreciated that. He hadn't told this story to anyone other than the people who were involved, and once he was finished, he didn't fancy sharing it ever again. "It was back when I was still walking the beat for Willowbrook P.D., before I knew about Adrian Marcon. I was just a young pup back then, wet behind the ears and still believing that a mook could do some good in the world. A couple of the boys had brought Josh in to the station. He'd had a few too many and tried to pick a fight with a cashier at Taco Bell when they got his bean burrito wrong."

Vinnie chortled, thinking of Josh now. It had been too long since he talked with him. He needed to set that right.

"Anyway, it was late, and I was working the desk that night when she walked in."

Flynn nodded. "Allison."

"Yep. Allison. Soon to be the love of my life. Josh was her older, no-good brother and she'd come to post his bail. I barely said three words to her, I was so stunned. Her long blonde hair, her shining bright eyes. And that smile. I think even in my darkest hour, I'll always see that smile."

Vinnie hadn't cried over Allison in a long while. His tears had been replaced by something darker. Anger had kept her memory alive, rather than love.

She would've been ashamed of him.

"With her deadbeat brother in tow, she walked out of the station…but thankfully not out of my life. Lucky for me, Josh was going through a rough spell. Three more run-ins with a Hardees, a Wendy's, and a McDonald's had left him with a regular reservation in the holding cells. Allison came each time. It was after the Wendy's incident that I finally said something to her." He grinned, fondly recalling that first awkward conversation, but decided to keep it to himself. Some things were still private. "We began to talk more and more, even when Josh wasn't in jail. I gave her my off-duty number and waited by the phone every night, hoping she'd use it. She did. A lot. I was living out on the West Side of town back then, in the loft above *Fishy's Feed and Supply*, and I was too afraid to invite her over. I figured that the smell alone would drive her away permanently. We met for pie and coffee a few times until she finally offered to bake me something homemade."

Flynn grinned. Vinnie liked that. It was good that Allison still made people smile.

"It was about ten months after that that we were married. Things were looking up for me. I had a good woman. A good job. The Captain was even looking to promote me to detective. Then… Boss Marcon started sticking his bony little fingers in everything. A lot of cops were turning on us, lining their pockets with some extra coin. I tried to be a good, honest cop. To lead by example. But, one by one, Marcon corrupted the whole station. My partner Frank, my friends. I was the only one left."

"What did you do?"

"I quit. Left the force and applied for my private investigator license. On my own, I decided to do what I couldn't while on the force—I tried to take down Marcon. Luckily, I had some help. Unluckily, my help was *Josh.*" He snorted through a smile, imagining Josh wearing his newsboy cap and that oversized jacket. He was a skinny thug, but had a good heart. Well, when you got his fast food order right. "It was Allison's idea, really. Josh was a shady guy. He'd been in and out of trouble with the cops for most of his life. He knew 'the element', and, for better or worse, he was my brother-in-law. It looked like I had a guy on the inside. Josh and me took some jobs. A couple missing persons, your garden variety cheating spouse. But all the while, I never wavered from my goal. I knew I had to take down Marcon. Make this town safe again. Me and Josh did a whole lot of digging and came up with truckloads of dirt. Came to a point where we had phone taps, address books, and receipts. We wrapped it up in a nice red bow and made plans to reveal it to the world."

The boy's eyes grew wide, impressed.

Yeah, Vinnie thought. *I was impressed, too. Really thought I had the bull by the horns.* "Then Marcon had Domingo take Allison to teach me a lesson, and my world fell apart."

He took a drink of his milk and set it down heavily. This was the part of the story he didn't know if he could stand to tell. Somehow, he didn't think time would ever heal all the wounds. Taking a deep breath, determined to get through it, he began, "They took her to a warehouse, to keep her out of the way while they threatened me to keep quiet about what me and Josh had found. Something spooked the guy who was watching Allison for Domingo, though. Malcolm was his name. He started shooting, and Allison was caught in the crossfire. Josh lost his sister…I lost my wife. The world lost an angel."

Growing respectfully sullen, the kid averted his eyes and drank from his milk, as well.

"I got my hands on the security tape and watched it over and over, trying to find what had got Malcolm to shooting. In one blurry image, I found my culprit."

Vinnie leveled his young protégé with a stern look. "It wasn't of this world."

Flynn sat straighter. "The Blue Skull."

Vinnie nodded, that name holding so much meaning to him. The monster had defined his life. "Malcolm hadn't missed, but the six slugs he'd pushed into the Blue Skull didn't stop it. No, the thing kept going. That's when I began to realize that there were scarier things than Boss Marcon in the world, and I was determined to find out what they were. I quit the P.I. biz the same way I quit being a cop. I needed to go *deeper* into that dark world and discover its mysteries. Maybe even find out what it was that cost me my Allison. Josh was there with me for a while, but…" *I pushed him away.* "He's got a wife and a couple kids now. Met his girl on one of our cases, actually. A nice lady thought her baby was an alien."

Flynn brightened behind his glasses. "Was it?"

"Nah. Just a demon cult, turns out. We cleaned it up. She and Josh hit it off and, well…he had his life to lead. I had my own path to follow. Things got dark for me…but I finally pulled out. Decided I was better off continuing my research, but leaving the huntin' to the pros."

"Vinnie, I'm sorry about Allison."

Simple words that never did any good, but Vinnie understood the boy was trying.

"So, you see," Vinnie stood, emptying his glass and taking it to the sink, "if it's Marcie who brought that thing out and told it what to do, then she sent the Blue Skull after Malcolm while he was watching Allison. And it's *Marcie's* fault that my wife is dead."

But was that true? Couldn't the blame have just as easily been placed at Adrian's feet?

Couldn't the blame be his own?

I never should have fought Adrian. If I had kept my fat nose out of it, Allison would still be here.

But it was so much easier blaming Marcie.

"Look, kid, I know my Allison is in heaven and one day I'll see her again, but I can't forgive Marcie for what she's done. She unleashed this thing. It's her burden now. Let her deal with it. I'm not getting involved. And as long as you're working for me, neither are you."

Flynn frowned. The kid was so full of conviction, of goodness. *I ain't been that noble in a long time.* "If we don't help, Molok will drag her soul to hell, Vinnie."

Vinnie darkened. "I know."

The kid just gave him that look. Like he still believed Vinnie would do the right thing if given enough time to wrestle with the decision. Like he still believed in the best in everyone. *I used to believe that, too, once.* "And you don't care?"

Vinnie considered for a while, then muttered, "Let her burn."

Marcie sat in Eli's living room. He'd done his best to make her comfortable, cleaning up the piles of clothes and empty take-out boxes that lay scattered on every flat surface. He'd given her one of his clean work shirts to wear to replace the gown. In the morning they'd find her some new clothes. How many, he didn't know. He didn't know how long she'd be staying. He supposed that depended on her—on how long she was going to put off doing the right thing and fighting Molok in the only way that mattered.

She sat on the couch, her shoulders raised, as if preparing for an attack. She looked ready to run at any moment, on edge. Eli crossed by her, handing her a newly poured cup of coffee.

"Thanks." She took it. Sipped it tentatively.

Eli sat beside her, feeling thrilled to be this close to her, just like every time he'd ever had the opportunity to brush against her skin. It was suddenly as though no time had passed at all since they'd been together. "Wanna tell me what happened tonight?"

She lowered the mug. "I tried another spell."

He shook his head, huffing a sad sort of laugh.

"I didn't know what else to do, okay?" she snapped. "It was a bad idea. I get that now."

"What are you going to do?"

She looked at him, surprised. "What, no sermon? Don't tell me you quit believing, choir boy."

"I still believe. But you're not ready to give up yet, so why bother? You still think you can solve this on your own? Your demon hitman's not going to go away. It's only a matter of time before he finds you. When that happens, only God can stand in for you."

"You don't know that."

Eli stood, feeling his blood boil. "Why don't you fall back on Plan B, then. Hire more men to hunt him down and when they're dead, what? Just keep throwing money at this problem until it's solved, right? Just like the Old Man. And you saw where that got him."

Marcie recoiled as though he'd struck her, and Eli chastised himself for being so cruel. But just when he expected Marcie to come back swinging and begin one of their legendary fights, she only grew quieter, staring into her coffee. "There is no money, all right?"

Eli narrowed his eyes. "What?"

"It's gone. All of it."

"But the family—"

"The family died with my father and you know it. I've been so busy trying to get rid of Molok that Rufus swooped in and bought out most of Daddy's old business. I haven't even ever *seen* this guy, but he's everywhere, taking what's left of my family. He's already bought off the other family heads. I'm the last holdout. But… all I've got left is that house in the woods now. I had to sell off all the other property. I was trying to keep the business going, but there was only me and Domingo. Now that he's… I'm all alone."

"Sounds to me like you've got a chance to start over."

She scoffed, rolling her eyes. "What, and be like you? Hiding and hoping that no one will find out who I really am, *Paul?* No thanks. I've had enough of that now. Why didn't you ever turn yourself in, anyway? I would think that would be the first thing you'd do after being 'born again' and all. Shouldn't you be out there confessing your sins and making sure justice is getting served?"

He tensed and looked away, angry. She always knew how to strike where it would hurt the most. And maybe she was right—maybe he was just like her. Running and hiding and hoping his past wouldn't catch up.

"Hey," she said, softening. She set her mug on the coffee table and moved towards him. Touched his shoulder. He missed her so much. "Sorry. Don't take it so personal, all right? You're the only friend I've got left. I don't want to tick *you* off."

But the words had already been said. Eli felt more confused than ever about who he was, what he was meant to do. "It's getting late," he said, not looking at her. "We should get some sleep. Tomorrow we'll try and figure out our next move."

"Our?" She grinned seductively. "Does that mean you're on my team now?"

"No. You're on *my* team."

He tried to remain stoic, but eventually cracked and smiled. "You take the bed. I'm good with the couch."

"You know…it doesn't have to be that way," she said, tracing her finger along his arm. "Big bed like that…I could use some company."

Eli's heart raced. He wanted nothing more than to take her into his bed, to be with her as they'd been together so many times before. But he couldn't. "That's not a good idea."

Marcie batted her eyes at him. "Let me guess. The Bible says, 'no sex before marriage', right?"

"Actually, it's closer to 'sex *is* marriage'." Chuckling, he added, "You ready for that?"

She blushed—actually *blushed*. Looking away, but leaving her hand resting on his arm, she replied, "Good night, lover."

Her touch lingered another moment before she left for his bedroom. Eli considered the woman in his apartment, noting that the place—after all the time he'd lived here—finally felt like home.

He turned off the lamp, got cozy on the couch, and drifted to sleep.

CHAPTER NINE

Eli blinked sleep out of his eyes, sunlight greeting him from the facing window. He squinted against it and growled. He'd slept hard and felt fully rested, something he'd not enjoyed in a long, long time. Sitting up on the couch, he stretched, savoring the quiet morning. He was supposed to work today at Jed's garage, but he'd call in sick and use that time to help Marcie.

He heard a cabinet shut in the kitchen, some shuffling around. For an instant, he nearly grabbed his gun to go investigate, but, remembering that he had a house guest, realized it was time to put some of that paranoia behind him. Feeling naked without his SIG, Eli entered the kitchen. Marcie stood at the counter fussing over something, wearing only her panties and his oversized shirt, her bare legs and feet tantalizing him. She was absolutely beautiful.

"Morning," he greeted.

She turned without fright and handed him a small stoneware plate from his cupboard. On the plate, a single piece of toast. It was a little burnt, and he wondered if Marcie had ever cooked a day in her life. She paid people to do that. Domingo, he knew, had been known to make a mean risotto.

"Here," she said, curt. She took a plate of her own with matching burnt toast and sat at his kitchen table. He noticed she'd tidied his clutter of papers and bills, forming a neat stack on the corner of the counter.

"You made me breakfast?"

She shrugged, peeling at the crispy crust. "It's just toast."

"You never made me breakfast before."

"Fine," she huffed. "Don't eat it then."

He grinned. "No, no, I *like* it. It's just …domesticated. That's all."

Sparing her any more embarrassment, Eli sat opposite her, hesitantly biting into his crunchy breakfast. It tasted like sawdust, but he chewed it all the same. Here they were—eating breakfast together. They'd done a lot of things while they dated, but nothing so ordinary.

He could get used to this.

"So, what's the plan, fearless demon killer?" Marcie asked, sounding grumpy.

"I think I know a guy who can help. But we can't do this alone. We need some friends right now. I think we need to find that private investigator who used to give your dad such a hard time. Vinnie—"

Marcie laughed sardonically. "Ha. Try again."

"Seriously. I've seen his website. He's all into the paranormal and he's been following the Blue Skull case for a while now. He seems to be on the level."

"I tried that already. He won't help."

"Why not?"

Marcie's face hardened. "He didn't exactly say, but my guess is it has something to do with how his wife died. You remember that?"

"Yeah, it was Malcolm. Adrian had him holding her for leverage and the guy got jumpy when—"

Then he recalled the footage. The Blue Skull had been there. Eli set down his toast and rubbed his face. It seemed there was no end to the hurt Marcie had caused with her selfishness.

"I *know*, all right?" she bit back, leaving the table. "I wish I had never brought that thing here, but it's too late now. Best thing to do is just…I don't know. Go away."

"You're leaving town?"

She did not face him. "I thought about it."

He blew steam out of his nostrils and shook his head. "That's just great. Good plan, Marcie."

"Eli. Vinnie knows the truth now. I can't face him again. I'm the reason his wife is dead! What am I supposed to say? 'Oops, sorry about that'. When, if you think about it, it's Malcolm's fault. He's the one who was a crappy shot and hit the girl instead of the Blue Skull in the first place." Under her breath, she grumbled, "That idiot never could get anything right."

Eli stood and reached out to her, but she pulled away. Leaning over the counter, holding her face in her hands, she asked, "How did you ever do it, Eli?"

"Do what?"

"Get that first night of sleep without having nightmares about all the people you hurt."

A familiar heavy silence settled between them. The gulf that always kept them apart. "It was hard. It took me a long time to forgive myself. The only thing I could hold onto was that I believed God had forgiven me. I didn't deserve it…but that's how love works. You can't earn it. It's just given to us."

Why can't you just accept that?

But Marcie didn't know a whole lot about love. Eli pitied her for that.

"I'm really scared, Eli," she confessed, still not meeting his eyes. "I'm afraid to face Molok again…because I know I won't be coming back."

Eli shared that fear. He'd been losing Marcie since the day he met her. It seemed some people just wanted to be lost.

Dad was at work, and Flynn was home alone. He spent the morning watching MTV and flipping through magazines, trying to anchor himself again in reality. But he knew he had to deal with what he'd seen at the park. So, around noon, Flynn settled down in front of his computer, replaying the footage he shot at Greensboro Park Lake. He watched it on repeat for the better part of an hour, but the sight of what took place still made him a bit queasy. He saw Marcie, hovering in the air; the Blue Skull, storming their way like a train, pumping black exhaust; and Domingo, firing wildly before being dragged, screaming, off-screen by the monster. Flynn heard his own shrieks and couldn't believe he had produced a sound so terrifying.

Finally, after the tenth or eleventh viewing, he closed the media player on his desktop, unable to stomach any more. The fact that he had survived the ordeal filled him with continual awe. All the same, the knowledge that they had failed— that Big Blue was still out there—filled him with unspeakable dread. His whole body shook with nerves; it had since Vinnie brought him home last night. Dad had been too immersed in paperwork to notice, except to ask Flynn once this morning if he'd had a good time hanging out with his friend the previous day. It took Flynn a moment to remember that he'd told his dad he was going out with Chigger, so he simply nodded mutely and replied it'd been "okay". That seemed to appease his father's curiosity as the man promptly left for work and Flynn began his morning of trying to forget the horror at the lake.

When a knock sounded at his front door, he welcomed the distraction from his own dark reflections. Peeking outside the front window, and subsequently spotting a familiar paint-chipped Taurus, Flynn crossed the living room and opened the door for Vinnie. The big guy looked a lot calmer than he had last night, but his face remained tight, his drooping eyes preoccupied.

"Hey, kid," Vinnie began hesitantly, slipping off his fedora to clutch it in his two large hands. "Got a sec?"

Flynn stepped aside without a word and Vinnie entered, giving the house a quick once-over.

"Your…uh…pop here?" he asked.

Flynn's brow creased. "No, he's at work. Why?"

Vinnie shook his head once, looking almost relieved. "Listen… About yesterday, I'm sorry I blew up at'cha. But you don't understand—"

"I understand," Flynn said. "You blame Marcie for what happened to Allison. I get it. But she needs our help and you don't want to give it to her."

Vinnie closed his eyes for a moment, as if drawing strength, then shook his head weakly. "Trust me, that little chickadee has flown the coop. She doesn't care about you. She doesn't care about stopping that *monster* for the good of all mankind. She only cares about saving her own tail. Don't fool yourself."

Eli drove over the train tracks and pulled up to the creaky old house on Buckingham Road, staring it down like a dragon he'd have to kill to complete his quest. He'd not been back to Willowbrook since he left after that night in James' house. Little had changed about the town, like a photo from the darkest time of his life.

Marcie fidgeted in the Jeep's passenger seat. After breakfast he had gone to the store and bought Marcie a couple outfits. Nothing fashionable, he realized, but a few shirts and pairs of jeans would be enough for now. He remembered her size, even after all this time. Dressed in new clothes and hiding behind a pair of Eli's sunglasses, she slouched in her seat, eyeing the house.

"This is where his partner lives?" Eli asked.

Marcie nodded to the car parked out front. "And that's Vinnie's car. Super."

Their first stop had been Vinnie's apartment, but the urban mythologist wasn't at home. It was Marcie's suggestion that they give his partner a try—some boy named Spanger. Eli was reluctant to bring a kid into this mess, but he hoped the boy could direct them to Vinnie.

He hadn't known that Flynn Spanger lived in James Lenderman's old house.

Eli shut off the engine and stepped out of the Jeep, his hands sweaty. The place looked a little different—it'd been repainted and there were new decorations on the porch and a nicely kept yard. Still, enough remained the same that he half-imagined he'd find James inside, arguing with Theresa about something stupid like always, or playing with his baby.

How old would his child be now? *I took that kid's dad away.*

It surprised Eli how raw the pain still felt. Now he knew why he'd avoided this place. He supposed he and Marcie had that in common; they both were hiding from demons. Maybe together they'd have the strength to finally face them.

"So…" Marcie began, standing at his side and watching him as though he were about to shatter. "This is it, huh? This is where…"

"Yeah."

Marcie faced the house. Her father had died in there. This was where both of their lives had changed forever. To his knowledge, she'd never been here.

A flurry of emotions churned in his stomach. Guilt, excitement, relief, regret. Everything all at once, each shouting to be heard over the other. He had arrived back at the beginning, here at the end. The irony concerned him, like an omen foretelling of dark times ahead. Without a doubt, they were headed for a battle, and he didn't know if he or Marcie would survive.

"You know it's not too late to get in the Jeep and skip town," she piped up, a nervous titter in her voice. "I hear Canada's nice this time of year."

He headed for the front porch. "Come on."

She hung back a moment before following. "It was worth a shot."

"You don't know that," Flynn argued. "She's trying to fix this. Can't you see that?"

Vinnie turned a brighter shade of crimson. "That may be, but it's not something you need to get mixed up in."

Flynn's mind flashed back to the scene at the lake yesterday, a familiar fear taking hold. "But I'm *already* mixed up in it! He was in *my* house and we let him out!" The boy quieted, surprised by the conviction in his own voice.

Vinnie stepped closer, his tone softening. "Is that what this is about? You think this is somehow your fault?"

Flynn kicked absently at the hardwood floor. "I don't know…"

"Kid, *I'm* the one who burnt the money. I'm the one who let him out. That's my fault."

Leveling hard eyes at the large man, Flynn said, "Then why aren't you doing something about it?"

Vinnie closed his mouth and looked away. "You want me to save Marcie after what she did. I…" He sighed, wringing his hat.

Then the doorbell rang.

Flynn moved to the window and pulled back the curtain. "It's her," he whispered harshly, looking sharply at Vinnie.

The urban mythologist grimaced and nodded towards the door. "I'll cover you."

Flynn hurried to the front door and popped it open, cautious. Marcie waited for him, looking annoyed. Behind her stood a lean man with a hard face. He looked lethal and fast.

"Marcie?" Flynn asked, surprised.

Vinnie had his gun out in a heartbeat, in the woman's face. "What did I tell you?"

But the man behind Marcie had his own gun drawn and against Vinnie's cheek almost instantly. *Where did that gun come from?* Marcie's hitman wore an expression like ice, but Vinnie faltered.

"Easy there, fella."

"Vinnie," Flynn soothed his friend.

Marcie seemed unaffected by the stand-off. "You got a minute?"

With the silent man's gun pushing into his chubby jaw, Vinnie said, "Who's this? Another one of your cronies?"

"Can we put the guns away, boys?"

The hitman did not move. Vinnie didn't either, at first, until Flynn patted his arm. At last the urban mythologist surrendered, holstering the gun. Just as fast as he'd drawn it, Marcie's man put his weapon away. His face never twitched. "I'm Eli."

Flynn looked to Vinnie, then back to the duo on his doorstep, recalling all the research they'd done on the Blue Skull massacre that happened in Flynn's own home a couple years ago. "Eli *Ross?*"

Marcie replied, "Yep. *Now* can we be in the Monster Club?"

CHAPTER TEN

Vinnie sat across from Marcie at Flynn's kitchen table. This close to the woman he now knew was behind Allison's death… It was hard to focus on the task at hand. But the kid sat next to him, ready to help. Vinnie wasn't an idiot, nor entirely blinded by his hatred for Marcie. Yes, Molok was after her—and he couldn't care less what happened to her—but until the demon succeeded, others were in harm's way. Marcie told them about how she escaped the hospital and the butchery the Blue Skull had left behind. *No one* was safe while that thing was on the loose, and Vinnie couldn't turn a blind eye to their suffering.

"So, what do we do?" Flynn asked, very serious. Too serious for a thirteen-year-old kid. Once again, Vinnie was reminded of how young the boy was. How much he stood to lose if this thing went south.

"Marcie and I have been talking about it," Eli said evenly.

Vinnie still didn't know what he thought of Marcie's stoic protector. He'd heard the stories, of course, of Eli Ross and all the trouble he made for Rufus and Adrian, both, when he'd first come back to town following a tour overseas. The guy was Adrian's top lieutenant. Some of the boys on the force thought Eli would take over one day. The shaggy-headed guy in worn-out jeans and a t-shirt sitting in front of him, however, didn't do the legends of the slick killer in a suit justice.

Flynn jumped at the possibility of a plan. "Did you find out something else?"

Marcie nodded, not quite as cold or arrogant as Vinnie remembered her. Was the kid right? Was she changing?

"Yes," she said. "I think Eli, here, is protected from Molok."

At this, both Vinnie and Flynn eyed the stranger in their midst with fresh perspective.

Eli finished for her, "I've run into him twice, now, and both times he spared me when he could've killed me without a thought."

"The last time," Marcie cut in, "Eli was able to hide me from Molok by using his blood. When he did that, I saw…" She glanced to Eli, then to the table. "I saw something. A mark. On his forehead."

"Tav," Vinnie uttered the word like an ominous gong, and shared an understanding look with Marcie. He reached into the inside pocket of his trenchcoat and produced a creased and crumpled sheet of paper that he'd been carrying around for months now. He unfolded it and tossed it on the table.

"Did it look like that?"

Marcie nodded, locking eyes with him.

Flynn turned to Vinnie, nearly coming out of his chair. "You knew?"

Vinnie regarded the kid. "Yeah. It's on *your* head, too, remember? We saw it that night—right over there—after we chased off the Blue Skull. Ever since then, I'd been looking into it, trying to figure out what it meant."

"You never told me."

He shrugged. "Hadn't learned anything worth noting."

"Tav is the twenty-second letter in the Hebrew alphabet," Marcie said. "It means 'mark'."

"It also represents Truth," Vinnie added. "'Repentance', 'prayer', 'redemption', 'Torah'—in Hebrew all these words start with 'tav'. It's a holy letter, you might say." He scratched his chin in thought. "When I first read up on it, I wondered about its shape." He reached out a finger and traced the contours of the letter. "Up, across, down." To Flynn, he said, "Like I told you about in the Book of Exodus. God had His chosen people mark their posts and the tops of their doors in blood to ward off the Destroyer."

Flynn studied the picture. "Like a giant 'tav' over their doors, then?"

"Could be."

"It's also in the Book of Ezekiel," Marcie said, drawing everyone's interest.

None more so than Vinnie's. "*You* actually read the Bible?"

She smirked, playful but conniving. "I told you. I've tried everything."

"Tell them about what it says," Eli prodded her, all-business.

Marcie shot him an annoyed look, then groaned. "In chapter nine, God *supposedly* showed Ezekiel a vision of Jerusalem. God's people had profaned the temple with idols and filled the land with violence. That loving God you all are so fond of decided to slaughter His people for their sins. He called forth six executioners—*angels*—and told them to start at one end of the city and sweep to the other end, killing everything in their path." She rolled her eyes. "Sound familiar?"

"You think Molok could've been like one of those 'executioner angels' before he fell?" Flynn asked, animated.

Marcie shrugged. "Beats me. It's *your* Bible."

"Go on," Eli said, straight-faced.

"Fine," she sighed. "Anyway, before the angels started, a seventh angel—seven being the mystic number for perfection—was to go ahead of them with a writing case. Anyone who had *not* participated in the idol worship, those who 'sigh and groan over all the abominations' committed in their midst—whoever remained faithful to God—got a mark on the forehead: *Tav*. Whoever had that mark, the angels spared, preserving a remnant of God's people."

Flynn's eyes widened as he eased back in his chair. "And that's on my forehead?"

"And mine," Eli said.

Marcie grinned and pointed at the urban mythologist. "And *yours*."

Vinnie stiffened. Even Eli seemed surprised by this. "What?"

"It's true," she said. "When I was about to die out there in the woods, and you so valiantly came to my rescue, I saw it." Chuckling sardonically, she said to Eli, "Looks like we found your people, Eli. Praise God, hallelujah."

Eli ignored her and said, "We've been marked. Molok can't touch us. We're in his blind spot. That gives us an advantage over him."

Flynn nearly bounced in his seat, brimming with excitement. "What do we do, then?"

"Marcie thinks that, because we have the mark, we might have a little bit of control over the demon."

Vinnie's eyes narrowed in curiosity. "How so?"

Marcie hooked a thumb in Eli's direction. "Handsome, here, locked it up. Right here in this very house."

"The briefcase of money!" Flynn exclaimed, then pointed to the hitman across from him. "You hid that here, in my room!"

Eli fidgeted a bit in his chair. "At the time, I felt like that money represented every bad thing I had ever done. I thought Molok was payment for those sins. I left the money, and I—" his dark blue eyes flicked to Marcie and his cheeks flushed, "—prayed that God would bind the monster to the money, to my sin, and just throw out the whole thing."

"Why didn't I think of that?" Marcie drawled in mockery.

"I didn't really think about it," Eli said. "It's not like I knew what I was saying. I just wanted all of it gone and out of my life."

Vinnie rubbed his chin. "'I will give you the keys of the kingdom of heaven; and whatever you bind on earth shall have been bound in heaven, and whatever you loose on earth shall have been loosed in heaven.'" He caught Flynn watching him and clarified, "Matthew 16:19."

Flynn's eyes roamed about the table. "So, you think we might actually have a shot at stopping Molok."

Eli rubbed his hands, staring at them. "I did it once. Maybe I can do it again."

"But that was different," Vinnie said quickly. "You were operating on instinct when you prayed that prayer. On desperation. Perfect faith. Now you've had a chance to think about it, to wonder if it'll work. Doubt creeps in like that—"

"He's right," Marcie said, looking at Eli with something like affection, which surprised Vinnie. "Black magick or white magick—it works the same. You only have one shot at this, Eli. It's too risky. There's got to be a way to exploit Molok's weakness against you three in a different way."

Eli spoke to Marcie quietly, as thought they were the only ones in the room. "I have to try."

Vinnie raised a hand. "I got a question: Why? In Ezekiel's time, the land was filled with violence and corruption, just like Willowbrook. God brought their abominations down on their own heads, same as He's doing now. We really gonna try and stand in the way of that?"

Marcie laughed cruelly. "This is great. You holy rollers are all the same. Hellfire and damnation for everyone else. What does it matter, huh, so long as you have the Mark and get your free ticket to the pearly gates? Screw the rest of us, right?"

"Just you, doll," Vinnie seethed. "Just you."

Eli clenched his jaw, speaking tersely, "No way. I know what Marcie's done." He dipped his chin in Vinnie's direction, with great care. "Especially to you. But God didn't give up on me when I did terrible things. I'm not giving up on her."

Vinnie watched Marcie as Eli spoke and saw a different woman before him. Eli's words seemed to weigh down her tipped chin and slump her proud shoulders. Gone were the biting remarks and general conceited air. For the first time, he simply saw her as a girl in trouble with a man who loved her at her side.

Just like he'd loved Allison.

"I'm not either," Flynn said almost immediately and with great enthusiasm. "I'll help you, Marcie." The boy looked to Vinnie, almost daring him to object. "If you're so worried about protecting me, then you'll just have to come along. But I'm not sitting this out."

Vinnie pursed his lips, fuming inside—but at the same time pleased with his protégé. Flynn really was a good kid. Relaxing, if only a fraction, Vinnie pulled a Dum Dum out of his coat, tore off the wrapper, and popped the sucker in his mouth. "What's your thinking?"

Marcie brightened and even Eli seemed to release a held breath. "First off," he said, "we need help. I think I know where we need to go."

The drive was uncomfortable. Eli and Marcie sat up front in the Jeep, with Vinnie and Flynn occupying the backseat. Journey was on the radio, Steve Perry singing about that city by the bay. Eli thought to change the station or turn it off, but feared that would be even more awkward.

"I ain't making any promises," Vinnie reminded them once again. "We'll go talk to this guy of yours and see where we stand then."

Marcie folded her arms, staring out her window, affecting her best cold shoulder. Eli had seen her use it many times, but by now he could tell that underneath she was hurting. "Suit yourself," she said. "I guess I just thought you were still one of the good guys."

"*Hey*—" he interjected, but Eli shot Marcie a reproachful look.

"Enough. Don't we have enough problems without you guys fighting?"

Vinnie retracted, looking uptight. Marcie shrugged it off, arms still crossed.

Eli returned his attention to the road and spotted their destination. "We're here." He pulled the car into the church's empty lot. It seemed he was destined to re-trace his steps from the night he'd first encountered the Blue Skull. First James' house, now the Little White Church. He'd talked to Pastor Loomis on the phone occasionally over the last couple years, but he hadn't been back here.

"You really trust this guy?" Marcie asked quietly.

Eli nodded. "He's a crank, but a well-meaning one. Besides, he knows about the paranormal—in ways most preachers these days don't. He helped me then. If we're going to beat Molok, we'll need his knowledge."

As soon as they parked, Vinnie was out of the vehicle, adjusting his hat, looking hot under the fedora and coat. Flynn followed, and Eli watched the two talking in low tones. No doubt the kid was trying to keep his friend in check.

"I'm not going in there," Marcie mumbled after a quiet moment. "I mean, the place might fall down on me, right?" She offered a weak grin. "Howabout I stay and watch the car?"

That sounded like a bad tactic. Eli was determined to keep his team close. Keep them safe. In spite of his gut instinct, he understood Marcie's reluctance to step on holy ground. He'd felt the same way when he first came to Pastor Loomis. She still just wasn't ready. "Okay. Honk—"

"—if I see anything." She nodded like a teenager with an overprotective guardian. "Got it, lover."

Eli found the frumpy pastor in his study, just as disheveled as always. Loomis' salt-and-pepper hair was nearly standing on end, as though he'd been wringing it in frustration. The man leaned crookedly over his desk, grumbling to himself, as he dug around in mounds of papers, some of them spilling to the floor. Eli smiled softly. He supposed he wouldn't want to find the man any other way.

"Hello, Pastor Loomis."

The preacher turned with a start, his beady eyes growing wider behind his thick, tinted glasses. "Eli! It's good to see you, m'boy." The man eased out of his chair and approached, straightening the hem of his turtleneck and shaking hands with Eli. He bowed just a bit too formally. "I welcome you on the Good Lord's behalf."

"Good to see you, too."

Behind Eli, Vinnie and Flynn waited. Loomis eyed them in curiosity. "Well, what brings you my way after all this time?"

"Sorry to say it, but I have another problem."

Loomis touched a knuckle to his head and sighed dramatically, if not good-naturedly. "I've come to suspect that problems follow you, my dear boy."

You have no idea.

Flynn had finally gotten over his fear that Eli was going to shoot them all. In fact, the more time he spent with the reformed killer, the harder he found it to imagine Eli being a hitman *at all.* He seemed really nice. Almost do-goody. He wondered what had happened that led Eli to become an assassin for Boss Marcon, but he knew that now wasn't the time to get into detailed backstories. Maybe if they survived all of this…

Eli's friend Pastor Loomis led the visitors into the sanctuary. Flynn marveled at the old structure. He could feel the tradition here, the age. It felt comforting and intimidating all at the same time. He and Vinnie took seats in the pews while Eli explained to the preacher what they were up against. Vinnie was still quiet. Flynn was thankful his friend was along, but wished he could get a handle on his emotions. What they were facing was too important for rivalry. They all needed to be on the same team.

Eli sat in the pew across the aisle. Loomis braced against the pulpit for a minute, as though he were about to deliver a sermon. "Ah, yes. Molok."

"So, you've heard of him," Eli said.

Loomis stepped down, moving for a pew of his own. He tapped his temple, thoughtful and disturbed. "I have. From the Malitivar Codex."

Flynn leaned in to Vinnie. "Has everybody heard of this book but me?"

Vinnie simply shrugged, but Loomis interrupted, "Believe me, my son, I wish I'd never heard of that dreadful book. It is full of darkness, and I fear the world's destruction may be bound in its pages."

"Then why not destroy it?" Flynn asked.

In a raspy, reverential voice, the pastor whispered, "You cannot destroy something so powerful."

The man seemed to know such things from experience, and Flynn was anxious to hear more. He couldn't deny that talking about these macabre matters stirred in him a certain sense of lordship over them.

Vinnie spoke at last, though his tone was curt. "So, tell us, preacher, what do you know about Molok?"

"When the Ammonites worshipped him, they sacrificed their children in blue-hot fire in his honor. The skies were filled with the smoke of charred innocent flesh."

Flynn frowned. "Marcie told us he was a powerful demon."

Loomis lifted his chin, striking a pose of quiet nobility. "No, not just *a* demon, but the general of a massive army. It is written in other manuscripts that he would lead an army of the damned—souls corrupted by What Is Yet To Come—to devour the worlds."

"How do we kill him?" Eli asked, right to the point. Maybe he had more hitman in him than Flynn had given him credit for.

"In the Books of Carvac—"

"Waitaminute," Vinnie cut in, leaning over. "You've read the Books of Carvac?"

Flynn had never heard of the books and didn't understand Vinnie's visceral reaction to hearing the pastor mention them.

Burdened, Loomis groaned. "I assure you, Mr. Caponi, I am well-versed in many arcane texts. The Codex, the Books of Carvac…even the mad writings of Abdul Alhazred."

Flynn didn't know who that was, either. But judging by the stern look that came across Vinnie's usually easy-going face, *he* did.

"Well, what do they say?" the boy finally asked.

"There is talk of a dagger forged in the fires of hell called the Aztaroth

Dagger. Everything I've read spells out quite plainly that this is the only weapon that can kill Molok."

"Where is the dagger?" Eli again. Aiming for the heart, making the kill.

Loomis pursed his lips in deep concentration, no doubt recalling from a long catalog of mental references. Flynn was amazed by the man's knowledge. "I'm not sure… Some manuscripts claim it was lost in the second World War when Hitler tried to summon Molok to fight against the Allies."

Flynn couldn't contain his excitement. Not only were they fighting a real, Biblical demon, but they had to use a weapon coveted by Hitler to destroy him! "We have to find it!"

"I ain't so sure that's a good idea, kid," Vinnie said.

He turned to his mentor. "But it's the only way. How else are we going to survive against him?"

"You've seen it yourself. It's *faith*."

Flynn bristled. "But what about people who don't have faith? How are we going to save *them*?"

Vinnie grew sullen.

"We need that dagger," Eli said.

CHAPTER ELEVEN

Flynn spent the rest of the afternoon at Vinnie's. They were in full-on research mode, scouring Vinnie's book collection and the internet, trying to glean every little bit of information on the Aztaroth Dagger and where it might be located. Not surprisingly, they turned up very little. Were it not for Loomis' assurance, Flynn would have doubted the thing even existed.

Master and apprentice barely spoke during their investigation. As angry as Flynn was at the thought of Vinnie keeping the deeper occult secrets from him, it hurt him more to think that their friendship was somehow broken, and maybe it was his fault. He worried that he should apologize again for pursuing the Blue Skull case when Vinnie would rather drop it altogether, but this was a just cause, and Vinnie had to know that. He was just consumed by resentment.

Flynn kept quiet, trying to pick the best opportunity to talk to Vinnie about everything. Finally, dusk settled, and Vinnie drove him back home. As they sat in the driveway, Flynn held off exiting the vehicle, desperate to think of something to say.

"I guess tomorrow we keep trying to figure out how to get this Aztaroth Dagger, huh?"

"Guess so," Vinnie replied without much enthusiasm. He seemed a million miles away.

Flynn frowned, but carried on with the chit-chat. "That preacher sure did know a lot."

"Yeah. A little too much if you ask me."

Barely able to contain his frustration, his unending questions, Flynn blurted, "I don't understand you, Vinnie. I thought you wanted to know the truth."

Rather than retaliate, Vinnie remained calm. He looked weary. "Kid, let me tell you something. There's some things in this world that maybe we're better off not knowing."

"How can you even say that after all we've been through?"

He shrugged, nonchalant. "Maybe God didn't mean for us to know certain things. You can't study the occult that extensively and not have it affect you. Black magick is black magick, and it can change a person, no matter what your intentions are. Trust me."

Flynn sensed a deeper meaning behind Vinnie's words, and decided to venture further. "Marcie said something about you being big into magick once."

Vinnie frowned and stared out the window. "Told you that, did she?" He took a breath and released it through his nose. "Yeah. After I lost Allison, I...started down a dark path. Found myself one of the Books of Carvac. Did some things that...I'm not proud of. It's a scary place to be, kid. If it weren't for Josh, I might never have come back." He glanced at the boy. "I don't want that for you. Getting involved in that stuff... It's not good for the soul and it just ain't smart."

Flynn supposed the man was speaking truth. It was *biblical*, even. But the truthfulness of Vinnie's words did not quench his thirst for more. Together he and Vinnie had scratched at the surface of a kind of understanding that went way beyond human reasoning. They'd peeked into the dark places of the universe. How could they just turn back? What was in there, buried in the deepest shadows? Flynn needed to know, for reasons he couldn't even articulate. It had to do with losing Mom, yes. It had to do with feeling awkward and overlooked for most of his life, yes. But there had to be more behind it. He was learning this arcane knowledge in order to *help* people.

Wasn't he?

Vinnie kept his hands on the wheel, the parked car idling. He gazed into the twilit night, somber. "Sometimes, I think maybe I did wrong by you when I took you in and taught you the trade."

Flynn frowned. "Vinnie..."

"A kid like you, you got your whole life ahead of ya. You shouldn't be getting mixed up in this business with Boss Marcon's family. It only leads to heartache. Trust me, I know. I see a lot of myself in you, kid. You want to know the truth, and that takes guts. But you gotta know where to draw the line and realize you ain't gonna know everything, and that's okay, too. That's where faith comes in. If you go this way with Marcie, you're gonna end up with a gun in your hand and a bullet in your noggin and that'd kill me. You're a good kid. A little overzealous, sometimes, but a good kid."

Hearing such praise from his mentor meant a lot to him.

"This should be the best summer of your life," Vinnie said. "At your age, you should be racing bikes with the neighborhood kids, playing 'til dark." He chuckled and finished, "Getting the number of that pretty little canary we saw at Carl's."

Flynn blushed at the thought of the mystery girl, but put her lovely face out of his mind. "But I don't want any of that stuff," he said, suddenly feeling very sad having said it aloud. Like he'd signed part of his life away. But resolving himself, he affirmed, "*This* is what's important."

"Nah, kid. That's where you're wrong. That other stuff—that's what we're all fighting for." His voice almost a whisper, the man finished, "I didn't get that. Not until it was too late. It's about time you started living, Flynn."

There was a sense of finality in the sentiment. Flynn grew worried and asked, "Are you…firing me?"

Vinnie didn't immediately reply. He just kept staring through the windshield, letting the seconds tick away. At length, he met Flynn's eyes. "I'm just saying maybe you need to talk to the Good Lord about what He wants you to do with your life. I became an urban mythologist to find out what happened to my wife, and now that I know…I'm at peace with that. The truth has set me free, as they say."

"But you're *not* free," Flynn declared. "Not yet. Not until you forgive her."

His friend turned back to the night, reflective. "I know, kid," he answered, almost to himself. "But it's so frickin' hard…"

The wall that Vinnie had built around himself was crumbling and Flynn felt closer to his friend than he had in weeks. He no longer felt angry with him or denied. He just saw a hurting man he'd come to respect and wanted to help. He wanted nothing more now than to make Vinnie whole. "But isn't that what we're supposed to do? Go the extra mile to do the right thing? We have to put our faith into action. What good is it if we don't?"

Just like that, the wall went up and Vinnie's face became unreadable. "You'd better scram. Your dad's probably wondering about ya."

Flynn wondered if he'd ever see Vinnie again, or if this was the end of it all. He tried to imagine life without the big lug. "Are you coming tomorrow?"

"I don't know."

Knowing that he might die fighting the Blue Skull, Flynn didn't want those to be the last words they spoke to each other. Feeling sick in his heart, he said, "You gotta do what you believe is right. And so do I. Good night, Vinnie."

"See you around, kid."

Flynn climbed out of the car, preparing himself for the path ahead, bracing himself to face it without Vinnie Caponi at his side.

Eli opened the door to his apartment, but stopped just short of stepping inside. He kept his gaze direct, alert, and waved Marcie behind him.

"Hold on a second. Let me check."

She blew out an aggravated breath and pushed ahead of him, switching on a light and dropping down onto his sofa with an exaggerated sigh. "Please," she drawled, tired but somehow playful as well. "He's not here. With your Bible and all your crosses, your place is practically a church." She grinned at him coyly. "You big choir boy."

He relented and entered as well, closing the door behind him and locking it tight. Despite her relaxed demeanor, he still made a quick once-over of the apartment, SIG dangling at his side as he peeked in every room. "Better to be safe than sorry."

"Suit yourself," she called out to him from the couch.

Once satisfied, he moved back into the living room, tucking his pistol in the small holster behind his back.

She cocked an amused eyebrow at him. "Happy?"

Marcie had been mostly quiet on the drive back to Greensboro, telling Eli she just wanted to go back to his apartment and "be normal". Watch bad TV, eat some take-out Chinese from the joint down on the corner, and soak up all the mundane idle chatter that most people took for granted. He couldn't blame her—the way she told it, she'd been trapped in her house for months, alone except for bodyguards and Domingo.

But following their meeting with Loomis, Eli's mind swam with all that they had to do: find the dagger, lay a trap for Molok, and finally kill the beast. It was a nigh insurmountable task, and Eli needed to prepare. Adaptability was any soldier's greatest asset, and the more he knew of any given situation, the more maneuvers he could foresee.

"We really need to go over the plan," he said, his brow furrowed.

Marcie stood in a hurry. "No."

He watched as she moved across the room to his stereo by the wall. She knelt down and sifted through his selection.

"Marcie—"

She selected a song. The opening chords of Creedence Clearwater Revival's "Long as I Can See the Light" played softly. Marcie stood, slow and purposeful, turning to face Eli. She watched him, her gaze fixed intently on him, and he knew that look. He flushed, his heart beginning to dance.

"What are you doing?" he asked, trying to be stern.

She eased upon him, wide brown eyes beseeching. "I don't want to talk about 'the plan'. I've gotten my hopes up too many times."

"This time will be different," he said immediately. "It'll work."

She shrugged, looking away. "Maybe it will. Maybe it won't." Locking eyes with him, she carefully undid the first couple of buttons on his shirt. "And if this is my last night on earth, I don't want to spend it talking about *him*." Pausing to search his eyes, she said, "I've wasted enough of my life on him as it is. Just give me this one night." Softer now. Sad. "Just this one."

Eli considered her, gently touching her face. She closed her eyes, savoring the moment, a single tear escaping. His thumb brushed her cheek, then her chin, then her lips. She parted them slightly to offer a kiss against his palm.

He embraced her as their lips finally met, and the song played on.

Kids' toys dotted the slightly overgrown lawn. Vinnie stepped one boot over a multi-colored big-wheel tricycle, heading for the front door. It was a little later than he liked to pay house calls, but he needed to talk.

At the doorstep, he heard movement inside, the sound of a child's voice, a woman urging someone to pick up toys and get ready for bed. Vinnie smiled despite himself. Could this have been his life? He supposed he'd never know now.

Raising a fist after a moment's doubt, he knocked on the door. Muffled voices followed, then the door opened. A young woman stood there, raven-haired and svelte with a delicate complexion. Her dark eyes widened, followed by an infectious smile. "Vinnie!"

"Hey, Zoe," he greeted casually, submitting to a friendly hug.

"What are you doing here?" she asked with a pleased enthusiasm.

"Is he in?"

"Yeah, yeah, come on in. He'll be happy to see you."

Zoe eagerly stepped aside, and Vinnie entered, feeling instantly at home. A pint-sized blond boy in airplane-patterned pajamas ran up to him and swatted him with a glowing toy lightsaber. "Die, Sith Lord!" he roared.

"*Zeke*," Zoe chided, looking horribly embarrassed.

Vinnie just laughed. "He's getting big. How old is he now?"

She groaned. "Old enough to know better." Turning to the boy, she took away the lightsaber and gave him a playful tap on the backside. "Go. Pick up."

"I don't want to," he groaned in barely decipherable toddler-speak.

"*Go.*"

He slumped and skulked away. Zoe closed the front door behind Vinnie. "You want me to get you a drink? A beer?"

"Yeah. Sure. Whatever you got."

"Great. He's around here somewhere."

Zoe disappeared into the kitchen, but not before shooing Zeke once again. Vinnie smiled and moved into the living room, where Zeke twirled around in a circle, making laser gun noises for no particular reason. In the corner, a little girl—maybe six months old—in footie pajamas and sucking a pacifier, rolled around on the floor, kicking her feet into the air, quiet and content. The last time Vinnie had seen Jordan had been at the hospital when she was born.

Has it really been that long?

"Babe?" Zoe hollered from the other room. "Could you *please* help with the kids?"

A familiar put-upon wise-guy voice filled the house and Vinnie warmed. "Yeah, yeah, I'm on it, already."

A lanky man—minus the old newsboy hat and oversized jacket—hurried into the living room, frustrated. "Zeke, what did your ma say? Pick up your toys already."

Zeke reluctantly obeyed just as his father spotted Vinnie. Long seconds passed like an eternity. "Hey!"

Vinnie stuck his hands in his pockets, giving a nonchalant shrug. "Hey, Josh."

His brother-in-law dodged toys, picking up speed, and wrapped his arms around Vinnie. "Man, it's been too long, brother. What're you doin'?"

"I thought I'd come by and talk."

Josh stood speechless, a dazed excitement on his face. Zoe arrived on cue with two beers, handing one to each of them.

"Come on outside, man," Josh said.

Vinnie followed him to the back porch, passing by wedding pictures, family photos, and candid vacation shots. He couldn't have been prouder. *He got out. He got to have his happy ending.*

Josh slid the patio door open and Vinnie took a seat at the table on the porch, next to the grill. The mental image of Josh barbecuing was especially hysterical. The last time he'd put Josh in charge of a fire, the guy managed to kill a banshee yet simultaneously took out a high school gymnasium. But that was Josh—crazy enough to make the impossible work.

I could really use him on this Blue Skull job, Vinnie thought. But...no. He'd made a promise to himself not to get Josh involved in any more monster hunts. The guy had people who were counting on him. Vinnie couldn't take him away from Zoe and the rugrats.

Once Josh settled in his chair, his euphoria darkened to reserved expectation. "So, what's up, man?"

"I got a lead on the thing that got Allison."

Josh sat in silence for a moment. Took a drink. "Skullface?"

"Well, we call him the 'Blue Skull' now, but yeah."

Another drink. Josh stood, blowing out a heavy breath. "Man..."

"There's a catch."

"There always is. What is it?"

"I gotta work with some unsavory types to get it. It's complicated, but I...I don't know."

Josh looked resolved. "I haven't fired my sawed-off in a while. I could get it outta the closet. Dust it off and come with."

"*No*," Vinnie said. "I don't want that. That's not why I came. You got a good thing going here." He grinned. "Better than you deserve."

"Ha," Josh chuckled and held up his beer. He and Vinnie clinked their bottles together, toasting to that. "You're telling me."

They shared a drink and Josh said, "So, why did you come?"

"I was actually thinking about not going after the goon."

Josh sat back. He didn't appear upset, just curious. "Yeah?"

"Like I said, there are factors that—"

"It's complicated," Josh repeated.

"Right. I guess I needed...your permission."

"Mine? Why?"

"I been chasing this guy for years. Used to think I was doing it for me, but maybe somewhere along the way I started doing it for us. Skullface took Allison from both of us. A part of me felt like I owed it to you, as much to myself, to kill it."

Now Vinnie needed a drink. Josh watched him, nodding like he was thinking it through. "So, you're asking me if I mind if you just sit this one out and don't go through with it?"

Vinnie couldn't reply except to nod. To do any more might unleash the tears threatening to build in his eyes, and he and Josh weren't in the habit of getting emotional if it wasn't absolutely necessary.

Josh sat in his chair again and leaned back, in his element in a backyard with faded plastic swings and barbecue grills and a nice family. The guy was a screw-up, but had somehow stumbled his way into a respectable life. "Look, Vin, losing Allison was the hardest thing I ever had to deal with. But...running with you, it made it better. And I think that's the way my sister would have wanted it. Man, you could spend your whole life trying to get payback or whatever. I was right there with you for a while. But ain't none of it gonna bring her back. Dude, *you* taught me that." Josh gestured to his home. "You talked me into this. You were the one who told me I should quit the job and see if what me and Zoe had was worth fighting for."

"And it was."

"Better believe it was. So, you gotta look at your life. What's worth fighting for? You can't do this crap for Allison, and she wouldn't want you to. That ship's sailed, man. If you go up against Skullface just outta payback, there ain't nothin' at the end of that rainbow, brother. If you *do* fight it, it's gotta be for the right reasons."

"What are the right reasons?"

Josh chugged his beer. "Beats me. Just sounds like something Allison would say."

"I'll drink to that," Vinnie replied, lifting his own beer high.

"You do what you gotta do. Just be sure why you're doin' it. Fight that bugger or don't—it's just gotta be for the right reasons, man. You do that, and we're square, you and me."

For a guy who landed in jail over a fast food joint getting his order wrong, Josh spoke a lot of wisdom.

"Thanks, Josh."

"Anytime."

The two stayed out on Josh's porch, talking and telling stories. They remembered the old times together, and Vinnie felt good, really good. Long after the kids and even Zoe had gone to sleep, the two buddies were still out back, laughing into the early hours of the morning.

Eli carried the fragrant bag of Chinese food past Corner Video, headed back to his apartment on foot. Headed home to Marcie.

The crisp night air revived him and the grin on his face refused to budge. He hadn't felt hopeful in a very long time, but something about tonight promised him rest. He didn't know how, but he was sure now that they would win. Somehow, they'd accomplish the impossible and destroy Molok once and for all, and Marcie would be freed from this nightmare. They *all* would be.

One more hill to take.

Buoyed by a fresh sense of anticipation for the future, Eli jogged across the street and entered his building, taking two steps at a time, ready to see Marcie again. He unlocked the door and entered, calling out in a sing-song voice, "Honey, I'm home."

No answer.

He chuckled uneasily, door still partly opened. "Marcie?"

When she didn't answer, he set the bag of Chinese on the nearby side table and drew his SIG. *Oh, God, please no.* Forcing himself to keep his cool, Eli swept the apartment, his gun ready to fire. Terror slowly built in the pit of his stomach, swelling to touch every nerve. *I shouldn't have left her.* If he found her body…if the Blue Skull had gotten to her first…

In the kitchen, he saw a note on the counter, folded so that it stood like a tent. It was in Marcie's handwriting:

DECIDED TO SKIP TOWN AFTER ALL. I SUCK AT GOOD-BYES. I'M SORRY. IT'S BETTER THIS WAY. DON'T BE MAD, OKAY?

—M

Eli crumpled the note and hurled it against the refrigerator.

She had brought light back into his life, and had taken it away just as quickly.

He sat alone in the dark all night, their Chinese dinner stuffed in the trashcan, untouched.

Marcie wasted no time in purchasing a bus ticket bound for anywhere out of town. She managed to make it three hours from Greensboro before the guilt set in. *Too late now.* It wasn't, she supposed. She could get off the bus and go back. But then what? Help Eli and those two bumbling ghost hunters save the world? What was so great about the world that made it worth saving, anyway? It wasn't like there was anything she could do. She'd tried everything in her bag of tricks and had only managed to further incense the demon. Caponi was looking for another magic bullet, but she'd gone down that path one too many times already. Didn't they see that it was useless? Molok was here to stay. Best thing to do was to keep out of its way. Eli had managed to do it. She knew he believed it was his God who had kept him safe, but Marcie hoped she could do this without the Almighty's help. She'd just keep her head down, mind her own business, and let her rebellious child throw his tantrum. Maybe the demon would forget about her. It wasn't like she was a threat to it anymore.

As for all the people it killed in the meantime, well…she'd just have to try and live with that.

Who knew? Maybe Eli and the others would actually kill that thing or send it back to the Other Side. She hoped they could. They would just have to do it without her.

"Where you headed?" the old woman sitting beside her asked in a syrupy sweet voice.

Marcie had been in fear that the lady was going to talk to her from the start of the trip, but after sitting so long in silence she'd finally abandoned that worry an hour ago. It seemed she'd given up too soon. "Uh, east." East was as about as accurate as Marcie could guess. She didn't know where she was going to land, and she certainly wasn't going to tell grandma, here, the whole story.

"Staying or just visiting?"

The woman clutched her purse on her lap, perfectly poised. The sickly smell of perfume wafted from her like the woman bathed in the stuff. "Visiting my mother," Marcie lied flawlessly. Of course, she'd never met her mom, but that seemed to be the kind of gooey sentiment a woman like this would tell all her bridge club about. *Yeah, my life's a Hallmark card waiting to happen.*

"Oh, that's wonderful," she beamed, her red lips turning up into a smile. "Are you and your mother close?"

"Oh, yeah. Best girlfriends," Marcie said, finding some cruel pleasure in exploiting this woman's friendly interest. "We used to do everything together. I was in pageants all the time when I was little, and she was always there. Not pushy like those moms on TV, you know? Just letting me do my thing. I took ballet, just like her. It's been hard being away at college, but I know we're going to have a *great* time when we see each other again." The lies rolled off Marcie's tongue, taking on a life of their own. She played the part to the hilt, gabbing excitedly as she imagined most girls did.

Once the fairy tale left her lips, though, a dark emptiness settled in her heart. *Wow, do I really wish all this nonsense were* true?

The elderly broad, of course, was near tears, her dentures a dazzling grin. "That's beautiful, dear. That really is."

Marcie hoped that'd be the end of it. That maybe the lady would conk out, since it ought to be past her bedtime, and Marcie could enjoy the rest of the ride in peace.

"Sadly, my daughter and I haven't talked in a couple years."

Great. It's going to be a long ride.

Without invitation, the woman carried on, matching Marcie's previous eagerness to share, "We used to be close, but after her divorce she got a little away from me. Started dating a lot of men who were just using her, if you ask me."

I didn't, lady.

"The one she's with now has got four kids—all with different mothers—and doesn't speak to a one of them. I told her he was no good for her, but, well…she doesn't call anymore."

Marcie weighed the option of pretending to be sleepy. The woman continued, talking to the air now, "But I love her anyway. I really do. Love forgives a multitude of sins, you know." Leaning over, she muttered, "That's from the Bible. Do you read God's Word, dear?"

Marcie glared at the woman, her teeth clenched. "No."

"Oh, I've got to read it every day. That's what keeps me going. Sometimes, I don't know how I'd carry on without my sweet Jesus."

"That's great. Look, I'm kind of tired and it's been a long day—"

"I think it's wonderful that you and your mother are so close. That's how it should be. So often, we don't appreciate the ones we love until it's too late. But I think God puts people in our lives for a reason and we need to be open to those opportunities."

Just as Marcie was about to raise her voice to shut the old biddy up, the woman took a worn tissue from her purse and dabbed at her eyes. Sniffling, she dug around until she retrieved a cell phone. "I'm sorry," she wept. "I just...I think God's brought you here for a reason. I think...I need to call my daughter. Tell her I love her. Excuse me." Marcie watched, stunned, as the woman stood on the bus, about to head to the lavatory in back. At just the last moment, she stopped and offered Marcie a truly appreciative smile, as if she'd just saved her life. "Thank you so much, dear. Bless you."

Dialing the phone, looking like she'd just won the lottery, the woman retreated to the back. Marcie could already hear her saying, "Suzanne? It's me, honey. I just wanted to say that I love you..."

The woman was grinning now, laughing through tears, just as she ducked into the bathroom for privacy. Marcie sat like a stone in her seat, numb. Much to her surprise, she felt her eyes begin to sting.

CHAPTER TWELVE

Vinnie steered his wrecked car to the curb with a cough and sputter and put it in PARK. He stepped out and opted to leave his trenchcoat behind. Rolling up his sleeves and adjusting his favorite *Scooby-Doo* tie, Vinnie propped his fedora on his head and grabbed a cardboard box from the passenger seat before walking up the sidewalk. Downtown Willowbrook had fallen into disrepair since Rufus had taken over. Chain link fences kept angry dogs at bay, while shirtless skinheads milled about broken-down cars, drinking and smoking. Vinnie kept to himself, respecting the fact that they were sharks, and these were their waters. Besides, he wasn't here for them.

He spotted the house—a drooping, dull sickly green two-story with a rotted wooden porch. Tar black shingles had fallen off the roof and littered the weed-covered lawn. Some of the siding was gone, exposing old boards. Cats scurried out of Vinnie's way, disappearing into crevices at the house's foundation. The front door was open, and Vinnie heard a man's deep, raspy voice through the screen door. "It's gotta be, man. It's *gotta* be the only way!"

The TV was on, as usual, loud enough for the whole neighborhood to hear. Vinnie climbed onto the shaky porch and knocked on the screen door.

"Yo, Vinnie, come on in, man."

Vinnie opened the door and stepped through, finding himself immediately enveloped in a cloud of cigarette smoke. The place was a sty, numerous shelves covered in thousands of worthless knick-knacks and trinkets. The floor was barely visible, and Vinnie had to navigate through stacks of DVDs and old VHS cases. At the center of this domain of junk sat a giant flat screen TV and a single recliner holding the lone resident of the house. The ashtray on the stand next to him was piled high with ash, two packs' worth of cigarette butts discarded with abandon. Plastic Mountain Dew bottles—at least a dozen—lay scattered like bowing servants at the man's feet. Puffing away on his latest cigarette and absently dropping ashes on a shirt that already bore a decade's worth of tiny cigarette burn holes, was Sam. Sam was like Jabba the Hutt dressed in athletic shorts and a faded t-shirt bearing images of motorcycles and wolves. The recliner he'd had for years was broken and tilting to one side under Sam's tremendous weight.

Sam puffed away, absorbed in his TV.

"Hey, Sam. Busy?"

Almost instantly, Sam waved him over. "Hey, man. Check this out. PCP, or what?"

"Huh?"

The man pointed at the TV, his smoke pinched in a couple fingers, sprinkling embers onto his belly unaware. "Come on, man. PCP. It's *gotta* be. There's no other way he can be that strong. Look, he's a sailor after all. Shouldn't be too hard for him to smuggle it into the country. I mean, how else are you gonna explain those swollen arms and legs? He's probably smokin' it in that pipe of his. *Gotta* be PCP. It's the only way he can take the licks from that big guy and still keep gettin' up again."

Vinnie lifted his hat and scratched his head. "You're losing me here."

"Popeye!" Sam exclaimed. Vinnie swatted away the smoky haze and saw an old Popeye cartoon on the tube. Currently the muscular sailor was punching out some Nazis in a submarine. "He has to be takin' PCP. His spinach must be laced with it. No ordinary spinach can make a man that strong, trust me. My Aunt Ruthie used to make me eat spinach and I was never able to tie two bulls' tails together."

Popeye started singing his trademark song and Sam shook his head in disgust. "I yam what I yam. I yam a *dope fiend* is what I yam. I'm onto you, Popeye the Sailor Man."

Knowing that Sam could go on like this for days, Vinnie kindly interrupted at the commercial break. "Sam, I need your help."

"Yeah?" Sam said casually, dousing one smoke and immediately lighting up another. "You still chasing the Yeti?"

"Nope. Already found him."

"Really? What was he like?"

"Surprisingly, he was a pretty good bowler. But that's not why I'm here."

With great difficulty, Sam pried himself from his chair, a day's worth of Cheetos bits raining from the folds of his shirt. "Aahh, here for an artifact, I suppose. On the trail of another monster, and you want something to lure it to you, so you can take its picture and sell it to one of those conspiracy theory websites, huh?"

If it had only been that easy.

Sam was a contact from the old days of his monster hunting career. The man was a hoarder with a not-so-healthy obsession with the strange. If he didn't have something, he knew how to get it. Vinnie hadn't had need of him since meeting Flynn. He'd hoped he could leave the killing behind from now on and just stick to the academic side of the hunt.

But there was still one more job he had to pull, it seemed.

Just do it for the right reasons. He reminded himself of what Josh told him last night.

"Actually, I'm looking to kill it this time."

Sam blinked. "Sounds serious."

"Ever hear of the Aztaroth Dagger?"

He whistled. "That *is* serious."

"You know where it is?"

He belched, then took a drag off his smoke. "Yeah. In the back."

It took a moment for that to sink in. "You've got it here?"

Sam shrugged like everybody had his own Aztaroth Dagger lying around. "Yeah. Found it about ten years ago at an estate sale of a Nazi war criminal. What's it do, you know?"

"I'm hoping it kills a demon."

"Well, I'd be happy to sell it to you, but…you know my price."

Now it came down to business. Sam was a good guy, but he wasn't generous. He expected to get his cut and made no qualms about that. Usually he had the good grace to at least look ashamed when he asked for his exorbitant fees—but one way or another it always came around to the price. Vinnie had made many sacrifices to acquire one of Sam's hidden treasures and this time was no different.

With a heavy heart, he reached into the box he carried and pulled out his offering. He handed it to Sam, who took it greedily, nearly salivating over the prize.

"Oh, man…The original 1992 VHS boxed set release of the *Star Wars Trilogy*…"

Vinnie nodded. He'd bought two when they came out. Watched one until the tapes wore out. The other—the one Sam currently held in his meaty hands— was still in plastic.

"Pre-Special Editions," Vinnie added poignantly.

Sam panted with glee. "Han shoots first?"

"You know it. Whattya say, Sammy? 'Bout an even trade for a demon-killing knife?"

Sam's once-childlike wonder faded. He frowned, cradling the boxed set, gazing longingly at it. "Look, Vinnie. I know you're my friend and I wanna help you out. But I can't pay the rent on Sailor Moon dolls anymore. There's gotta be a time when a man takes a stand and joins the real world."

So Sam was going to play hardball.

If parting from his collector's copy of *Star Wars* was painful, losing this was like having an arm amputated without painkiller.

Reverently, Vinnie passed Sam his one and only copy of the *Star Wars Holiday*

Special—taped off TV onto a Beta tape on November 17, 1978, the one and only time the bizarre variety show ever aired. Most of the Holiday Specials floating around on the black market were dubs of dubs of dubs. Generations of people re-recording the program on VHS tapes until the quality was so downgraded the audio was garbled and the video was washed-out.

But this is Beta, first gen.

Sam had been eyeing it for a long time.

The junk dealer just stared at it, tiny tears building in his eyes. Broken, he looked to Vinnie and nodded solemnly. "I'll go get it."

Sam returned a few moments later, holding something wrapped in a dirty rag. With a flourish, he removed the rag and presented the sheathed weapon to Vinnie. The urban mythologist carefully took the dagger out and examined it. The blade was stained black and still sharp. The hilt was an ornate silver skull with gleaming blue jewel eyes. It looked like something right out of an Indiana Jones movie, which Vinnie supposed was precisely why Sam picked it up in the first place.

"Is this what you're looking for?" Sam said.

"The Aztaroth Dagger…"

"Nice, huh?"

Vinnie slid the dagger back into its sheath. "Real nice. I just hope it does the trick."

Sam's forehead glistened with anxious sweat. "Uh…if it doesn't—"

"You can keep the Holiday Special."

"Whew. Thanks."

Since Vinnie was off the case, Flynn carried on the investigation, doing his best to utilize his computer skills to track down the elusive Aztaroth Dagger. He came across some more lore—something about Aztaroth being an arch-duke of hell or some such. The blade was said to be able to cut the very fabric of reality, opening up rifts into other planes of existence like the kinds Marcie said that Malitivar guy talked about. If that were true, that had to be how they were going to send the Blue Skull away. But it was going to require guts and crackerjack timing.

Both things that Vinnie seemed unwilling to contribute.

But Eli was still on board. He seemed to be one of those run-into-a-burning-building kind of guys. Flynn hoped he'd have the same courage when it came down to the final battle.

Final battle.

He'd barely been able to sleep the night before, those terrible words echoing through his mind. He was just a kid—how would he ever be able to go through with it? More importantly, why had it fallen to him? Why couldn't the responsibility have passed to someone else? Nevertheless, Eli and Marcie were committed to the cause, and Flynn wouldn't let them do it alone. He had to try.

If he died, it would ruin his dad. Losing Mom had been hard enough on his father, but to lose his only son, too? Flynn couldn't do that to him, but... He didn't see a lot of choice. Vinnie had taught him the number one rule: *Know what you're hunting.* Flynn believed he knew everything there was to know about the Blue Skull. Combine that knowledge with the Mark, Eli's tactical skills, and Marcie and Loomis' experience in the occult, and they were bound to have the upper hand against Molok.

Still, it would have been nice to have Vinnie along. He always felt safer with the big guy around.

The phone rang in the other room. Dad answered while Flynn kept searching online. After a minute, Dad poked his head in. "That was Vinnie on the phone."

"What did he want?"

"He said he needed you to meet him at that place where you did that thing that one time. He said something about having what you guys were looking for, and 'game on'."

Suddenly, Flynn's death seemed to have a countdown clock attached to it. *No, this is too soon. I thought we'd have weeks—months—to prepare.* How had Vinnie found the dagger so fast? *I'm not ready, God. Please, I'm not ready!*

But wasn't this what he wanted? To save people? To kill the monster?

I'm just a kid. I haven't even kissed a girl yet. I don't want to die.

His friends were waiting on him. Standing, taking good stock of his computer, his room, his posters, his video games—all the things he worried he'd never see again—Flynn replied shakily, "Okay...I'd better go."

"Off to hunt more monsters?" Dad asked with a grin. Clueless Dad who had no idea that his son was marching off to his death. *I'm sorry, Dad. I didn't want it to end this way.* "What is it this time? Alligators in the sewers? Trolls under the overpass?"

"Yeah. Something like that."

"Well, be careful. I don't entirely get what it is an urban mythologist does, but I *do* support you, Flynn. I just…call it Dad's intuition, but I think you might be getting in over your head with this stuff and…I just want you to be careful. Okay?"

Flynn couldn't promise that. All he could see in his mind were the pieces of bodies that the Blue Skull had left in its wake. "Okay, Dad. Will do."

"I love you."

Flynn tried not to cry. If Vinnie had found the dagger, that meant he was back on the team. Things were always better with Vinnie around—he was a pro. *I can do this. I'm going to get through this.*

He still felt like crying.

Flynn hugged his dad tight, holding onto him, praying his dad would remember this moment when his son was dead and gone. "I love you, Dad."

And I'm sorry.

Eli opened the blinds, allowing the sunlight to illuminate his work. Killing was such a dark thing, and he'd always found an unusual desire for daylight whenever he'd prepared for a hit in the past. Now, those old habits returned. On his bed, his equipment. Knives, the SIG Sauer P229, his M4 Carbine—all old friends. Seeing them lined up again brought back a lot of memories. He'd never quite learned how to deal with the feelings dredged up when he recalled those experiences. With the instruments before him he'd killed foreign enemies and local thugs in equal measure. Mixed with his disgust was also a sense of pride— he'd been good at his job.

Today he'd need to be the *best*.

Vinnie had phoned him half an hour ago. Told him he'd secured the dagger. "Game on," he'd said. Eli discussed it with the preacher and got back in touch with Vinnie. They were going to meet at the Little White Church in Willowbrook and talk strategy. It wouldn't be a long talk, Eli figured. The plan was simple: Stab the Blue Skull through the heart with the Aztaroth Dagger. The problem came in implementing the plan. Vinnie was a good man, but he was out of shape and more of an intel guy. Eli knew it would fall to him to make the kill. He had the experience, the agility, and the stupidity to charge a hulking behemoth with a pig sticker.

I'm really not walking away from this one.

He'd made peace with that, though. Marcie, as intolerable as she could be, had been exactly right about him. He'd grabbed his second chance and ran with it, taking the coward's way out, just as Marcie had last night. But he was done running. He'd had a good run of things, working at the garage, making friends, getting to pretend to be normal for a while. Yet, whatever path God had originally intended for Eli, he was a killer, through and through. It was in his blood. Would *always* be. Only this time, he'd be using his power for good. This was a holy mission, and Eli would not fail.

He holstered his SIG 229 under his left arm and zipped up his camo tactical vest. Strapped a sheath to his leg where he would put the Aztaroth Dagger once Vinnie handed it off to him. Slid his M4 into his duffel bag. He slipped a cross on a silver chain around his neck and tucked it under his vest, feeling its pleasant weight against his chest.

Go with me, God, as I descend into hell to kill the devil.

Eli stood before the window, watching the sunlight bathing peaceful Greensboro in its warm light. Clearing his mind, he absorbed the sight, taking comfort that, once his task was done—even if he died during it—life would carry on. If he did his job right, these people would never have to know how close they came to losing everything. After a moment of quiet reflection, Eli hummed a little hymn, praising God for this chance he had been given to preserve lives.

I'll see you soon.

When he was finished, he neatly folded his brother's leather jacket over the back of the straight-backed chair in his bedroom. He patted it, affectionately, saying good-bye. Then he gave his apartment a once-over, slung the duffel with the Carbine over his shoulder, and headed for the door, marching to war.

Seeing Marcie standing in the hallway was the last thing he expected.

She waited in front of his door as though she'd been deciding whether or not she wanted to knock. They faced each other without speaking, the silence comfortable and warm. He thought he should feel angry, but he couldn't muster any negative emotions towards her.

"You're late," he finally said.

She rolled her eyes. "Yeah, there was this lady on the bus— Whatever. It's not important."

He grinned. Maybe people *could* change. "We're meeting Vinnie at the church. You ready?"

Somber, she nodded, her eyes drifting to the floor. "This is it, isn't it?"

"Let's hope so."

"There're just so many things I wish I hadn't done."

"I know. Me, too."

That was the closest he believed she'd ever come to an honest apology for her actions. Even that simple statement seemed to be difficult for her. "Do you really think there's hope for people like us? That we can start over—"

"Yes."

She smiled at his interruption, but still wouldn't face him. "I want you to know that…if things don't go right out there today…If something goes wrong, I mean…I love you."

That's all he needed to hear. He was ready now.

He beamed back at her, though she didn't see it. "I love you, too."

Marcie lifted her chin, her face set. He could see it in her eyes. She was ready now, too. "Then let's go get him."

CHAPTER THIRTEEN

Vinnie arrived at the Little White Church, decked out in his fedora and trenchcoat. Beneath his coat, twin Colt M1911s. He crunched on a mystery flavor Dum Dum sucker, hands in his pockets, the steady pulse of his heart beating in his ears. Was it strawberry, or maybe fruit punch he tasted? On the outside, he played things cool, but inside he was alert. He felt primal, ready to attack at any moment. The Aztaroth Dagger was sheathed and resting in his inside pocket. He planned to give it to Eli. Vinnie was fair in a fight, but Eli was a soldier—if anyone had the best shot at taking out Big Blue, it'd be that guy.

Stepping into the sanctuary, Vinnie immediately spotted Flynn sitting in a pew, his head bowed down as if in prayer.

We can use all the prayer we can get.

Flynn was growing into a tall kid, but he still seemed dwarfed by the cavernous sanctuary. Stone statues of saintly figures watched Vinnie as he walked the aisle. They looked sad, as though they pitied him and the path before him, but he tried not to get spooked. Josh had told him to do this for the right reasons, and he believed he was now. This wasn't about payback for Allison. Molok was a villain, and Vinnie was a hero. At least, he tried to be.

When it came right down to it, maybe that comic book dichotomy was all that really mattered. All that is necessary for the triumph of evil is that good men sit on their butts like babies.

Or something like that.

Well, Evil wasn't winning today. Not if Vinnie Caponi could help it.

Flynn looked up from his quiet reflection and saw his friend. The boy stood and approached. "My dad gave me your message. What made you change your mind?"

Vinnie shrugged. "A good friend set me straight."

The kid grinned. All was forgiven. Now they had work to do.

Vinnie looked over Flynn's shoulder, scoping out the sanctuary. "Where's the preacher?"

"He said he had to get some things ready."

The side doors into the sanctuary opened behind them, and the urban mythologists turned to see Eli and Marcie enter. Eli was decked out like a commando in a tactical vest with an assault rifle attached to a loop at his shoulder, his face set in ice. He was here on business, and Vinnie felt a little better about their situation. *We really got a shot at this.*

Marcie looked totally different than the first time Vinnie had met her a few days ago. Where once an air of superiority dwelled on her face, now there was just a humble uncertainty. *She's got just as much to lose as the rest of us. More, even.* What surprised him most was that, looking at her now, seeing little more than a scared kid trying to shake a fist at the bogeyman, Vinnie couldn't hate her. What happened to Allison had been an accident, he admitted to himself at last. A dumb mistake made by a schoolgirl playing with fire. A tragic mistake, harmful and impossible to undo, but a mistake, all the same.

"We all set?" Eli asked, his eyes darting like he was ready to shoot something.

"Almost," Vinnie answered.

Flynn added, "We're waiting on the preacher."

Vinnie eyed Eli. "Glad you could make it." To Marcie, he nodded meaningfully. "Both of you."

The girl glanced to the floor, uncomfortable but somehow appreciative of the sentiment. Vinnie surmised she wasn't used to people being glad to see her. Trying to cover her embarrassment, she grumbled, "Yeah, well…somebody had to come along to make sure you didn't all get us sucked into hell or something."

"No," a voice corrected from the altar. "Not today at any rate."

The group of hunters faced the altar as Pastor Loomis emerged from his study wearing a dark cloak. Trailing behind him were more men and women— about thirty in all—dressed like they were coming to a Sunday afternoon church social. They were older, looked a little backwards, but seemed to be simple country folk. *Loomis' congregation*, Vinnie assumed, though he wasn't sure what they were all doing here. Judging by the looks on the faces of Eli, Marcie, and Flynn, they weren't sure, either. The church folk surrounded the altar, taking to their hands and knees, bowing as Loomis stepped into their midst. It was then that Vinnie realized a circle had been drawn on the floor boards in white chalk, its edges decorated with odd symbols.

"What's going on?" Eli asked.

"Yeah," Vinnie added, his hackles rising. "What's with your getup?"

"My congregation and I have been in prayer all morning, preparing for this moment."

A flicker warped the air behind the preacher, like an old TV with bad reception. But the static wasn't attached to any screen. Rather, it was as if reality itself were attempting to tune into another channel, and after a moment, the channel came through. Without warning, the flickering cleared, and the Blue Skull appeared.

"Loomis!" Eli hollered, pulling out a pistol. "*Behind you!*"

313

The worshippers gasped and cried, bowing their heads to the ground, weeping. Vinnie tensed upon seeing the demon, and Eli was in his ear, screaming. "Vinnie! The knife!"

Molok took a step towards the preacher and Vinnie wasted no time. He reached into his coat and pulled out the dagger. Yanking off the sheath and tossing it to the side, he slid the blade along the ground, straight for Loomis.

"Preacher! Catch!"

Loomis scrambled to his knees, grabbing the knife.

"Stab it in his heart!" Eli shouted, taking aim as if to provide backup. "Hurry!"

But Loomis just stood there, delighting in the dagger in his hands. "Yesss…"

The Blue Skull did not move.

Marcie slapped Eli on the arm. "*What are you doing?*"

"It's the Aztaroth Dagger!"

"I know what it is! *That's* your secret weapon?"

"It's the only thing that can kill Molok!" Flynn shouted back.

"Haven't any of you idiots ever *read* the Malitivar Codex? The Aztaroth Dagger is the key that Molok will use to open the gates of the Other Side and bring What Is Yet To Come to rule upon the earth! It's his *weapon!*"

The hunters froze. As one, they turned to the stage. The church people were raising their hands towards the Blue Skull, chanting, singing strange praises to it. The demon stood at the center of their adoration like a god.

Vinnie wanted to punch himself. *Aw, crap.*

Loomis turned to Molok, his head low and contrite, presenting the dagger to the beast. In raspy tones, near tears, the preacher said, "Hear me, creature. I hold your destiny in my hands. It is yours. And all I ask is that you spare me, your humble servant, in your kingdom."

The Blue Skull regarded the offering and stood down, deactivated. Loomis lifted the dagger to heaven, the loose-fitting sleeves of his robe drooping, exposing his arms. There Vinnie saw bizarre tribal tattoos in sickening patterns. He could've sworn they moved, writhing around the preacher's pale flesh.

Now he knew why the guy always wore turtlenecks.

The mad cleric proclaimed, "I have found favor in his eyes!"

"What are we going to do?" Flynn panicked.

Eli whirled on Marcie. "Marcie, is there anything in the Codex at all—anything on how we can stop this thing?"

"What do you think I've been trying to do? I've tried every spell, every incantation. There's nothing left. And now that he has the dagger, that's it. The end. Of *everything.*"

Eli stomped past Vinnie, facing the altar. "Pastor Loomis! What are you doing? You're supposed to be a man of God!"

Loomis lowered the dagger and sneered, shaking his head in derision. "My dear boy, not everyone who claims to be of the Lord actually *is*." His beady eyes were hidden beneath his cowl, but Vinnie saw a forlorn frown crease the plump man's lips. "I tried to serve the Lord, but could not find Him. In all my travels, in all that I have seen... I still saw none of His miracles and no real proof that He exists." Loomis looked to Molok, a mad grin spreading across his face. "But then, I glimpsed the darkness In-Between the worlds. There is a Beast in the Void, young sir. The Terror With a Thousand Faces *is* coming. When my new master arrives, he will see that I have brought him his greatest champion, and with an army of untold strength he will make me a king!" Back to Eli, he encouraged, "My poor boy, the Terror is coming, and the only way to be spared is to pledge allegiance to it."

Vinnie watched Eli. The hitman looked more disappointed than surprised.

"Besides," Loomis added loudly, "I told you once long ago that I answered to a *much* higher authority."

The door to the study opened once more, and another man stepped out of the shadows. A couple days' worth of stubble had grown on his pretty face, and his hair was tousled. Nonetheless, he still wore slacks and a loose-fitting button-up shirt. With his hands in his pockets, the man casually strolled into the middle of the unholy ceremony as though he were just back from a vacation in the Florida Keys.

Loomis inclined his head. "I answer to *him*."

A new level of shock set in among the Molok-hunters, and Marcie was the first able to speak. "*Domingo?*"

Darius Domingo stepped over the weeping cult members and took his place with Loomis and Molok at the altar—like a blasphemous trinity.

"Actually, love, the name's Rufus."

Marcie stood frozen, stung as though someone had slapped her. The knife of betrayal twisted in her back and she felt undone.

"It was you..." She glared at Domingo, her lip trembling. After everything Daddy had given him, everything *she* had given him. "My family trusted you!"

"Of course they did," he chuckled, smacking a piece of gum in his mouth. "That was the point. When I first came here, I tried to compete with your father, but he had too many loyal to him. So, I decided I'd work my way up through the ranks. If I couldn't beat him, I'd join him. I put myself in the position to inherit his empire—" His grin dropped to reveal real hate. Hate Marcie had never seen in him. He'd always been so together, so cool and carefree. But that had all been a lie. Here she saw wicked rage in his eyes, demanding to be let out. "—then *you* went and ruined everything with your little spells. I always knew you were special, Marcie. Your ruthless ambition. Your—" He paused and smirked. "—apparent lack of any moral center. That's why I carefully guided you into the black arts."

Marcie listened, thinking back with horror to the time when she'd begun her descent into witchcraft. Domingo had been there all along, introducing her to the simple texts that had led to her ruin. Looking back now, she understood that he'd never pressed her—simply suggested. Always letting her think that she was the one pushing *him*. Always letting her think that she was in control, when in reality, he'd played her from the start.

"You…" she began, but was too overwhelmed to finish.

Domingo went on, "I thought you'd be a useful ally, in time. But I had no idea just how powerful you really were. You brought Molok into the world—even when I could not—and ruined all my plans. Thanks to you, Adrian died way ahead of schedule, and *you* became the new Boss. So, I changed the plan. I remained with you, biding my time—"

Her eyes narrowed. "Until you learned how to control Molok for yourself."

"And now I have." Grinning again, chomping on his gum like some disrespectful teenager.

Marcie's mind whirled with the implications of all that Domingo had revealed. She stammered, "B-But we looked for a way to stop Molok. All those leads I sent you on—"

He smirked, arrogant. "And all those murders."

Marcie balked. "That wasn't Molok…that was *you*."

"Of course, love. I had to cover my tracks, obviously. Couldn't have you getting any ideas about how to dispose of our blue-faced friend." Domingo gestured to the preacher. "Pastor Loomis, here, was very instrumental in my ascension. You know, this town overlooked him for too long, but you really shouldn't have. He's very gifted."

Loomis said, "Rufus believed me when no one else would. In return for his charitable donations, and his friendship, I offered him my unique services."

Still more realization sunk into Marcie's understanding. "I tried to send the Blue Skull after you…but I never could. I always thought you had some kind of magick on your side."

Domingo sneered. "Powerful though you may be, you were still a schoolgirl, fumbling in the dark. I had a high priest of the Esoteric Brotherhood of the Sun in my pocket. Now I just won't be king over some little town, I'll be a *god*. Thanks, Marcie."

Eli railed against the phony preacher. "Pastor Loomis, how could you help him do this?"

Domingo grew serious and held out his hand. "Give me the dagger, preacher, so I can complete the ritual."

Loomis screwed up his face in confusion even as he passed the dagger to Domingo. "Complete the ritual?"

"Of course. The only way to open the portal to the Other Side is with blood. There *always* has to be a sacrifice."

The preacher eyed his partner suspiciously. "I never read that."

"Of course not," he replied brightly. "I tore out that page."

Suddenly, Domingo raised the blade high and brought it down in a flash of metal, burying it hilt-deep in Loomis' back. The preacher bucked against the attack, hissing in surprise. Hissing turned to shrieking as he flailed, collapsing to the floor. The man's followers cried out and backed away in shock as Domingo retrieved the knife and brought it down again. Again. *Again.* Loomis screeched like the Wicked Witch of the West in a rainstorm, until finally his groans and pleas tapered off.

At last the man lay dead, his blood pumping out of his body, running to the edge of the chalk outline—but not crossing. The church shook beneath Marcie's feet and the magick circle began to glow with rainbow-colored light.

Domingo turned to Molok, shouting over the panicked worshippers, and handing the bloodied dagger to the devil. "Remember! We had a deal. Your master comes, and I'll be made a god!"

The Blue Skull wrapped its gigantic hand around the Aztaroth Dagger— Arthur taking Excalibur. Domingo hurried off to the sidelines, loose dust shaking free from the rafters as the whole place trembled. Molok stepped out of the circle and held its dagger up, a general calling his army. The blade popped, snapped, and grew, turning into a jagged black sword. At the same time, horns grew out of Molok's skull and twisted like a bull's. The monster grew to at least double its original size, shredding its black coat to reveal armor, bone, and muscle underneath—its entire body a pillar of blue fire.

The thing lifted its chin and let out a warble that made Marcie immediately sick to her stomach. Without warning, the floor within the magick circle cracked, upended, then dropped into a black hole. The powerful vacuum pulled in the nearest religious zealots, sucking them screaming into the dark space *in-between* the worlds. Others fled for their very souls, and Marcie thought to do the same, but the doors slammed shut—the wood sucked in until the frames cracked.

She eyed her companions. They held their ground, either too petrified to move or still foolish enough to think they could stop this. "It's too late!" she shouted over the roaring wind and the sounds of the church breaking apart, threatening to be sucked into the vortex. "The portal's open! His army is coming!"

But Eli would not go down without a fight. Eli, who never gave up, never lost hope.

He raised the M4 dangling at his side and fired three-round bursts into Molok, still finding the presence of mind to *aim* in this chaos. Marcie watched him as he slowly advanced on the monster, dodging debris in the swirling maelstrom. Vinnie, too, pushed back his trenchcoat and withdrew two Colt 1911s from their holsters. He fired them—one-two, one-two—at the skull-faced devil, shouting at the few surviving church folk. "Get back! Get out of here!"

The urban mythologist provided cover for a few stragglers to hurry behind Marcie, near the door. They clawed at the exit, weeping and praying that their Dark Master would spare them.

Flynn tried to help them, his face ashen with terror. He worked at the doors, kicking, pulling, pushing, *anything* to get them to move. Eli and Vinnie fought on, their gunfire doing little but irritating their enemy. Molok twitched under their attacks, but stood its ground as the bullets dissolved into its blue fire.

"Push him toward the rift!" Vinnie roared to his partner. "Maybe we can drive him back through!"

Marcie heard Eli holler back, "But how do we close it?"

"I'm working on that!"

Molok loosed another trill, then swung at its attackers. The duo worked in perfect synchronicity with each other, dodging to either side of the beast's blade and coming up firing once more. The urban mythologist blasted at the devil until his guns ran dry. He ejected his clips without missing a beat, slapping in two fresh ones, and fired some more.

Both men's *Tav* mark burned like hot iron on their foreheads and the beast snorted and snapped at them in impotent rage. The mark was doing the trick, warding off the monster, forcing it back towards the shimmering rainbow rim of the vortex.

Flynn shouted over the winds, at Marcie's side, "It's working! They're doing it!"

Marcie's attention, however, was drawn to the vortex—to the terrible sounds coming from the pit. An angry hum, like the battle cry of locusts, slowly rose before bubbling over. Molok's army wasn't coming.

They were already *there*.

Ash-colored pincers shot out from the gateway, hooking into the floorboards as the creatures began to pull their way into her world.

We weren't fast enough. We lost.

Marcie whimpered in her heart and stepped back, protectively putting Flynn behind her. "Stay back!"

Perhaps emboldened that its blasphemous army was nearly birthed into the world, Molok pressed its attack. Shrieking in fury, it grabbed the nearest pew and hurled it at the humans. Eli narrowly ducked beneath it, but Vinnie was too slow and took the full brunt of the bench. The urban mythologist was carried across the church, landing in a heap on the other side and buried in rubble.

"Vinnie!" Flynn started and raced for his friend.

Marcie reached for the boy, but he was already off. "Flynn, wait!" She spun back to Eli, fearing for him now that he was on his own.

Eli knelt down, hurriedly ripping the spent clip out of his M4 and replacing it with a full one. Molok slowly turned and stood over him like a monument. "You can't kill me," Eli bellowed, his voice strong and sure.

Then Molok reared back with its sword and plunged it through Eli's shoulder.

"Eli!"

Eli screamed in pain as Molok lifted him into the air. The devil brought Eli's paling face close and studied it. Eli snarled in agony, and spat in the monster's flaming skull face. Molok growled, took one huge foot, and shoved Eli's body off its blade. The hitman tumbled through the air and caromed off the wall. He fell to the hard, wooden floor, his Carbine clattering down just out of reach.

Marcie slid to her knees beside him. Eli gripped his wound, gnashing his teeth. She hovered over him, touching his face. "Eli! *Eli!* What do I do? *What am I supposed to do?*"

Despite his pain, he looked into her eyes. "I'm sorry, Marcie."

"No! We can't give up! You can't die!"

Eli shivered—entering shock, Marcie feared—and she reminded herself once more that this was all her fault. Righteous rage coursed through her. She took Eli's M4 and slipped through the violent winds, headed for the altar where Molok stood.

"Marcie!" she heard Eli shouting after her. But her sights were set on the Blue Skull.

She charged, pushing aside the terrified congregation, ignoring their pleas for salvation, until at last she reached the edge of the portal where the Blue Skull stood. She held up the rifle and unloaded on its face, screaming with rage.

Molok recoiled under the gunfire, its grip on the sword loosening a bit.

Marcie would not let up, not until the gun clicked dry. Even then she hurled it at the monster, smacking it in the face.

The behemoth leveled its cerulean skull at her and growled, its fire dying down to a low, radiating glow. It hoisted up its magnificent blade and brought it down. Marcie's body seemed to react without her even being aware of it. In a flash, she hurled herself to the side, the blade cleaving a pew in half. Molok swung the blade again and she ducked under it, screaming. The giant charged her, hacking and slashing, leveling everything around her as she rolled, dodged, and ran. Enraged, the monster threw the sword, and it stuck in the wall next to her, a shard of wood cutting her cheek. Leaving the weapon behind, Molok reached for her, yanking her by the ponytail.

"AACH!"

It pulled her back, took her in its arms, and threw her across the room. She landed hard by the choir loft, rolling, slipping, sliding—

Falling towards the pull of the vortex.

Death was one thing—being lost in the Abyss was another.

"*NO!*" She dug at the floor with her fingers. Her fingertips scraped as the power of the opening drew her ever closer. Unable to stop herself, she looked into the maw and saw *them*—Molok's army.

The grey beasts were naked, crouched over on all fours, standing on nothing, poised to attack, with curled toes and giant curved blades for hands. They had no eyes or noses, just large, hungry mouths with dull, cracked teeth. Chattering those chipped incisors, the legions of lanky devils reached from the Void. Reached for her. And beyond them, there was only black.

From that black, she heard a hungry rumble and a chilling, malevolent Voice calling out to her in her mind.

{*Welcome home, daughter.*}

"NO, NO, NO!"

The insectoid beasts stretched for her, rubbing their pincers against her dangling legs, moving up her body. She trembled in stark terror, her mind threatening to snap as she sought to comprehend the legions of hell that were coming to Earth.

Hands suddenly wrapped around her wrists and pulled. She jerked from the Void and looked into the strained face of Vinnie Caponi.

"Y-You came back for me."

He grunted in effort, his fedora blown off his head by the high winds produced by the vacuum. Sweat ran in rivulets down his round face, and he pulled with all of his might. "I got you," he huffed through clenched teeth.

Marcie crawled up his arms, her legs kicking the air over the Abyss as she scrambled to free herself. "I'm so sorry," she repeated over and over in a garbled blur, truly repentant.

"I know, kitten," Vinnie heaved, finally wrenching her free of the portal. They landed on the floor, out of breath, smiling at one another. "Now," he caught his second wind. "We gotta close this portal."

"How?" She glanced past him. Flynn was sitting on his knees, holding Eli up. Her lover fired his pistol at the first wave of ash-grey demons whose heads were emerging from the portal, while Flynn helped him reload. Past them, Marcie watched the Blue Skull yank its embedded blade from the wall and storm her way.

"Blood," Vinnie coughed. "To open one of these rifts—to close it, too—you always need a sacrifice."

Vinnie nodded to the wall above Marcie. She spotted a crucifix, a dying Jesus gazing sympathetically down at her. The urban mythologist said, "Hell ain't never been beat without a sacrifice."

Marcie turned back to him, to ask what he meant, when her field of vision was filled with the sight of the Blue Skull. Molok towered over her, holding its sword with two hands. It reared back and Marcie wondered where Vinnie had gone. Maybe he'd abandoned her at the very end. Molok thrust the blade out, aimed right for her heart—

But she never felt it.

Vinnie had stepped in to take the blow.

He looked at her now, the *Tav* mark on his forehead blazing, his eyes turning glassy, his face restful. At peace. Red mist covered Marcie's face, her front. The Aztaroth blade's tip poked clear through the hero's body, extending to mere inches from her chest. She looked at it—at Vinnie—dumbfounded. From somewhere she heard Flynn screaming Vinnie's name and she realized she'd robbed the boy of his best friend.

Why can't I stop hurting people?

"Vinnie?" she whispered, beginning to sob.

"It's okay, kid…it's going to be okay, now. All part a' the plan…"

Molok ripped the blade out of Vinnie's back. The man's blood cascaded onto the floor, circling into the Void like water down a drain. The rumbling ceased. The church stood still.

Then the Blue Skull and all its minions screamed.

The foundations rattled once more, the vortex whining as it pulled, pulled, *pulled*. Marcie no longer felt the pull, but was only buffeted by the winds, as if by a gentle breeze. She stood at the edge, unaffected by the supernatural magnetism, as the few grey devils that had managed to enter her reality were already snatched back through the rainbow-colored lights. They dug their pincers into the church, fighting against the wind, but their efforts proved useless. One by one, they passed by Marcie and Vinnie, disappearing into the darkness.

Molok came last. It staggered against the powerful gale, reaching for Marcie. Even at the end, it hated her—was trying to drag her with it. She simply stepped back from it, watching it strain to grab her, but eventually the devil fell into the pit. At once, the floorboards that had previously fallen away were returned. The altar was broken up like someone had taken a sledgehammer to it, but the gate was sealed.

Vinnie had done it.

She turned back to him, smiling, but he lay on the ground, eyes staring at the ceiling, gasping for breath. His chest wound pumped blood, but he didn't look in pain. Marcie knelt down beside him, breathless.

"You did it. It's all over."

He reached up and gently stroked Marcie's cheek. "Allison…I missed you…"

Her heart broke, and Marcie clenched her jaw to hold in her cries.

"I'm not—" Then she stopped herself. Instead, she took his hand and gently kissed it, smiling as best she could. "It's me. You did great. You can come home now. I'm here…"

"Home," he whispered, with the ghost of a smile on his lips. Then he closed his eyes and passed away, the mark on his head dimming and finally fading away.

Marcie carefully laid the man's hand across his chest, staring through her tears.

"Vinnie!" Flynn shouted. The boy helped Eli hobble over to where Vinnie lay, then slipped out from underneath Eli's arm and fell to the floor beside his unmoving friend. Pushing on his chest, trying to stir him, Flynn wept, "Vinnie? Vinnie!"

Eli reached down with his remaining good arm, touching the boy's shoulder. "Flynn, come on…"

The boy buried his face in Vinnie's neck, crying.

Marcie looked to Eli, shaking her head. She'd run out of apologies. She was empty of words or tears. In their place was a resounding gratitude for what this one brave man had done for her. Eli seemed to understand.

"Look at what you've done!"

Marcie turned to see Domingo. She'd lost sight of him in the chaos, and now he stood at the base of the platform, a pistol aimed in his shaky hand. He was mad with rage, his cool veneer shattered for good. "You ruined it again! You keep taking things away from me! You sent Molok to hell!"

Flynn stood, eyes brimming with tears, his young face hard. "Maybe we should send you to hell with him." The boy drew a .38 snub-nosed revolver. The same one, Marcie realized, that Domingo had given him in the North Woods.

Flynn aimed the gun, his jaw tense, his arm stiff and focused.

Eli limped closer. "Flynn, put the gun down."

"Don't worry," the boy spat through strained teeth. "I know how to use one of these things. You take this end, point it at the bad guy, and squeeze—don't *pull!*—the trigger."

Domingo lowered his gun, but did not drop it, and held his hands out as if in surrender. "Whoa, whoa, let's not get hasty."

Eli put a hand on the boy's arm, careful not to set him off. "Flynn, you don't want to do this."

"*It's all his fault!*" Flynn was shaking, an angry heat pouring off his body.

Eli shuffled, placing himself in front of Flynn's gun.

"Get out of the way!" the kid screamed.

"Flynn," Eli said calmly. Forcing him to listen. "I was here once, too. Revenge won't solve anything."

It hurt Marcie to hear those words, thinking back on her long, strange journey with Eli. All that he'd lost, the pieces of his soul that were gone forever because of the decisions he'd made. He was a broken man, every bit as tarnished as she was, and yet he'd somehow found the strength to carry on. To reshape the scattered fragments of his life into something beautiful and whole.

She stood to be by Flynn's side, hoping to spare the boy their pain.

"Don't be like us," she offered. "You've got a choice, Flynn. Make the right one."

Flynn's gun wavered. He bit his lip. "Vinnie…he died for you."

Marcie hung her head. "I know. I wish—"

"No. He…forgave you."

Flynn glared at Domingo, then handed his gun to Eli. The kid's shoulders slumped, but he proved victorious. He'd faced his temptation and passed where Eli and Marcie had not. Eli patted him on the arm. "You did good, bud. Vinnie would be proud of you."

"Party's over, kids!" Domingo called out, raising his gun. A dazzling red dot projected from the laser sight fixed to the barrel, passing by Marcie's eyes on the way to her forehead. Domingo looked directly at her and sneered. "Spoiled brat."

The gunshot rang out.

After a moment, Marcie slowly opened her eyes. She felt no pain.

Domingo swayed on his feet, a widening blotch of blood on his chest. He dropped his gun, looking down to the bullet hole. "You…you…"

Marcie followed his line of sight to Eli. In his hand he held Flynn's .38. Wispy purple smoke billowed from the barrel. Eli kept the gun trained on Domingo, making sure the man was no longer a threat. When Domingo collapsed, Eli lowered the weapon and approached his fallen foe.

Domingo coughed up a mouthful of blood, still glaring at Marcie as though she were to blame for every wrong thing that ever happened in his life. "I'll see you in hell, darling…"

The traitor lay his head back, his eyes vacant. Dead.

Eli stood over him for the longest time. Marcie joined Eli, wanting desperately to touch him. To hold him and let him cry if he needed to. But her lover seemed okay. No tears were in his eyes, no regret. He was at peace. Marcie didn't know if she'd ever seen him so tranquil—not plagued by his past. He was beautiful.

Her eyes fell on Domingo. Was he in that Abyss now, with Molok and the others? Was that where the damned went? Was her father down there, waiting for her? "I…don't want to go to hell," she said at length.

Eli turned to her. "You don't have to."

"Do you still believe? Your famed preacher was a liar."

Eli crossed by her, taking painful steps up the platform towards the altar. She noticed now that the crucifix had fallen from the wall during the gate's closing. Wincing in pain, the reformed hitman took the cross and righted it once more. Finished, he reached out with a bloody hand, touching the foot of Christ in reverence.

She supposed that was the answer to her question. It was a good answer.

Taking a deep breath, Eli turned to Loomis' frightened flock. "We need to get them help," he said.

"What about you, tough guy?" she laughed. "You've got a big hole in your arm."

Sirens blared outside. Flynn raced to one of the stained glass windows, pressing his face to the glass. "It's the cops! What do we do?"

Marcie regarded the dead bodies surrounding her, not a devil in sight. They'd have a lot of explaining to do.

Panicked, Flynn headed for a door in back of the sanctuary, looking for another way out. "Come on! We have to get out of here!"

"I can't," Marcie said, without the least bit of fear. "I've got to take some responsibility for once."

Eli smiled at her. "You know, the cops would pin it on Domingo. You could leave, and they'd never know it was you."

He was testing her. She could tell by his grin. "But *I* would."

Eli stooped down and picked up Vinnie's discarded hat. Dusted it off. "Go ahead and go, Flynn."

"*What?*"

"This isn't your fight anymore."

Flynn seemed torn between saving his own skin and backing up his newfound friends. "Are you sure you guys will be okay?"

"Yeah." Eli tossed Flynn Vinnie's fedora, which he barely caught. "This is where we belong."

Flynn looked long and hard at the two of them. "Take care, you guys."

"Lead a good life," Marcie told him.

He nodded, then ran for it out the back.

Sighing dramatically, Marcie looked to her hero. "Guess we gotta make sure justice is served and all that, right, choir boy?"

"Right."

Their hands met at their sides and gripped tight.

A moment later, SWAT burst through the windows and rammed the broken front door off its hinges. They swarmed the place with guns and flashlights, barking commands.

But all Marcie saw was Eli.

CHAPTER FOURTEEN

TWO MONTHS LATER

The sky was a perfect shade of blue today. White clouds moved overhead, dancing in the wind. A peaceful breeze blew through the thick green manes of the trees surrounding the cemetery. Dad pulled up along the path and parked.

"Take as long as you need."

Flynn smiled, appreciative of the sentiment, and climbed out. Temperatures were dropping, with autumn moving in. Halloween would soon follow, and the streets would be filled with ghouls and goblins. Flynn imagined he'd think of Vinnie the most at Halloweentime. The two of them talking monsters and whatnot, planning another investigation. But Flynn was content to celebrate the paranormal from a safe distance now. He left the website online after a final report, detailing everything he'd learned about the Blue Skull, but he wasn't planning on renewing the domain name once the expiration date arrived. Chasing spooks wasn't the same without Vinnie. He couldn't entirely bury the feeling that he was somehow betraying Vinnie by quitting, but deep down he knew it was what the big lug would have wanted.

He grinned, thinking of the last real conversation he'd had with Vinnie in the car. They'd been at odds then, but Vinnie's wisdom still guided him.

Flynn stepped up to the marker, a bouquet of flowers in his hand. He laid the flowers on the grave—not Vinnie's, but Allison's beside it. For Vinnie, he retrieved a Dum Dum sucker from his pants pocket and placed it carefully on his friend's tombstone.

"Hey, Vinnie. It's me."

The quiet *shoosh-shooshing* of windswept leaves in the trees soothed him, and he hoped that was Vinnie's way of telling him he was still here, in some weird way.

"Just thought you'd like to know what's been going on. The cops blamed the Blue Skull murders on Pastor Loomis and Mr. Domingo—or *Rufus*, I guess. The official report was that the two were the ringleaders of a Satanic cult and were behind the killings. The police called you a hero for exposing them. You got a medal and everything. I've got it framed on my wall..." Flynn lingered in the silence, a light chill wind brushing his face. "Oh, you should know that Marcie and Eli turned themselves in and made a full confession about the Marcon crime syndicate, solving about seventy-five percent of the unsolved mysteries in this town. They couldn't directly pin anything on Marcie, so she got off with parole. Eli made a plea bargain and provided information. They only gave him five years. Boss Marcon's crime family is finally through. Rufus is gone. A lot of the dirty cops were exposed and fired or are facing trial. Willowbrook is cleaning up, like you always wanted, Vinnie, and I think that maybe that was God's plan all along."

Flynn smiled. "Marcie is doing good. She's got a fresh start. She's not sure what she's going to do with it, but she seems really at peace. She's different now. *Better.* You really made a difference in her life." The boy considered. "I think that maybe that was all part of God's plan too."

He stood by the stone in silence for a moment, unsure of how to continue. "I'm doing okay, mostly. Dad and I are spending a lot of time together. And I'm doing like you wanted—I'm leaving the ghost hunting to those guys on the '*tee-vee*'." Flynn chuckled, thinking of Leland O'Dell's interview months ago. Underneath the warm memory, though, was a fearful uncertainty in his heart that he couldn't shake. One that he didn't feel comfortable sharing with his dad. "School started back up. I'm doing better in class and I've tried a couple times to talk to the other kids, but, I don't know… After all that we've seen and done… What if I'm not any good at being 'normal'?"

He waited for a silent moment, hoping above all hope that Vinnie would give him one last piece of advice. In the end, no answer came, and Flynn knew he had to look out for himself now. *Maybe this is what growing up is like.* The quiet turned bittersweet and Flynn adjusted the black fedora on his head. It was his most treasured possession. After all, it had once belonged to Vinnie Caponi: Urban Mythologist—the man who saved the world. "Well, I'll be seeing you. Tell Allison I said 'hi' and that I can't wait to meet her one day."

Flynn tipped the bill of the hat—just as he'd seen Vinnie do—and turned to leave. As he raised his eyes, though, he saw her standing there. A tall girl with long blonde hair twisting gently in the breeze. The girl from school. The girl from Carl's. She jumped with a start as their eyes met, then grinned as her cheeks reddened, combing her wayward hair behind an ear. "Sorry. I didn't mean to bother you. I was just…uh…visiting my grandma. Over there." She quickly pointed down the row and Flynn saw her mother still standing over a gravesite, in quiet reflection. "I saw you over here."

Flynn nodded, realizing that he'd yet to offer a word in this conversation. She was actually standing here in front of him. Actually *talking* to him. His palms turned instantly slick with perspiration and he struggled to swallow his heart back into his chest.

"Uh…"

She nodded sympathetically in the direction of Vinnie's grave. "Is this a friend?"

Flynn's joints grew stiff, but he managed to shove his hands in his pockets as he, too, looked back at the tombstone. "Yeah. My best friend."

"I'm sorry."

He shrugged, feeling suddenly giddy. "He's in a better place now." From his own experience in losing Mom, Flynn knew most people said that about the ones they loved—but in Vinnie's case, Flynn really believed it was true.

"Yeah," she echoed the sentiment, sounding genuine.

Their words drifted to silence, the wind whistling through the empty space between them. In Flynn's mind, he could almost hear Vinnie.

Never hurts to make a new friend.

After quickly toweling off his palm on the inside of his pants pocket, Flynn took a breath and extended a hand. "I'm Flynn, by the way."

Her smile widened to light up every dark space in Flynn's heart. She took the proffered hand, giggling a little. "I'm Mikaela."

"Hi."

Her giggle turned to outright laughter. It was, perhaps, the most lovely thing Flynn had ever heard. "*Hi.*"

FIVE YEARS LATER

An angry buzzer blared, and the chain link fence slid open. Armed guards watched him with eyes of steel, and Eli was glad he'd never have to see them again. Outside, beautiful flatlands waited for him. It had been five years since he'd seen life beyond barbed wire. All he had were the clothes on his back, now. He suspected the first thing he'd need to do was find a job. Maybe a garage was hiring somewhere. He wasn't worried about it right now; God had gotten him this far, he just had to trust Him a little farther.

Eli stepped into the parking lot, taking one last look at the old place. Wexler State Penitentiary stood like a monument to the Middle Ages, but he'd fared all right in there, considering. Lucky for him, his reputation from his days on the street was still the stuff of legend, and he spent more time signing autographs than fending for his life. He wouldn't miss it, though. He'd already lost five years.

Got a lot of catching up to do.

It'd be a long walk back to the City. He imagined he'd walk to the gas station down the road and use a payphone. Call a taxi or—

He paused. Grinned.

Marcie leaned against a dusty old convertible in a halter top and jeans, her hair in pigtails, a straw cowgirl hat atop her head. Her brown eyes sparkled, even across the parking lot, and Eli felt faint. With her thumbs hooked in her belt loops, she looked comfortable and absolutely stunning, backed by the painted sky. *Five years…*

She'd visited him, of course. He'd seen her, but always behind glass, a beautiful butterfly that he could never catch, always flitting away. She'd been like that for most of their time together, he supposed.

His mind whirled with a thousand things he wanted to say to her. All he could manage was, "Hey."

"Hey, back."

"You look good."

She laughed. "You look like crap."

Eli rubbed at the dark stubble on his chin. "Yeah, I could use a shower and shave, I guess."

They stood in not-so-awkward silence, with Eli wondering where they would go from here. They'd been lovers, enemies, and finally, at the end, friends. It had been the most insane ride of his life. *Are we ready for another round?* "You know…I could kill for some toast."

Smirking, she shook her head. "Isn't killing what got us into all this trouble in the first place? Why don't I just make you some?"

"That sounds nice." Her eyes were dazzling, inviting. "What about some scrambled eggs?"

"Now you're just pushing it."

At last, Marcie wrapped her arms around him. He held her by the waist, her body bringing him to new life.

The kiss that followed lasted for a long time.

METAMORPHOSIS

(Originally appearing in *Occult Detective Tales, Vol. 1—A Cat of Nine Tales*)

Josh Banks turned his key and entered the country shack. The place seemed colder these days without *her* there. On the wall, where portraits of her pretty face once smiled back at him, there was only bare wood-paneling. Vinnie had already removed all the painful reminders of her beauty, her warmth. Dirty clothes lay draped over furniture and empty bottles of Bourbon were scattered on the carpet, but what bothered Josh most were the stacks of strange books. Vinnie's new obsession.

"Vin?" Josh called out into the evening gloom, barely broken by the glow of a lamp in the corner. Silence answered him. Maybe Vinnie was off doing more research on the case. Vinnie had always been thorough—that was what had made him such a great private investigator. But this new Vinnie—one without Allison—was driven in a new and terrible way.

Drawn by morbid interest, Josh plucked a thin book off the top of the nearest stack. The spine read: *White Magic, Black Magic.* "Aw, Vin…I hope you know what you're getting yourself into."

The cell phone stashed in his baggy jacket blitzed and Josh nearly dropped the book. He fumbled to bring the phone to his ear. "Yeah?"

"Josh."

Vinnie sounded hollow and distant, a shadow of the jovial giant he had been only a month ago. "Vinnie? Where you at? You told me to meet'cha."

"There's been a change of plans. Meet me at the lake."

Not that again. "What for?"

"I'm gonna summon Tanner's spirit and I need your help."

Josh's blood froze in his veins. He felt like the Devil himself was standing behind him. At last, he swallowed hard. "I'm on my way."

Vinnie Caponi pressed the chalk to the dock boards, finishing the runic configuration, mumbling the incantation as he did so. With each syllable, he felt himself slipping into darkness, crossing a line he'd never even known existed a few weeks back. Allison had been a faith-driven woman and he respected her beliefs, though he never entirely shared them. Since he was a boy, Vinnie had been a practical thinker, observing physical facts to draw conclusions about the unknown. That, coupled with his desire to mimic the two-fisted detective stories he enjoyed in his youth, had led him to join the Willowbrook P.D. However, reality was not as rewarding as fiction, and corruption on the force drove him away. He went into business for himself, with Allison's brother Josh at his side. It was an unlikely partnership, as his brother-in-law was lazy and undisciplined, but Vinnie had done it for Allison. He would have done anything to make her happy. To repay her for noticing him when so many others hadn't. Vinnie better resembled John Candy than John Wayne, yet Allison made him feel accepted and loved.

But Allison was gone... Was she in heaven now? Had her faith rewarded her? Or was she someplace dark and cold and alone, waiting for him to save her? Or, at the very least, avenge her?

He'd watched the camera footage a thousand times. The thing that was there when Allison died...it wasn't human. It took six slugs like someone was throwing pebbles at it. It bled dust. Its face was a ghostly skull, nearly luminescent in the dark. Vinnie had never believed in ghosts, but the way that thing—that *Skullface*—flickered out of sight and vanished...

The world had opened to him and proven itself a terrible, unknowable place, shattering every perception he held, ruining his life—and triggering his rebirth. He was shuffling around in the cocoon and wasn't quite sure how he would emerge when the transformation was complete.

He straightened as he finished his task, readjusting the black trenchcoat and fedora that warded off the encroaching cold. Josh materialized from the shadows onto the small pier, stepping into the white-blue beam of the overhead lights. The string bean looked worn, reminding Vinnie that Josh had lost Allison, as well. *But I'm going to make this right. I can fix this. For both of us.*

"What do ya think you're doin'?" Josh sighed, looking more annoyed than angry.

Vinnie regarded his intricate scribbling on the ground, mindful of the instruction book he held in his hand. It hadn't been easy—or cheap—procuring the text. "It's a summoning spell."

"Dude," Josh groaned, "what is your *problem*? Will you just listen to yourself? Spells, ghosts...this is *dark stuff*, man."

Vinnie knew Josh was right. He'd buried himself in research the last few days, taking a crash course in the occult. Even from what little he'd read, he understood he was dabbling in powers he couldn't control. He was aware of the thin line he walked between salvation and damnation. "If it gets me closer to the thing that killed Allison, then it doesn't matter."

"It does, too, Vin! What does it matter if you get your revenge, or whatever, but you lose your own soul in the process? *Allison* wouldn't want that."

No. She wouldn't. There were a lot of things Allison wouldn't have wanted. "Allison's dead."

Vinnie saw Josh flinch and marveled at how well he was holding it together. Josh was calm, clear-headed, though he had to be hurting inside. Sad as it was, losing Allison had been good for Josh, maturing him overnight into a good man. *Am I a good man anymore?*

"She is," Josh reflected. "But that doesn't mean you have to die, too."

Vinnie set his teeth on edge, his heart pierced. "Are you going to help me or not?"

"I ain't touching that magick stuff, man," Josh snarled like Vinnie held a plate of spoiled sour kraut. Eyeing the tome in Vinnie's hand, he asked tentatively, "What *is* that, anyway?"

"It's one of the Thirteen Books of Carvac. It contains spells for conjuring spirits and binding them to corporeal form."

Josh stared at him for a long moment. "Great plan, Sherlock. What do you plan on doin' after ya got this Tanner cat where you want 'im?"

The spirit in question was Jimmy Tanner, a twenty-six-year-old man who drowned in the lake back in the 1960s. He was backward and probably mildly retarded—but he was far from innocent. He was known to mutilate animals and spent too long lurking around playgrounds for parents' liking. Tanner was a hulking man, and Willowbrook feared him. Then one day, he turned up missing. Years went by until, in the mid- '80s, a group of men confessed to running afoul of Tanner when they were thirteen, returning from a Little League game. The boys teased the man, called him names, and provoked him into a fight. When Tanner lashed out, the frightened kids retaliated, nearly beating the man to death, and pushing his body into the water where he met his demise. The secret had stayed with the boys into their adulthood, until guilt moved them to confess what they'd done.

But Tanner's body was never recovered.

Instead, his vengeful ghost became the stuff of stories told at the nearby summer camp. There had been a few unexplained accidents out there, often attributed to Tanner's lingering fury.

Allison had died near those woods. Near the lake. Vinnie found a photo of Tanner—huge and lumbering—and believed it matched the shape of the phantom he glimpsed on the video.

At least, he *wanted* to believe.

"Check the bag."

It was only then that Josh noticed the duffel on the ground, a sawed-off shotgun protruding from the open top. Josh knelt and handled the weapon with respect and awe, then looked back to the detective, his eyes betraying a broken heart. "Vinnie…"

Vinnie detected the hurt in Josh's voice, knowing he had let down his friend. Vinnie had always owned a pistol as a cop and later a P.I.—had been trained to use one—but as a pacifist by nature, he preferred to make friends of his enemies and reason his way out of difficulties. Resorting to violence was traitor to so many things he once stood for. But he was changing. "The bullets are enchanted. I used one of the spells on them, so they should be lethal to a supernatural being."

Josh stood, shaking his head. "You're losing it."

Vinnie could not argue.

Relenting, Josh exhaled. "So, after you kill this guy or send him back to hell or whateva', *then* what?"

Vinnie hung his head. "I don't know."

"Because it won't bring back Allison, you know?"

The truth stung like a slap to the face. Then again, what was truth anymore? Vinnie was starting to understand that the rules could be rewritten. With the right symbols, the right incantations, anything was possible. *Anything…* "Yeah…I know…" He felt the weight of the Book of Carvac in his hand. His eye was drawn to its yellowed pages. They held so many secrets about death— and life beyond. Maybe he could find a way to breach that veil and see Allison again. Maybe…bring her back. "This book is powerful…" he muttered, his heart tripping in his chest, as he felt himself sink a little further into darkness.

Looking up, he saw Josh's eyes widen. The kid wasn't stupid. He fixed an accusing glare on the book, then Vinnie. "No! Don't even think it!"

"But if it works on Tanner, it could work on—"

In a display of anger Vinnie had never seen in him, Josh charged and slapped the book from his hand. "*Stop it!*"

In the second it took the book to drop, Vinnie drew his Colt 1911 from his shoulder holster and pressed it to Josh's nose. Ice surged through him—hate and pain and grief—as he leveled the gun.

Josh paled. "What are you doin', Vin? You gonna shoot *me* now?"

Vinnie's hand trembled, his pulse pounding in his ears. Josh was standing in his way. Hadn't he promised himself he would do anything to make things right? To bring Allison back into the world and make everything *whole* again?

Josh stared him down, growing bolder in the silence. He had Allison's eyes. Maybe he had her heart, too.

What are you doing? Vinnie asked himself, echoing his friend's words. He really didn't know anymore.

Slowly, he lowered the pistol. Slid it back into its holster.

"I'm so lost, Josh…I miss her so much…"

Josh's familiar easygoing, lopsided grin returned. He patted Vinnie on the shoulder. "I know, big guy. I do, too."

Vinnie had lost Allison: his wife, his friend, his reason to get up in the morning. But maybe in the end, he'd gained a brother. Josh's goodwill warmed his soul and he found himself smiling again at last.

"Come on," Josh said, nodding towards the end of the pier, away from the lake and its temptations. "Let's get rid of this crap and go get a pizza. I'll even let you buy."

It sounded wonderful, but there was one catch. "We can't."

"Why not?"

Vinnie looked to his boots and the chalk drawing beneath them. Already the symbols began to glow a faint red. He frowned. *Too late to turn back now.* "Because…I already did the spell. I already summoned Jimmy Tanner."

A soul-shivering howl split the night and the screaming giant exploded out of the lake's cold depths. Josh let out a curse and tumbled back onto his seat as the behemoth landed on the pier, cracking the boards under his weight. Vinnie stepped back, his hand hovering over his pistol, but not drawing it. The thing before him stood over six feet tall and wore coveralls and a discolored flannel shirt. Its shriveled skin was white as marble and bloated, its hair a strange shade of green. But Vinnie recognized the overbite, the bushy eyebrows.

This was Tanner. But…this was *not* Skullface.

"*Is it him?*" Josh screamed, scrambling in a crab-walk, desperately retreating as the waterlogged giant clomped closer.

"No," Vinnie said at length, his heart breaking. It wasn't Skullface. He had disturbed this murdered man, stirring those decades of rage…for no reason at all.

Tanner's grotesque body raised its arms for Vinnie, and the thing bellowed a hungry, hate-filled cry. Josh screamed like a small girl, but Vinnie steadied himself. Without fear or anger—even the grief was gone—he slid his pistol into his hand, took aim, and fired one magickally enhanced bullet. The spinning projectile flew from the barrel and struck the Goliath's forehead. Tanner went limp, tumbling forward on the dock.

The waters bubbled, lit from below by a green light. Vinnie trembled, wondering what else he had released. Suddenly, the boards snapped, jutting skyward. Vinnie stumbled and was saved from impalement by Josh's quick thinking and quicker feet. "Come on!" he squeaked, lugging Vinnie off the pier.

The two of them stood on shore watching as an eerie fog rose from the waters, moaning as if alive, and encircled Tanner's limbs. Slowly, the mist dragged Tanner down into the lake, sealing what remained of his soul in its final resting place. As he sunk below the surface, the ghostly echoes faded, and the waters grew dark and still once more.

Vinnie and Josh stood without speaking for a long time.

But Josh was never very good at keeping his mouth shut. "Did...we just see that?"

Feeling an odd sense of peace, Vinnie reached into his deep pockets and retrieved his favorite treat while on a stakeout—a Dum Dum sucker. He unwrapped a bubble gum-flavored one and popped it into his mouth. "Yep."

"I vote we never do this again."

Vinnie felt the same. He couldn't save Allison. He couldn't bend the laws of the universe to his own whims—the consequences were too dire.

But before he could voice his agreement, he realized he had emerged from the cocoon that her death had spun around him and knew what he had become. "I'm not so sure."

Josh did a double-take. "Come again?"

Vinnie chuckled. "Easy. No more meddling with the Books of Carvac. I get that. But...I know, now, that there are some *strange things* hiding in the shadows. I can't turn my back on all I've learned. There are monsters out there, and somebody's gotta fight 'em back. Maybe that's me. Maybe I'm—"

"What? An urban mythologist?" Josh snickered.

Vinnie grinned around his Dum Dum. "That ain't got a bad ring to it."

The two of them contemplated the idea in the cool autumn breeze. After a moment, Josh stuck his hands in his pockets and shrugged. "So, you, uh, think you'll need a partner?"

"It never hurt before. You interested?"

As they gathered their things and headed away from the lake and the ghosts they'd laid to rest, Josh explained, "Well, it just so happens that I used to work for this private investigator, but he quit the business. So, you could say I'm in between internships. What does an urban mythologist pay anyway?"

Vinnie crunched on the sucker. "It pays in truth."

"Aw, man, that's really cheesy."

"Really? I was thinking of putting it on the new business card."

"You mean you're gonna have a real card now?" Josh exclaimed.

Vinnie considered the stack of Fishy's Feed and Supply cards he still had in his possession, with his name and number scrawled on the back. He shrugged with a smirk. "Well…we'll see."

Josh groaned, and Vinnie laughed for the first time since his world turned dark, and felt sure that somewhere Allison was laughing too.

"Infernal City *is a mesmerizing story. Captivating. And Quinn Holbrook is a dude you just have to root for. Mitchell's way with words puts you right in the middle of the action. This is a story that will linger long after completion.*"

-Mike Dellosso, author of *Centralia* and *Kill Devil* (Jed Patrick novels)

There is a City
where the sun never shines
and the rain never lets up...
...where your every dream
can come true
for a price.

AVAILABLE IN PRINT AND EBOOK
FROM:

ISBN: 978-1542392044

www.ingramcontent.com/pod-product-compliance
Lightning Source LLC
Chambersburg PA
CBHW021444240626
47153CB00001B/291